THE BOOK OF
COMIC AND DRAMATIC MONOLOGUES

THE BOOK OF
COMIC AND DRAMATIC
MONOLOGUES

Compiled and introduced by

MICHAEL MARSHALL

ELM TREE BOOKS /
EMI MUSIC PUBLISHING

For my father, from whom I inherited my love of the halls, and for my mother, in appreciation of her performing skills

First published in Great Britain 1981
by Elm Tree Books/Hamish Hamilton Ltd
Garden House 57–59 Long Acre London WC2E 9JZ
and EMI Music Publishing Ltd
138–140 Charing Cross Road London WC2H 0LD
Second impression March 1982
Third impression February 1984

Music trade distribution by
International Music Publications
60–70 Roden Street Ilford Essex

Introductions copyright © 1981 by Michael Marshall
See also further copyright acknowledgements on page xii

British Library Cataloguing in Publication Data

The Book of monologues.
1. Humorous poetry, English
2. Humorous recitations
I. Marshall, Michael, *1930*–
821′,07   PR1195.H8

ISBN 0-241-10738-5
ISBN 0-241-10670-2 (Pbk)

Filmset by Pioneer
Printed and bound in Great Britain by
Richard Clay (The Chaucer Press) Ltd, Bungay, Suffolk

CONTENTS

PART III — PERFORMERS AND WRITERS 1938 — 1981

ACKNOWLEDGEMENTS

I owe a special debt of gratitude to Greatrex Newman: he has not only contributed samples of his work which demonstrate his monologue writing over the last seventy years, but he has also made freely available his memories of writers and performers over the same period. In tracing rare material, I have been helped, as in the past, by Derek Bromberg of the BBC and, also, on this occasion, by Leslie Wilkinson of the British Music Hall Society. My thanks are also due to my editorial team, Patrick Howgill of EMI and Roger Houghton and Caroline Taggart at Elm Tree and, above all, to my wife, for her continued forbearance.

The author and publishers would like to thank the following for their kind permission to reproduce copyright material in this book: Arthur Askey for *The Worm* © 1939; *The Seagull* © 1940; *The Ant* © 1962; *The Foreign Legion* © 1941; Campbell Connelly Ltd for *Walter Walter* © 1928; *The Biggest Aspidistra in the World* © 1928; *In My Little Bottom Drawer* © 1928; *Mrs Binns's Twins* © 1938; *Out in the Cold, Cold Snow* © 1948; Chappell Music Ltd for *The Budgerigar* © 1941; *The Pixie* © 1941; *The Death Watch Beetle* © 1941; *The Bunny Rabbit* © 1942; *I Took My Harp to a Party* © 1933; *There's a Hole in My Budget* © 1953; *A Transport of Delight* © 1956; *Design for Living* © 1956; *Have Some Madeira, M'Dear* © 1956; *The Hippopotamus* © 1956; *A Gnu* © 1956; *Bedstead Men* © 1963; *The Gas Man Cometh* © 1963; *A Song of Patriotic Prejudice* © 1963; *In the Bath* © 1965; *The Warthog (The Hog Beneath the Skin)* © 1977; *The Wom Pom* © 1980; Archie de Bear for *Many Happy Returns* © 1933; Joan de St Hellyer for *George Lashwood Monologue* © 1942; Dick James Music Ltd for *Bunger-Up o' Rat-'Oles* © 1968; B. Feldman & Co Ltd for *The Other Department Please* © 1912; Francis, Day & Hunter Ltd for *And Yet I Don't Know* © 1919; *My Word You Do Look Queer!* © 1923; *I Might Marry You* © 1923; *The Cautious Lover* © 1925; *She Was Poor But She Was Honest* © 1930; *Please Let Me Sleep on Your Doorstep Tonight* © 1930; *Heaven Will Protect an Honest Girl* © 1933; *Whiskers and All* © 1933; *Old Sam* © 1929; *The Lion & Albert* © 1932; *Three Ha'pence a Foot* © 1932; *Gunner Joe* © 1933; *With Her Head Tucked Underneath Her Arm* © 1936; *The Battle of Hastings* © 1937; *The Magna Charter* © 1937; *Brahn Boots* © 1941; Ronald Frankau for *Shootin' and Huntin' and Fishin'* © 1934; Cyril Fletcher for *Ode of the Fletcher* © 1940; *Song of The Fletchers* © 1940; *The Mermaid* © 1939; *The Fan* © 1939; *Theophelus and His Operation* © 1939; Mrs M Longmire for *Yorkshire Pudden!* © 1940; Sweeney Todd The Barber © 1957; Greatrex Newman for *What Did You Do in the Great War Daddy?* © 1919; *Come Into the Garden More* © 1981; *No News is Good News* © 1981; *Piscatorial Pastime* © 1981; *Turn Again Whittington* © 1981; *Hat Trick* © 1981; *Prehistoric Prattle* © 1981; *Wakey! Wakey!* © 1981; *That's That* © 1981; *It Pays to Advertise* © 1981; *Mr and Mrs Whistler* © 1981; *Heads Tucked Underneath Their Arms* © 1981; *Animal, Vegetable or Mineral?* © 1981; *The Big Tale of Hoo Flung Mud* © 1981; *Sour Grapes* © 1981; *Cursory Nursery Versery* © 1981; Novello & Co Ltd for the following copyrights of Paxton & Co Ltd *(The Charge of) The Tight Brigade* © 1926; *The Tightest Man I Know* © 1927; *The Member of Parliament* © 1929; *Mandalay* © 1929; *Christmas Day in The Cookhouse* © 1930; *The Bookmakers Daughter* © 1934; *The Foreign Legion* © 1934; *The Old School Tie* © 1934; The Executors of the Will of the Late Nicholas Phipps for *Maud* © 1951; Reynolds Music/EMI Music Publishing Ltd for *The Future Mrs 'Awkins* © 1898; *A Fallen Star* © 1898; *The Yankee In London* © 1900; *An Old Bachelor* © 1904; *Wot Vur Do 'Ee Luv Oi?* © 1905; *The Village Constable* © 1909; *My Old Dutch* © 1911; *'E Can't Take a Roise Out of Oi* © 1911; *Napoleon's Last Dream* © 1914; *'Is Pipe* © 1905; *Devil-May-Care* © 1905; *Jim Bludso* © 1905; *The Hindoo's Paradise* © 1907; *For A Woman's Sake* © 1908; *How We Saved the Barge* © 1908; *The Student* © 1908; *Jack* © 1910; *The Portrait* © 1911; *The Caretaker* © 1912; *The Coward* © 1913; *Joe's Luck* © 1913; *Uncle George* © 1914; *"Rake" Windermere* © 1914; *The Lounger* © 1914; *Spotty* © 1914; *A Backwood Penance* © 1915; *The Flying Boatman* © 1916; *The Plumber* © 1916; *The Shooting of Dan McGrew* © 1917; *Wild Bill Drives the Stage* © 1918; *The Pigtail of Li Fang Fu* © 1919; *Orange Blossom* © 1921; *Black Roger* © 1922; *The Last Bottle* © 1925; *The Green Eye of The Little Yellow God* © 1911; *The Dream Ring of the Desert* © 1912; *The Whitest Man I Know* © 1914; *Merchandise* © 1920; *Orange Peel* © 1920; *My Old Football* © 1920; *You Know What I Mean* © 1923; *A Soldiers Reminiscences* © 1915; *If We Only Knew* © 1897; *Johnnie, Me and You* © 1907; *When Father Laid the Carpet on the Stairs* © 1911; *The Kid* © 1914; *Up and Down The Strand* © 1915; *Periodicals* © 1916; *Reflections of A Penny* © 1916; *Charm* © 1922; *The Madman's Will* © 1925; *Auction of Life* © 1928; *The Scot's Lament* © 1929; *Soliloquy of A Tramp* © 1932; *The Twirp* © 1942; *Pity The Boy Who's Grown Out of His Clothes* © 1943; *The Grand Old Girls of Britain* © 1944; *Pull Together* © 1949; *Thanks, Johnnie* © 1951; *The Lesson of The Water Mill* © 1897; *What Is A Gentleman?* © 1897; *The Last Token* © 1898; *The Man With the Single Hair* © 1902; *A Tragedy in One Act* © 1904; *Laugh and The World Laughs With You* © 1904; *11.69 Express* © 1906; *The Lighthouse Keeper's Story* © 1909; *A Dickens Monologue* © 1910; *The Girl at the Station* © 1911; *Charge of The Night Brigade* © 1911; *Bill* © 1911; *What Will the Child Become?* © 1912; *Reward of the Great* © 1913; *The Hinglishman* © 1913; *A Clean Sweep* © 1913; *The Waster* © 1913; *An East End Saturday*

Night © 1914; *The Man Who Stayed At Home* © 1914; *The Steam Roller Man's Story* © 1914; *Answered* © 1914; *The Scrapper and The Nut* © 1915; *'Erbert, A.B.* © 1915; *Broom & Co* © 1915; *The Answer of the Anzacs* © 1916; *The Gardener's Story* © 1916; *Conscientious Alf* © 1916; *Pincher, D.C.M.* © 1916; *A Little Guttersnipe* © 1916; *Cheerful Charlie* © 1916; *The 'Oxton 'Ero* © 1917; *Phil Blood's Leap* © 1918; *The Mercantile Marine* © 1918; *Afterwards* © 1919; *The Duet* © 1920; *The Cabman's Railway Yarn* © 1920; *Thrilling Stories* © 1920; *My Love Affairs* © 1921; *Our Grandparents' Yarns* © 1921; *When You Figger It Out* © 1921; *Girls! (According to a 14-year-old Boy)* © 1922; *Jimmy Johnson* © 1922; *Supplanted* © 1923; *Sally's Ups and Downs* © 1923; *Lizette, Queen of the Apaches* © 1924; *Aren't Men Funny?* © 1924; *Old Flames* © 1924; *Square Deal Sanderson* © 1925; *'Arf A Cigar* © 1925; *The Girl at the Ball* © 1926; *When the Road's (H)Up, It's (H)Up* © 1926; *He Did* © 1926; *Wheels* © 1926; *My Leetle Rosa* © 1927; *Two Men* © 1928; *Penny For Da Monk* © 1929; *Memories of Waterloo* © 1930; *Suicide* © 1931; *The Man With The Swollen Head* © 1931; *Tommy Out East* © 1932; *The Old Barnstormer* © 1933; *A Tattoo Tragedy* © 1933; *The Sufferer* © 1934; *Sam's Parrot* © 1933; *The Road to La Bassée* © 1934; *When I'm Cross* © 1934; *What's it For?* © 1935; *The Touch of the Master's Hand* © 1936; *The Killjoy* © 1937; *Loyalty* © 1937; *Bill's Trombone* © 1938; *Providence* © 1938; *Common Sense* © 1938; *Lor' Lumme! You'd Never Believe It* © 1938; *Life is Like a Game of Football* © 1938; *Frisco Sam, Bad Man* © 1938; *Nell* © 1939; *Cigarette Cards* © 1939; *The Human Touch* © 1939; *Goodbye and God Bless You* © 1939; *Me and My Pipe* © 1940; *The Glutton* © 1940; *The Voyage of the 'Saucy Jane'* © 1941; *If You'll Pardon My Saying So* © 1941; *My England* © 1941; *The Civilians* © 1941; *Dawn Patrol* © 1942; *Merchant Navy* © 1943; *Legs* © 1945; *Timmy's Sacrifice* © 1946; *Thank You* © 1946; *Dreamin' of Thee* © 1938; *The Bee Song* © 1947; *Chirrup* © 1947; *The Seaside Band* © 1947; *The Moth* © 1947; *Pukka Sahib* © 1940; *The Street Watchman's Story* © 1957; *Eving's Dorg 'Ospital* © 1957; *On Strike* © 1957; *The Parson of Puddle* © 1923; Richard Scott Simon Ltd for the following copyrights of the late Joyce Grenfell *Oh Mr du Maurier* © 1945; *Three Brothers* © 1953; *Old Tyme Dancing (Stately as a Galleon)* © 1964; *Rainbow Nights* © 1964; *At The Laundrette* © 1964; *The Countess of Coteley* © 1964; *Picture Postcard* © 1964; *Dear François* © 1964; Robert Rutherford for *All To Specification* © 1939; *The Flu Germ* © 1942; *The Villain Still Pursued Her* © 1935; Dr Jan Van Loewen Ltd for *The End of the News* © 1945 by Chappell & Co Ltd. We would also like to thank Mrs Claudia Flanders for her kind permission to use a 1981 version of *There's a Hole in My Budget*.

We are grateful to the following for the use of photographs and illustrations: Tony Barker and 'Music Hall' magazine for photographs of Billy Bennett, Stanley Holloway and Milton Hayes; the Raymond Mander and Joe Mitchenson Theatre Collection for the photograph of Joyce Grenfell; Greatrex Newman for the photographs of the Fol de Rols Concert Party and of himself; EMI Music Publishing Ltd. for the other illustrations from their music archives.

We would also like to acknowledge the valuable help of Tony Barker, Peggy Jones, Mark Newell, Harry Shaberman and John Whitehorn in researching the monologues and illustrations; also the work of Diana Chilvers, Eileen Izon, Peggy Jones and Debbie Leach in transcribing the monologues, sometimes from very worn recordings.

No. 2305.

6D NET.

WHISKERS AN' ALL!

WRITTEN BY
R.P. WESTON & BERT LEE.
COMPOSED BY
HARRIS WESTON.

SUNG BY

GRACIE FIELDS.

London: FRANCIS, DAY & HUNTER LTD
138-140, CHARING CROSS ROAD, W.C. 2.
NEW YORK AGENTS: LEO FEIST, Inc., 56, COOPER SQUARE.
SYDNEY AGENTS: J. ALBERT & SON, 137-139, KING STREET.
PARIS AGENTS: PUBLICATIONS, FRANCIS-DAY S.A., 30, RUE DE L'ECHQUIER
BERLIN AGENTS: FRANCIS DAY & HUNTER G.m.b.H. LEIPZIGER STR 37, W.8.
PRINTED IN ENGLAND.

PART ONE

PERFORMERS 1897 — 1951

The Monologues in Part 1 are derived from the British Music Hall at the turn of the century. As the Victorian era ended, many turns on the halls were seeking an increased professional dignity and status more in keeping with the spirit of the age. They achieved it through the dramatic monologue.

Such monologues, in contrast with the cheerful vulgarity of the popular music hall song, were based on moral and patriotic appeal. This in turn stemmed from the 'uplift' songs of the 1860s — numbers like the Great Vance's *Act on the Square Boys* and Harry Clifton's *A Motto for Every Man.* But unlike these rollicking songs which often invited the audience to join in, the piano accompaniment to the dramatic monologue was secondary to the emphasis on the spoken word. These words were strung together in simple poetic form, mainly with rhyming couplets on the second and fourth lines.

The first "big name" music hall performer to bring all these elements together was Albert Chevalier (1862-1923). Our selection of his performances between 1898 and 1914 shows how he made the transition from the traditional music hall act to his eventual billing as the Coster Laureate. *The Future Mrs 'Awkins* (sometimes subtitled *A Cockney Carol*) is a typically sentimental ballad. What made it unusual was Chevalier's decision to speak the verse as indicated in the text. In 1898, the year in which this song was introduced, Chevalier asked his brother-in-law, the musician Alfred H. West, to collaborate with him in writing a purely dramatic monologue. The old actor's lament *A Fallen Star* was the result. Both this and *The Future Mrs 'Awkins* were considered of sufficient stature to justify a concert performance at the Queen's Hall in London in 1898 when Chevalier was supported by the Concert Party work of Pellisier's Follies.

A string of monologues were the result of continued collaboration between Chevalier and West: *An Old Bachelor* was the best known. Some of the others such as *The Yankee in London* and *Wot Vur Do Ee Luv Oi?* allowed Chevalier to show his versatility in using American and West Country dialects respectively. However, he never lost his enthusiasm for song monologues which bridged the gap with more traditional musical offerings and in *My Old Dutch* achieved his greatest personal success.

If Albert Chevalier was the first really well known performer to develop the dramatic monologue, it was one of his contemporaries, Bransby Williams, who brought acting to the halls with monologue works of a scale and variety which have never been surpassed. Born in 1870, he started his working life as a tea taster in Mincing Lane. He made his professional debut doing impersonations of Dan Leno and other music hall stars in working men's clubs and, in 1890, appeared as Sydney Carton in *The Noble Deed* at the Oxford. The presentation of Dickensian characters was the foundation of his music hall act and lasted throughout his career, from his first appearance at the London Shoreditch on 26th August 1896. In addition to Sydney Carton, Williams presented such varying Dickensian characters as Scrooge, Uriah Heep and Little Nell's Grandfather. To these he added his impressions of leading actors of the day such as Henry Irving, George Alexander, Fred Terry and Martin Harvey in some of their most histrionic Shakespearean and other roles.

Much of the fascination of Bransby Williams' act lay in the skill with which the young man, suitably dressed for each part, made his lightning costume and make-up changes from youth to old age and back again in full view of his audience.

By 1897, Williams was so well established that he shared "Top of the Bill" with Dan Leno at the London Pavilion and, in 1903, consolidated his career in the halls by signing a three year contract for eighteen weeks a year at the Empire, Leicester Square. In that same year, partly no doubt in keeping with the new monarch's more relaxed views (and certainly at the end of the official mourning for Queen Victoria) both Dan Leno and Bransby Williams became the first variety artists to appear by royal command at Sandringham.

Certainly Bransby Williams could claim credit for lifting the whole tone of the halls: following his Dickensian success — and noting Albert Chevalier's song monologue popularity — he decided to extend his repertoire by including several dramatic monologues. He chose material which still allowed him to dress in character and demonstrate his versatility. In *'Is Pipe*, Williams would appear in a smoking jacket following the action to the words as he lit his pipe. In such Charles Winter monologues as *The Caretaker and the Lounger,* Williams would dress accordingly while changing into the round cap and heavy oriental make-up required of *The Pigtail of Li-Fang-Fu.*

The musical background for most of this work was produced by Cuthbert Clarke, the musical director (and Williams' first accompanist) at the Empire, Leicester Square. It was while appearing at the Empire that Williams truly established his dramatic monologue success with *Devil May Care*, the work of Charles H. Taylor. Taylor, a charming personality, was to die young, but not before achieving a great success with *Tom Jones*. Of the other regular Williams writers, Arthur Helliar was popular in amateur circles; F. Chatterton Hennequin was a branch manager for Keith Prowse; Ridgwell Callum and Robert Service wrote Canadian and Wild West material based on their own travels and Sax Rohmer (born Arthur Sarsfield Ward and creator of the Fu Manchu character we know today) provided the main oriental input. In order to absorb an appropriate atmosphere for his work, Rohmer took to living in Limehouse where he would sit dictating to his secretary hidden behind an oriental screen.

Sax Rohmer, who also used his pen name Carolus Rex when contributing material for George Robey and Little Tich, was one of the many writers whom Bransby Williams gathered around him at his famous Sunday night suppers in the years before the First World War, at his house in Brixton. Others came from even more unusual sources. Colonel John Hay was the American ambassador in London and *Jim Bludso*, his story of the Mississippi steam boat captain whose ship goes down in flames, was first performed by Williams when crossing the Atlantic on the *Caronia* in 1905. By a strange coincidence, there was a fire on the *Caronia* on the same voyage. Despite this, Bransby Williams' southern accent was much admired by the many Americans on board, including his ship's concert party chairman Charles Hughes, Chief Justice of the United States.

This interest and enthusiasm for original material served Williams well and he performed over a hundred monologues, most of which he recorded. The range of his repertoire was to provide material — and inspiration — for monologue performers both professional and amateur. Williams' own career suffered badly when, in the early thirties, he broke a five year contract while appearing at the London Palladium to be with his wife after she had been in a car accident. The subsequent black-listing, the demise of the music hall and an ill-fated "legitimate" theatrical overseas touring venture reduced him from one of the highest paid performers to near poverty. However, with the introduction of television, he bounced back and, for many years, his performance as Scrooge was an annual event on Christmas Eve. He died in 1961 at the age of 91.

Milton Hayes, known as Micky Hayes, is included in the performer section as he was originally a concert party artist (and later appeared on the halls and made many recordings). He was smitten by the Fol-de-Rols' leading lady, Doris Lee, in Scarborough and, with her encouragement, took to writing. He became another of Bransby Williams' Sunday night guests and, in 1911, wrote for him probably the best known (and certainly most often parodied) of all the monologues, *The Green Eye of the Little Yellow God*.

When, in the twenties, Hayes took to performing again (with his *Monty* monologues) a certain professional jealousy grew up between him and Bransby Williams, particularly in the matter of *The Green Eye*. Hayes felt that he should be free to perform his own material but this ran counter to the performing rights agreement he had made with Willaims.

You Know What I Mean is one of the items which Milton Hayes made popular with his own performance and recording. Items in this selection were intended for wider use. Some of these, like *The Whitest Man I Know* (originally written for Bransby Williams) reflect the prejudices of the day and read strangely to modern eyes — although this piece was, as we shall see, to lend itself to many parodies. *Merchandise* was obviously inspired by the trade-promoting globe trotting activities of the Prince of Wales in the twenties, and is a rare example of Elsie April's monologue work. She was a pianist who originally worked with Fred Allendale on the Central Pier in Blackpool. When she graduated to the West End it was as a rehearsal pianist for C.B.Cochran and it was here that she came to the attention of Noel Coward and subsequently transposed and arranged much of his work. *Orange Peel* is also of interest since its military "passing the buck" theme is one which inspired Stanley Holloway's *Old Sam* (see page 61).

My Old Football also has a military connection which was typical of many immediate post-war pieces. *A Soldier's Reminiscences*, on the other hand, is a timeless piece about an old soldier's fading memory. It was the first of more than forty recordings made by Ernest Hastings, a bald-headed man with a pince-nez who became one of the first widely popular performers of the comedy monologue accompanying himself on the piano. In 1919 he had great success with *And Yet I Don't Know* and, in 1923, capped it with *My Word You Do Look Queer*. These classic comedy pieces were written by Bob Weston and Bert Lee, composers of the wartime hit *Goodbyee*. Bert Lee was a cheerful little Northerner who had started life as a piano tuner while Bob Weston, the ideas man, was a Cockney. *I Might Marry You* was also one of their contributions and its origins are evident from another Hastings hit *The Cautious Lover* which was originally performed (and composed) by an early monologue performer, Corney Grain.

This derivative approach was developed on the grand scale in the form of burlesque monologues by Billy Bennett. Born in 1887, he grew up in that great breeding ground of comics, Liverpool. He served as a regular cavalryman and was decorated during the 1914-1918 war with the M.M. and the D.C.M. (which, he would later claim, he was awarded for dumping horse salts in a French village well so that — ever afterwards — people came to take the health-giving local waters). Towards the end of the war, he took his "Shell Fire Concert Party" to perform in fields, barns, schools and hangars. As a result of this wartime experience, his first appearance on the halls (apart from one brief interlude as the rear end of a property horse) came as "The Trench Comedian". Gradually he got rid of the khaki uniform, retained his sergeant-major walrus moustache and hob-nailed boots and appeared, billed as "Almost A Gentleman" in a badly stained dress suit.

Bennett's speciality lay in parodying the best known dramatic monologues and poems as in *The Green Tie on the Little Yellow Dog, Devil-May-Not-Care, The Charge of the Tight Brigade* and *The Tightest Man I Know*. These take-offs of Bransby Williams and Milton Hayes ran into many published versions so that, for example, *The Green Tie on the Little Yellow Dog* would, on other occasions, start:

"There's a cock-eyed yellow poodle to the north of Waterloo
There's a little hot cross bun that's turning green . . ."

In introducing this and similar pieces, Billy Bennett would use quick-fire patter like, "Here's a little song written by my wife and composed by my mother-in-law entitled, 'I shall love you when your money has gone — but I shan't be with you'. Put that light on me. Not that green one. It makes me look as though I've been drinking cabbage water."

In the twenties, Bennett's monologues covered, as well as the parodies, a wide variety of original themes which made irreverent fun of, among others, actors, the night club set and, happily for the present editor, Members of Parliament. Much of this material was written by Billy Bennett himself, although a substantial part (and many entire pieces) were the work of his regular collaborator, T.W.Connor. Connor had contributed comic material for many years to leading pantomime dames like Herbert Campbell and Harry Randell and had even — before his success with dramatic monologues — sold *Mary, the Mudpusher's Daughter* to Bransby Williams for five shillings.

Many others attempted to emulate the Billy Bennett parody — especially amateur performers. Bennett's advice to them is revealing. As he said in the introduction of one of the many monologue booklets he produced with T.W.Connor:

"If you wish to be a success as a burlesque or mock-dramatic monologuist, the most important factor in your repertoire must be *sincerity*. You must apparently mean every word you utter, and as your lines become more ridiculous you must become more serious, even to the point of appearing indignant with the audience for daring to laugh at you!

Never laugh at your own gags whilst reciting burlesque poetry — even the heartiest scream from your listeners should not bring a semblance of a smile to your sphinx-like countenance.

Never stress or over-emphasise a point, let the gag do its own work, with the exception of a purposely bad rhyme (like hindoo and windoo) — this should be accentuated.

When the laugh comes, don't wait until it dies down before starting again, catch the tail-end of it and try to make your monologue one continuous ripple of laughter. Judge the speed you work at according to the reaction of your audience. By that I mean quicken up slightly until you get them going, then slow down a little; but at all times speak clearly and distinctly so that everyone can hear you.

Very little action is required during the recitation, and what little movements you employ should be those of a dramatic actor, *slightly* but not over-exaggerated. If the laughs are very big, fill in the time with these actions, but always with a straight face — and remember, the watch-word of the successful burlesque comedian is *Sincerity*."

In the thirties, Bennett joined those who used Bob Weston and Bert Lee's material as he turned to the newly-popular song monologue and, in *She Was Poor But She Was Honest*, he introduced what has become virtually the Cockney hymn — especially in the closing chorus:

"It's the same the whole world over,
It's the poor that gets the blame,
It's the rich that gets the pleasure,
Isn't it a blooming shame?"

Gracie Fields was another enormously popular performer who used Weston and Lee's song monologues with great comic effect, particularly in *Whiskers and All* and *Heaven Will Protect an Honest Girl*, an almost autobiographical tale of a Lancashire lass in London.

In fact, Gracie Fields can claim to be first exponent of the "big time" song monologue. When George Black presented the "new look" variety at the London Palladium in 1928, Gracie introduced a range of comic song monologues written for her by Will E. Haines and Jimmy Harper of which *The Biggest Aspidistra in the World, In My Little Bottom Drawer* and, above all, *Walter, Walter* became, in their way, as clearly identified with her as her romantic signature tune, *Sally*.

But "Our Gracie" had served a long apprenticeship before she became the legitimate successor to Marie Lloyd as

"Queen of the Halls". She was born over her grandmother's fish and chip shop in Rochdale in 1898. Encouraged — indeed driven — by her ambitious mother, by the time she was twelve she was a "half-timer" — one of the children who worked in a cotton mill from six o'clock in the morning and went to school afterwards. At the same time, she was singing in every amateur talent contest she could, seeking the ten shillings first prize and, more importantly, a chance to work in dancing troupes, concerts parties and pierrot shows.

When she was sixteen, Archie Pitt (whom she was to marry nine years later) put her into one of his touring shows. This led to her first West End success in the revue "Mr. Tower of London" at the Alhambra in 1923 when Hannen Swaffer described her strong singing voice and northern humour as "Beatrice Lillie, Florence Mills, Ethel Levey and Nellie Wallace all rolled into one."

It was this versatility which made her song monologues so effective and led from variety to some of the few really successful British film musicals of the thirties (Mrs Binns's Twins is from "Keep Smiling" in 1938). This led her to Hollywood and extensive wartime troop concerts in virtually every battle zone.

Teddy Holmes has described how she retained her humility. When she returned to Rochdale for the first time after the war, she learnt one of the latest song hits, *You'll never Know* especially for the occasion she could "sing it over the wall" or, in other words, on the balcony of the Town Hall. Afterwards, she slipped away to meet Mr Brierley, the cobbler who had made her clogs many years before.

In 1948, *I Took My Harp to a Party* and *Out in the Cold, Cold Snow* were two of her long established favourite song monologues which she chose for her return to the London Palladium. She continued to use them with other old favourites in periodic breaks from her retirement in Capri until her recent death.

Gracie Fields also played a major part in Stanley Holloway's emergence as the world's greatest exponent of the comic song monologue. When they were working together on location in Blackpool for the film "Sing as We Go" in 1933, Gracie asked Stanley why he did not go into variety. "Because I don't think I belong there," said Stanley, who was then heavily committed to musical comedy and film appearances. "Don't be silly," replied Gracie, "you've got those monologues you've made popular — let the people hear them."

The monologues to which she referred were the adventures of the old soldier Sam Small and "that grand little lad" young Albert Ramsbottom. Stanley Holloway, who was born in 1890, had developed the first of these characters to balance his singing act when invited to appear at the London Palladium in 1929. The idea of a soldier who would not pick up his rifle had been suggested to him by his old friend and fellow performer Leslie Henson. One night when his children had whooping cough, Stanley, banished to a spare room, found he could not sleep for thinking about Sam. Turning on his bedside light, he tore open an envelope and wrote a rough outline of *Old Sam*.

With this character, Stanley added to his already well established recording career, which had thrived through the whole of the nineteen twenties as a result of his success in the West End concert party, "The Co-Optimists". His usual collaborator then and for virtually all his monologues in the thirties was Wolseley Charles, a brilliant musician always known as "Harry". With the success of the Sam monologues, there was evident demand for a new character. Marriot Edgar, Edgar Wallace's half-brother and always referred to as "George" Edgar, had been on several Co-Optimist tours with Stanley and had studied the Sam monologues closely. A press report of a lion mauling a small boy at the London Zoo caught his attention, but when George mentioned this as a likely plot, Stanley replied, "Yes, I think it has possibilities, but you'll have a hell of a job with that gruesome ending." George Edgar persevered, however, and, by changing the venue to Blackpool, was able to inject the kind of northern humour which is so often displayed in the face of adversity. *The Lion and Albert* was first tried out in the formidable atmosphere of the Northern Rugby League Annual Dinner at the Grand Hotel, Newcastle and, as Stanley recently recalled, "It succeeded then and I knew I had a sure fire winner which has been a good friend to me for almost fifty years".

George Edgar was to write fifteen more monologues for Stanley Holloway.* He was joined by others like Archie de Bear, a co-founder and the publicity manager for the Co-Optimists, who produced *Many Happy Returns* which Stanley performed in a "schoolmaster's voice" on the many occasions when he was asked to appear before school children.

When he accepted Gracie Fields' advice to tour in variety, Stanley also became a member of the Weston and Lee song monologue club. *With Her Head Tucked Underneath Her Arm* was considered daring in 1934 in referring to the Bloody Tower. Indeed, high level conferences were held at the B.B.C. before it was accepted that this could be broadcast as an historical reference rather than an unparliamentary description. *Yorkshire Pudden* and *Brahn Boots* were also extremely popular on the halls during the thirties. The 1940-41 entries shown against them reflects their wartime recording dates. (They have also been part of Stanley Holloway's post-war repertoire which is covered in Part III).

---

* All these other George Edgar compositions, together with twenty-six other Holloway monologues have been published in *The Stanley Holloway Monologues* (Elm Tree 1979) and *Stanley Holloway — More Monologues and Songs* (Elm Tree 1980).

The "Miscellaneous" section which begins on page 68 is a representative sample of other monologue performers over the first half of the century, many of whom composed their own material. There is another Holloway link with the first two. Both Mel B. Spurr and Corney Grain were entertainers at the piano who sharpened Stanley Holloway's monologue interest when he saw them prior to his own first appearances on the halls, at the Tivoli, in 1912. Once their work was published, it was taken up and repeated by many other performers.

Tom Kilfoy and Lawrence Vane were typical of a number of pianist composers who performed their own monologues and seemingly had "one off" publications. Sam Walsh was rather better known, having published two works before *Up and Down The Strand* about the time he toured South America with Stanley Holloway and the Grotesques Concert Party in 1914.

Tom Clare was a monocled songs-at-the-piano specialist in the style of Ernest Hastings. He was one of a whole range of piano entertainers represented in this section who can be regarded as the successors to Harry Fragson. Fragson had been the biggest name of them all as a result of his success in both the London and Paris music halls where his magnetic personality and almost insolent attitude to his audience (in a style of which Max Wall is today's master) were unique. He died aged only 44 when he was shot by his insane father in Paris in 1913.

Both before and during the 1914-1918 war, a number of other piano entertainers flourished on the halls and as a recording artists. Nelson Jackson's *When Father Laid the Carpet On the Stairs* was very popular; Margaret Cooper made *Johnnie, Me and You* even more widely known than Corney Grain had done, and Dorothy Varick's *The Reflections of a Penny* was only one of half a dozen successful monologues which she performed during the war years.

What all these piano entertainers had in common was the use of songs — usually written by others — which were more spoken than sung. They can therefore claim to have developed the comic or dramatic monologue form in the style which, today, is demonstrated to perfection by Rex Harrison.

Fred Lewis gained much of his experience of the halls as a writer for the famous comedian Wilkie Bard. As a concert party comic himself, Lewis was a regular performer and obviously appreciated George Arthur's card playing word dexterity in *Auction for Life*.

Will Fyffe was a music hall giant who achieved success relatively late in life, when he made his debut at the London Palladium in 1921 at the age of 36. The epitome of Scottish humour, his signature tune became *I Belong to Glasgow*. Strangely, there were few Scottish monologues written and *The Scot's Lament* is an almost over-obvious piece about Scottish thrift. It was written by an unusual family combination: Kennedy Allen, a concert party comedian married to Georgina de Lara (best known for her dramatic work in *Anybody's Wife*), wrote the words and their daughter Kitty Kennedy Allen provided the musical background.

Chesney Allen's name will always be associated with his partner for over thirty years, Bud Flanagan, and the other members of the Crazy Gang. *Soliloquy of a Tramp* is an example of his solo work just before his partnership with Bud Flanagan began in 1931. The Cockney tramp role is in sharp contrast with Allan's usual suave straight-man work, but he had wide experience on the halls after his London debut at the Bedford, Camden Town in 1911 at the age of seventeen. Still remarkably active in 1981, he appeared in the Chichester Festival Theatre's tribute to his partnership with Bud Flanagan.

During the thirties, competition from cinema and the radio (and later television) saw the steady decline of the music hall. The newer monologue performers, while seen on the halls, tended to achieve their main recognition in the more intimate atmosphere of cabaret and, in the home, through radio and recordings. Many of them, like Gillie Potter or John Tilley used the prose form for their material, which takes them outside the scope of the rhyming monologues in this book. Those who came nearest to song monologue were performers like the Western Brothers and Ronald Frankau who appealed to West End audience with a new, slightly mocking approach, as in *The Old School Tie* and *Shootin' and Huntin' and Fishin'*.

Jack Warner, on the other hand, was a reversion to Cockney humour but, again, he owed his main success to radio. Born in 1900, he trained as an engineer and, influenced by the success of his sisters, Elsie and Doris Waters, tried his luck on the halls. In the late twenties, he worked as a comedy singer but, before his success in films and television as Dixon of Dock Green, he achieved his main recognition on radio during the Second World War. In the B.B.C.'s "Garrison Theatre" he wrote and introduced several monologues on which *Bunger Up of Rat 'Oles* is a typical example of his jokes at the expense of those with "necessary occupations". It was especially popular with service audiences and was one of his many wartime recordings.

Norman Long, often described as "Teeth and Trousers" and billed as "A Song, A Smile and A Piano", was another concert party performer who achieved his main success on the radio. He had also been successful as a recording artist from 1922 onwards, specialising in sharp social distinctions such as the joy of being a Smythe opposed to a Smith. In *The Twirp* he added his musical talents to the prolific pen of Robert Rutherford (some of whose work for Arthur Askey is included in Part III). There is a certain poignancy in this piece, with its references to "packed houses" and earning three hundred pounds a week, at a time when the music hall was so soon to disappear from the British scene.

Harry Hemsley was another artist who appeared on the halls but who achieved his major breakthrough on the radio and in many recordings. He specialised in child impressions, particularly in nursery rhyme and pantomime parodies. *Pity the Boy Who's Grown Out of his Clothes* is a typical example of his work.

Suzette Tarri worked as a comedienne with Harry Hemsley in recordings in the late thirties and as a cockney charwoman "Our Ada" in wartime radio broadcasts. Born in 1881, she had originally performed as a child violinist and contralto and was one of the generation of women musicians and singers who turned to comedy and monologues (Gladys Palmer and Edith Faulkener were others) with the growing popularity of the comedienne. *The Grand Old Girls of Britain* was written by her husband, David Jenkins, and was the kind of material she liked to use in balancing her comedy work and songs such as her signature tune *Red Sails in the Sunset*.

The last two performers, Nosmo King and Jack Watson, are a rare example of father and son monologuists. Nosmo King was the name chosen by Vernon Watson after his success in revues at the Empire, Leicester Square in 1912 and 1913 on the sound principle that, thereafter, his name would always be up in lights whenever "No Smoking" signs appeared.

His early success was gained with impressions of Harry Lauder, George Robey, George Formby (senior), Wilkie Bard and Alfred Lester (in which last role his first understudy was Jack Buchanan). He turned his hand to writing and performing monologues in the late thirties. (Other examples of his work are found in Part II.)

His style leaned heavily on the sentimental, but *Pull Together* in 1949 showed a new, almost political message as he expressed his dissatisfaction with many aspects of post-war Britain. (Note his thinly disguised disgust at the electorate's rejection of Winston Churchill.) The monologue has a special poignancy as Nosmo King died a few days after recording it on 4th January 1949.

Earlier he had recorded two other monologues *Common Sense* and *Providence* (see pages 134 and 135). These feature an introductory dialogue with a small boy, Herbert, played by his son Jack Watson, now best known as a television actor. After his father's death, Jack Watson carried on the family tradition and *Thanks Johnny* can be seen as one of the links between the monologue of the halls and its post-war variations as illustrated in Part III.

The Future Mrs 'Awkins (A Cockney Carol)
By Albert Chevalier (1898)

I knows a little doner, I'm about to own 'er,
　She's a goin' to marry me.
At fust she said she wouldn't, then she said she
　　couldn't,
　Then she whispered 'Well, I'll see.'
Sez I, 'Be Mrs. 'Awkins, Mrs. 'En'ry 'Awkins,
　Or acrost the seas I'll roam;
So 'elp me bob I'm crazy! Lizer, you're a daisy,
　Won't yer share my 'umble 'ome?'
(Spoken or Sung:) 'Won't yer?'
　Oh! Lizer! Sweet Lizer!
If you die an old maid you'll 'ave only yerself to
　　blame!
　D'y'ear Lizer? Dear Lizer!
'Ow d'yer fancy 'Awkins for your other name?

I shan't forgit our meetin', 'G'arn,' was 'er greetin'
　'Just yer mind wot you're about;'
'Er pretty 'ead she throws up, then she turns 'er nose
　　up,
　Sayin' 'Let me go, I'll shout!'
'I like your style,' sez Lizer; thought as I'd surprise 'er
　Cops 'er round the waist like this!

Sez she, 'I must be dreamin', chuck it I'll start
　　screamin' '
　'If yer do,' sez I, 'I'll kiss.'
(Spoken or Sung:) 'Now then'
　Oh! Lizer! Sweet Lizer!
If yer die an old maid you'll 'ave only yerself to blame!
　D'y'ear Lizer? Dear Lizer!
'Ow d'yer fancy 'Awkins for your other name?

She wears a artful bonnit, feathers stuck upon it,
　Coverin' a fringe all curled;
She's just about the sweetest, prettiest and neatest
　Doner in the wide, wide, world!
And she'll be Mrs. 'Awkins, Mrs. 'En'ry 'Awkins
　Got 'er for to name the day;
Settled it last Monday so to church on Sunday
　Off we trots the donkey shay!
(Spoken or Sung:) 'Now then'
　Oh! Lizer! Sweet Lizer!
If yer died an old maid you'd 'ave only yerself to
　　blame
　D'y'ear Lizer? Dear Lizer!
Mrs. 'En'ry 'Awkins is a fust class name!

A Fallen Star
By Albert Chevalier & Alfred H. West (1898)

Thirty years ago I was a fav'rite at the 'Vic.'
　A finished actor, not a Cuff and Collar shooting
　　stick.
I roused the house to laughter, or called forth the
　　silent tear,
　And made enthusiastic gods vociferously cheer.
Those were the days, the palmy days, of historic art,
　Without a moment's notice I'd go on for any part.
I do not wish to gas, I merely state in self-defence,
　The denizens of New Cut thought my Hamlet was
　　immense.
Thirty years ago! I can hear them shout 'Bravo,'
　When after fighting armies I could never show a
　　scar,
That time, alas! is gone, and the light that erstwhile
　　shone
　Was the light of a falling star.
From patrons of the circle too, I had my meed of
　　praise,

The ladies all admired me in those happy halcyon
　　days.
My charm of manner, easy grace, and courtly old-
　　world air,
　Heroic bursts of eloquence, or villain's dark despair.
I thrilled my audience thrilled 'em as they never had
　　been thrilled
　And filled the theatre nightly as it never had been
　　filled!
Right through the mighty gamut of emotions I could
　　range
　From classic Julius Caesar to the 'Idiot of the
　　Grange'.
Thirty years ago! I was someone in the show,
　And now I pass unrecognised in crowded street or
　　bar!
The firmament of fame holds no record of my name,
　The name of a fallen star!
The dramas that I played in were not all up on the stage.

Nor did I in an hour become the petted of the age.
Oft in my youthful days I've sung 'Hot Codlins' as the
    clown,
    And turned my face away to hide the tear-drops
      rolling down.
And when the pit and gallery saw I'd wiped the paint
    away,
    They shouted 'Go it, Joey. Ain't 'e funny? Hip
      hooray!'

My triumphs, and my failures, my rise, and then my
    fall!
    They've rung the bell, the curtain's down, I'm
      waiting for my call!
Bills — not those I owe — but old play-bills of the show!
    My name is Hamlet, Lear, Virginius, Shylock,
      Ingomar!
The laurel on my brow — a favourite — and now —
    Forgotten! a fallen star!

The Yankee in London
By Albert Chevalier & Alfred H. West (1900)

I've just arrived from New York, and I'm real glad that
    I came.
    This city's out of sight! Yes sir! It's worthy of its
      fame.
I've visited Chicago, Paris, Berlin, Cairo, Rome.
    But here I somehow kind of, sort of, feel that I'm at
      home.
America just owns the sun — you get it here in bits.
    We loan it — we're not selfish, we have more than
      we require,
Besides our hearts are warm enough to generate a fire.
    We're quicker on the other side, we can't afford to
      wait.
We always like to get in first, you bet, we're seldom
    late.
    There is, I know, some difference in Transatlantic
      time,
That may not p'r'aps explain it, but it helps me with a
    rhyme.
    Your buses and your cabs strike us Americans as
      slow.
Your theatres are O.K. when New York supplies the
    show.

You can't say we're remiss, no sir, we send you of the
    best,
Why in your aristocracy we've been known to invest.
    We've many points in common with our cousins over
      here.
We come of good old stock, our sires were men who
    knew no fear.
    We may at times run England down, I'm sorry, but I
      know
That relatives will squabble, it's their priv'lege, that is
    so.
    The only real difference so far as I can see,
Is the language that you speak, which is not pure
    enough for me.
    You have a horrid accent, you should hustle round
      and *git*
A genu*ine* New Yorker just to tone it down a bit.
    Great country sir, America, my own, I'm proud to
      state
And Britain is its 'mommer', so Great Britain's vurry
    great!

An Old Bachelor
By Albert Chevalier & Alfred H. West (1904)

They call me an old bachelor, I'm known as poor old
    bachelor,
    Although I'm really rich in what this world
      considers wealth.
But money can't buy everything, No! money is not
    everything,
    It cannot bring you happiness, it cannot purchase
      health.
I'm hale and very hearty too,

Play 'poker' and écarté too,
To pass the time away at home —
    My only home the Club!
The boys all know my Christian name!
    They call me by my Christian name!
And if they're running short of cash, and want a
    modest sub —
They know I've more than I can spend,
    I may say that I will not lend,

But still they get it in the end,
    From a poor old bachelor.
I've heard I save my money up —
    I scrape and hoard my money up,
Why don't I have a trifle on a gee gee now and then.
    A modest little flutter,
Yes, it's called, I think, a flutter,
    By some of my acquaintances who think they're
        sporting-men.
You're old, they say, and out-of-date,
    A trifle slow, at any rate.
I tell them they're so go ahead and p'r'aps I've lived
        too long.
    I only back the winners — and I do pick the
        winners —
Although before the race they always tell me that I'm
        wrong.
    They envy me my luck, they say,
And I? — Well I can only pray

That know my luck they never may. A poor old
    bachelor.
I've been advised to settle down,
    To choose a wife and settle down,
To find some homely body who is sensible and good.
    A tempting combination. An unusual combination.
I only smile and say I wouldn't marry if I could.
    They little guess when chaffingly
They question me and laughingly
    I answer how each thoughtless word recalls
        a dream of youth.
A dream from which I cannot wake,
    Of life lived for remembrance' sake,
They call me woman-hater! If they only knew the
        truth!
    But way out where the flowers are seen,
A white cross marks the place I mean,
    Who keeps a little grave so green? A poor old
        bachelor!

Wot Vur Do 'ee Luv Oi?
By Albert Chevalier & Alfred H. West (1905)

Oi've got a sweet'eart now Oi 'ave
    She be in love wi Oi,
Thought Oi should never 'ave the pluck
    Oi be that mortal shoy!
'Ay makin down at Varmer Giles
    Oi comes along side she,
An' Oi sez, to er Oi sez, sez Oi,
    'Wot's oop wi' you an' me?'
Oi sez 'Meg,' Oi sez 'Oi luv 'ee,'
    She sez 'Garge Oi luv 'ee too!'
She sez 'Wot vur do 'ee luv Oi?'
    Oi sez 'Wot vur? — coz Oi do!'
Us walks vur moiles, an' moiles, an' moiles,
    She'll let Oi take a 'buss' —
Soomtoimes she'll gi' Oi one as well,
    But Lard! she makes a fuss!
Us sets vur hours a 'oldin' 'ands,
    An' when 'er gives a soigh,

Oi knows it's toime to talk, and so
    Oi sez to 'er sez Oi:
Oi sez 'Meg,' Oi sez 'Oi luv 'ee,'
    She sez 'Garge Oi luv 'ee too!'
She sez 'Wot vur do 'ee luv Oi?'
    Oi sez 'Wot vur? — coz Oi do!'
Folks laugh at we, but us don't care!
    Sez Oi Oi'll tell 'ee wot,
'Us be in luv,' sez Oi, 'us be,
    An' pities them that's not!
Don't take no notice — don' 'ee moind —'
    Oi tells 'er on the sloy.
'We'll make un jealous: then Oi sez
    To 'er, Oi sez, sez Oi:
Oi sez 'Meg,' Oi sez 'Oi luv 'ee,'
    She sez 'Garge Oi luv 'ee too!'
She sez 'Wot vur do 'ee luv Oi?'
    Oi sez 'Wot vur? — coz Oi do!'

The Village Constable
By Albert Chevalier & Alfred H. West (1909)

Ah! wot a moighty wicked place our village it 'ud be,
    If 'twasn't vur the care Oi takes from crime to keep it
        free,

Oi've taught 'un to respect the law since Oi've been in
    the force,
    An' wot Oi sez, they 'as ter do, they 'as ter do, of course.

Oi can't 'ave that, Oi sez, Oi can't, Oi bean't agoin' to
    tell 'ee why,
  An' don' 'ee try no tricks on 'cos Oi'm moighty sharp
    and floy —
Oi can't 'ave that, Oi sez, Oi can't, Ah! you may stan'
    an' gi' Oi jaw,
  But when Oi sez a thing, Oi sez, the thing Oi sez be
    law.
They troies all koinds o' broibes wi' Oi, but Lor!
    Oi knows their game,
  There's nowt Oi can't see through at once, Oi puts
    un all to shame.
Oi be that quick they knows wi' Oi they don't stan' arf a
    chance,
  Oi be a reg'lar master-piece to see things at a glance.
Oi can't 'ave that, Oi sez, Oi can't, Oi bean't agoin' to
    tell 'ee why,
  An' don' 'ee try no tricks on 'cos Oi'm moighty sharp
    and floy —

Oi can't 'ave that, Oi sez, Oi can't, Ah! you may stan'
    an' gi' Oi jaw,
  But when Oi sez a thing, Oi sez, the thing Oi sez be
    law.
It's hard work tho', vor Muddleton's a moighty busy
    place.
  There's foive-an'-forty people an' they loikes to go
    the pace.
But Lor! Oi've got un all inside the 'oller o' my 'and,
  They dursent call their souls their own, Oi tell 'ee as
    it's grand.
Oi can't 'ave that, Oi sez, Oi can't, Oi bean't agoin' to
    tell 'ee why,
  An' don' 'ee try no tricks on 'cos Oi'm moighty sharp
    and floy —
Oi can't 'ave that, Oi sez, Oi can't. Ah! you may stan'
    an' gi' Oi jaw,
  But when Oi sez a thing, Oi sez, the thing Oi sez be
    law.

My Old Dutch
By Albert Chevalier & Charles Ingle (1911)

I've got a pal,
  A reg'lar out an' outer,
She's a dear good old gal.
  I'll tell yer all about 'er.
It's many years since fust we met,
  'Er 'air was then as black as jet,
It's whiter now, but she don't fret,
  Not my old gal!

Chorus
We've been together now for forty years,
  An' it don't seem a day too much,
There ain't a lady livin' in the land
  As I'd 'swop' for my dear old Dutch.

I calls 'er Sal,
  'Er proper name is Sairer,
An' yer may find a gal
  As you'd consider fairer.
She ain't a angel — she can start
  A-jawin' till it makes yer smart,
She's just a *woman*, bless 'er 'eart,
  Is my old gal!

Chorus.

Sweet fine old gal,
  For worlds I wouldn't lose 'er,
She's a dear good old gal,
  An' that's what made me choose 'er.
She's stuck to me through thick and thin,
  When luck was out, when luck was in,
Ah! wot a wife to me she's been,
  An' wot a *pal!*

Chorus.

I sees yer Sal —
  Yer pretty ribbons sportin'!
Many years now, old gal,
  Since them young days of courtin'
I ain't a coward, still I trust
  When we've to part, as part we must,
That Death may come and take me fust
  To wait . . . my pal!

Chorus.

'E Can't take a Roise Out of Oi!
By Albert Chevalier & Alfred H. West (1911)

Oi've sarved a many masters, an' Oi've travelled in my
    toime,
    Oi've been as fur as twenty moile from 'ere;
Oi'm eighty-four coom Christmas, an' Oi feels just in
    my proime,
    An' never was moi yed an' thoughts more clear!
Moi son 'e left the village nigh on thirty year ago,
    An' drat un! 'e coom back 'ome t'other day:
'Tain't that Oi grumbles at, at all, tho' that there were a
    blow —
    It's 'is 'Oi knows all about it' sort o' way!

Oi've been moindin' the farm 'ere fur forty-five years,
    An' afore that, the pigs in the stye,
An' Oi knows wot Oi knows, an' Oi 'ears wot Oi 'ears,
    An' 'e can't take a roise out of Oi!

'E sez as Oi'm be'oind the toimes, wotever that may
    mean,
    Becos Oi don't take kindly tew 'is ways,
'E tells about play-actors, an' all sich like as 'e's seen,

An' sez as 'ow theayter bizness pays.
Lord sakes! Oi gits that roiled, as Oi could 'it un when
    'e talks,
    A-sayin' as 'ow actors roides in style,
Oi've seed un ride at circus, but on comin' out they
    walks,
    'E laughs at Oi, an' that makes my blood bile!
Oi've been moindin' the farm, etc.

'E musn't think as 'ow becos 'e's lived i' Lunnon town
    'E's ev'rybody — me amongst the rest!
Oi've 'arf a moind to show un up, or reyther take un
    down,
    Oi 'ardly knows which way ud be the best.
Soomtoimes I lets un talk, and then Oi busts into a
    laugh,
    Oi never did 'ear sich a pack o' loies.
'E sez as 'ow 'e's seed a thing they calls the 'fonygraph!'
    You turns a 'andle, an' it talks an' croies!
    Oi've been moindin' the farm, etc.

Napoleon's Last Dream
By Albert Chevalier & Alfred H. West (1914)

I dreamed last night of ev'ry fight
    Where in my might I conqu'ring led.
Of battle cries; of lung-pierced sighs;
    Of glazing eyes; of all my dead!
For I had killed and stormed and stilled,
    As I had willed, in ruthless fray.
I knew — too late — relentless fate
    Had marked a date — had fixed — a Day!
There stood revealed, that hated field
    Where doomed to yield, I bowed the knee.
My bravest slain; my courage vain!
    A cup to drain Grief filled for me.
Once more, in trance, I saw my France a prey to
    chance,
    A conquered land — and 'ere surprise
Had stunned my eyes
    Beheld her rise erect and grand!
And at her side there stood, allied,
    A Pow'r world-wide, my conqu'ring foe!
The brave all came,

And loud their claim
In freedom's name
    To lay Lust low —
The lust of greed, of braggart breed;
    Of War Lord's lead 'gainst Peace, grown bold.
True friends in need, in word and deed,
    Close bound they bleed
Their faith to hold.
    Their faith — in PEACE,
In earth's increase,
    When war shall cease — when Caesars die!
For this they fight in all their might,
    And they are right, *I* say it — I!
For good or ill my iron will, unrivalled still,
    Can know no peer. Stern fate will see who copies me,
Shall bow the knee in abject fear.
    I know when Peace the whole world seeks,
When Peace, on War, grim vengeance wreaks,
    The Dawn is near — Napoleon speaks:
God sends — The Day!

11

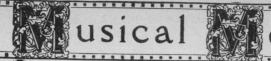

Musical Monologues

RECITATIONS WITH ❧ MUSICAL ACCOMPANIMENTS

An early Reynolds & Co. publication featuring Albert Chevalier

No. 23.

The Yankee in London.

Composed by

ALFRED H. WEST.

Written and Performed by

ALBERT CHEVALIER.

Bransby Williams on another Reynolds cover, 1925

RECITATIONS WITH ❧ MUSICAL ACCOMPANIMENTS

No. 306.

THE LAST BOTTLE

WRITTEN BY

PETER CHEYNEY

MUSIC BY

HAROLD ARPTHORP

PERFORMED BY

BRANSBY WILLIAMS

Jim Bludso

By Colonel John Hay & Eric Mareo (1905)
Performed by Bransby Williams

Well no! I can't tell where he lives because he don't
    live, you see!
    Least ways, he's got out of the habit of livin' like you
    and me.
Where have you been for the last three years, that you
    haven't heard folks tell,
    How Jimmy Bludso passed in his checks the night of
    the Prairie Belle?
He weren't no saint — them engineers is all pretty
    much alike;
    One wife in Natchez-under-the-Hill and another one
    here in Pike.
A keerless man in his talk, was Jim, and an awkward
    man in a row,
    But he never funked and never lied, I reckon he
    never knowed how;
And this was all the religion he had to treat his engines
    well;
    Never be passed on the river: to mind the Pilot's
    bell:
And if ever the Prairie Belle took fire a thousand times
    he swore,
    He'd hold her nozzle agin the bank till the last soul
    got ashore.
All boats has their day on the Missisip and her day
    came at last.
    The Movastor was a better boat, but the Belle she
    wouldn't be passed.

And so come tearin' along that night the oldest craft on
    on the line
    With a nigger squat on her safety valve, and her
    furnace crammed, resin and pine.
The fire burst out as she cleared the bar and burnt a
    hole in the night,
    But quick as a flash she turned and made for that
    willowbank on the right
There was runnin' and cursin', but Jim yelled out over
    all the infernal roar.
    'I'll hold her nozzle agin the bank till the last galoot's
    ashore!'
Throught the hot black breath of the burning boat, Jim
    Bludso's voice was heard
    And they all had faith in his cussedness, and knowed
    he would keep his word.
Sure as you're born they all got off, afore the
    smokestack fell.
    And Bludso's ghost went up alone in the smoke of
    the Prairie Belle.
He weren't no saint, but at judgement I'd run my
    chance with Jim:
    Longside of some pious gentlemen, that wouldn't
    shook hands with him
He'd seen his duty a deadsure thing and went for it
    there and then:
    And Christ ain't goin' to be too hard, on a man that
    died for men.

'Is Pipe

By Charles H. Taylor & Cuthbert Clarke (1905)
Performed by Bransby Williams

You're not as 'andsome as you was,
    Old pipe, if truth be told,
But we ain't parting just becos
    You're black, and worn, and old.
I'm not in many many ways
    The cove I used to be;
And ain't a flattering when I says
    You're stronger now than me.
You cost a bob at first, may be;
    You ain't no fancy touch,
But there, you're worth as much as me,
    And that, Gawd knows, ain't much.
We draw'd together from the fust;
    We knows each other's ways;

And you're a pal as I can trust —
    That's somethink nowadays.
She give yer to me, my old gal —
    My gal wot used to be;
Wot 'appy times we 'ad ol pal,
    Eh? 'er and you and me!
Times lightly passed, like 'arf a ounce
    Of 'bacca, keerless drawn
An' blown away, they all amounts
    To somethink when they're gone.
She says: 'Yer won't forgit me Bill!
    I knows yer, I can tell;
But sometimes of a evening, will,
    You act I'm there as well?

An' when you're smoking quiet,
    Will you talk to me? becos
I might be very near you, Bill.'
    Supposin' now she was!
She's gone to heaven, and that's the place
    Where all the past's forgot.
So some religious covey says —
    Who knows a blooming lot!

Lord! if I thought she could forgit
    Them days wot used to be —
Well it 'ud 'urt above a bit,
    Old pal, eh? you, and me.
Let's wait a while — what must be must,
    The time ain't far off when
You'll be ashes, an' I'll be dust,
    For ever, an' ever, Amen.

Devil-May-Care
By Charles H. Taylor & Cuthbert Clarke (1905)
Performed by Bransby Williams

Fly, if you see me in the street
    Leave me to drift — to drift.
Turning aside if by chance we meet,
    Pray that the end come swift.
Once I was spick and span like you,
    Had money and all to spare:
Do you remember me? Yes you do!
    Dear old Devil-may-Care.
Devil-may-Care who paid your debts
    When you'd gone the pace too fast;
Devil-may-Care whom the world forgets,
    But Devil-may-Care to the last.
Some of you tell today with pride,
    Aye! brag of it here and there.
How you scattered the Pathans side by side
    With Dashing Devil-may-Care.
You were plucky enough in days gone by
    But you haven't the saving grace,
To look at me boldly in the eye
    When you meet me face to face.
Not that I want it, Heaven knows;
    Shabby with wear and tear,
Little remains now I suppose,
    Of what once was Devil-may-Care.
How do I live? Well — never mind,
    That's a secret I can keep;

I manage a sort of meal to find
    And a place where I crawl to sleep.
To sleep, and see in a fitful dream
    The wraith of a face once fair,
And a woman's eyes, whose tender gleam
    Once dazzled old Devil-may-Care.
To wake, and wonder what might have been
    Had the game been fairly played;
To wearily fumble the tangled skein
    That a woman's fingers made.
We waltzed together the night we met —
    'Twas an Indian summer night
And I gazed my fill in her eyes deep set
    And her soul seemed pure and white.
Every one told me she was false,
    And by Heaven! I proved it well;
And I danced the Devil's eternal waltz
    That spins on the brink of Hell;
Till I reeled from the verge with a heart that broke,
    And with pockets with nothing in.
And the world took the first for a lively joke,
    But the last was a deadly sin.
What does it matter? It soon will end
    With the sentinel's 'Who goes there?'
And to Death I shall cheerfully cry — 'A friend!'
    And he'll say 'Pass, Devil-may-Care.'

The Hindoo's Paradise
By Herbert Harraden (1907)
Performed by Bransby Williams

A Hindoo died.
    A happy thing to do
When twenty years united to a shrew.
    Released, he hopefully for entrance cries
Outside the gates of Brahma's Paradise.
    'Hast been through Purgatory?' Brahma said.

'No, I've been married, I have been married,'
    And he hung his head.
'Come in! Come in! And welcome, too, my son,
    For marriage and Purgatory are as one.'
With joy supreme he entered Brahma's door,
    And knew *that* bliss he ne'er had known before.

He scarce had entered in the garden fair,
    Ere another Hindoo craved admission there.
The selfsame question Brahma asked again.
    'Hast been through Purgatory?' 'No! What then?'
'Thou canst not enter,' did the God reply.

'But he who went in had been no more than I.'
'All that is true, but he has married been.
    And so on earth *he* suffered for his sin.'
'Married! 'Tis well! For I've been married *twice.*'
    'Begone! Begone! We want no fools in Paradise!'

For a Woman's Sake
By Lorna Fane & Cuthbert Clarke (1908)
Performed by Bransby Williams

He fought for his country as brave men will,
    Who *die* for their country's sake,
But there was a mightier motive still
    And a higher prize at stake.
He fought for the fame where glory lies:
    To win a smile from a woman's eyes.
He spurred on his horse to its utmost speed,
    And thick in the fight rode he,
And many a noble heroic deed
    Was done in his bravery.
But the one reward he craved was this,
    To feel the touch of a woman's kiss.
He lived in the saddle from dawn till night,
    And often till dawn again.
And the sun rose red on a ghastly sight,
    Of wounded amidst the slain:
But thro' the horror of time and place,
    His thoughts were full of a woman's face.

He stuck to his colours until the last,
    Then sailed for his native land,
For his heart was hungry to feel the clasp
    Of a woman's tender hand.
But life had something to teach him yet, —
    That women of fashion soon forget.
He had staked his all on the woman's vow,
    His life on a woman's kiss,
And nothing that mattered could happen now,
    Since what had happened was this:
That he, who fearless had faced the foe,
    Passed from her presence with head bowed low.
He went to the dogs at a quicker rate
    Than many a man grown grey,
For it's very easy to find Hell's gate
    When the Devil leads the way.
And one more soul was damned in despair;
    For the sake of a woman false and fair.

How We Saved the Barge
By Arthur Helliar & Cuthbert Clarke (1908)
Performed by Bransby Williams

I'm a Captain, that's what I am, sir, a nautical man by
        trade,
    Though I ain't tricked out in a uniform with buttons
        of gold and braid.
I ain't the Captain it's true of one of these floating
        grand hotels, —
    It's true as I ain't the skipper of one of these Clacton
        or Yarmouth Belles.
I'm the Captain of this 'ere barge, sir, wot's known as
        the 'Slimy Sal,'
    And a faster boat there ain't on the length or breadth
        of the whole canal.
Though I'll own so far as the breadth's concerned that
        ain't much praise o' course,
    And the number of knots an hour she makes has
        summat to do with a horse.

Have I ever had any adventures, the same as one
        meets at sea?
    I should rather just think I 'ave, sir, not *one* but a
        dozen may be.
If it wasn't as 'ow my throat's so dry as to almost stop
        my breath,
    I'd tell yer the way as the missis and me was
        snatched from the jaws of death. —
Her courage it was too as saved us, 'er courage what
        pulled us through,
    Or I wouldn't be standing here thirsty — well thank
        'ee, don't mind if I do.
One morning some two or three weeks ago, our cargo
        had all been stowed,
    We'd 80 odd tons of coal aboard which o' course was
        a fairish load, —

15

We'd got a new 'orse that day, sir, too good for the job a lot,
    He'd once been a Derby winner, though 'is name I've clean forgot.
He was standing harnessed on to the barge, the missis and I was aboard.
    When all of a sudden we feels a jerk and he starts of his own accord.
Something or other had startled him, what it was I never could think,
    Though I fancy he'd 'eard some gent like you wot 'ad offered to stand me a drink.
I flew like a flash to the rudder, and I pushes it 'ard alee,
    And the missis 'ad 'oisted a flag of distress to the chimbly, I could see.
We 'adn't a fog 'orn or whistle aboard but the missis she yells like two,
    But the louder she screamed out 'Clear the course' the faster the old 'orse flew.
He thought he was back in the days gone by, a-winning some famous race,
    'Twas a race with death for the missis and me at that awful 'eadlong pace.
'Ouses and trees went flying by — a mighty splash and a shock —
    And we'd passed bang through, without paying too, the closed up gates of a lock.
Just then when we'd whizzed through a tunnel she yells from the lower deck
    And says 'If that 'orse ain't pulled up pretty quick, I can see as we're in for a wreck.'
We only got thirty or forty miles till we gets to the end of the course,
    It's a case of which 'olds out the longest the bloomin' canal or the 'orse.

But before I tells 'ow we was saved, sir, there's one thing I'd like yer to know,
    My missis was once in a circus as a h'artist I mean, years ago.
She used to perform on the tightrope and wonderful tricks too she done,
    But of course, that's all finished and over, her weight being seventeen stun.
Then she stood on the deck where I stood sir, and I sees a gleam come in her eye,
    She says 'It's a chance in a thousand, but it's one as I'm willing to try.
The 'eadlong career of the 'orse must be stopped, it's our last and our only hope.
    There's only one way to get at 'im, I must walk to his back on the rope.'
She gives me one farewell 'ug sir, takes an oar for a pole in 'er hands,
    Then smiling, as tho' in a circus, on the tow-rope a second she stands.
I closed both my eyes after that sir, for the sight would a made me unnerved,
    For a 'orrible death 'twould 'ave meant for 'er if the barge for a moment had swerved.
But I opens 'em wide in a moment, for I 'ears a loud kind of a crack,
    And I sees that there 'orse all collapse in a 'eap, for the missis 'ad broken 'is back.
As soon as the crisis was over, on the deck in a swoon sir I dropped,
    But the barge went on for a mile and a 'arf on its lonesome afore it was stopped.
Why didn't we cut thro' the rope, sir, and 'ave let the 'orse loose instead?
    Just fancy you thinking o' that now, why it never came into my 'ead!!

The Student

By John Edwards (1908)
Performed by Bransby Williams

At a certain University not many years ago
    There lived a student, learned, wise and slow.
From flighty feelings he was quite exempt
    And all frivolity held in contempt.
In fact for knowledge he was widely noted
    And as a model was oft-times quoted.
One fatal day, on serious thoughts intent,
    Our hero o'er a ponderous tome was bent,
Extracting wisdom from its musty pages,
    For knowledge is not gained by easy stages.

When a light foot-fall at his door he hears,
    And in his room a fair damsel appears.
'What, Sister Madge,' cried he with unfeigned glee,
    'Sit down my dear, we'll have some tea.'
They whiled away the hours with pleasant chat
    Of plays, pictures, and her last new hat.
When suddenly at the door there came a loud rat-tat.
    Brother and sister both exclaimed 'Tut tut. What's that?'
'Oh,' said the youth, with reassuring look,

'Twill be some fellow student for a book.
You get behind those curtains there — just so
  And in a moment I'll make him go.'
Then turning to the door which he opened wide,
  There a grey wizened old man espied.
'Excuse me, sir,' the ancient one began,
  'I occupied these rooms some fifty years ago,
And thought I'd like to see them once again before I
    died.'
  'With pleasure sir, just step inside and look around.
You'll find them interesting, I'll be bound.'
  'Ah me! the same old place I see once more,

The same old ceiling and the same old floor.
  The same old grate where I have often sat till very,
    very late.
The same old window and the same old view.'
  Then he the curtains wide apart withdrew,
His quick eye resting on the dame, he chuckled,
  'Aye, aye, aye, and the same old game.'
'Excuse me, sir,' said the youth, hurt at the slur,
  'This lady is my sister sir!'
The old man smiled and quick to make reply
  Said, 'I beg your pardon, Sister? Oh!
Aye, aye, aye and the same old lie!'

Jack
By Fred Rome & Ada Tunks (1910)
Performed by Bransby Williams

'Tis ten long years since first we met,
  He came not from a famous set,
A tiny pup, a precious pet
  My little Jack.
He was not born of high degree,
  He had no lengthy pedigree,
But he was all the world to me
  My little Jack.
Folk may think my ways absurd,
  For I told him all that had occurred,
He understood most every word
  My little Jack.
Once the victim of a heartless theft
  Of home and all I was bereft,
I was happy for I'd one thing left,
  My little Jack.
And when the funds and food were low,
  The same affection he'd bestow,
How different from the world we know,
  Was little Jack.
And when I once was taken ill,
  He lingered by my bedside still,
The only one my heart to thrill
  Was little Jack.
Each morn upon my humble bed,
  He'd greet me with a drooping head,

What sorrow on his face I read,
  My little Jack.
And when our hardship days had flown,
  And many hardships we have known,
Still he ate his humble bone,
  My little Jack.
One night I lost him on his way,
  Some friends had led my Jack astray,
I watched and waited day by day,
  For little Jack.
And when a weary week passed by,
  One night I heard a piteous cry,
My Jack returned to me to die,
  Poor little Jack.
My only friend in pain and play,
  My life's sunshine had passed away,
My only pal in stillness lay,
  My little Jack.
He was but a dog, a beast I know,
  I'm a fool perhaps to worry so,
But my only friend on earth below
  Was little Jack.
His tiny life is at an end,
  But Heaven never more can send,
A stauncher pal, a truer friend
  Than little Jack.

The Portrait
By Owen Meredith & Eric Mareo (1911)
Performed by Bransby Williams

Midnight passed! not a sound of aught thro' the silent
    house, but the wind at his prayers.
  I sat by the dying fire and thought of the dear dead
    woman upstairs.

A night of tears for the gusty rain had ceased but the
    eaves were dripping yet;
  And the moon looked forth, as tho' in pain, with her
    face all white and wet.

Nobody with me, my watch to keep but the friend of
    my bosom, the man I love;
    And grief had sent him fast asleep in the chamber up
      above.
Nobody else in the country place all round, that knew
    of my loss beside,
    But the good young priest with the Raphael-face,
      who confessed her when she died.
That good young priest is of gentle nerve and my grief
    had moved him beyond control.
    For his lips grew white, as I could observe, when he
      speeded her parting soul.
I sat by the dreary hearth alone; I thought of the
    pleasant days of yore.
    I said 'The staff of my life is gone; the woman I
      loved is no more.
On her cold dead bosom my portrait lies, which next
    to her heart she used to wear.
    Haunting it o'er with her tender eyes, when my own
      face was not there.
It is set all round with rubies red and pearls which a
    Peri might have kept,
    For each ruby there my heart hath bled, for each
      pearl my eyes have wept.'
And I said 'The thing is precious to me, they will bury
    her soon in the church yard clay.
    It lies on her heart and lost must be, if I do not take
      it away.'
I lighted my lamp at the dying flame and crept up the
    stairs that creaked for fright.
    Till into the chamber of Death I came, where she lay
      all in white.
The moon shone over her winding sheet, there stark
    she lay on her carven bed,
    Seven burning tapers about her feet and seven about
      her head.
As I stretched my hand I held my breath; I turned as I
    drew the curtains apart.
    I dared not look on the face of Death: I knew where
      to find her heart.

I thought at first, as my touch fell there, it had warmed
    that heart to life with love;
    For the thing I touched was warm, I swear, and I
      could feel it move.
'Twas the hand of a man, that was moving slow o'er the
    heart of the dead from the other side,
    And at once the sweat broke over my brow, 'Who is
      robbing the corpse?' I cried.
Opposite me, by the taper's light, the friend of my
    bosom, the man I loved.
    Stood over the corpse, and all as white, and neither
      of us moved.
'What do you here, my friend?' The man looked first at
    me and then at the dead. —
    'There is a portrait here' — he began. 'There is. It is
      mine.' I said.
Said the friend of my bosom 'Yours, no doubt, the
    portrait was till a month ago.
    When this suffering angel took that out, and placed
      mine there, I know.'
'This woman loved me well,' said I. 'A month ago,' said
    my friend to me
    'And in your throat,' I groaned. 'You lie!' He
      answered 'Let us see.'
'Enough!' I returned. 'Let the dead decide, and
    whosoever the portrait prove,
    His shall it be, when the cause is tried, where death
      is arraigned by Love.'
We found the portrait in its place: we opened it by the
    taper's shine.
    The gems were all unchanged: the face was —
      neither his or mine.
'One nail drives out another, at least! The face of the
    portrait there,' I cried,
    'Is our friend's, the Raphael-faced young priest, who
      confessed her when she died.'
The setting is all of rubies red and pearls which a Peri
    might have kept.
    For each ruby there my heart hath bled: for each
      pearl my eyes have wept.

The Caretaker

By Charles J. Winter (1912)
Performed by Bransby Williams

We've had a fine time and no kid, puss,
    We've been 'ere two year come next week.
Still the 'ouse isn't let, and not likely,
    Although we've oft 'ad a near squeak.
But the yarn that I pitch is so creepy,
    Not a soul cares the 'orrers to face,
So we can rest easy and sing, puss,

There's no place like 'ome.
You want to look over the 'ouse sir?
    Why certainly, step this way.
It's a 'ouse anyone might be proud of,
    So the 'undreds that's seen it say.
Don't mind the cat jumping about sir:
    Maybe she is after a rat,

She's at it from morning to night sir,
    But there's swarms of them still for all that,
'Ow they get 'ere I'm sure is a marvel,
    Leastways 'twas a marvel to me,
Till one morning I spots on the reason,
    When a hextra big fat one I see.
I figgers it out like this 'ere sir,
    Their numbers would not always swell
If they didn't come out from the sewer,
    And besides that accounts for the smell.
Is the smell very bad? well not always,
    Why *sometimes* the air is quite clear.
And I've only 'ad three bouts of typhoid
    In the two years I 'ave been 'ere.
No, the smell's not so bad as the damp sir,
    For that fairly gets into your bones,
And you'll never be free from rheumatics
    While the damp rises off of them stones.
But there — what's the good of complaining,
    There's even some blessing in that,
For the fungus and moss on the 'earthstone
    Makes a lovely soft bed for the cat.
And if I don't sweep over the floors, sir,
    For a day or two after some rain,
The mildoo's that white and that pure, sir,
    It's as pretty as snow in a lane.
Any sounds? well not doorin' day sir,
    But at midnight there's moans and there's groans,
And a 'orrible smell of blue brimstone,

With shrieks and the rattlin' of bones.
As a fact that's the one serious drawback,
    And I'm sorry I let an 'int drop,
(Don't give me away to the owner,
    Or he'll 'ave me kicked out neck and crop.)
But the sounds that we get 'ere at midnight
    Forget them, well I never shall.
I'm sure I'd go stark, staring balmy,
    If I 'adn't the cat for a pal.
It comes of that there Jack the Ripper,
    What once used to live 'ere they say,
'E made this a kind of 'eadquarters
    When putting his victims away,
And now all their ghosts come to 'aunt 'im,
    A shrieking and dragging great chains.
Well, I'm sure I'm a pretty tough 'andful,
    But that there beats the rats and the drains.
What! you *like* the house from my description?
    And you wish that you'd come 'ere before?
Well, I'm 'anged if that don't take the biscuit!
    Then I shan't be wanted no more!!
I suppose you're some newspaper feller
    That wants in a ghost house to hide?
Or a chap that's been chucked by 'is sweetheart,
    And wants to commit suicide?
Or perhaps you are studying 'hefluvias,'
    If so you've a chance that is prime!
Beg pardon? *What! You are the landlord!!*
    O hang it! I've done it this time!

The Coward
By F. Chatterton Hennequin & Harry May Hemsley (1913)
Performed by Bransby Williams

It was muttered in his club-room, it was whispered in
    the mess,
    As the rumour grew with telling, men believed it
    more or less.
Over cards they say it happened, grew to earnest from
    a joke,
    And tho' twenty heard the insult, yet the coward
    never spoke.
He had friends of course who waited, said his reasons
    must be good,
    But he did not give his reasons, and they never
    understood.
One by one they drifted from him, till the tale of
    friends was done,
    Tho' they shunned him like a leper, yet the coward
    spoke to none.
So the poison quickly spreading, reached at length his
    lady's ear,

And she proudly said 'I trust him,' tho' her heart was
    chill with fear,
All in vain she waited, hoping, till her faith in him
    grew weak,
    Then she gave him back his freedom, yet the coward
    would not speak.
Next his grim old Colonel heard it, and his brow grew
    black as night.
    'By the love I bore your father, by the God of truth
    and right,
They are liars all who say it' — then the man's heart
    nearly broke,
    'Tell your father's friend the truth boy,' yet the
    coward never spoke.
So his Colonel sorely puzzled, got him transferred to
    the front,
    Where the snarling Hills-men squabble, and our
    Tommies bear the brunt,

They were ambushed in a donga, with all hope of
    rescue past,
  Came a whisper of surrender, then the coward spoke
    at last.
'We were sent here for a purpose, to uphold our
    Country's fame,
  If these dogs shall take us living, they will spit upon
    our name,
We must take the fighting chances, till our paltry lives
    are sped,
  'Ere I give the word surrender you shall see me
    damned and dead.'
On the Afghan border lying with his secret
    unconfessed

Is the coward, with his story locked for ever in his
    breast.
Were the reasons for his silence, such as you or I might
    guess?
  Should he speak a friend's dishonour, or a woman's
    shame confess?
More than this we may not question, for the truth is
    with the dead,
Till our secrets are discovered when the lives of men
    are read.
But the Judgment Book will show it, clear of blame,
    free from disgrace,
When the coward gives his reasons, to his Maker face
    to face.

Joe's Luck

By L. Waldron & Cuthbert Clarke (1913)
Performed by Bransby Williams

Dear old Joe he was one of the best
  And everyone's pal without doubt
The sort of chap that would give you his boots
  And swear he walked better without.
Why I've known him to give his last dollar away
  To some other fellow in need,
And explain that he fasted from choice don't you
    know,
  He was seedy and gone off his feed.
He told us they called him a waster at home,
  We knew that he'd both grit and pluck,
Yet somehow things never went rosy with him,
  But we chaps put it down to Joe's luck.
A gentleman's son we all knew him to be,
  And the breed in him showed plain enough,
But he never let on to the boys who he was
  And he chummed in with sundry and rough.
The life of a cowboy is not very soft,
  But he stuck it quite well for all that,
And though he rode reckless and faster than most
  Like a toff in the saddle he sat.
Jack and I were his pals right away from the first
  And we showed him the ropes all we could,
Tho' mind you his pride would prevent us sometimes
  From doing so much as we would.

He told us the story of how he left home,
  How he'd got in the hands of a Jew,
And the guv'nor — the name that he gave to his dad
  Faced ruin to pay what was due.
How he bid his own people good-bye in remorse
  And swore to repay all the debt.
But fortunes he found even out in the West
  Were not quite so easy to get.
He liked nothing better — a pipe, and a chat
  Round the fire of a night just we three.
Then he'd talk of old England and how he'd return
  With the money — when wealthy was he.
One evening we sat in our usual way
  When the mail brought a letter for Joe,
A solicitor's name was embossed on the flap,
  He showed it with face all aglow.
'Maybe it's the money boys — coming at last,'
  He said with a shake in his voice.
We gave him a thump on the back for good luck,
  Just to show him how we should rejoice,
He opened the letter with quivering hands
  His face turning white as he read —
'It's come boys,' he shouted, 'I knew luck would
    change',
  Then he gasped — just fell back — and was dead.

Uncle George

By Greatrex Newman & Fred Cecil (1914)
Performed by Bransby Williams

It's plain as I ain't a policeman,
  An' likewise I ain't a Boy Sprout,

I'm a Bailiff! Yes, that's my perfession,
  The bloke wot goes round chuckin' out.

Last Toosday I went to an 'ouse to distrain,
  When the door was thrown open quite wide,
An' a woman, all smilin', takes old o' me 'and,
  An' ses *'Dear Uncle George come inside.*
We all was *so* pleased,' 'er goes on, smilin' still
  'When we got yer last letter what say'd
As 'ow you was comin' back 'ome from Noo York,
  To retire now yer fortune yer'd made.'
Then 'er 'usband 'e 'eartily shakes both me 'ands,
  An' 'e gets a chair for me to sit:
'It's twenty long years since yer left us,' ses 'e,
  'But lumme, *you ain't changed a bit!'*
O' course it was plain they was thinkin' as I
  Was their h'uncle jus' back from the States,
So thinks I to meself, this 'ere h'uncle's got brass
  So p'r'aps I shall 'touch' if I waits.
So I sits meself down, an' I ses:— 'Well me dears,
  I've come back at last from me roam;
Arter twenty long years in the wilds o' Noo York,
  I'm glad, once agen, to be 'ome.'
Then the 'usband, 'e gets out 'is pipe, an' 'e ses:—
  'Me terbacca I've gone an' forgot:—
I'll try yours if yer like Huncle George?' — An' 'e did!
  An' 'e very near took all I'd got.
Then 'e ses — 'Now we'll all celebrate yer return

By drinkin' yer jolly good 'ealth, —
So lend us a bob;— An' I couldn't refuse,
  Or else 'e'd a-doubted me wealth.
Well then it got late, Uncle George 'adn't come,
  But I thought 'e'd come next day all right,
So I ses: 'My 'otel's a good distance from 'ere
  P'r'aps *you'd* put me up for the night?'
'We've jus' sent our h'only spare mattress away,
  To 'ave the springs cleaned' the wife said,
'But we've got some *old sacks* in the garret upstairs' —
  I ses: 'Right, them'll do for a bed.
I've slep' on wus beds than sacks many a time,
  Yer should be in *Noo York,* that's the place, —
Why h'out there I've slep' *on the prairies for weeks,*
  Wi' tigers a-lickin' me face!'
'What a brave 'un you is h'uncle George to be sure,
  You're an 'ero,' the bloke proudly said,
Then 'e touched me for fourpence;— 'twas all as I'd got,
  So I left 'em and went up to bed.
When I got up next day, all the furniture'd gone!
  Exceptin' a rusty old fork,
An' a note, left beside it, said:
  'Dear Uncle George, *Good-bye, we're just off ter*
    Noo York!'

'Rake' Windermere

By Leonard Pounds & Herbert Townsend (1914)
Performed by Bransby Williams

Disgrace he'd brought on an ancient name;
  A smirch on an honoured crest.
He'd blotted the page of glorious fame
  That his family once possessed.
Eton he'd left beneath a cloud,
  And left in the greatest haste.
He'd proceeded whilst there in revels loud,
  Life's choicest hours to waste.
Sent down from Oxford next was he,
  The result of orgies wild.
He'd filled the cup of vice with glee,
  And a noble stock defiled.
A nickname he'd earned by his acts of shame,
  'Mong comrades of many a bout.
From the broken shell of his own true name
  'Rake' Windermere stepped out.
As a fitting end to an angry scene,
  He had quitted the family home.
With a tearless eye and a smile serene,
  He had started the world to roam.
Still lower he'd sunk than e'er before,
  And never a vice he'd shun,

Till even his roystering friends of yore
  Forsook him one by one.
He'd drifted at length with a tourist band
  To the land of the war-like Moor.
And there on the dreary desert sand
  Had disaster attacked the tour.
Approached by a tribe of bandit brand,
  The party had turned and fled;
But first a shot, fired by some foolish hand,
  Had pierced a Moorish head.
Besieged for a week on a mound of stone,
  And with water getting low,
The bandit chief had appeared alone
  And said 'Thou art free to go,
If thou first deliverest up to me
  Of thy number any one,
So that True Believer's blood may be
  Avenged ere to-morrow's sun.'
Each looked at each as he rode away.
  Grim silence reigned supreme.
The sun went down, and the moon held sway,
  Flooding all with silver stream.

Then a muffled form crept down the mound,
   With a wistful glance about.

Then with head erect but without a sound,
   'Rake' Windermere stepped out.

The Lounger

By Charles J. Winter (1914)
Performed by Bransby Williams

I've 'ad a shock this last few years what's nearly turned
   me white.
   I mean the shutting up of pubs for 'arf the day and
   night.
Wy wot's the use of leavin' bed to try an' earn a bob
   By leaning 'gainst a empty 'ouse, when workin' at my
   job?
The pub is shut till 12, so there's no customers d'yer
   see,
   That makes my bloomin' spirits fall to thirty five
   U.P.
I've been supportin' of this 'ouse for fifteen year or
   more,
   And as for drink, — I've 'ad enough to float a man
   o'war.
I'm such a reg'lar landmark, and I keep so still yer see,
   That people often come along and tie their 'orse to
   me!
Now no one comes till 12, and then they walks, or
   comes by car;
   And I get all the *smell* outside while they *taste* at the
   bar.
I reely don't know 'ow I'd live by workin' of this pub,
   But the missis goes out charrin' just to git me a bit o'
   grub.
I've told 'er she must put in for a rise and get more tin,
   Or a hextra job as night nurse just to bring more
   money in.
We've 'ad to give up something. Now we 'ave no
   Sunday's jint,
   For they've put the people's food up, yuss to
   fivepence 'arf a pint!
And when you get it, wot's it like? It's bad, and it ain't
   cheap,
   With not sufficient biff in it to promote a 'ealthy
   sleep.
You git a chance to drink from six till ten I will agree,
   And if you can't get canned by then — well you *ain't
   a-tryin' see!*
It's just the same with *all* our food, we works for every
   crust,
   Yuss, *works* for it, and swallers it, but *'as to chew it fust!*
Then look at the unfairness — take the bloke wot
   sweeps the road

'E's gettin' nigh four quid a week to 'elp 'im with 'is
   load;
And take the case of bricklayers at about a quid a day,
   It's fair if they 'ave only twenty bricks an 'our to lay;
I often 'as to nod my 'ead, and sometimes 'as to shout,
   And from my pocket take my 'and to point a buildin'
   out,
Each day I'm workin' at my job for quite three hours
   or more,
   With only — p'raps six drinks, and yet they say *we
   won the war!*'
And then there's Joe what works the pitch outside the
   private bar,
   I've chucked 'im, 'e's got uppish and 'e don't know
   where 'e are.
Today 'e finds some baccy, and 'e's gettin' such a dude,
   'E wouldn't put it in 'is pipe because it 'ad been
   chewed!
And then last week 'e washed 'is 'ands at the old road-
   mender's tank!
   I dropped 'im after that, what O! I can*not* stand sich
   swank.
I never wash *my* 'ands and I am dirtier than 'im
   I told 'im so: and 'e says '*well, you're three year older,
   Jim!*'
There's work agoin' up the street at very decent pay,
   But I ain't takin' none myself; I've done enough
   today.
I starts my job at ten o'clock as usual feelin' grand,
   I 'ad a drink inside, and filled my match-box at the
   stand,
I gets a clay pipe while I stands to 'ave my mornin'
   sup.
   (I likes a clay 'cause if it falls you needn't pick it up)
And then I 'as a think about what job I'd tackle first.
   I drink much better when I think, it 'elps to bring a
   thirst.
Some say that beer kills more smart men than bullets
   in a war,
   If *I'm* to 'ave a skinful — I prefer the beer by far.
Well, fust I 'eld a 'orse leastways I watched 'e didn't
   fall,
   And twice I carried parcels when I seed that they
   was small,

I fetched the guv'nor's dog 'is meat and got a nasty
    sneer,
    The bloke says 'shall I wrap it up, or will you eat it
      ere!!'
And then I minds some kiddies while their mother 'ad
    a drink,
    She'll git me on that job again *for tuppence* I *don't* think!

It's 'arf past two, the missis will be 'ome now with 'er
pay,
    So I'll be knockin' off too as it's early closin' day.
'Old 'ard! they say there's work down there for them
    that want a bit,
    What an escape! I might 'a gone *and run right into it!*

Spotty
By F. Chatterton Hennequin & Phyllis Norman Parker (1914)
Performed by Bransby Williams

Spotty was my chum, he was, a ginger-headed bloke,
    An everlasting gas-bag and as stubborn as a moke.
He give us all the 'ump he did before it come to war,
    By sportin' all 'is bits of French, what no-one asked
      him for.
He says to me 'old son,' he says, 'you won't have 'arf a
    chance,
    When I gets in conversation with them demerselles
      of France.'
I says to 'im 'you close yer face,' he says, 'all right bong
    swore,'
    Don't 'urt yourself mong sher amy,' then 'so long!
      oh re-vore!'
When we got our marching orders you can bet we
    wasn't slow,
    A-singing, 'Tipperary! it's a long, long way to go.'

On the transport 'ow he swanked it, with 'is parley
    vooing airs,
    Till I nearly knocked 'is 'ead off cos he said I'd 'mal
      de mares'.
When we landed, what a beano, how them Frenchies
    laughed and cried,
    And I see old Spotty swelling fit to bust 'iself with
      pride,
He was blowin' of 'em kisses and was singing 'Vive la
    France,'
    Till the Sergeant-Major copped 'im, then he says,
      'Kel mauvay chance!'
But we didn't get no waitin', where we went nobody
    knows,

And it wasn't like the fighting that you sees in
    picture shows.
We 'ad days of 'ell together, till they told us to retire,
    And then Spotty's flow of language set the water-
      carts on fire.

'Im and me was very lucky, for two-thirds of us was
    dead,
    With their greasy 'black Marias' and the shrapnel
      overhead.
And every time they missed us when the fire was
    murderous 'ot,
    Old Spotty says 'Honcore! Honcore!' that's French
      for 'Rotten shot.'
And then at last there came the time, we got 'em on the
    go,
    And 'im and me was fightin' at a little place called
      Mo (Meaux)
A-lying down together in a 'ole dug with our 'ands,
    For you gets it quick and sudden if you moves about
      or stands,
We was sharing 'arf a fag we was, Yus! turn and turn
    about,
    When I felt 'im move towards me, and he ses, 'Oh
      mate I'm out.'

'Is eyes they couldn't see me — they never will no
    more,
    But 'is twisted mouth it whispered, 'So long matey,
      Oh Re-vore!'

A Backwood Penance
By Harry Kenneth Wynne & Cuthbert Clarke (1915)
Performed by Bransby Williams

He's away across the Prairie,
    Growing lean and lank and hairy,

Slinging booze across a counter in some hole that
    God's forsook;

But the Angel who's recording
Knows the secret that he's hoarding,
  And he's got a credit balance in the Lord Almighty's
  Book.
They had followed him from Dover,
  Half the length of Europe over,
Till they thought they had him corner'd near to
  Barcelona Town,
  Then they drew their meshes tighter,
But they found he was a fighter,
  And he slipp'd between their fingers, tho' they
  nearly ran him down.
He had laid his plans so neatly
  That he disappear'd completely,
And they couldn't spot his hiding, tho' they followed
  ev'ry clue,
  Till, at last, thro' ceaseless working,
They'd a hint that he was lurking
  Somewhere round the River Niger, not so far from
  Timbuctoo.
Then they thought that they could find him,
  For a trail he'd left behind him,
And they traced him back to Turkey, and from there
  to Aden Bay,
  But he dar'd not cut it finer,
So he slunk aboard a liner,
  And I found him, sick and helpless, in the streets of
  Mandalay.
Then I fed him from my table,
  And as well as I was able
I nurs'd him thro' a fever, hiding him the while from
  sight;
  Why he came remain'd a myst'ry,

Till I chanc'd to learn his hist'ry
  As I watch'd beside his pillow thro' the silent, tropic
  night.
He spoke in rambling phrases when the fever touch'd
  his brain
  Of a girl he'd lov'd in England; and his suit was not
  in vain.
But her brother, high in office, had been brib'd, and
  gave away
  A diplomatic secret it was treason to betray.
The girl, of course, knew nothing, so to save her from
  disgrace
  Her lover took the onus in her guilty brother's
  place;
He fled away from justice, and an outcast he became,
  A hunted, homeless wand'rer, with a slur upon his
  name.
I saw, as he grew stronger,
  That I could not keep him longer,
Though I begg'd him not to leave me his brave spirit
  knew no rest;
  A handgrip, and we parted,
Then, silently, he started
  To seek a safer hiding in the Backwoods of the West.
So he's far across the Prairie,
  Growing lean and lank and hairy,
Slinging booze across a counter in some hole that
  God's forsook;
  But the Angel who's recording
Knows the secret that he's hoarding,
  And he's got a credit balance in the Lord Almighty's
  Book.

The Flying Boatman
By Charles J. Winter (1916)
Performed by Bransby Williams

Stick to your trade is the motter for me,
  And a wonderful good motter too,
The cobbler should stick to 'is wax so I say,
  And the joiner should stick to 'is glue.
I've follered the sea for forty odd year,
  But I once by mistake broke away,
And I follered the air just by way of a change,
  For the whole of one perishing day.
It 'appened like this some aeronaut chap
  To the village 'ad brought a balloon,
And 'e anchors it down in a field, for next day
  'E was giving a show about noon.
Well I leant on some rails looking seaward,
  And dreamed of the bar at the Magpie and Stump,

When my pipe was sent flying right out of my mouth,
  And I gets an almighty great thump.
The wind 'ad sprung up, the balloon 'ad broke loose,
  I was lifted right clean off my feet,
For in passing, the anchor 'ad dragged on the ground
  And then stuck in my trousers' seat!
I often 'ave 'eard of a rise in the world,
  But *this* rise would be 'ard to match,
And I blessed my old woman who'd done such good
  work
  When she sewed on my trousers that patch.
Up went the balloon, and I dangled beneath
  Like a worm on a fisherman's line.
Down below were my boats all let out by the hour

24

Not a penny of which would be mine.
I 'ollered and screamed till my voice got quite hoarse
  And my throat got uncommonly dry,
But all I could 'ear was some kids who cried out
  'Look, old Ben's going up to the sky!'
I travelled all day with the 'ot sun above
  And the blue rolling waters beneath,
When I 'ears a loud hiss, the balloon sprung a leak
  And the gas rushes out of the sheath.
Then I 'ad an idea, I'd been often blown out
  By the drinking of bottles of Bass.
So I climbed up and placed my mouth over the hole
  And sucked in the Hydrogen gas!
I started to swell and my buttons flew off
  With the sound of a crackling spark,
And as the balloon 'ad quite shrunk, why I
  Chopped it away with a cutting remark.
Relieved of its weight I bobbed up so 'igh
  I thought I'd bash into the stars.
Then I gently and gracefully fluttered to earth
  Like the man in the 'Message from Mars.'
Down below was the land I'd crossed over the sea
  So I knew I should come down in France,
But the Frenchies it seems didn't quite like the look
  Of me doing my aerial dance.
They started off firing their pistols and guns
  Till the shots flew about me like rain,
So I kicked off me boots, rose, and caught some fresh
    wind
    And then sailed back to England again.

But when I touched ground why I bobbed up again
  Till I'd covered a furlong or two,
And so I proceeded with bounds and with 'ops
  Like a terrible great kangaroo.
In the village the news of my going 'ad spread
  And the people were running about,
They'd rung all the bells, they 'ad let the dogs loose
  And old Jack the Towncrier was out
Announcing they'd give a reward of ten bob
  Which the mayor 'ad made up to eleven
To the one who would bring them back old Boatman
    Ben
  Who 'ad taken a trip up to heaven.
But up to the evening they'd not heard a word.
  They were all of them getting the pip,
When they see me come bounding and bouncing along
  Like springheeled Jack out on the rip.
They threw me a line which I caught in the air
  And 'eld firmly grasped in my 'and.
They they 'auled me to earth to the toon of the
  'Conquerin' Hero' played by the Town Band.
They thought I'd float off so they sat on my 'ead
  Till I couldn't see out of my eyes,
But the gas I got rid of cussing and swearing
  Redooced me about half the size.
I ain't got well yet, but I'm getting along
  With the 'elp of some Guinness and Bass.
But still you can tell by the way that I talk
  I have still got a good deal of gas!

The Plumber

By Harry Kenneth Wynne & Cuthbert Clarke (1916)
Performed by Bransby Williams

I'm a plumber, I ham, an' I'm proud o' me trade,
  An' I tells yer I can't hunder-stand
Why Kiplin' should talk o' 'is soldiers and squads
  When there's 'eroes like me in the land.
I was once called from bed on a cold, frosty morn
  Fer ter go to the 'ouse of a toff,
Jest ter look at the tap in the scullery sink,
  What they seys as they couldn't turn hoff.
Well, I shoves on me clothes, an' I puts on me 'at,
  An I goes ter the 'ouse right away.
Ter hinspect this 'ere job, an' ter see if the case
  His has bad has they'd sent round ter say.
They shows me this tap as they couldn't turn hoff,
  They was right, 'cos I tried hit ter see,
Then I studies hit like, an' I scratches me 'ead,
  An' I asks what they wanted wiv me.

The toff 'e explains as 'e wanted hit stopp'd,
  So I asks for some hink an' a pen,
An' I makes hout a list o' the tools I shall want,
  And I shoves 'em hall down, there an' then.
Then I goes ter the shop fer ter fetch 'em along,
  But me wife, she was fryin' a chop,
An' there was me breakfast, hall tasty an' nice,
  An' the smell of it tempts me ter stop.
I gets thro' me grub an' I puts on me pipe,
  An' I sits down to wait fer me mate,
'E's a feller what fancies 'ome comforts, like me,
  An' 'e never gets hup afore height.
When hat larst 'e arrives we goes round ter the place,
  An' we starts on the job in a trice,
While the boys of the tradesmen, what call'd ter the
    'ouse,

Stands hadmirin' an' givin' hadvice.
First we tries fer ter plug up the tap wiv a cork,
  But the water squirts hall round the place,
An' the toff, what was jest comin' hin hat the door,
  Gets a gallon or two in his face.
'E dances about hin a terrible rage, An' 'e treads hon
  the kitten's 'ind legs,
  An' the cook 'ears hit squeal, an' she faints hin han
  'eap,
An' falls 'flop' hin a basket hof heggs.

By this time the water was hup to our knees,
  An' the tables an' chairs was afloat,
  So the toff 'e yells hout, 'Save the women an' kids,'
An' runs hoff ter borrow a boat.
  Then the greengrocer's boy, what was watchin' the
  scene,
Comes a-pokin 'is nose hin again,
  An' the himpudent feller seys, 'Take my hadvice,
An' jest turn it hoff at the main!'

The Shooting of Dan McGrew
By Robert Service & Cuthbert Clarke (1917)
Performed by Bransby Williams

A bunch of the boys were whooping it up in the
  Malamute Saloon,
  The kid that handles the music box was hitting a
  rag-time tune;
Back of the bar, in a solo game, sat Dangerous Dan
  McGrew,
  And watching his luck was his light o' love, the lady
  that's known as Lou.
When out of the night, which was fifty below, and into
  the din and the glare,
  There stumbled a miner fresh from the creeks, dog-
  dirty and loaded for bear.
He looked like a man with a foot in the grave, and
  scarcely the strength of a louse.
  Yet he tilted a poke of dust on the bar, and he called
  for drinks for the house.
There was none could place the stranger's face though
  we searched ourselves for a clue:
  But we drank his health, and the last to drink was
  Dangerous Dan McGrew.
There's men that somehow just grip your eyes, and
  hold them hard like a spell,
  And such was he, and he looked at me like a man
  who had lived in hell;
With a face most hair, and the dreary stare of a dog
  whose day is done,
  As he watered the green stuff in his glass, and the
  drops fell one by one.
Then I got to figgering who he was, and wondering
  what he'd do,
  And I turned my head and there watching him was
  the lady that's known as Lou.
His eyes went rubbering round the room, and he
  seemed in a kind of daze
  Till at last that old piano fell in the way of his
  wandering gaze.

The rag-time kid was having a drink, there was no one
  else on the stool,
  So the stranger stumbled across the room, and flops
  down there like a fool.
In a buckskin shirt that was glazed with dirt he sat, and
  I saw him sway.
  Then he clutched the keys with his talon hands —
  my God but that man could play!
Were you ever out in the Great Alone, when the moon
  was awful clear
  And the icy mountains hemmed you in with a
  silence you 'most could hear;
With only the howl of the timber wolf, and you
  camped there in the cold,
  A half-dead thing in a stark dead world, clean mad
  for the muck called gold.
While high overhead, green, yellow and red the North
  lights swept in bars.
  Then you've a hunch what the music meant, hunger
  and night and the stars.
Then on a sudden the music changed, so soft that you
  scarce could hear,
  But you felt that your life had been looted clean of
  all that it once held dear.
That some one had stolen the woman you loved, that
  her love was a devil's lie;
  That your guts were gone, and the best for you was
  to crawl away and die.
'Twas the crowning cry of a heart's despair, and it
  thrilled you thro' and thro',
  And it found its goal in the blackened soul of the
  lady that's known as Lou.
Then the stranger turned and his eyes they burned in
  a most peculiar way,
  In a buckskin shirt that was glazed with dirt he sat,
  and I saw him sway.

Then his lips went in, in a kind of grin, and he spoke
and his voice was calm,
And 'Boys,' says he, 'you don't know me, and none of
you care a damn,
But I want to state, and my words are straight and I'll
bet my poke they're true,
That one of you here is a hound of hell and that one
is Dan McGrew'.

Then I ducked my head, and the lights went out and
two guns blazed in the dark
And a woman screamed, and the lights went up, and
two men lay stiff and stark:
Pitched on his head, and pumped full of lead was
Dangerous Dan McGrew
While the man from the creeks lay clutched to the
breast of the lady that's known as Lou.

Wild Bill Drives The Stage

By Ridgwell Callum & Cuthbert Clarke (1918)
Performed by Bransby Williams

It was Bill that bossed the outfit, and Job's Flat knew its
man.
He'd throw a bluff, and back it, as only a live man
can.
He was chock-full of hell inside, and as mean as a she
coyote
For the feller who'd hurt a hoss, or a dog, or a kid,
or a woman's repute.
He'd 'straddled' the fill of a jackpot when the news
reached Minkey's Saloon
That a gang had held up the gold stage that very
afternoon.
They'd robbed it for thousands of dollars in dust, the
work of a week,
The keep of the women and kiddies and the boys of
Suffering Creek.
He was raging mad as he pitched down his hand and
quit the table dead,
But he gave no sign of the thoughts he had lying
aback of his head,
Till the day came along when he handed it out,
chalked on a slab of wood —
'You can tote your dust on the stage today, Wild
Bill's standing Good.'
But even then there was none of 'em guessed the things
about to begin,
Till ten thousand dollars of horseflesh swept round
from the barn — then their grin
Changed like a streak of lightning and the 'hooch'
drained out of their brains,
For Bill was hunched in the teamster's seat, clawing
the bunch of reins.
His eyes never quit those horses, and it made you
wonder — well —
He looked like an evil image on the trail of a red-hot
hell.
He'd a halo of guns round his middle, and his eyes
froze you through to the bone

P'r'aps he was reck'ning the game out — the game
he'd to play alone.
With careless jest they loaded the chest,
Bill passed his horses the word,
They leapt at their bits, stark mad for the run,
Their prairie blood full-stirred.
Across the flat to the hills beyond where the pine-trees
rake the sky
Bill raced his team with a master hand at a pace
you'd hate to try.
Far in the hills the hold-up gang were waiting their
golden haul —
With merciless guns and coward hearts, blood-
steeped beyond recall.
On came the thunder of racing hoofs — and each man
held his breath —
As Bill flung his team with fearless grip deep in the
jaws of death.
Swift as a flash the scene was changed by a rain of
speeding lead,
The leaders swerved from the broken trail, and the
'wheelers' pulled up dead.
Astride of the chest that held the gold of the folk he'd
sworn to serve,
Cold as a 'berg from a Polar flow Bill crouched with
an iron nerve.
He hadn't a care for chances, tho' the odds were one to
eight:
He was drunk with the scent of battle and the fire of
a deadly hate.
A hail of lead swept down on the head of the man
whose law was the gun.
His flesh was ripped and his lifeblood dripped as he
shot 'em *one by one*.
The vicious yap of his barking guns ne'er ceased from
their screech for blood
Till five stark bodies had yielded life there on the
crimsoning mud.

Shot up in twenty places, bleeding and broken in limb,
  Hunched like a crouching panther, savage and ready to spring.
Like the swirl of a raging blizzard the bullets round him sang
  Till he'd sent the last to his reckoning: the last of the hold-up gang.
He raised a hand to bloodblind eyes, and smeared 'em clear with his sleeve,
  His brain lived on while his body drained — holed like a human sieve.
Out of the silence there came a sound like the sigh of a soul that's lost;
  A shuffle of desperate movement, with its tale of the awful cost;
Of a victory well and truly won, of a cruel wrong set right,
  A half-dead thing, Bill clutched his seat — even with Death he'd fight.
With shaking hands he blindly groped in the box beneath his feet,
  He sought a rawhide picket rope and lashed him to his seat.
The reins made fast to bloodstained wrists 'By God! my hands shan't fail
  To drive you home, my beauties.' Again he hits the trail.
The miles flew by under speeding hoofs of a team that asks no rest.
  The man they knew was behind them, helpless, and needing their best.
He lolled about — a broken thing — scarce life in his ghastly face
  For Death was sitting beside him, and Death was making the pace.
The shades of night in the City were lit by the twinkling stars
  The lamps on the wooded side-walks and the garish light of the bars.
When out of the far off distance came the rattle of speeding wheels
  And the ghostly race of a team nigh spent, with terror lashing their heels.
Jolting and swaying behind them came the stage from Suffering Creak;
  Pitched like a storm-tossed vessel it flashed thro' the town like a streak.
On to the barn beside the bank — how well they knew that place —
  Right to the door — not a yard beyond — Bill's horses finished the race.
The boys rushed out with lanterns, and found Bill there in the seat
  Held by the rawhide picket rope, the gold chest safe at his feet.
He'd fought his fight to a finish, no matter tho' riddled with lead,
  He'd pledg'd his word — he'd kept it —
He'd driven for three hours *dead!*

The Pigtail of Li-Fang-Fu

By Sax Rohmer & T. W. Thurban (1919)
Performed by Bransby Williams

They speak of a dead man's vengeance; they whisper a deed of hell
  'Neath the Mosque of Mohammed Ali.
  And this is the thing they tell.
In a deep and a midnight gully, by the street where the goldsmiths are,
  'Neath the Mosque of Mohammed Ali, at the back of the Scent Bazaar,
Was the House of a Hundred Raptures, the tomb of a thousand sighs;
  Where the sleepers lay in that living death which the opium-smoker dies.
At the House of a Hundred Raptures, where the reek of the joss-stick rose
  From the knees of the golden idol to the tip of his gilded nose,
Through the billowing oily vapour, the smoke of the black *chandu,*
  There a lantern green cast a serpent sheen on the pigtail of Li-Fang-Fu.
There was Ramsa Lal of Bhiwâni, who could smoke more than any three,
  A pair of Kashmiri dancing girls and Ameer Khân Môtee;
And there was a grey-haired soldier too, the wreck of a splendid man;
  When the place was still I've heard mounted drill being muttered by 'Captain Dan'.
Then, one night as I lay a-dreaming, there was shuddering, frenzied screams;
  But the smoke had a spell upon me; I was chained to that couch of dreams.
All my strength, all my will had left me, because of the black *chandu,*
  And upon the floor, by the close-barred door, lay the daughter of Li-Fang-Fu.

28

'Twas the first time I ever saw her, but often I dream
    of her now;
    For she was as sweet as a lotus, with the grace of a
      willow bough.
The daintiest ivory maiden that ever a man called fair,
    And I saw blood drip where Li-Fang-Fu's whip had
      tattered her shoulders bare!
I fought for the power to curse him — and never a
    word would come!
    To reach him — to kill him! — but opium had
      stricken me helpless — dumb.
He lashed her again and again, until she uttered a
    moaning prayer,
    And as he whipped so the red blood dripped from
      those ivory shoulders bare.
When crash! went the window behind me, and in leapt
    a greyhaired man,
    As he tore the whip from that devil's grip, I knew
      him: 'twas Captain Dan!
Ne'er a word spoke he, but remorseless, grim, his brow
    with anger black.
    He lashed and lashed till the shirt was slashed from
      the Chinaman's writhing back.
And when in his grasp the whip broke short, he cut
    with a long keen knife,
    The pigtail, for which a Chinaman would barter his
      gold, his life —
He cut the pig-tail from Li-Fang-Fu. And this is the
    thing they tell
    By the Mosque of Mohammed Ali — for it led to a
      deed of hell.
In his terrible icy passion, Captain Dan that pig-tail
    plied,
    And with it he thrashed the Chinaman, until any but
      he had died —
Until Li-Fang-Fu dropped limply down too feeble, it
    seemed, to stand.
    But swift to arise, with death in his eyes — and the
      long keen knife in his hand!
Like fiends of an opium vision they closed in a fight
    for life,

And nearer the breast of the Captain crept the blade
    of the gleaming knife.
Then a shot! a groan — and a wisp of smoke. I
    swooned and knew no more —
    Save that Li-Fang-Fu lay silent and still in a red pool
      near the door.
But never shall I remember how that curtain of sleep
    was drawn
    And I woke, 'mid a deathly silence, in the darkness
      before the dawn.
There was blood on the golden idol! My God! that
    dream was true!
    For there, like a slumbering serpent, lay the pigtail
      of Li-Fang-Fu.
From the House of a Hundred Raptures I crept ere the
    news should spread
    That the Devil's due had claimed Li-Fang-Fu, and
      that Li-Fang-Fu was dead.
'Twas the end of that Indian summer, when Fate — or
    the ancient ties —
    Drew my steps again to the gully, to the Tomb of a
      Thousand Sighs;
And the door of the house was open! All the blood in
    my heart grew cold.
    For within sat the golden idol, and he leered as he
      leered of old!
And I thought that his eyes were moving in a sinister
    vile grimace
    When suddenly, there at his feet I saw a staring and
      well-known face!
With the shriek of a soul in torment, I turned like a
    frenzied man,
    Falling back from the spot where the moonlight
      poured down upon 'Captain Dan'!
He was dead, and in death was fearful; with features of
    ghastly hue —
    And snakelike around his throat was wound the
      pigtail of Li-Fang-Fu!

Orange Blossom
By Sax Rohmer (1921)
Performed by Bransby Williams

My little Orange Blossom — light of my life
    Sleep on, tender flower — sleep on!
Hist! — Wu Chang! — Greetings! greetings!
    Ha! Wu Chang, long have I waited.
But that my friend would answer to my call

I had not fear. See, old friend, the tea awaits,
It is the famous Pekoe!
    Sit! My friend, Wu Chang, Wu Chang, my friend!
I love you for your heart of gold.
    Alas! Wu Chang, much water's flown from Honan

To the Yellow Sea since you and I were playmates —
    Playmates in the valley where the opium poppies
        grow.
The tea is to your liking? Then we smoke.
    You gaze 'round for my wife?
Ah! The little Orange Blossom. I know you loved her
    well
    For my sake? Yes, Wu Chang, my friend!
Have Courage! Courage! Heart of gold!
    It is the incense that you smell —
The little Orange Blossom's dead!
    You start! 'Twas sudden? Yes!
She died at dawn. But let us smoke.
    At dawn she lived, Tonight her soul is free.
Her body lies in yonder.
    Come! Come! Wu Chang and kiss her. No?
Her red lips smile, her eyes are kind.
    So slender is the thread of life, that even I,
Or you, Wu Chang, might die to-night! How pale you
    grow!
    The tea is to your liking? Is the incense so
        oppressive?
Well, the flowers are fresh. For she, too, was a flower,
    Wu Chang,
    A lily, slender white — so frail a flower — my wife.
My journeys left her much alone.
    But when I placed her in your care,

My old and trusted friend Wu Chang,
    I deemed her safe, but see!
Your tea grows cold. Drink up!
    Her lips were red, her heart was young
How fair she was! and I so far away!
    You shudder yet, your brow is wet, nor do you
        smoke.
Your face is grey, and how you twitch and clutch with
    clammy fingers.
    You thought me safe in far Honan! Yes!
So did the little Orange Blossom! —
    Sit!! — Look well into your empty cup —
The same from which your mistress drank at dawn,
    Wu Chang — her last! Your whispered vows, each
        stolen kiss,
All reached my ears!
    I heard, I saw, my friend, Wu Chang!
In yonder room, the room where now our little
        Orange Blossom lies —
    I lay, concealed!
No, no! You have no strength to raise your knife!
    The poison cup has done its work.
Her lips were sweet? Her arms were soft?
    You writhe, and why, your eyes are glazed!
'Twas so with her, at dawn, as 'tis with you to-night
    Go sleep in hell — in HELL! my friend, Wu Chang!

Black Roger

By Carolus Rex (1922)
Performed by Bransby Williams

Watchin' the tide go out,
    Over the shiny sand,
Leavin' it there, as smooth an' as bare,
    As the back of a baby's 'and!
Only a quarter to twelve.
    Fifteen minutes from now
Afore I can dip my bow sprit
    In a pint at the Bull an' Cow.
After the life I've led.
    Perils by land and sea,
Nobody knows wot a dog I've been, —
    Nobody — not even me!
Think o' the wrecks I've seen,
    Through my spy-glass standin' 'ere.
Think o' the gallant lifeboat lads,
    Wot I've watched from the end o' the pier!
It's a pretty spot — Dozey Bay —
    As any I've been to or seen,
Tho' as I've stood just 'ere for the past forty year
    I don't know *when* I've been!

I knows ev'ry winkle an' crab,
    Wot lives in this part o' the sea.
First thing I says is 'Good mornin', crabs,'
    An' the crabs all wink at me!
The pirate of Dozey Bay —
    That's wot they calls me down 'ere.
They asks me to pitch yarns of bloodshed an' sich,
    An' they stands me pints o' beer.
I'm the fisherman's sailin' mark,
    Which 'as earned me many a swipe.
Comin' in they all steer in a line with the pier
    An' the end o' my old clay pipe!
Old ladies they offers me tracts —
    An' I makes little children cry
When I leans on the rail an' I pitches my tale
    Of the 'orrible days gone by.
Yes! I was a pirate once —
    That's wot I used to be!
Scuttlin' a boat or cuttin' a throat
    Was all alike to me!

Now that my whiskers is grey,
  It sounds a queer remark
To tell you once I was known I was
  As Black Roger the Ocean Shark!
From Clyde to Vigo Bay —
  Wherever that may be!
You only 'ad to whisper the words
  In pidgin or Portugee.
'Black Roger the Ocean Shark' —
  Lor' lummy, you'd 'ave seen
Strong men feel queer, upset their beer,
  An' ev'ry face turn green!
Mine was a name o' dread.
  Wot a black 'eart I'd got —
Black as my whiskers used to be,
  An' as 'ard as a galleypot.
I owned 'alf the Spanish Main,
  No cat's 'ad so many lives,
I'd a couple o' score of a crew or more,
  An' I 'ad about ninety wives!
There was white 'uns an' brown 'uns too —
  An' some just as black as my boot,

Two dozen was fair, with long golden 'air,
  An' one was as bald as a coot!
Ho! I didn't *know* she was bald.
  I might never 'ave tumbled the game,
Only one night she left 'er thingummyjig
  On top of the wot's-is-name!
There was one 'ad a wooden leg!
  Ah! she was a lucky wife!
I reckon I owe to that timber toe
  As I didn't lose my life.
We was cast away in a boat,
  We'd been wrecked in a dreadful gale.
'Alf barmy with thirst, our 'eads fit to burst,
  When 'A sail!' I ollers — 'A sail!'
'Ow to attract their heye?
  We was crazy with despair
When I ties my shirt to 'er timber toe
  An' she waves 'er leg in the air!
Watchin' the tide go out
  Good mornin' mum, thanks! Tails win! Tails! —
Ho! the door's open now at the old Bull an' Cow.
  It's time that the tide come in!

The Last Bottle
By Peter Cheyney & Harold Arpthorp (1925)
Performed by Bransby Williams

Good night, good Toby — old servant, faithful friend,
  As sound as this old wine throughout the years,
And faithful still — Good night!
  So you are the end of many dozens of a famous blend
That links these days up to the olden time,
  When men could ride and drink, and drank like
    men,
And loved good horses as they loved good wine.
  Gad! I remember — It seems but yesterday,
When shouts and laughter made the rafters ring,
  When from the table top, proudly I'd give the toast:
Friends! charge your glasses! Gentlemen — the King!
  For we were all King's men in those old merry days,
Loyal to the land we tilled — the land we trod.
  Men who were proud to count their Country and
    their King
Second to none other — save their God.
  And when they laid my father to his rest
In that quiet country churchyard on the hill,
  We drank a silent toast.
Deep in each breast
  The thought that he had loved you as I love you
    still.
Old wine, companion of our bygone days
  In time of trouble, happiness and stress,

You bound each friend to us with splendid faith,
  And drove dull care away with your caress.
Tonight across the silence comes a whisper,
  My Father's voice from outside earthly bounds.
The words sound clearly on my listening ear,
  The words he spoke when first I rode to hounds:
'Ride straight my son, and teach your son the same,
  Choose carefully your horses and your wife,
Remember that you bear an ancient name,
  And guard your honour as you guard your life'.
And I remembered and my heart I steeled
  To play the game as he would have me play.
And then I met her on the hunting-field.
  'Twas golden sunset at the close of day,
In fancy I can see her dear eyes shine,
  And hear her murmured word of soft consent.
That night I drank to her in this old wine,
  Before I knew what life or true love meant.
I can remember the birthday of our boy,
  How bon-fires flared, and life was full of joy
Because of him.
  He would have been a man of thirty years —
Full-voiced and courage fine,
  If he were here, together we would sit,
And laugh o'er this last bottle of good wine.

But he, my son, sleeps soundly on the hill, with my
    fore-fathers.
Boy, I drink to you!
    To all you might have been and might have done
If you had stayed the course. But you were gone,
    Ere your first race of life was yet begun.
I see your young face smiling through the years,
    Your eyes a-flashing with the joy of youth,
Just as your mother's eyes smiled through her tears,
    And she has left me too.
My dear, she waits for me, sending her love
    In many a happy thought, until I join her.
For, like this old port, my drops of life are running
    low,

And I await, with patient happiness
The call to walk the way we all must go.
    Sweetheart, in fancy I can see you smile
So sweetly, as you nod your snow-white head.
    I shall be with you in a little while,
And when I go our ancient race is dead.
    My dear, I drink to you.
To all the bygone days,
    To all our times of happiness and cheer.
To all our ventures on life's pleasant ways.
    To our next meeting. My love! My dear!

The Green Eye of the Little Yellow God
By Milton Hayes & Cuthbert Clarke (1911)

There's a one-eyed yellow idol to the north of
    Kathmandu;
    There's a little marble cross below the town;
And a brokenhearted woman tends the grave of 'Mad'
    Carew,
    While the yellow god for ever gazes down.
He was known as 'Mad' Carew by the subs at
    Kathmandu,
    He was hotter than they felt inclined to tell,
But, for all his foolish pranks,
    He was worshipped in the ranks,
And the Colonel's daughter smiled on him as well.
    He had loved her all along,
With the passion of the strong,
    And that she returned his love was plain to all.
She was nearly twenty-one,
    And arrangements were begun
To celebrate her birthday with a ball.
    He wrote to ask what present she would like from
      'Mad' Carew:
They met next day as he dismissed a squad:
    And jestingly she made pretence that nothing else
      would do . . .
But the green eye of the little yellow god.
    On the night before the dance
'Mad' Carew seemed in a trance,
    And they chaffed him as they puffed at their cigars,
But for once he failed to smile,
    And he sat alone awhile,
Then went out into the night . . . beneath the stars.
    He returned, before the dawn,
With his shirt and tunic torn,
    And a gash across his temples . . . dripping red
He was patched up right away,

And he slept all through the day,
While the Colonel's daughter watched beside his bed.
    He woke at last and asked her if she'd send his tunic
      through.
She brought it and he thanked her with a nod.
    He bade her search the pocket, saying, 'That's from
      "Mad" Carew,'
And she found . . . *the little green eye of the god*.
    She upbraided poor Carew,
In the way that women do,
    Although her eyes were strangely hot and wet;
But she would not take the stone,
    And Carew was left alone
With the jewel that he'd chanced his life to get.
    When the ball was at its height
On that still and tropic night,
    She thought of him . . . and hastened to his room.
As she crossed the barrack square
    She could hear the dreamy air
Of a waltz tune softly stealing thro' the gloom.
    His door was open wide, with silver moonlight
      shining through;
The place was wet and slippery where she trod;
    An ugly knife lay buried in the heart of 'Mad'
      Carew . . .
Twas the vengeance of the little yellow god.

There's a one eyed yellow idol to the north of
    Kathmandu;
There's a little marble cross below the town;
    And a brokenhearted woman tends the grave of
      'Mad' Carew,
While the yellow god for ever gazes down.

The Dream Ring of the Desert
By Milton Hayes & R. Fenton Gower (1912)

The Merchant Abu Khan shunned the customs of his
   race,
  And sought the cultured wisdom of the West.
His daughter — fair Leola — had the desert's supple
   grace,
  With an English education of the best.
The suitors for her hand were as grains of desert sand,
  But the merchant bade the Arab swarm begone:
And he swore a mighty oath, she should only make her
   troth
  With an Englishman — an Englishman or none!
The chieftain Ben Kamir, tho' rejected, stayed to
   plead,
  But Abu Khan replied, 'Thy suit is vain.
I cast aside my kinsmen and I scorn the prophet's
   creed;
  So get thee to thy tents, across the plain.'
'Enough,' the Chief replied, 'Thine eyes are blind with
   pride,
  But Allah hears my prayers and guides my star,
With patience I shall wait till I am called by Fate,
  And then I shall return to Akabar.'
The right man came at last in the month of Ramadhan,
  An Englishman who learned to love her soon.
His suit was proudly sanctioned by the merchant Abu
   Khan,
  And the wedding was to be at the full moon.
The merchant, in his pride, thought the news too good
   to hide,
  And it circled round the desert near and far:
Circled round and caught the ear of the chieftain Ben
   Kamir,
  And he turned his camel's head to Akabar:
The chieftain wore his robe of green, an emblem of his
   rank.
  And many bowed in honour of the man.
But heedless of their reverence he beat his camel's
   flank,
  And rode on to the house of Abu Khan.
The merchant, from his roof, saw the chief, but held
   aloof,

A suitor twice dismissed was one to shun —
But Kamir declared his ride was in homage to the
   bride,
  And the merchant's fears vanished one by one.
'Leola,' said the Arab, as she came to greet the guests,
  'Thy praises are beyond what I can sing,
But let this little token bring the fortune of the best.'
  And he placed upon her hand an opal ring.
''Tis more than what it seems, and its spell shall gild
   thy dreams,
   For 'twas carried by Mahomet, Allah's Priest.'
Then the chieftain said goodbye, and she watched him
   with a sigh,
  As he rode across the desert to the East.
Leola dreamt a dream most strange, and nightly 'twas
   the same,
  And love within her breast began to peep.
A voice from out the burning sandhills called and
   called her name,
  And waking she would long again for sleep.
The wedding eve's bright moon saw her rise as from a
   swoon,
  With the dream voice ringing still within her ear,
Saw her glide toward the sand, where the stately palm-
   trees stand,
  To the desert, and the arms of Ben Kamir.
The chieftain pointed Eastward to the plains he loved
   so well,
  And told her of his plans for hasty flight.
The dream-ring on her finger held her soul within its
   spell.
  And they rode across the desert thro' the night.
On the morrow, lined with care, at the Maghrib sunset
   prayer,
  The merchant joined the worshippers unshod.
And he cried with spirit broken, as the Mueddin's
   chant was spoken,
  'Mahomet *is* the prophet — God *is* God.'

The Whitest Man I Know
By Milton Hayes & R. Fenton Gower (1914)

He's a-cruisin' in a pearler with a dirty nigger crew,
  A-buyin' pearls and copra for a stingy Spanish Jew,

And his face is tann'd like leather 'neath a blazin'
   tropic Sun,

And he's workin' out a penance for the things he
   hasn't done.
Round the Solomons he runs, tradin' beads and cast-off
   guns,
   Buyin' pearls from grinnin' niggers, loadin' copra by
    the ton;
And he'll bargain and he'll smile, but he's thinkin' all
   the while
   Of the penance that he's workin' out for sins he
    hasn't done.
We'd been round the Horn together, and I'd come to
   know his worth;
   The greatest friend I'd ever had, the whitest man on
    earth.
He'd pull'd me out of many a scrape, he'd risk'd his
   life for me,
   And side by side, for many a year, we'd rough'd it on
    the sea;
But a woman came between us; she was beautiful as
   Venus,
   And she set her cap at him until she hook'd him
    unawares:
And I sailed off on my own
   Leavin' him and her alone:
Sign'd aboard a tramp for 'Frisco, leavin' them in
   Bu'nos Ayres.
   When I met him in a twelvemonth he was goin' to
    the deuce,
For she's blacken'd all the good in him, she'd play'd
   him fast and loose,
   And she'd gone off with a Dago who was lettin'
    dollars fly,
And she'd left my mate to drink his precious soul away
   and die.
   Well, I talk'd and talk'd him over, and we sign'd
    aboard 'The Rover.'
It was just like good old times, until we shor'd at Rio
   Bay;
   Then the hand of Fate show'd plain — brought us
    face to face again
With the woman, and the Dago who had taken her
   away.
   We were sittin' in a cafe when the couple came
    along,
She simply smil'd and pass'd us by, then vanish'd in
   the throng.
   My mate jump'd up to follow, but I wouldn't let him
    stir,
And later on a waiter brought a note that came from
   her:
   She pretended she regretted
What she'd done, and that she fretted
   For the wrong that she had done him, and she
    wanted to atone;

There was so much to explain,
   Would he meet her once again?
After midnight, in her garden — she would watch for
   him, alone.
   'Course he went, but unbeknown to him I follow'd
    on behind.
I watch'd, and saw the shadows of two figures on the
   blind —
   The woman — and the Dago — and I heard the
    Dago shout,
They quarrell'd, and the woman scream'd — and then
   a shot rang out.
   My mate dash'd thro' the curtain —
And I follow'd, makin' certain
   That my little gun was ready — case I had to make a
    stand:
There I saw the Dago — dead,
   With a bullet thro' his head,
And the woman standin' near him with a shooter in
   her hand.
   Before the Civil Guard came in my mate had
    snatch'd her gun,
And he ask'd them to arrest *him* for the thing he hadn't
   done.
   I tried madly to explain things, but they shook their
    heads at me,
And the woman let them take him, so that she might
   get off free.
   In the court I sat and heard her
Tell them all *he'd done the murder,*
   And I pray'd she might be stricken into some
    shape,
He was sentenc'd for his life —
   But out there corruption's rife,
And I brib'd and brib'd, until at last I manag'd his
   escape.
   Then I stow'd him on a hooker sailin' far from
    woman's wiles,
And he's workin' his salvation out amongst the South
   Sea Isles;
   And the woman's there at Rio, and she's weavin' of
    her spell,
With a crowd of fools awaitin' her commands to burn
   in hell;
   Whilst the whitest man I know
Runs a Christy minstrel show,
   Buyin' pearls from dirty niggers — 'neath a blazin
    tropic sun,
And he'll cuss 'em, and he'll smile —
   But he's thinkin' all the while —
Of the penance that he's workin' out for things he
   hasn't done.

Merchandise

By Milton Hayes & Elsie April (1920)

Dedicated, by gracious permission,
to H.R.H. THE PRINCE OF WALES.

Merchandise! Merchandise! Tortoise-shell, spices,
  Carpets and Indigo — sent o'er the high-seas;
Mother-o'-Pearl from the Solomon Isles —
  Brought by a brigantine ten thousand miles.
Rubber from Zanzibar, tea from Nang-Po,
  Copra from Haiti, and wine from Bordeaux;
Ships, with top-gallants and royals unfurled,
  Are bringing in freights from the ends of the
    world —
Crazy old windjammers, manned by Malays,
  With ratridden bulk-heads and creaking old stays,
Reeking of bilge and of paint and of pitch —
  That's how these ocean-girt islands grew rich:
And tramps, heavy laden, and liners untold
  Will lease a new life to a nation grown old.

Merchandise! Merchandise! England was made
  By her Men and her Ships and her OVERSEAS TRADE.
Widen your harbours, your docks and your quays,
  Hazard your wares on the seven wide seas,
Run out your railways and hew out your coal,
  For only by trade can a country keep whole.
Feed up your furnaces, fashion your steel,
  Stick to your bargains and pay on the deal;
Rich is your birthright, and well you'll be paid.
  If you keep in good faith with your Overseas Trade.
Learn up geography, work out your sums,
  Build up your commerce, and pull down your
    slums;

Sail on a Plimsoll that marks a full hold:
  Your Overseas Trade means a harvest of gold.
Bring in the palmoil and pepper you've bought,
  But send out ten times the amount you import:
Trade your inventions, your labour and sweat:
  Your Overseas Traffic will keep ye from debt.
Hark to the song of the shuttle and loom,
  'Keep up your commerce or crawl to your tomb!'
Study new methods and open new lines,
  Quicken your factories, foundries and mines,
Think of what Drake did, and Raleigh and Howe,
  And waste not their labours by slacking it now:
Work is life's currency — earn what you're worth,
  And *send out your ships to the ends of the earth.*
Deep-bosomed mothers with wide-fashioned hips
  Will bear ye good sons for the building of ships:
Good sons for your ships and good ships for your
    trade —
  That's how the Peace of the World will be made!
So send out your strong to the forests untrod,
  Work for yourselves and your neighbours and God,
Keep this good England the home of the free,
  With Merchandise, Men and good Ships on the Sea.
Merchandise! Merchandise! Good honest
    Merchandise!
  Merchandise, Men and Good Ships on the Sea.

Orange Peel

By Milton Hayes & Cuthbert Clarke (1920)

The Colonel stopped, and glared around,
  Then, pointing sternly to the ground,
'What *does* this mean?' demanded he,
  'A piece of orange peel I see!'
The Major called the Captain then,
  And said, 'By Gad! Your fault again!
Now what the blazes do you mean
  By letting all this filth be seen?'
The Captain sniffed, but took the snub,
  Then, calling to the Junior Sub.,

Observed, 'Look here, what's all this mess?
  It's fit for pigs, sir, nothing less!'
The Junior Sub. blushed crimson red,
  Then, to the Sergeant-major, said,
'I'm quite fed up, and all that rot!
  I mean to say — a pig-sty! What?'
The Sergeant-major, filled with rage,
  Attacked the Sergeant at this stage,
'You careless swab! Jump to it smart.
  Oh strewth! You break my blinkin 'eart!'

The Sergeant, starting in to cuss,
   Apostrophized the Corporal, thus,
'You lazy, lumberin', boss-eyed lout!
   Who chucked this crimson fruit about?'
The Corporal frowned, and turned his eye
   On Private Atkins passing by;

'Hi! you! Come 'ere, you slobberin' sweep,
   Just shift this festerin' rubbish 'eap!'
And Private Atkins, filled with gloom,
   Applied himself with spade and broom:
'They talk a ruddy lot,' quoth he,
   'But 'oo does all the work? *Why me!*'

My Old Football
By Milton Hayes & Cuthbert Clarke (1920)

You can keep your antique silver and your statuettes of
   bronze,
   Your curios and tapestries so fine,
But of all your treasures rare there is nothing to
   compare
   With this patched up, worn-out football pal o' mine.
Just a patched-up worn-out football, yet how it clings!
   I live again my happier days in thoughts that
   football brings.
It's got a mouth, it's got a tongue,
   And oft when we're alone I fancy that it speaks
To me of golden youth that's flown.
   It calls to mind our meeting,
'Twas a present from the Dad.
   I kicked it yet I worshipped it,
How strange a priest it had!
   And yet it jumped with pleasure
When I punched it might and main:
   And when it had the dumps
It got blown up and punched again.
   It's lived its life;
It's played the game;
   It's had its rise and fall,
There's history in the wrinkles of
   That worn-out football.
Caresses rarely came its way —
   In baby-hood 'twas tanned.
It's been well oiled, and yet it's quite tee-total,
   understand.
   It's gone the pace, and sometimes it's been absolutely
   bust,
And yet 'twas always full of bounce,
   No matter how 'twas cussed.
He's broken many rules and oft has wandered out of
   bounds,
   He's joined in shooting parties
Over other people's grounds.
   Misunderstood by women,
He was never thought a catch,
   Yet he was never happier

Than when bringing off a match.
   He's often been in danger —
Caught in nets that foes have spread,
   He's even come to life again
When all have called him dead.
   Started on the centre,
And he's acted on the square,
   To all parts of the compass
He's been bullied everywhere.
   His aims and his ambitions
Were opposed by one and all,
   And yet he somehow reached his goal —
That plucky old football.
   When schooling days were ended
I forgot him altogether,
   And 'midst the dusty years
He lay a crumpled lump of leather.
   Then came the threat'ning voice of War,
And games had little chance,
   My brother went to do his bit —
Out there somewhere in France.
   And when my brother wrote he said,
'Of all a Tommy's joys,
   There's none compares with football.
Will you send one for the boys?'
   I sent not one but many,
And my old one with the rest,
   I thought that football's finished now,
But no — he stood the test.
   Behind the lines they kicked him
As he'd never been kicked before.
   Till they busted him and sent him back —
A keep-sake of the war.
   My brother lies out there in France,
Beneath a simple cross,
   And I seem to feel my football knows my grief,
And shares my loss.
   He tells me of that splendid charge,
And then my brother's fall.
   In life he loved our mutual chum —

That worn-out old football.
  Oh, you can keep your antique silver
And your statuettes of bronze,
  Your curios and tapestries so fine,

But of all your treasures rare
  There is nothing to compare
With that patched-up worn-out football —
  Pal o' mine.

You Know What I Mean
By Milton Hayes (1923)

I've noticed this happen,
  When everything is black,
When I'm down below zero and cannot get back,
  When I feel like a sort of a National Debt,
That will go on for ages and never be met,
  When my will is all bagged at the knees and dead
    beat,
It is then, don't you know, that I'm certain to meet
  With some prodigal lifeless dejected old bean,
Who is worse off than I — you know what I mean.

Someone or other who's entered the race,
  With a sense of intention but can't stay the pace,
He tells all his troubles and heaven knows what,
  Talks about Fate and all that sort of rot,
And it makes all my own little troubles look small,
  Till I find I've no cause to be worried at all,
And it doesn't seem cricket to grouse when I've seen,
  That he's worse off than I — you know what I mean.

No matter how hard one may fall down the hill,
  There's always a somebody lower down still,
And it makes you feel — well, it seems mean to repeat,
  All your own little troubles to people you meet.
One learns in the end, that self pity's a curse,

And to talk of your cares only makes them seem
  worse.
It takes courage to stand where it's easy to lean,
  But it makes you feel better — you know what I
  mean.

The chap we all like is the chap who can smile,
  Though his heart may be breaking with sorrow the
  while,
He just keeps them all secretly locked in his breast,
  Keep's the worm to himself, gives the world of his
  best.
He has losses like we have, yet never gives in,
  But goes silently back to his task with a grin.
And the lesson we learn from this priceless old being,
  Is to smile all the while with some laughs in
  between.
Though you're empty and broke, meet your fate with a
  joke,
  For the sake of the folk who can't see what you mean.
And it may be in turn even they will yet learn,
  And they'll smile all the while when they see what
  you mean.
Do you get me?
  Ah — well — that's what I mean.

A Soldier's Reminiscences
By Bert Lee & Ernest Hastings (1915)

I am an old Soldier with hair iron grey,
  My mem'ry's not bad tho' I'm sixty today;
Or else sixty-two; I can't be sixty-four,
  Well, maybe I am, but I'm not a day more.
I can reckon it out, I was born in — dear me!
  Why at that rate I must be turned seventy-three.
Dear me, this confusion it makes me upset,
  Why I'm eighty I think — I forget — I forget!
Only loved once, 'twas a girl called Elaine,
  Elaine or Priscilla, no! perhaps it was Jane —
However, one evening my brain in a whirl,
  I went to her father and asked for the girl.

Said he 'Which girl is it? for I possess three,'
  I said 'Gladys Maud is the best girl for me.'
Now did he consent in a tone of regret,
  Or say 'Take the three?' — I forget — I forget!
I first joined the Army in seventeen ten,
  No, that can't be right for I wasn't born then,
'Twas eighteen six three, wrong again, it was not,
  No, that's somebody's telephone number I've got.
They asked me what regiment I'd like to choose,
  Would I join the Hussars? I said 'No, the Who's
  Who's.'
'Twas with General Buller we captured De Wet,

Or did he catch us? I forget, I forget!
Ah! well! I suppose that I get very old,
    And I'm not so much use in the Army I'm told,
So I just jog along as the days come and go,
    And wait for the call that is coming I know,

When the final halt comes, and I hear the last call,
    That comes from the Greatest Commander of all,
Then whatever there is in the past to regret,
    I shall hand up my sword and just hope He'll forget.

And Yet I Don't Know

By Bob Weston & Bert Lee (1919)
Performed by Ernest Hastings

Now, my sister's daughter Elizabeth May
    Is going to get married next Sunday, they say.
Now, what shall I buy her? She's such a nice gel!
    I think a piano would do very well.
I saw one today, only ninety-five pound:
    A decent piano, I'll have it sent round.

And yet I don't know! And yet I don't know!
    I think she's the rottenest player I know.
And if she keeps thumping out that 'Maiden's Pray'r'
    The husband might kill his young bride, and so
      there!
I won't buy the piano! It's not that I'm mean;
    I think I'd best buy her a sewing machine.

And yet I don't know! And yet I don't know!
    A sewing machine is a 'tenner' or so!
A tenner would buy lots of needles and thread,
    And things that are hand-made are best, so it's said.
So it's not that I'm mingy, although I'm half Scotch —
    I know what I'll buy her: an Ingersoll watch!

And yet I don't know! And yet I don't know!
    In five or six years they're too fast or too slow.
And when she's turn'd seventy, that's if she's spar'd,
    'Twill have cost her a fortune in being repair'd.
Or else she'll have pawn'd it, and lost it, so there!
    I know what I'll buy her: a jumper to wear!

And yet I don't know! And yet I don't know!
    The girls won't wear jumpers in ten years or so.
Besides she might start getting fat before long.
    And fat girls in jumpers show too much ong bong!
And open work jumpers give ladies the 'flu.
    I'll buy her some handkerchiefs, that's what I'll do!

And yet I don't know! And yet I don't know!
    Good hankies cost twelve bob a dozen or so.
And twelve bob's too much for her poor Uncle John.
    Why, anything does just to blow your nose on.
And talking of noses, hers looks red enough!
    I know what I'll buy her: a nice powder puff.

She can't powder her nose with a grand piano,
    Nor yet with a sewing machine.
She can't powder her nose with an Ingersoll watch:
    Well, it's silly! You see what I mean!

She can't powder her nose with a jumper:
    She would find it a little bit rough;
So I'll go round to Woolworth's tonight, God bless her!
    And buy her a powder puff.

And yet I don't know! And yet I don't know!
    Sixpence ha'p'nies don't grow in backyards,
So I don't think I'll send her a powder puff,
    I'll send her — my kindest regards!

My Word! You Do Look Queer

By Bob Weston & Bert Lee (1923)
Performed by Ernest Hastings

I've been very poorly but now I feel prime,
    I've been out today for the very first time.
I felt like a lad as I walk'd down the road,
    Then I met old Jones and he said, 'Well I'm blow'd!'

'My word you do look queer! My word you do look
    queer!

Oh, dear! You look dreadful: you've had a near
    shave,
You look like a man with one foot in the grave.'
    I said, 'Bosh! I'm better; it's true I've been ill.'
He said, 'I'm delighted you're better, but still,
    I wish you'd a thousand for me in your will.
My word, you do look queer!'

That didn't improve me, it quite put me back,
  Still, I walk'd farther on, and I met Cousin Jack.
He look'd at me hard and he murmur'd, 'Gee whiz!
  It's like him! It can't be! It isn't! It is!
By gosh! Who'd have thought it? Well, well, I declare!
  I'd never have known you except for your hair.

'My word you do look queer! My word you do look
    queer!
  Your cheeks are all sunk and your colour's all gone,
Your neck's very scraggy, still you're getting on.
  How old are you now? About fifty, that's true.
Your father died that age, your mother did too.
  Well, the black clothes I wore then'll come in for
    you.
My word! You do look queer!'

That really upset me; I felt quite cast down,
  But I tried to buck up, and then up came old Brown.
He star'd at me hard, then he solemnly said,
  'You shouldn't be out, you should be home in bed.
I heard you were bad, well I heard you were gone.
  You look like a corpse with an overcoat on.

'My word you do look queer! My word you do look
    queer!
  You'd best have a brandy before you drop dead.'
So, pale as a sheet I crawl'd in the 'King's Head'.
  The bar-maid sobbed, 'Oh you poor fellow,' and
    then

She said, 'On the slate you owe just one-pound-ten.
  You'd better pay up, we shan't see you again.
My word you do look queer!'

My knees started knocking, I did feel so sad.
  Then Brown said, 'Don't die in a pub, it looks bad!'
He said, 'Come with me, I'll show you what to do.
  Now I've got a friend who'll be useful to you.'
He led me to Black's Undertaking Depot,
  And Black, with some crepe round his hat said,
    'Hello,

'My word you do look queer! My word you do look
    queer!
  Now we'll fix you up for a trifling amount.
Now what do you say to a bit on account?'
  I said, 'I'm not dying.' He said, 'Don't say that!
My business of late has been terribly flat,
  But I'm telling my wife she can have that new hat.
My word, you do look queer!'

I crawl'd in the street and I murmur'd, 'I'm done.'
  Then up came old Jenkins and shouted, 'Old son!'
'My word you do look well! My word you do look
    well!
  You're looking fine and in the pink!'
I shouted, 'Am I? Come and have a drink!
  You've put new life in me, I'm sounder than a bell.
By gad! There's life in the old dog yet.
  My word I do feel well!'

I Might Marry You!
(The Cautious Lover)
By Bob Weston & Bert Lee (1923)
Performed by Ernest Hastings

Introduction: spoken
In these days of commercialism I'm afraid the old
fashioned sentimental love ballads like 'I passed by
your window' will soon be obsolete. I can't imagine a
young man of the present day going up to a girl and
saying, 'I will love you till the sands of the desert grow
cold.' A man wants to know a bit more about what he's
getting before he rushes into a thing of this kind, and
the following is the sort of love ballad which I imagine
a hard headed business man might sing to his girl. I
call it 'The Cautious Lover'.

I've passed by your house and next time I'm coming
    in,
  Oh yes, I am! — you bet I am!
Some hang round a house when a girl they want to
    win,

But not for Sam — no, not for Sam!
Besides, it's not a cert I'm going to have you.
  It's time that I was married, I'll admit;
But would I ask a girl before I'd found out all about
    her?
  Would I WHAT — would I hamlet — not a bit!
I've other girls in view, but still I fancy you,
  And if you answer my requirements, possibly you'll
    do.

Now, what is your father worth? Has he a thousand or
    two?
  Will he be sure to pop off quick and leave it all to
    you?
Is the old boy a sport? Are his cigars all right?
  Has he a drop of the 'doings' if I bring you home at
    night?

What is your mother like — What is she like, I say?
  Has she the sort of mouth that hasn't an early closing
    day?
I couldn't stand a ma that sniffs and murmurs 'Jane,
  I'm fed up with that young man of yours, he's here
    to tea again.'

What's your house like inside? I want you to tell me,
  do —
  Is it the sort of house that you can ask a young man
    to?
What is it furnish'd like? Don't think I want to grouse,
  But it's no use courting a girl if there's no sofa in the
    house.

Oh! oh! that's what I want to know,
  For I'm looking for a wife, it's true,
And probably, probably, very, very possibly, I might
  marry you.

Now, some fellows rush things and take a girl for keeps
  I wonder why — I wonder why;
For I like a young man who looks before he leaps,
  And so shall I — yes, so shall I.
Besides, as I am now, I'm very comfy.
  My mother's just as good as any wife.
So would I marry one in haste and then repent at
    Brixton?
  Would I WHAT — would I NO! Not on your life!
But still I'm getting on — I'm just turn'd thirty-three.
  I'll have a wife — if I can find one good enough for
    me.

Do you know how to bake? What is your pastry like?

Will it go down the mine all right, or will it go on
  strike?
Have you expensive tastes? Can you shun temptation?
  Can you walk past John Barker's when the Bargain
    Sales are on?

Say if you've got cold feet — I want you to make that
  clear.
  I couldn't stand a refrigerator ruining my career.
Can you darn all my clothes; and when my shirts you
    see,
  Can you fix an extension where the tail part used to
    be?

How is your general health, for tho' you're looking
    prime,
  A wife is an awful drag on a chap if she's ailing all
    the time.
Are your teeth all your own? They look all right, and
    yet
  I don't want to marry you and find you need a new
    top set.

Oh! oh! that's what I want to know,
  For I'm looking for a wife, it's true,
And probably, probably, very, very possibly* I might
  marry you.

*Spoken passage in last Chorus
Mind you — I don't want to take anything for granted
— I don't want you to build on it — I don't want to
lead you up the garden and leave you stranded in the
summer house — but, I'll think it over for a week or
two and if I don't hear of anything better . . .
(sing) I might marry you.

The Cautious Lover
By Corney Grain (1925)
Performed by Ernest Hastings

I love thee and would make thee mine, sweet maid!
  Thy form and features are divine, sweet maid!
But ere I yield to Cupid's fatal dart,
  I think I'd like to know how really old thou art,
I think I'd like to know how really old thou art.
  No red, red rose that I could seek, sweet maid!
Could match the bloom upon thy cheek, sweet maid!
  But ere by Cupid's fatal dart I'm shot,
I think I'd like to know if it comes off or not,
  I think I'd like to know if it comes off or not!

How wondrous and divinely fair, sweet maid!
  Thy glorious wealth of golden hair, sweet maid!
But ere I yield to Cupid's dart outright,
  I think I'd like to know if it comes off at night,
I think I'd like to know if it comes off at night.
  So do not deem me too unkind, sweet maid!
To give thee pain I have no mind, sweet maid!
  But when a swain a modern maiden wins,
It's hard to know where Nature ends and Art begins,
  It's hard to know where Nature ends and Art begins.

Milton Hayes, writer and performer of perhaps the most famous dramatic monologue of all, *The Green Eye of the Little Yellow God*

Billy Bennett, 'Almost A Gentleman', and the cover of one of his many publications offering valuable advice to aspiring performers

Supplement . .

TO......

BILLY BENNETT'S BUDGET.

The Treasure Trove of Futurist Humour.

¶ This Budget is used and recommended by every Contortionist, Equilibrist, Russian Dancer, and Humpsti-Bumpsti act of repute.

¶ Mr. Bennett has submitted songs to every Star Artiste in the Profession and has only had one song returned; this was when he enclosed a stamped addressed envelope.

WILLSONS' PRINTERIES, NOTTINGHAM.

The Green Tie on the Little Yellow Dog
By Billy Bennett (1926)

There's a little sallow idle man lives north of Waterloo,
  And he owns the toughest music hall in town.
There are broken hearted comics, there's a grave yard
    for them too
  And the gallery gods are ever gazing down,
He was known as Fat Caroo in the pubs round
    Waterloo
  And he wore a green tie with a diamond pin;
He was worshipped in the ranks
  By the captain of the swanks and the coal man's
    daughter
Loved his double chin.
  He had loved her all along
And, despite his ong-bong-pong,
  The fact that she loved him
They say was right,
  Though her complexion was a fake
And her teeth were put and take
  (Put in by day and taken out by night).
'Twas the fifteenth anniversary of her twenty-second
    year,
  So he smiled at her as sweetly as a hog
And asked what present she would like and jestingly
    she said,
  'Your green tie for my little yellow dog.'
Fat Caroo seemed in a trance
  And his heart slipped through his pants,
But he tried his utmost not to look a wreck.
  So he handed her the tie and kissed her hand
    goodbye —
When he bowed his head she bit his neck.

Later on Caroo came to —
His tie had gone it's true
  And his tie pin with it.
He seemed in a fog,
  He rushed like mad to find, that she'd tied that tie
    behind
To the tailpiece of her little yellow dog.
  She was screaming like a child,
The dog was running wild,
  Biting policemen as he galloped up the straight;
For the little dog caled Tom
  When he wagged his to and from
Felt the tie pin urged him on to meet his fate.
  The dog returned at dawn with his windscreen
    slightly torn
And on seeing took something from the lady's room.
  To another room he flew, saying, 'That's for Fat
    Caroo'
And silently he slunked out in the gloom.
  When Caroo jumped into bed he'd 've wakened up
    the dead,
With a scream as he fell like a hog.
  Her false teeth they were buried in the seat of Fat
    Caroo —
'Twas the vengeance of that little yellow dog.
  There's a cockeyed yellow poodle to the north of
    Gonga Pooch,
There's a little hot cross bun that's turning green,
  There's a double jointed woman doing tricks in
    Choo-Chin-Chow —
And you're a better man that I am Gunga Din.

Devil-May-Not-Care
By Billy Bennett (1926)

Fly if your pigtail catches fire,
  Dive down the nearest sink,
Remember if you wash a pancake,
  It's underwear's sure to shrink.

Once I was a twister, just like you,
  Had ricketts, false teeth and no hair.
Do you remember when we first met,
  You do? You're a liar, Devil-May-Care.

Devil-May-Care who trampled corn,
  To cover his awful past.

Devil-May-Care, the cowheel taster
  And a bachelor's son to the last.

Some of you tell how you beat the bull,
  Aye, brag on a flush of hair,
When you scattered the giblets in the tube,
  With dirty old Devil-May-Care.

You were lucky at finding things not lost,
  As a milkmaid milks with pliers.
Your mothers nurse your baby
  If you can't use Dunlop tyres.

Dog at the lamp-post wags its tail,
  'Cos the dirty legs are square.
What little remains of the crystal set,
  Of dirty old Devil-May-Care.

How do I live? On the Parish.
  Where do I sleep? In a tomb.
I was born in a sardine's graveyard,
  Where treacle and sausages bloom.

Asleep on your back in a haunted house,
  And dreaming of rats with bobbed hair.
Fighting boss-eyed bulls and knock-kneed cows,
  Puts the wind up Devil-May-Care.

But we can find you a three-quid short,
  The lady lodger's out.
It makes you think what the Parson knows,
  When the feathers are lying about.

We got drunk together the night we met,
  At a Japanese Yiddish wake.
And I slipped my hand deep down in her purse,
  And I pinched her currant cake.

Everyone said her legs were false,
  And I proved it so in the dark.
But we tried to dance the can-can in Paris,
  But her magneto wouldn't spark.

So I reeled up the aisle with me braces broke,
  While crowds pelted me with bad eggs.
When the Parson said, 'Look what the wind's blown in',
  She hit him with one of her legs.

What does it matter if rock cakes rock,
  And pineapples fly in the air.
'Cos at death I shall cheerfully cry, 'I'm sticking'
  But he'll say 'Pontoons only, Devil-May-Care.'

Nell
By Billy Bennett (1926)

Nell was a collier's daughter, innocent, sweet seventeen.
  Shall I tell you the story of Nellie? Yes, tell us it,
    Bill, if it's clean.
Nell was a collier's daughter, with a coal-black daddy
    so fine,
  At the close of the day to the theatre he'd stray to
    forget the dark toil of the mine.

Once he sat in the gallery with some of the lads,
  They started to quarrel a bit.
It wasn't his shift, but they gave him a lift,
  And the collier went down in the pit.

Years have rolled on since that happened,
  Time soothed the widow's pain.
One morning she met a diver
  And the girl's mother married again.

Nell was a diver's daughter —
  He used to dive under the ships.
He'd walk on the bed of the ocean
  And tread on the fishes and chips.

But the mother and he could never agree,
  And they quarrelled for hours and hours.
Once he called her a dog, so she picked up his clog,
  And then came a coach filled with flowers.

Years have rolled on since that happened,
  Time soothed the widow's pain.
One morning she met a plumber
  And the girl's mother married again.

Nell was a plumber's daughter,
  Aye, Nell was a plumber's lass
She ran like mad to fetch her dad
  When she smelt an escape of gas.

Dad went upstairs with a lighted match
  Singing 'Grannie's Song at Twilight.'
We heard a crack, and Dad came back
  Through the next-door neighbour's sky-light!

Years have rolled on since that happened,
  Time soothed the widow's pain,
One morning she met an engineer
  And the girl's mother married again.

Nell was an engineer's daughter
  She once took his mid-day meal,
He was oiling a shaft, and she stood and laughed
  When his boko got caught in a wheel.

He was picked from the ground, whirled round and
  round,
  And poor Nell started shrieking.
He came down down with a smack on the back of his
  back
  And his oil-can started leaking!

Years have rolled on — no, I've said that once!

Then Nell fell in love with a sailor
  And married a jolly Jack Tar.
He had eyes of blue, he was sixty-two,
  But you know what sailors are!

He'd a son called John who was twenty-one,
  And it's very strange to say
He fell in love with Nell's mother
  And married her right away.

Now Nell is her mother's new mother,
  Her father becomes her own son,
Her mother's first child is her father-in-law,
  And her daughter's the son-of-a-gun.

Her mother's first cousin looks after Nell's child,
  For they found on the day of its birth
That its uncle's step-sister's its grandmother's aunt
  And I'm the biggest liar on earth!

The Charge of the Tight Brigade
By Billy Bennett (1926)

Half a league, half a league, football league, onward.
  In fifteen char-a-bancs rode the 600.
This is the tale of a football match, where men fought
  to their death,
  A tale of forward backs and fronts, and footballs
  filled with breath.

The famous Chelsea Totspurs — what a name! (there's
  nowt to kill it)
  Were playing Woolworth's Arsenic for the cup (and
  beer to fill it).
There in the stands they stood, hoping the match was
  good.
  Up to their knees in mud — noble 600!

The band was blowing bubbles, trills and frills and
  rolls,
  And a pair of cows were busy chewing grass from
  round the goals.
The good old Totspurs came on first, a hefty lot of
  kickers,
  They all wore shinguards on their shins, and
  mudguards on their knickers.

Bring out the busted ball cried stop-me-and-buy-one
  Wall,
  Answer your country's call, who killed Rob
  Cocking?
Pass, shouted Porky Flynn, pass me a double gin,
  Who kicked the captain's chin — pushed all his
  dimples in?

Rude girls began to grin, his pants were giving in,
  Lend him a safety pin, or — pop goes the weasel!
Half backs to right of 'em, draw backs to left of 'em,
  Switch backs in front of 'em.

Tuck in your jersey,
  Centre, and have a shot,
Cannon in off and pot.
  Don't hit the baby's cot,
Someone has blundered.

They tackled them and tickled them,
  But give the men their due,
The ball bounced swiftly to and fro
  And sometimes fro and to.

When they'd scored fifty goals,
  Postmen delivered coals,
Boy scouts climbed up their poles,
  All waving sausage rolls.

Navvies in camisoles
  Went to their better 'oles,
Back, back to draw their doles
  And buy silk pyjamas.

Then came an awful smash,
  Goal posts fell with a crash,
Hit one bald head and bash,
  Shingled a bloke's moustache —
But don't tell his mother.

44

The referee put his foot down, with a most decided
    smack,
  He ordered eight men off the field and fetched
    eleven back,
He tried to blow his whistle, but they pushed it
    through his face,
  He'd two black eyes, and his trousers torn in a very
    awkward place.

Offside for leg before, inside to have one more,
  Outside the canteen door stood the 600.
Oh! what a charge they made. Oh! what a canteen raid,
  All drank and no one paid,
Honour the Tight Brigade,
  Chockful of lemonade,
Noble 600.

The Tightest Man I Know
By Billy Bennett (1927)

The tightest man I know is an Irish Eskimo,
  He's selling grapes with whiskers on beneath a
    burning sun.
And he's working night and day, though his feet are
    turning grey,
  Trying to straighten out bananas, and that's a thing
    he hasn't done!

Jim and I were pals together in the days of Auld Lang
    Syne,
  We were even chums at college when his cell was
    next to mine.
He's pulled me out of many a scrape, and I've pulled
    corks for Jim,
  I'd risk my life for myself, and he'd do the same for
    him!

Then a woman came to part us. She was pretty as a
    cart-horse,
  And she didn't rest till Jim and I did part.
He'd her picture in a locket, which he wore in his back
    pocket,
  So he always had her photo next his heart!

I sailed away to 'Frisco, leaving him and her alone,
  She dragged him to the gutter bit by bit.
She blackened both his eyes, and then to Jim's surprise
  Tried to hand him out another, but he'd nowhere it
    would fit.

Then she left him for a Dago, a hokey-pokey man,
  Supposed to be the richest gink in town.
He was making money fly, throwing dollars to the sky,
  And he always used to catch them coming down.

This Dago, slippery Joe, was the tightest guy I know,
  And he'd had one pair of trousers round his legs
For nine years, it is true, and the pockets were bran
    new.
  And he used to look in cuckoo-clocks for eggs.

I returned from 'Frisco's gates on a pair of roller
    skates,
  And I met Jim with a face just like the Sphinx.
He'd incurred some gambling losses, playing foolish
    noughts and crosses,
  And so doped he sometimes bought a round of
    drinks.

He said he'd like a bottle, so we walked into a Hottle
    (sorry, Hotel),
  Where a fat girl rose and gave us both her seat.
At the table we were sipping at a glass of bread and
    dripping
  When I saw the cursed woman face to feet — feet to
    feet — face to face!

She was sitting with the Dago, he'd his whiskers full of
    sago,
  You'd think they owned the blessed earth to watch
    them dine and sup,
And Jim said, 'For two pins I'd kick him on the
    shins' —
  Well I had two pins, but needed them to hold my
    trousers up!

So we sat there for a second, 'till the woman to us
    beckoned,
  We went over to her table just to listen to her chin.
She said that she regretted, she wept and cried and
    fretted,
  The tears rolled down until our whisky looked like
    drops of gin.

Then a shot rang through the night, and bang out went
    the light,
  We heard the crash of falling steel and glass.
The head waiter gave a curse as he dived down for his
    purse —
  It was his turn for a penny for the gas.

When the lights went up again, we'd been tricked, 'twas
    very plain,
    For uncannily the place was calm and still.
And the woman and the Dago had vamoosed upon
    their way-go
    And left my poor chum Jim to pay the bill!

There's a custom over there, if you haven't got your
    fare,
    You're branded with hot irons as an outcast from the
    Greeks.

Jim was seized by six Hussars, made to sit on red-hot
    bars,
    But he stuck it like a hero — that's how he got rosy
    cheeks!

When they call the final rolls, and we just wear
    camisoles,
    In a land that's far away from earthly woe;
When Jim hands in his cheque, if they don't include
    his neck,
    I'm sure he'll be the whitest man I know!

'She's Mine'
By Billy Bennett (1927)

You see pretty girls' photos on magazine covers,
    But no fella's got one like that;
For I've got a wife who's really quite nice
    But the looking glass tells her she's fat.
She's so very plump to get in a room once
    She has to go twice through each door.
There's a terrible lot and then not so much
    And men help yourself to some more.

Still she's mine, all mine, she's nobody else's but mine.
    I think she was built when it comes to the worst
To show how far the skin will stretch before it will
    burst
    On the day we were wed a rude fella said,
'Why he's brought back a tank from the Rhine.'
    I paid 7/6d and I got a treat, 19 stone 4 in her
    stocking feet —
That's three pounds a penny all good English meat
    and
    It's mine, all mine.

She's mine, all mine, she's nobody else's but mine.
    Skipping would bring down her weight so they said;
She skipped but she brought down the ceiling instead.
    She was washing last week but the weather was bleak
Her lingerie blew off the line
    I searched from eleven to twenty past three;
I found some boy scouts who had made a marquee
    With five yards to spare, so I said 'Give it me
cos she's mine, all mine.'

We wanted a holiday one day last summer,
    So went to the seaside for luck.
The luggage went on in a five seater car
    And the wife came along in a truck.
She's fond of the water excepting for drinking,
    The morning was lovely and clear,
She dived in the sea but she made such a splash
    That she washed the jazz band off the pier.

Still she's mine, all mine, she's nobody else's but mine.
    I thought she looked grand as she swam in the foam,
But a sailor said, 'Crikey the fleet's coming home.'
    He stuck a harpoon in the captive balloon
And pulled her ashore with his line.
    The crowd stood and cheered as she lay soaking wet;
One said 'It's a whale
    Or a porpoise I'll bet.'
I said, 'No sir it's only a girl men forget
    But it's mine, all mine.'

She's mine, all mine, she's nobody else's but mine.
    We'd our photographs taken before we came home,
With me as St. Pauls and the wife as the dome.
    We jumped on a tram but she caused such a jam,
She took up enough room for nine.
    She sat on a man's hat and he said 'Now my dear,
Do you know what you've sat on?'
    She answered, 'Look here, I ought to,
I've sat there for thirty five years
    And it's mine, all mine.'

The Member of Parliament

By Billy Bennett (1929)

I've just been elected to Parliament,
    At Westminster I'm the big cheese,
I'm also a Knight of the Garter, it's right —
    In fact, I've got one on both knees.

Whilst my maiden speech I was making,
    Someone opened the door for some air,
And my maiden speech was blown out of reach,
    So I sang them the 'Maiden's Prayer.'

Ye Gods, how the Members applauded,
    I raised my voice, drowning the cheers,
I was straining my glands, while they clapped their
        hands,
    They clapped their hands over their ears.

I cried 'What will I do for England?
    For England, what would I do?'
Then young Locker Lam said, 'We don't care a damn,
    But we know what we'll do to you.'

Britain, I say, for the British,
    There's some good British firms even yet,
There's Edgar & Duck, and Salmon & Gluck,
    And the Galleries Lafayette.'

I cried 'I will throw out a challenge —
    Have you read your "Exchange & Mart" '
Then a voice loud and shrill said 'Let's throw out the
        bill
    And let's throw out this Bill for a start.'

To the member I shouted out, 'Order.'
    He ordered nine bottles of stout,
He drank every one, and the son of a gun
    Pinched the doormat as he staggered out.

'What do we need to unite us?' I cried,
    Then a voice like a bolt from the blue
Shouted 'Social Reform, Party Reform,
    And a good dose of chloroform, too.'

'Why not improve our Air Force?
    We're a bit behind times,' I declared,
'For taking air trips we want plenty of ships,
    We've already got plenty of air!'

'Let's open an air route to Russia,
    To Poland, and Czecho-Slovak,
It takes us by air two days to get there,
    And three and a half years to get back.'

'Now, let us talk about Labour,
    And if the worst comes to the worst
There's work for you, and work for me too,
    But *you* make a start on it first.'

'What's wrong with our Prison System?
    Are the Judges all 'Bats in the Belf'?
I'll tell you what's wrong, the terms are too long,
    I've just done twelve years myself.'

'Our railways, they want improving,
    On more engines let's squander the bunce,
Let's have one on the front and one on the back,
    And then we'll go both ways at once.'

'Why can't shopkeepers all be like Woolworths?
    Then shopping would be all sublime,
Sell motors and boots, and houses and suits,
    Nothing over a tanner a time.'

'Why go to Belgium for bloaters
    And Camembert cheese over-ripe?
Why go to Peru for fresh eggs, like we do,
    And why trip to the tropics for tripe?'

'For six months the House has been sitting,
    Not one single egg have we got,
We wear trousers, not frocks,
    We're not hens, we're all cocks, and that's why we all
        crow such a lot.'

'Why have we so many waifs and strays?
    It's a dirty trick, you must agree,
Who's right and who's wrong, I don't care so long
As you don't put the blame on to me.'

'And then, there's the great drinking question,
    The answer must be brief and short —
Put the question to me and the answer will be
    Same again, only this time a quart.'

My Mother Doesn't Know I'm On The Stage
By Billy Bennett (1929)

I'm cherishing a secret in my bosom
　About this dreadful stage life that I lead,
I've heard it said that pro's are decent people,
　But according to the papers that I read
Both actresses and actors are dead wrong 'uns
　Whether from the Palace or the Hippodrome
The chaps I meet outside know I'm an actor
　But I never breathe a word of it at home,
So me mother doesn't know I'm on the stage.

It would break her poor old heart if she found out.
　She knows I'm a deserter from the Scottish Fusiliers,
She knows I stole a blind man's can that got me seven
　　years,
　She knows I have been connected with a gang of
　　West End pests
And the police have had me twice inside the cage,
　And she knows I mix with ladies that have got a
　　shady past
But me mother doesn't know I'm on the stage.

Some times she sees the powder on me clothing
　And then it's such a nuisance to explain.
If she thought it was powder she'd go crazy —
　Of course, I have to tell her it's cocaine.
The day she met me out with Gladys Cooper
　She started screaming murder and police
And would have caused a dreadful scene in public
　So I told her that the girl was Crippin's niece —
Cos me mother doesn't know I'm on the stage.

And when I draw six hundred pounds each week
　If she knew where it came from she'd shoot me like a
　　dog,
So I said I stole the money box, from an Irish
　　Synagogue,
　She can think that I'm a murderer
Before she'll know the truth,
　I have to have respect for her old age.
And she knows that I'm a bigamist, a blaggard and a
　　crook,
　But thank heaven she don't know I'm on the stage.

The Club Raid
By Billy Bennett (1929)

I'm a lover of night life in London
　When I start I can go pretty fast
I've blotted me copy book I must admit
　When I think of my future that's past.
I've been a bad lad to my parents,
　I'm a rip and I just live for crime.
The last thing I ripped was me nightie
　Coming down the stairs two at a time.
I've bumped round some bends in my travels
　And was told I would come to no good
When I told them that day at the workhouse
　What to do with their old Christmas pud.
My curse has been ladies and lime juice;
　In the West they call me The Big Noise;
The fat of the land's what I live on —
　Grease dripping and pork saveloys.
Scotland Yard's got a photograph of me
　In me gaiters and dolly dyed vest,
But I'll tell of the raid I was in once
　At the Cat Gut Club somewhere up West.
I started at night with a gamble —
　Fourpence is nothing to me.

With a couple of chinks
　I stood tossing for drinks,
Roast peanuts and saucers of tea.
　That night I shall never forget, sir,
The band playing Home Sweet Home
　I sat sucking a lemon and shouting good health
To the old crock who played the trombone.
　I lounged with a girl in the Palm Court;
She had a low neck chest at the back,
　Her blouse it was cut to and from
And all but the tips of her fingers in black.
　She'd come from a very big family
Who knows perhaps a publican's daughter.
　On Reggie's settee she got rather too free —
with the champagne I very near bought her.
　Later on we danced round and I noticed she took
　　size elevens
In shoes — I said to myself, 'She's a copper,'
　When she asked me if I knew the Blues.
Round went the Tic Tac, 'Police, Boys,'
　So I smuggled my soda and milk.
I grabbed a sea shell from the fire grate

And disguised myself there as a wilk.
Just then someone switched off the lights —
  In the dark I got quite a shock:
I was feeling my way and heard one girl say
  'Will you stop your tickling, Jock.'
It was a case of Blindman's Buff then,
  'Strike a Match' I heard one copper holler.
It was my rotten luck when the match had been struck
  It set light to my celluloid collar.
An officer pulled out his handcuffs
  And whispered, 'I must do my bit.'
But he said 'It's no use I apologise'
  When he found the darn things wouldn't fit.

So they took us all off for a joyride
  To the sergeant Mr. Everyman.
I said 'Please put us in with the lino
  And cart us there in a plain van.'
Next morning we turned up at Bow Street and stood
  looking solemn and sad —
  We had to stand there cos there was only one chair,
That's the one that the Magistrate had.
  He fined us he did, for each one paid a quid
And the Judge said, 'I'll soon stop your row.'
  But it's cured me of dancing with policemen —
only sailors and chorus boys now.

Mandalay
By Billy Bennett (1929)

By an old whitewashed Pagoda
  Looking eastward to the west
There's a Burma girl, from Bermondsey,
  Sits in a sparrow's nest.

She's as pretty as a picture,
  Though she lost one eye, they say,
Through the black hole of Calcutta —
  Perhaps the keyhole of Bombay!

Look as far as you can see, boy;
  Look a little further, son,
For that Burma girl is burning —
  Stick a fork in, see if she's done.

Oh, there's not a drop of water
  In that waste of desert land,
And the soldiers' tongues are hanging out
  And trailing in the sand.

Oh, they're hanging out like carpets,
  And you'll hear the natives say
Mr. Drage has laid the lino
  On the road to Mandalay!

As the temple bells are ringing
  Comes a soldier from his hut.
Will he be in time for service?
  No, too late, the canteen's shut!

There's a pub three miles behind us
  And we've passed it on the way;
Come you back, you British soldiers,
  There's a Scotsman wants to pay!

See, the desert moon is rising,
  For the golden sun has dropped,
And the Burma girl is sleeping —
  Sleeping sleeps she never slopped.

She is lying on an ant hill;
  Soon the ants come out to play;
Then she wakes and finds she's bitten —
  On the road to Mandalay!

See that stately dromedary
  As it walks along with pride,
On its back there's two mosquitos,
  Cheek to cheek and side by side.

On its humps there sits a Hindoo
  And, as up and down he bobs,
All the troops shout, 'Stop your swanking,
  'Cos you're sitting with the knobs.'

Oh, that land of plague and pestilence,
  Where the natives die in shoals,
And they have to vaccinate them
  Till their torso's full of holes!

Where they have to sit on red hot stones
  To keep the flies away;
It's no wonder they get sunburnt
  On the road to Mandalay.

There's a farm on the horizon,
  Looking eastward to Siam;
We could have some ham and eggs there —
  If they had some eggs and ham!

But they've only got one hen —
   They call her Mandy by the way;
But they've found out she's a cock,
   That's why they can't make Mandy-lay!

The poor sandpiper cannot pipe,
   He's all wheezed up and croaked,
He's swallowed so much sand
   His blinking carburettor's choked!

He cannot whistle through his throat,
   He's in a sorry plight;
So he sticks his beak into the sand
   And whistles through the night.

There were no maps for soldiers
   In this land of Gunga-Din,
So they picked the toughest warrior out
   And tattooed on his skin.

On his back he's got Calcutta,
   Lower down he's got Bombay,
And you'll find him sitting peacefully
   On the road to Mandalay!

Daddy
By Billy Bennett (1929)

How nice to see the picture of a father and his son.
   My father is my mother's wife and I'm his hot cross
   bun.
Our home sweet home's his castle, my daddy is the
   king.
   Cos mother's crowned him once or twice and that is
   why I sing.
Father, dear father, come home with me now,
   For the clock in the steeple strikes none.
We've got dover soles, lemon soles, camisoles too,
   And polonys with pullovers on.
Custard and jelly to fill up your evening,
   And onions that put up a barrage.
We'd a toad in the hole but the toad has flown out,
   And we can't get him back in the garage.
The twins have been crying for daddy all night,
   And mother's too tender to slap 'em,
So she gave them a bath and one slipped through the
   plug,
   And he's stuck in a drainpipe in Clapham.
The other poor darling keeps screaming for milk,
   But the dairy sent news that's upset us.

Their cows have been feeding on lots of ice-cream,
   And they've frozen their poor carburettors.
There's only one button left now on your pants,
   And these things are not done in this nice land.
For everyone knows if that last button goes,
   There'll be a depression in Iceland.
So picture this scene and take warning,
   Oh father stand up perpendicular.
And mother beware 'cos sailors don't care,
   And soldiers are not too particular.
Who made London today what Johannesburg is?
   Why the fathers of England we know.
And daddy I know you're my father,
   Cos dear mother told me it's so.
And you can't part a boy from his father,
   You can't part a boy from his dad.
You can't part a Scotchman from money,
   No matter how many he's had.
You can't part the skin of a sausage,
   Or a dad from his fond son and heir.
And you can't part the hair on a bald-headed man,
   For there'll be no parting there.

She was Poor but She was Honest
By Bob Weston & Bert Lee (1930)
Performed by Billy Bennett

She was poor but she was honest,
   Though she came from 'umble stock,
And her honest heart was beating
   Underneath her tattered frock.
But the rich man saw her beauty,
   She knew not his base design

And he took her to a hotel
   And bought her a small port wine.
It's the same the whole world over,
   It's the poor what gets the blame,
It's the rich what gets the pleasure,
   Isn't it a blooming shame?

In the rich man's arms she fluttered
  Like a bird with a broken wing,
But he loved her and he left her,
  Now she hasn't got no ring.
Time has flown — outcast and homeless
  In the street she stands and says
While the snowflakes fall around her,
  'Won't you buy my bootlaces.'
It's the same the whole world over,
  It's the poor what gets the blame,
It's the rich what gets the pleasure,
  Isn't it a blooming shame?

Standing on the bridge at midnight
  She says 'Farewell, blighted love!'
There's a scream, a splash, good 'eavens!
  What is she a doing of?
Soon they dragged her from the river
  Water from her clothes they wrang
They all thought that she was drownded
  But the corpse got up and sang:
It's the same the whole world over
  It's the poor what gets the blame
It's the rich what gets the pleasure
  Isn't it a blooming shame?

Please let me Sleep on your Doorstep Tonight
By Bob Weston & Bert Lee (1930)
Performed by Billy Bennett

'Twas Christmas Eve at midnight
  And a tramp with haggard face
Was knocking at the door
  Of a rich millionaire's palace.
The rich man in pyjamas
  Trimmed with gold and costly fur
Said 'What are you a-wanting of?'
  The tramp replied, 'Dear sir,
Please let me sleep on your doorstep tonight,
  I'm homeless and cold and the snow's falling white,
The fire through your keyhole looks cosy and bright,
  So please let me sleep on your doorstep tonight.'

The rich man said 'How dare you?'
  In a manner cold and chill
And from his freezing nose
  He proudly wiped an icicle.
That night while his rich brother
  slept on silk sheets trimmed with lace
The poor man slept and then the snowflakes fell
  On his cock ace.
'Please let me sleep on your doorstep tonight,
  I'm homeless and cold and the snow's falling white,
The fire through your keyhole looks cosy and bright,
  So please let me sleep on your doorstep tonight.'

The rich man called a constable and said,
  'Remove this man.'
He shone his lamp — the rich man cried,
  'Why it's my brother Dan!
You want to sleep upon my doorstep,
  You my brother Fred,
You shall sleep on my doorstep
  I didn't know you when yer said,
"Please let me sleep on your doorstep tonight,
  I'm homeless and cold and the snow's falling white,
The fire through your keyhole looks cosy and bright,
  So please let me sleep on your doorstep tonight." '

The rich man caught pneumonia
  Through standing in the cold
And soon at heavens pearly gates
  He claimed his wings of gold.
The angel to the rich man said,
  'You can't come in, oh no.'
The rich man said, 'Well as it's late and they're full up
    below,
  Please let me sleep on your doorstep tonight,
I'm homeless and cold and the snow's falling white,
  The fire through your keyhole looks cosy and bright,
So please let me sleep on your doorstep tonight.'

Christmas Day in the Cookhouse
By Billy Bennett (1930)

'Twas Christmas Day in the cookhouse, and the place
    was clean and tidy,
  The soldiers were eating their pancakes — I'm a liar,
    that was Good Friday.

In the oven a turkey was sizzling and to make it look
    posh, I suppose,
  They fetched the Battalion Barber, to shingle it's
    parson's nose!

Potatoes were cooked in their jackets, and carrots in
    pants — how unique!
  A sheep's head was baked with the eyes in, as it had
    to see them through the week.
At one o'clock 'Dinner Up' sounded, the sight made an
    old soldier blush,
  They were dishing out Guinness for nothing, and
    fifteen got killed in the crush!

A jazz band played in the mess-room, a fine lot of
    messers it's true,
  We told them to go and play Ludo, and they all
    answered 'Fishcakes' to you!
In came the old Sergeant Major, he'd walked all the
    way from his billet,
  His toes were turned in, his chest was turned out,
    with his head back in case he'd spill it.

He wished all the troops 'Merry Xmas,' including the
    poor Orderly Man;
  Some said 'Good Old Sergeant Major,' but others
    said 'San Fairy Ann.'
Then up spoke one ancient warrior, his whiskers a nest
    for the sparrows,
  The old man had first joined the army when the
    troops used to use bows and arrows.

His grey eyes were flashing with anger, he threw down
    his pudden' and cursed,
  'You dare to wish me a Happy New Year, well, just
    hear my story first.

Ten years ago, as the crow flies, I came here with my
    darling bride,
  It was Christmas Day in the Waxworks, so it must be
    the same outside.

We asked for some food, we were starving — you gave
    us pease pudden' and pork.
  My poor wife went to the Infirmary, with a pain in
    her Belle of New York.
You're the man that stopped bacon from shrinking, by
    making the cook fry with Lux,
  And you wound up the cuckoo clock backwards, and
    now it goes 'oo' fore it 'cucks'.

So thank you, and bless you, and b—low you, you just
    take these curses from me,
  May your wife give you nothing for dinner, and
    then warm it up for your tea.
Whatever you eat, may it always repeat — be it soup,
    fish, entrée, or horse doovers,
  May blue bottles and flies descend from the skies
And use your bald head for manoeuvres.

May the patent expire on your evening dress shoes,
    may your Marcel waves all come uncurled,
  May your flannel shirt shrink up the back of your
    neck and expose your deceit to the world.
And now that I've told you my story, I'll walk to the
    clink by the gate,
  And as for your old Xmas Pudden', stick that — on
    the next fellow's plate.'

The League of Nations
By Billy Bennett (1930)

Friends, Romans, Countrymen, lend me your ears. I
    have a story to tell.
  Lend me your ears, if you've not got them with you,
    your noses will do just as well.
What we want today is social reform, parish reform
    and more than likely chloroform.
  What did Gladstone say after '99? Why, 100 of
    course. And he was right.
I represent the common people and nobody is more
    common than I am.
  We have the Press behind us and if there is one
    thing I like to see in a newspaper it's a good feed
    of fish and chips.
I've just arrived from the League of Nations and I'll
    tell you all about it.

The League of Nations met in Berwick Market,
To discuss on which side kippers ought to swim.
  There were Hottentots and Prussians playing
    honeypots on cushions,
And a Greek with bubble and squeak upon his chin.
  Some drove up in taxis that were empty,
Some arrived to say they couldn't come.
  The Hindus had their quilts on, the Hebrews had
    their kilts on,
A Scandinavian rose and said 'By Gum,
  Think of what we have done in the future,
Shall we do our duty in the past?'
  The Japanese Prime Minister got up and said 'Tush,
    tush'.

Someone threw a shepherd's pie that hit his Shepherd's
    Bush.
    A Scotsman from the north land got up and spoke in
      shorthand,
Like a vegetarian straight from Botany Bay.
    He said, 'Where has the kidney bean? What made
      the woodbine wild?
Is red cabbage greengrocery? And tell me friends,' he
      smiled,
    'Can a bandy-legged gherkin be a straight
      cucumber's child?
That's what Crosse and Blackwell want to know today.'

The League of Nations met at Marks and Woolworths,
    And asked them if a discount they'd allow.
A farmer with his tanner said he wished to buy a
      spanner,
He could use when he was milking of the cow.
A Turk said 'We want work, and not much of it,
    A job like giving gooseberries Marcel waves.'
A Zulu most courageous said, 'Brothers it's outrageous,
    Black puddings should be treated as white slaves'.
Shall we ever do so if we can't do,
    Would we, would we, if we, p'raps we won't.
Admiral McNestle of the Swiss Navy arose shouting
      'Where would Turkey be without the parson's
      nose?'
    The Rajah of Shlemozzle got up and blew his nozzle,
He had these few well-chosen words to say,
    'Can a sausage keep its figure if its burberry is flat?
If a duck has had its tonsils out where does it keep its
      quack?
    We know a hen can lay an egg but can it put it back?
That's what Levy and Franks are fighting for today.'

The Bookmaker's Daughter
By Billy Bennett (1934)

Nell was a bookmaker's daughter;
    On the day she was born there was trouble:
In addition to Nell came a sister as well —
    Nell's mother had brought off a double.

Nell was the eldest twin sister,
    But by only two minutes at most;
The other they reckoned came in a good second,
    But Nellie was first past the post.

Poor father went wild when he heard there were two,
    He was found in a pub drinking gin;
He said, 'I'll get tight; I won't go home to-night
    In case any more runners come in.'

But Nell's sister was not a long liver,
    Though the girl was as strong as a haddock,
But one day on the course she got kicked by a horse
    Between the grandstand and the paddock.

Now Nellie's grown up into manhood,
    She's buxom and all in full bloom,
She's useful to Dad on the racecourse
    Parking betting slips in her boosoom.

It's a sight to see Nell at the racecourse,
    Her beauty can not be concealed;
All the young knobs bet their tanners and bobs
    To see Nellie lay on the field.

Yes, all the young bloods fall for Nellie,
    Though against them her dad used to warn her.
For he knew if they placed one arm round her waist
    They'd be halfway round Tattenham Corner.

One day Nell's dad said, 'I'm in trouble,
    I've a thousand on Black Pudding to win;
Now I hear they're all backing Polony —
    At all costs I must save my skin.

'If Black Pudding loses I'm ruined;
    I thought that the horse was a good-un,
But his skin's got so shiny and slippy
    The jockey can't stick on his pudden'.

Nell cried, 'Tell the jockey I'll ride it,
    I'll borrow his clothes all complete —
That is, all excepting the trousers,
    He's rubbed Ronuk all over the seat!

'And that's why he slips off Black Pudding,
    But, Daddy, I'll save you your quids:
I'll stick on the mare, for I'll ride in a pair
    Of my mother's red flannel non-skids.'

The day of the race — what excitement!
    They both started off like the wind;
Polony was making the running,
    With Black Pudding just two links behind.

Nell looked a safe bet in her red flannelette
   As over its neck she kept bending;
Every time the horse jumped in the air Nellie
    bumped,
   And we saw her invisible mending.

The pace was too hot for Polony,
   She began to curl up with the heat;
The people were all shouting, 'Blimey,
   She's trying to make both ends meet!'

We could all see Polony was beaten;
   The trainer was shouting out, 'Cuss it,
They've forgotten to sew her tights up at one end
   And the stuffing's dropped out of her gusset.'

Nell won and she's got a new motto:
   It's this — and you never will match it —
If you run on life's course, take a chance with your
    horse —
   It'll never do well if you scratch it!

The Foreign Legion
By Billy Bennett (1934)

I've served in the French Foreign Legion —
   It's Hell! The life couldn't be harder,
For it's war to the knife as you run for your life
   On the plains of Cascara Sagrada.

Mixed with the sewer rats of Europe,
   Hobos and tramps of all kinds;
Several outcasts trying to wipe out their pasts
   And some Bums with no future behind.

Scum of the earth they all called us!
   That made my blood boil in a trice.
I said, 'There's no doubt that we're all down and out,
   But scum, oh s'come, s'come, that's not nice!'

But at best we were just human wreckage
   Cast up on Life's shore — like a toy.
Ships of misfortune, just Flotsam and Jetsam
   And Flanagan and Allen — OI! OI!

Persians and Medes, Parsnips and Swedes,
   But I'm British, I'm not like the rest,
My birthplace was Bow, I'm bowlegged also,
   And that's why they call me Beau-geste.

Think of the life of the poor Legionnaire,
   Risking his life, limb and blood,
'Mid the shot and the shells and the sand and the
    smells
   That remind you of Southend-on-Mud.

I've had the rheumatics from basement to attics,
   Had a sneeze and a wheeze and a whinny.
Neuritis, gastritis and Eddystone lighthouse,
   And a pain in the crease of my pinny.

The pet of the ranks was Sergeant Vin Blancs,
   With nice teeth, and hair curled so fancy.
He said: 'Qu'est ce que vous dit' (KESS KER VOO
    DEE).
   I said: 'Kiss you, not me, my name is Willie, not
    Nancy!'

Out there on the sands of Morocco
   One day with a foreign Field Marshal
An entrenchment I'd made, with my bucket and spade,
   When two Riffs came and kicked down my castle.

I went for those Riffs in their little short shifts,
   And I gave them two biffs with my boot.
If you biff a Riff he'll run back to his wiff
   On a jiff with a rift in his lute.

I speak fluid French when I've had a few drinks —
   You can ask the French girls if you doubt it —
I say *Hors de combat* and *Paté de foie gras* —
   That's French for 'Now then, what about it?'

On the slopes of Girvana I met Wheezy Anna,
   Half Hindoo and half Hottentot.
She was half-caste, it's true, but which half no one
    knew,
   Till one night she cast off all the lot.

She was blistered with heat from her head to her feet
   And her skin was beginning to crack,
So the poor little thing jumped out of her skin
   And it took half an hour to get back.

Alas and alack, when we got the skin back
   She looked big round the Avoirdupois — so,
We looked and we found she'd the skin wrong way
     round,
   Now she has to sit down on her torso!

Oh! it's not very grand when you sleep on the sand
   With a bunch of stiffs lying together.
As you grunt and you snore on your back there's a
     corps
   Of mosquitos who sing, 'Stormy Weather'!

And the hot summer days with the sun's burning rays,
   When you feel like a well-toasted muffin.

One day the heat scorched all the clothes off my back
   And I sat on the sands in my 'nuffin.'

As I sat there sizzling, frying and frizzling,
   An ice cream cart came my direction,
So like a soft geezer I jumped in the freezer
   And sat there to cool my affection!

Then old Sergeant Stringer said, 'Come on, lead
     swinger,
   Get out of that, do as you're told.'
I shouted, 'No fear. I'm not shifting from here
   'Till the sands of the desert grow cold!'

Walter, Walter
By Will E. Haines, Jimmy Harper & Noel Forrester (1928)
Performed by Gracie Fields

Walter and me 'ave been courtin' for years,
   But he's never asked me to wed.
When Leap Year comes round I give three hearty
     cheers,
   And I do the asking instead.
I don't want to die an old maid,
   So I sing him this serenade:

Walter! Walter! Lead me to the altar,
   I'll make a better man of you.
Walter! Walter! Buy the bricks and mortar,
   And we'll build a love nest for two.
I've kept my bottom draw'r together,
   My bridal gown's as good as new.
Walter! Walter! Lead me to the altar,
   And make all my nightmares come true.

I took him round to the furniture shop
   And I showed him a nice double bed.
But when I felt sure that the question he'd pop,
   He popped to the pictures instead.
I still have to play the same part,
   He must know this chorus by heart:

Walter! Walter! Lead me to the altar
   I don't cost much to keep in food,
Walter! Walter! Mother thinks you oughter
   So take me while she's in the mood.
You know I'm very fond of chickens,
   We'll raise a lovely little brood.
Walter! Walter! Lead me to the altar,
   And I'll show you where I'm tatooed.

Walter! Walter! Lead me to the altar,
   Don't say I've met my Waterloo.
Walter! Walter! Tears are tasting salter
   And I've lost my handkerchief too.
Don't muck the goods about no longer,
   My old age pension's nearly due.
Walter! Walter! Lead me to the altar
   It's either the Workhouse or you.

The Biggest Aspidistra in the World
By Will E. Haines, Jimmy Harper and Tommy Connor (1928)
Performed by Gracie Fields

For years we 'ad an Aspidistra in a flower pot,
   On the What-not, near the 'at stand in the 'all.
It didn't seem to grow, till one day our Brother Joe,

Had a notion that he'd make it strong and tall.
So 'e crossed it with an acorn from an oak tree,
   And 'e planted it against the garden wall.

It shot up like a rocket till it nearly touched the sky
   It's the biggest Aspidistra in the world.
We couldn't see the top of it — it got so bloomin' high
   It's the biggest Aspidistra in the world.
When father's 'ad a skinful at his pub the 'Bunch of
    Grapes'
   He doesn't go all fighting mad, and getting into
    scrapes,
You'll find 'im in 'is bearskin playing 'Tarzan of the
    Apes'
   Up the biggest Aspidistra in the world.

We 'ave to get it watered by the local fire brigade,
   So they've put the water rate up 'arf a crown.
The roots stop up the drains, grow along the country
    lanes
   And they come up 'arf a mile outside the Town.
Once we 'ired the Crystal Palace for an 'ot-'ouse
   But a jealous rival went and burned it down.

The Tom Cats and the Moggies love to spend their
    evenings out
   Up the biggest Aspidistra in the world.
They all begin miaowing when the buds begin to
    sprout
   From the biggest Aspidistra in the world.

The dogs line up for miles and miles a funny sight to
    see —
   They sniff around for hours on end and wag their
    tails with glee,
So I've 'ad to put a notice up to say it's not a tree,
   It's the biggest Aspidistra in the world.

It's getting worn and weary and its leaves are turning
    grey,
   It's the oldest Aspidistra in the world.
So we water it with 'alf a pint of Guinness ev'ry day
   It's the stoutest Aspidistra in the world.
The Borough Council told us that we've got to chop it
    down.
   It interferes with aeroplanes that fly above the Town
So we sold it to a woodyard for a lousy 'alf a crown
   It's the biggest Aspidistra in the world.

In my Little Bottom Drawer
By Will E. Haines and Jimmy Harper (1928)
Performed by Gracie Fields

For years and years I've been a lonely spinster on the
    shelf,
   I'm right fed up with spending all me wages on
    meself.
I'm all prepared for married life — its secrets I've been
    taught
   And here's some little odds and ends I've been and
    gorn and bought.

One bridal gown — one eiderdown, I've been saving
    'em up since eighteen ninety-four,
   Got me ribbons and me bows and me these and
    thems and those
All packed up in my little bottom drawer.
   One baby's cot — one flower pot
Where I've planted a rambling rose bush for the door;
   Got a motto for the wall — it says 'Heaven 'elp us
    all' —
All packed up in my little bottom drawer.
   Got a pianer under the staircase

And I'm teaching meself to play the 'Maiden's Prayer'.
   One toilet set — one basinette,
Now I'm waiting for love to open up the door.
   Got me Aristotle's works and a case of eggs from
    Pearks.
All packed up in my little bottom drawer.

I've answered ev'ry advert in the Matrimonial Times,
   I've bought me own confetti and a set of wedding
    chimes.
At night I count me treasures, just to see they haven't
    strayed;
   I'm very patriotic, ev'ry one is British made.

One cheffoneer — one keg o' beer
   And some orange and purple lino for the floor.
Got a new pyjama set made of bright red flannelette,
   All packed up in my little bottom drawer.
One Persian rug — one china jug

And some beautiful silver ware from Woolworth's
  store,
With a book by Doctor Fife, 'How to be a perfect wife',
  All packed up in my little bottom drawer.
We'll have a bathroom Oh! what a bathroom

With a wonderful bath where we can keep the coals.
Horse-shoe for luck — pail for the muck
  And a President Hoover's cleaner for the floor.
If the plans go all to pot I can sell the bloomin' lot —
  All packed up in my little bottom drawer.

Heaven will protect an Honest Girl
By Bob Weston, Bert Lee & Harris Weston (1933)
Performed by Gracie Fields

On the day I left the village, my dear Mother
  whispered 'Nell,
  Take this piece of bread and dripping and your fare,
And remember when in London, though you're just a
  servant gel,
  You're a blonde, the sort that gentlemen ensnare.
With your youth and fatal beauty, when you get to
  Waterloo,
  There'll be crowds of dukes and millionaires all
  waiting there for you' — 'But

Heaven will protect an honest gel,
  An an-gi-el will guard you, little Nell,
When these rich men tempt you, Nelly,
  With their spark-el-ling Moselly,
Say 'Nay-nay!' and do be very carefu-el!
  And if some old bloated blasé roué swell
Says 'I'll kiss you, we're alone in this hotel',
  Breathe a prayer he shall not do it,
And then biff him with the cruet,
  Then Heaven will protect an honest gel!'

When I got to wicked London, in my little clogs and
  shawl,
  And my bit of bread and dripping in my hand,
I went up to that big Lifeguard on his horse outside
  Whitehall,
  And I asked him to direct me to the Strand.
But he didn't even answer, he just sat there with his
  sword,
  In a helmet that had whiskers on, so I said, 'Thank
  the Lord — For

Heaven will protect an honest gel,
  And I reached Piccadilly safe and well,
There I saw a red light showing,
  But across I started going,
When a P'liceman pulled me back I nearly fell.
  'You're a silly little fool' he starts to yell,

'Don't you know what that red light means?' I said
  'Well,
  Red's for danger if you please sir,
But don't switch it on for me sir,
  'Cause Heaven will protect an honest gel!'

Heaven will protect an honest gel,
  That night I got a job at some Hotel,
But the Chef was most improper,
  For he sat me on the copper
And said, 'Kiss me or I'll boil you, little Nell.'
  But I slapped him on the face and in I fell,
And I came up for the third time with a yell,
  'In the soup I'm going to simmer
But I'll come out clean and slimmer,
  For Heaven will protect an honest gel!'

I wandered round Li-cester Square from six o'clock till
  nine,
  But no millionaire came tempting me to stray,
'If he does,' I thought, 'I'll let him take me to the Ritz
  to dine,
  Then I'll gollop up his tripe and run away.'
Eh by gum, I did feel hungry, eh, I hadn't had a bite
  Since my bit of bread and dripping, and I knew that
  Ma was right — For

Heaven will protect an honest gel,
  Next day I pawned my shawl in Camberwell,
Then my skirt and blouse, I sold 'em
  And went tramping back to Oldham;
When a fortnight passed, then I rang at the bell.
  'Eh, but Mother dear' I said 'it's little Nell,
I have lost my sole, my uppers too, as well;
  And I've walked home in my undies,
But I'll tell my Class on Sundays
  That Heaven will protect an honest gel!'

Whiskers an' All!

By Bob Weston, Bert Lee & Harris Weston (1933)
Performed by Gracie Fields

Uncle Ebenezer's whiskers were a wild and woolly
    mass,
  But those whiskers were the pride of Auntie Lou.
When he courted her and whispered 'Do you love me,
    little lass?'
  She would stroke them and caress them, and say 'I
    do! I do!'

Whiskers an' all — aye, whiskers an' all!
  And when they knelt in Church and our old Parson
    with a drawl
Said 'Now will you take Ebenezer; Love and cherish
    him, Louisa?'
  Auntie said 'Not half! Yes please sir; Whiskers an'
    all!'

But our Uncle Ebenezer used to gamble, drink and
    swear,
  And his raspb'ry nose was just as red as paint.
Then he went and got converted, and out in the open
    air
  He would preach to all the people, and look just like
    a Saint.

Whiskers an' all! — aye, whiskers an' all!
  'Dear friends I used to be a wicked sinner,' he would
    bawl.
'In beer and rum I used to 'waller'. Dirty shirt and
    dirty collar!
  Now I'm clean,' and they'd all holler, 'Whiskers an' all!'

But our Uncle Ebenezer died; one night he drew a
    breath,
  And he swallowed all his whiskers in his sleep.
And the Doctor said they'd accident'lly tickled him to
    death,
  But the Undertaker buried dear Uncle very cheap.

Whiskers an' all! — aye whiskers an' all!
  And still they grew and grew right thro' the Earth; it
    may sound tall
But in Australia playing cricket, Bradman shouted, 'I
    can't stick it
  Look what's growing round the wicket; Whiskers an'
    all!'

Poor old Auntie sat one night upon his grave-stone
    cold and damp,
  Saying, 'Ebenezer tho' we used to fight.
And the neighbours still declare you were a good for
    nothing scamp,
  Oh! I miss you, yes, I miss you upon a winter's
    night.'

Whiskers an' all! — aye, whiskers an' all!
  Then Riley's goat came us and poked his head
    beneath her shawl
She felt the beard upon his chin, an' said, 'It's not a
    ghost, it's him
  An' up to his old games agin! Oh! Whiskers an' all!'

Mrs Binns's Twins

By J. P. Long, Will E. Haines & Jimmy Harper (1938)
Performed by Gracie Fields

Behold in me a member of a family called 'Binns,'
  Me mother's just increased the population wi' some
    twins;
A lovely girl, a bouncing boy, they've neither mumps
    or quinsies,
  We had a fam'ly gatherin' to name the Binns's
    twinsies.

'Eric and Veronica,' suggested Auntie Monica
  To Nurse, as she removed the safety pins.
Cecil and Celia, Clarence and Ophelia,
  Were some o' the names they tried to bung on
    Missus Binns's twins.

'Call the girl child Pansy,' said the curate, looking coy; —
  'Nay,' said sister Susie, 'Folks'll think she is a boy.'
Call 'em what the heck you like,' said Uncle Benje Binns,
  'But what about summat to drink the health of Missus
    Binns's twins.'

Owd Bill, the Captain of a barge, suggested Ebb and Flo,
  Bob Brown, who's breeding rabbits, gave his vote for
    Buck and Doe
Then just as we'd made up our minds to call 'em 'Kate
    and Sidney'
  Old Silver-side the Butcher, said 'Well, why not
    Steak and Kidney?'

'Algernon and Angeline,' suggested Cousin Geraldine
  To Mother, as she strok'd their chubby chins,
Rudolph and Felicity, Simon and Simplicity
  Were some o' the names they tried to bung on
    Missus Binns's twins.
'Call the she one Clarabelle,' said fat old Farmer Joe,
  'Once I 'ad a cow that name took prizes in a show.'
The tom cat started mewing and the goldfish flapped
    its fins!
  When the parrot suggested some terrible names for
    Missus Binns's twins.
Then mother said, 'We ought to name the girl for
    Auntie Flo,
  She's saved a heap o' money and she can't have long
    to go.'
But when they'd filled their glasses wi' another
    appetiser,

They went and mucked up ev'rything and named
  'em Bill and Liza.

'Boneypart and Josephine,' suggested Great Aunt
    Clementine,
  Who'd had about a dozen double gins.
Archibald and Adeline, Claudius and Caroline
  Were some o' the names they tried to bung on
    Missus Binns's twins.
'Call 'em Bright and Breezy,' said the servant girl
    Maria,
  'Call 'em Wet and Windy,' said Doctor Macintyre.
Father said, 'If I weren't scared o' adding to me sins
  I'd tell you a few o' the names I've got for Missus
    Binns's twins.'

I took my Harp to a Party
By Desmond Carter & Noel Gay (1948)
Performed by Gracie Fields

Christmas is coming, Christmas is coming, Christmas is
    coming again,
  But that never thrills me,
The thought of it chills me,
  I tell you it fills me with pain.
It makes me remember
  A Christmas gone by when I was extremely upset.
A night in December,
  An evening that I would very much rather forget.

Chorus
For I took my harp to a party
  But nobody asked me to play.
The others were jolly and hearty,
  But I wasn't feeling so gay.
They might have said 'Play us a tune we can sing.'
  But somehow I don't think they noticed the thing.
I took my harp to a party
  But nobody asked me to play,
So I took the darn thing away.

Christmas is coming, Christmas is coming, Christmas is
    coming once more,
  But I'm not delighted
Or even excited
  My hopes have been blighted before.
I felt so elated
  With joy in my heart to join in the revels I rushed.
But then I just waited
  A chance to depart,
Forgotten, neglected and crushed!

Repeat Chorus
They asked Missus Morgan to play her mouth organ,
  And somebody else did a dance.
They let Missus Carter perform a sonata
  But I wasn't given a chance.
A North Country person call'd Sandy Macpherson
    play'd bagpipes and took off his coat
  While both the Miss Fawcetts
Burst out of their corsets in trying to take a top note.

Repeat Chorus
They sang 'Home Sweet Home' and 'The Banks of
    Loch Lomond'
  Than 'All the King's Horses' then 'Trees'
While nephews and nieces kept playing their pieces
  And spreading their jam on the keys.
A daughter call'd Lena play'd her concertina
  We all play'd ridiculous games
Till old Mister Dyer
  Set his whiskers on fire and a fire engine play'd on
    the flames.

I took my harp to a party
  But nobody asked me to play
The others were jolly and hearty
  But I wasn't feeling so gay.
I felt so ashamed at not striking a note
  That I tried to hide the thing under my coat.
I took my harp to a party
  But nobody asked me to play,
So I took the darn thing away.

No. 153.

Periodicals

Composed by
FRED CECIL

Written and Performed by
GREATREX NEWMAN

Also Performed by
TOM CLARE

A Reynolds cover dated 1916, featuring the work of one of the most durable of monologue writers, Greatrex Newman, and the songs-at-the-piano style of performer Tom Clare

Will Fyffe in character for *The Scot's Lament*

Norman Long, billed as 'a song, a smile and a piano'

Out in the Cold, Cold Snow

By Will E. Haines & Jimmy Harper (1948)
Performed by Gracie Fields

I wander alone through the city.
  Not a friend in the world do I know;
Not a crust, not a bite as I trudge thro' the night
  OUT IN THE COLD, COLD SNOW.
They think I'm a tramp or a hiker,
  But it's pride that compels me to go
Past the homes of the posh thro' the slush and the slosh
  OUT IN THE COLD, COLD SNOW.

Chorus

Out in the cold, cold snow,
  Out where the cold winds blow:
No-one to love me and nowhere to go
  OUT IN THE COLD, COLD SNOW.

It's all through the bloke that I married,
  When he gambled and spent all the dough;
Then he slung me, Oh Heck!
  By the back of the neck,
OUT IN THE COLD, COLD SNOW.
  He left me with one little off-spring,
Cast your eye on our John Willie Joe:
  Does it seem worth a kiss to be landed like this
OUT IN THE COLD, COLD SNOW.

Repeat Chorus

One dark night I jumped in the river
  For to end all my weal and my woe;
But I just missed the flood, so I stuck in the mud,
  OUT IN THE COLD, COLD SNOW.
I've only the rags that I'm wearing.
  All my silks went in pawn long ago:
But I keep out the wet with my red flannelette,
  OUT IN THE COLD, COLD SNOW.

Repeat Chorus

Last night I was chased by a bandit,
  He took me for the Duchess of Bow;
'Where's your town house?' he cried, and to him I
    replied,
  'OUT IN THE COLD, COLD SNOW.'
I don't seek revenge on my 'usband
  'Cause to blazes I'm sure he will go:
Then how glad he would be to change places with me,
  OUT IN THE COLD, COLD SNOW.

Old Sam
(Sam, Pick Oop Tha' Musket)
Stanley Holloway & Wolseley Charles (1929)

It occurred on the evening before Waterloo
  And troops were lined up on Parade,
And Sergeant inspecting 'em, he was a terror
  Of whom every man was afraid —

All excepting one man who was in the front rank,
  A man by the name of Sam Small,
And 'im and the Sergeant were both 'daggers drawn',
  They thought 'nowt' of each other at all.

As Sergeant walked past he was swinging his arm,
  And he happened to brush against Sam.
And knocking his musket clean out of his hand
  It fell to the ground with a slam.

'Pick it oop,' said Sergeant, abrupt like but cool,
  But Sam with a shake of his head
Said, 'Seeing as tha' knocked it out of me hand,
  P'raps tha'll pick the thing oop instead.'

'Sam, Sam, pick oop tha' musket,'
  The Sergeant exclaimed with a roar.
Sam said 'Tha' knocked it doon, Reet!
  Then tha'll pick it oop, or it stays where it is, on't
    floor.'

The sound of high words very soon reached the ears
  Of an Officer, Lieutenant Bird,
Who says to the Sergeant, 'Now what's all this 'ere?'
  And the Sergeant told what had occurred.

'Sam, Sam, pick oop tha' musket,'
    Lieutenant exclaimed with some heat.
Sam said 'He knocked it doon. Reet! then he'll pick it
        oop,
    Or it stays where it is, at me feet.'

It caused quite a stir when the Captain arrived
    To find out the cause of the trouble;
And every man there, all excepting Old Sam,
    Was full of excitement and bubble.

'Sam, Sam, pick oop tha' musket,'
    Said Captain for strictness renowned.
Sam said 'He knocked it doon. Reet!
    Then he'll pick it oop, or it stays where it is on't
        ground.'

The same thing occurred when the Major and Colonel
    Both tried to get Sam to see sense,
But when Old Duke o' Wellington came into view
    Well, the excitement was tense.

Up rode the Duke on a lovely white 'orse,
    To find out the cause of the bother;
He looks at the musket and then at old Sam
    And he talked to Old Sam like a brother.

'Sam, Sam, pick oop tha' musket,'
    The Duke said as quiet as could be,
'Sam, Sam, pick oop tha' musket
    Coom on, lad, just to please me.'

'All right, Duke,' said Old Sam, 'just for thee I'll
        oblige,
    And to show thee I meant no offence.'
So Sam picked it up. 'Gradeley, lad,' said the Duke,
    'Right-o, boys, let battle commence.'

The Lion and Albert
By Marriott Edgar & Wolseley Charles (1932)
Performed by Stanley Holloway

There's a famous seaside place called Blackpool,
    That's noted for fresh air and fun,
And Mr and Mrs Ramsbottom
    Went there with young Albert, their son.

A grand little lad was young Albert,
    All dressed in his best; quite a swell
With a stick with an 'orse's 'ead 'andle,
    The finest that Woolworth's could sell.

They didn't think much to the Ocean:
    The waves, they was fiddlin' and small,
There was no wrecks and nobody drownded,
    Fact, nothing to laugh at at all.

So, seeking for further amusement,
    They paid and went into the Zoo,
Where they'd Lions and Tigers and Camels,
    And old ale and sandwiches too.

There were one great big Lion called Wallace;
    His nose were all covered with scars —
He lay in a somnolent posture,
    With the side of his face on the bars.

Now Albert had heard about Lions,
    How they was ferocious and wild —
To see Wallace lying so peaceful,
    Well, it didn't seem right to the child.

So straightway the brave little feller,
    Not showing a morsel of fear,
Took his stick with its 'orse's 'ead 'andle
    And pushed it in Wallace's ear.

You could see that the Lion didn't like it,
    For giving a kind of a roll,
He pulled Albert inside the cage with 'im,
    And swallowed the little lad 'ole.

Then Pa, who had seen the occurrence,
    And didn't know what to do next,
Said, 'Mother! Yon Lion's 'et Albert',
    And Mother said, 'Well, I am vexed!'

Then Mr and Mrs Ramsbottom —
    Quite rightly, when all's said and done —
Complained to the Animal Keeper,
    That the Lion had eaten their son.

The keeper was quite nice about it;
  He said, 'What a nasty mishap.
Are you sure that it's *your* boy he's eaten?'
  Pa said, 'Am I sure? There's his cap!'

The manager had to be sent for.
  He came and he said 'What's to do?'
Pa said, 'Yon Lion's 'et Albert,'
  And 'im in his Sunday clothes, too.'

Then Mother said, 'Right's right, young feller;
  I think it's a shame and a sin,
For a lion to go and eat Albert,
  And after we've paid to come in.'

The manager wanted no trouble,
  He took out his purse right away,
Saying, 'How much to settle the matter?'
  And Pa said, 'What do you usually pay?'

But Mother had turned a bit awkward
  When she thought where her Albert had gone.
She said, 'No! someone's got to be summonsed —'
  So that was decided upon.

Then off they went to the P'lice Station,
  In front of the Magistrate chap;
They told 'im what happened to Albert
  And proved it by showing his cap.

The Magistrate gave his opinion
  That no one was really to blame
And he said that he hoped the Ramsbottoms
  Would have further sons to their name.

At that Mother got proper blazing,
  'And thank you, sir, kindly,' said she.
'What, waste all our lives raising children
  To feed ruddy lions? Not me!'

Three Ha'pence a Foot
By Marriott Edgar & Wolseley Charles (1932)
Performed by Stanley Holloway

I'll tell you an old-fashioned story
  That Grandfather used to relate,
Of a joiner and building contractor;
  'Is name, it were Sam Oglethwaite.

In a shop on the banks of the Irwell,
  Old Sam used to follow 'is trade,
In a place you'll have 'eard of, called Bury;
  You know, where black puddings is made.

One day, Sam were filling a knot 'ole
  Wi' putty, when in thro' the door
Came an old feller fair wreathed i' whiskers;
  T'old chap said, 'Good morning, I'm Noah.'

Sam asked Noah what was 'is business,
  And t'old chap went on to remark,
That not liking the look of the weather,
  'E were thinking of building an Ark.

'E'd gotten the wood for the bulwarks,
  And all t'other shipbuilding junk,
And wanted some nice Bird's Eye Maple
  To panel the side of 'is bunk.

Now, Maple were Sam's Mon-o-po-ly;
  That means it were all 'is to cut,
And nobody else 'adn't got none;
  So 'e asked Noah three ha'pence a foot.

'A ha'pence too much,' replied Noah,
  'Penny a foot's more the mark;
A penny a foot, and when rain comes,
  I'll give you a ride in me Ark.'

But neither would budge in the bargain;
  The whole daft thing were kind of a jam,
So Sam put 'is tongue out at Noah,
  And Noah made 'Long Bacon' at Sam.

In wrath and ill-feeling they parted,
  Not knowing when they'd meet again,
And Sam had forgot all about it,
  'Til one day it started to rain.

It rained and it rained for a fortni't,
  And flooded the 'ole countryside.
It rained and it kep' on raining,
  'Til the Irwell were fifty miles wide.

The 'ouses were soon under water,
  And folks to the roof 'ad to climb.
They said 'twas the rottonest summer
  That Bury 'ad 'ad for some time.

The rain showed no sign of abating,
  And water rose hour by hour,
'Til the only dry land were at Blackpool,
  And that were on top of the Tower.

So Sam started swimming to Blackpool;
    It took 'im best part of a week.
'Is clothes were wet through when 'e got there,
    And 'is boots were beginning to leak.

'E stood to 'is watch-chain in water,
    On Tower top, just before dark,
When who should come sailing towards 'im
    But old Noah, steering 'is Ark.

They stared at each other in silence,
    'Til Ark were alongside, all but,
Then Noah said: 'What price yer Maple?'
    Sam answered: 'Three ha'pence a foot.'

Noah said 'Nay: I'll make thee an offer,
    The same as I did t'other day.
A penny a foot and a free ride,
    Now, come on, lad, what does tha' say?'

'Three ha'pence a foot,' came the answer,
    So Noah 'is sail 'ad to hoist,
And sailed off again in a dudgeon,
    While Sam stood determined, but moist.

Noah cruised around, flying 'is pigeons,
    'Til fortieth day of the wet,
And on 'is way back, passing Blackpool,
    'E saw old Sam standing there yet.

'Is chin just stuck out of the water;
    A comical figure 'e cut.
Noah said: '*Now* what's the price of yer Maple?'
    Sam answered: 'Three ha'pence a foot.'

Said Noah: 'Ye'd best take my offer;
    It's last time I'll be hereabout;
And if water comes half an inch higher,
    I'll happen get Maple for nought.'

'Three ha'pence a foot it'll cost yer,
    And as fer me,' Sam said, 'don't fret.
The sky's took a turn since this morning;
    I think it'll brighten up yet.'

Many Happy Returns

By Archie de Bear & Wolseley Charles (1933)
Performed by Stanley Holloway

Down at the school house at Runcorn,
    The 'eadmaster walked in one day
Looking all 'appy and cheerful,
    Which wasn't his habit, they say.

The boys were completely dumbfounded,
    And whispered 'Hello, what's to do?'
But the headmaster still went on smiling
    And said, 'Boys, I've some good news for you.'

It's like this. Today is my birthday,
    So it's no time for classes and such —
You can go,' but the boys were too staggered
    To even say 'Thanks very much.'

They could scarcely believe their own earholes
    As they welcomed these tidings so bright;
But soon they all cheered to the echo,
    And very near busted with delight.

Said headmaster 'Now there's no hurry,
    Before very long you'll be free;
But seeing as how it's me birthday,
    How old would you take me to be?'

Well, the boys didn't like this delaying.
    And one of the younger ones swore
At the silly old fool of a master,
    And the satisfied smile that he wore.

He didn't swear any too loudly,
    Or he'd have been out on the mat
For calling the master a silly old beggar —
    Or something that sounded like that.

'I bet you won't guess it correctly,'
    The headmaster went on with a wink,
''Cos I've got a sort of notion
    I'm not quite as old as you think.'

A new boy jumped up and guessed twenty,
    In the hopes that he'd get off for a week;
While another one guessed ninety-seven —
    Although with his tongue in his cheek.

Said the headmaster 'Don't let's be funny,
    Or you'll be here all day I can see;
So who'll give a serious guess now,
    Come on, just between you and me.'

Then in walked the junior tutor,
   In a very old mortar board hat.
He said 'I hear there's a game on,
   Well, I'd like a baisin of that.'

Said the headmaster 'Mind your own business,
   And kindly do not interfere —
Or you'll lose half your rasher of bacon,
   And all your allowance of beer.'

The tutor said 'Don't be a cad, Sir,
   I don't wish to make any noise;
But you might at least try to be sporting,
   If only in front of the boys.'

With that he swep' out of the classroom,
   Fearing the look that he saw —
For he knew that in less than two seconds,
   He'd get such a sock in the jaw.

Then in came the language professor,
   French teaching was one of his jobs,
So he bowed to the Head and said *'Bonjour,'*
   And the Head said *'Bonjour, avec* knobs.'

'But if you've come here to give lessons,
   You can take it from me — it's no *bon*
Because today's a holiday. Savvy?
   So you might as well *allez-vous en.'*

Then a small voice called 'Sir, why it's easy,
   Forty-four is your age I should say.'
Said the master 'Now what a remarkable thing.
   You've guessed my right age to the day.'

Said the boy 'Well my brother is just twenty-two.'
   Said the headmaster 'What's that to me?'
'Well, Sir, if he's twenty-two you must be forty-four,
   'Cos he's only half barmy — see.'

Then the whole class joined in the school anthem,
   Which nobody wanted to shirk:
'For he's a jolly good fellow,
   So long as we don't have to work.'

Gunner Joe

By Marriott Edgar & Wolseley Charles (1933)
Performed by Stanley Holloway

I'll tell you a seafaring story,
   Of a lad who won honour and fame
Wi' Nelson at Battle Trafalgar —
   Joe Moggeridge, that were his name.

He were one of the crew of the Victory,
   His job when a battle begun
Was to take cannon balls out o' basket
   And shove 'em down front end o' gun.

One day him and Nelson were boxing —
   The compass, like sailor lads do,
When 'Ardy comes up wi' a spyglass
   And pointing, says "Ere, take a screw!'

They looked to where 'Ardy were pointing
   And saw lots o' ships in a row.
Joe says abrupt-like but respectful,
   "Oratio lad, yon's the foe.'

'What say we attack 'em?' says Nelson,
   Says Joe 'Nay, lad, not to-day,'
And 'Ardy says, 'Aye! well, let's toss up.'
   'Oratio answers 'Okay.'

They tossed — it were heads for attacking
   And tails for t'other way 'bout.
Joe lent them 'is two-headed penny,
   So the answer was never in doubt.

When penny came down 'ead side uppards,
   They was in for a do it were plain,
And Joe murmur'd 'Shiver my timbers,'
   And Nelson kiss'd 'Ardy again.

And then, taking flags out o' locker,
   'E strung out a message on high;
'Twere all about England and duty —
   Crew thought they was 'ung out to dry.

They got the guns ready for action,
   And that gave 'em trouble enough,
They 'adn't been fired all the summer
   And touch-holes were bunged up wi' fluff.

Joe's cannon it weren't 'alf a corker,
   The cannon balls went three foot round,
They wasn't no toy balloons neither,
   They weigh'd close on sixty-five pound.

Joe, selecting two of the largest,
   Was going to load double for luck —
When a hot shot came in thro' the porthole
   And a gunpowder barrel got struck.

By gum! there weren't 'alf an explosion,
   The gun crew was filled wi' alarm
As out of the port-hole went Joseph
   Wi' a cannon ball under each arm.

At that moment up came the 'Boat-swine',
   He says 'Where's Joe?'
Gunner replied "E's taken two cannon balls with 'im
   And gone for a breather outside.'

'Do y'think he'll be long?' says the 'Boat-swine',
   The gunner replied 'If as 'ow
'E comes back as quick as 'e left us,
   'E should be 'ere any time now.'

And all this time Joe, treading water,
   Was trying 'is 'ardest to float.
'E shouted thro' turmoil of battle —
   'Tell someone to lower a boat.'

'E'd come to the top for assistance,
   Then down to the bottom 'e'd go;
This up and down kind of existence
   Made ev'ryone laugh except Joe.

At last 'e could stand it no longer,
   And next time 'e came to the top
'E said 'If you don't come and save me
   I'll let these 'ere cannon balls drop.'

'Twere Nelson at finish who saved him
   And 'e said Joe deserved the V.C.,
But finding 'e 'adn't one 'andy
   'E gave Joe an egg for 'is tea.

And after the battle was over,
   And vessel was safely in dock,
The sailors all saved up their coupons
   And bought Joe a nice marble clock.

With Her Head Tucked Underneath Her Arm
By Bob Weston & Bert Lee (1934)
Performed by Stanley Holloway

In the Tower of London, large as life
   The ghost of Ann Boleyn walks, they declare.
Poor Ann Boleyn was once King Henry's wife —
   Until he made the Headsman bob her hair!
Ah yes! he did her wrong long years ago
   And she comes up at night to tell him so.

With her head tucked underneath her arm
   She walks the Bloody Tower!
With her head tucked underneath her arm
   At the Midnight hour —
She comes to haunt King Henry,
   She means giving him 'what for',
Gad Zooks, she's going to tell him off for having spilt
   her gore.
   And just in case the Headsman wants to give her an
   encore
She has her head tucked underneath her arm!

With her head tucked underneath her arm
   She walks the Bloody Tower!
With her head tucked underneath her arm
   At the Midnight hour.

Along the draughty corridors for miles and miles she
   goes,
   She often catches cold, poor thing, it's cold there
   when it blows,
And it's awfully awkward for the Queen to have to
   blow her nose
   With her head tucked underneath her arm!

Sometimes gay King Henry gives a spread
   For all his pals and gals — a ghostly crew.
The headsman carves the joint and cuts the bread,
   Then in comes Ann Boleyn to 'queer' the 'do';
She holds her head up with a wild war whoop,
   And Henry cries, 'Don't drop it in the soup!'

With her head tucked underneath her arm
   She walks the Bloody Tower!
With her head tucked underneath her arm
   At the Midnight hour.
The sentries think that it's a football that she carries in,
   And when they've had a few they shout, 'Is Ars'nal
   going to win?'
They think it's Alec James, instead of poor old Ann
   Boleyn

With her head tucked underneath her arm!

With her head tucked underneath her arm
  She walks the Bloody Tower!
With her head tucked underneath her arm
  At the Midnight hour.

One night she caught King Henry, he was in the
    Canteen Bar,
  Said he 'Are you Jane Seymour, Ann Boleyn or
    Cath'rine Parr?
For how the sweet san fairy ann do I know who you are
  With your head tucked underneath your arm!'

Yorkshire Pudden!

By Bob Weston & Bert Lee (1940)
Performed by Stanley Holloway

Hi waitress, excuse me a minute, now listen,
  I'm not finding fault, but here, Miss,
The 'taters' look gradely — the beef is a' reet
  But what kind of pudden is this?

It's what? — Yorkshire pudden!, now coom coom coom
    coom,
  It's what! Yorkshire pudden d'ye say!
It's pudden I'll grant you — it's some sort o'pudden,
  But not Yorkshire pudden, nay nay!

The real Yorkshire pudden's a poem in batter,
  To make one's an art not a trade,
Now listen to me — for I'm going to tell thee
  How t'first Yorkshire pudden wor made.

A young angel on furlough from Heaven
  Came flying above Ilkley Moor
And this angel, poor thing — got cramp in her wing
  And coom down at owd woman's door.

The owd woman smiled and said 'Ee, it's an angel,
  Well I am surprised to see thee,
I've not seen an angel before but thou'rt welcome,
  I'll make thee a nice cup o' tea.'

The angel said 'Ee, thank you kindly I will,'
  Well she had two or three cups of tea,
Three or four Sally Lunns, and a couple of buns —
  Angels eat very lightly you see.

Then t'owd woman looking at clock said 'By Gum!
  He's due home from mill is my Dan,
You get on wi' ye tea, but ye must excuse me,
  I must make pudden now for t'owd man.'

Then the angel jumped up and said 'Gimme your
    bowl —
  Flour and t'watter and eggs, salt and all,
And I'll show thee how we make puddens in Heaven,
  For Peter and Thomas and Paul.

Then t'owd woman gave her the things, and the angel
  Just pushed back her wings and said 'Hush!'
Then she tenderly tickled the mixture wi' t'spoon
  Like an artist would paint with his brush.

Aye, she mixed up that pudden with Heavenly magic,
  She played with her spoon on that dough
Just like Paderewski would play the piano
  Or Kreisler now deceased would twiddle his bow.

And when it wor done and she put it in t'oven
  She said t'owd woman 'Goodbye',
Then she flew away leaving the first Yorkshire pudden
  That ever was made — and that's why.

It melts in the mouth, like the snow in the sunshine
  As light as a maiden's first kiss:
As soft as the fluff on the breast of a dove
  Not elephant's leather like this!

It's real Yorkshire pudden that makes Yorkshire lassies
  So buxom and broad in the hips,
It's real Yorkshire pudden that makes Yorkshire
    cricketers
  Win County championships.

It's real Yorkshire pudden that gives me my dreams
  Of a real Paradise up above,
Where at the last trump I'll queue up for a lump
  Of the real Yorkshire pudden I love!

And there on a cloud — far away from the crowd
  In a real Paradise, not a 'dud' 'un,
I'll do nowt for ever and ever and ever
  But gollup up real Yorkshire pudden!

Brahn Boots

By Bob Weston & Bert Lee (1940)
Performed by Stanley Holloway

Our Aunt Hannah's passed away,
　We'd her funeral today,
And it was a posh affair —
　Had to have two p'licemen there!

The 'earse was luv'ly all plate glass,
　And wot a corfin! oak and brass!
We'd fah-sands weepin', flahers galore,
　But Jim, our cousin — what d'yer fink 'e wore?

Why brahn boots! I ask yer — brahn boots!
　Fancy comin' to a funeral in brahn boots!
I will admit 'e 'ad a nice black tie,
　Black finger nails and a nice black eye;
But yer can't see people orf when they die in brahn
　　boots!

And Aunt 'ad been so very good to 'im,
　Done all that any muvver could fer 'im,
And Jim, her son, to show his clars
　Rolls up to make it all a farce
In brahn boots — I ask yer — brahn boots!
　While all the rest
Wore decent black and mourning suits.

I'll own he didn't seem so gay,
　In fact he cried best part the way,
But straight, he reg'lar spoilt our day
　Wiv 'is brahn boots.

In the graveyard we left Jim,
　None of us said much to him,
Yus, we all give 'im the bird,
　Then by accident we 'eard

'E'd given 'is black boots to Jim Small,
　A bloke wot 'ad no boots at all,
So p'raps Aunt Hannah doesn't mind
　She did like people who was good and kind.

But brahn boots! I ask yer — brahn boots!
　Fancy coming to a funeral in brahn boots!
And we could 'ear the neighbours all remark
　'Wot, 'im chief mourner? Wot a bloomin' lark!
'Why 'e looks more like a Bookmaker's clerk — in
　　brahn boots!'

That's why we 'ad to be so rude to 'im,
　That's why we never said 'Ow do!' to 'im,
We didn't know — he didn't say.
　He'd give 'is other boots away.
But brahn boots! I ask yer — brahn boots!
　While all the rest
Wore decent black and mourning suits!

But some day up at Heaven's gate
　Poor Jim, all nerves, will stand and wait
Till an angel whispers 'Come in, Mate,
　Where's yer brahn boots?'

If We Only Knew

By Mel. B. Spurr & Bond Andrews (1897)

It's a curious thing to reflect sometimes
　On the various incidents passing around.
To think of the number of horrible crimes
　Whose authors have never as yet been found.
A murderer's hand may be clasped in ours,
　In the grasp of friendship, warm and true.
Should we love it the less or cease to caress,
　If we only knew?
If we only knew?
　How many a tie that once was sweet
Has been cruelly snapped by a slanderer's tongue!
　How many a friend whom we used to greet
With welcoming words, and to whom we clung
　In joy or in sorrow, in pleasure or pain,

Has suddenly seemed to be false and untrue:
　How oft should we find that our doubts were
　　unkind,
If we only knew!
　If we only knew!
There are some will sigh and whisper low
　Of a love that is changeless, and deep, and pure:
And we think — do we not? when they tell us so,
　That of *somebody's* heart, at least, we are sure.
But fancy is apt to wander about,
　And to sip from a hundred flowers the dew:
Would our love be as deep, would our jealousy sleep,
　If we only knew? If we only knew?
Then comes the time when 'the knot' is tied:

Surely of life its most charming scene!
The bridegroom looks on his beautiful bride,
  And dreams of a future all bright and serene.
Let the lad dream on: shall his hopes be fulfilled?
  One turns out a slattern? Another a shrew?
How many would pause at the very church doors?
  If they only knew! If they only knew!
This world is composed of rich and poor,
  And each sees life in a different way:
Whilst Lazarus begs door to door,
  Dives fares sumptuously every day.
But, which is the happier, peasant or lord?
  That is a problem solved by few:
For the rich man may sigh, as the peasant goes by
  If we only knew! If we only knew!
A tradesman fails, and his credit is gone!
  He has hardly a shilling to call his own.
He may have been patiently struggling on,
  But his prospects are blighted, prosperity flown.
The world, in its wisdom (?) no doubt, will condemn,

But don't let *us* treat him as heedless men do:
Tho' he failed so ignobly, he may have fought nobly.
  If we only knew — If we only knew!
We are ever too apt to be hard on a man
  Who doesn't appear to have success:
Instead of helping him all we can
  We strive to render his chances less.
A kindly word, or a friendly hand,
  May help him — who knows? — to pull easily thro:
It may give him fresh life to renew the strife.
  If we only knew — If we only knew!
It's each for himself, and the weak to the wall!
  So runs the world for ever and aye.
The stout hearts advance — whilst the feeble ones fall.
  To perish alone, on the world's highway.
Let us succour the frail ones, bearing in mind
  That though in this world we meet not our due,
For a kind act done, a crown may be won
  In the world to come — If we only knew!

Johnnie! Me and You
By Corney Grain (1907)

Oh! Johnnie! 'ere's a dinner party
  Look at all them things!
Oh! look at all them dishes
  Wot that powder'd footman brings!
Well if they eat all that there food
  'Ow poorly they will be!
'Ere jump upon my back Johnnie!
  Now then you can see!
Oh! Johnnie! look at that ole gent,
  They've took 'is plate away!
Afore 'e's finished 'arf 'is food,
  That is a game to play!
No! that ain't beer they're drinkin' of
  Not likely, why that's fizz!
Oh! look at that great pink thing there,
  That's salmon fish, that is!
I think there's some mistake 'ere Johnnie!
  We ain't arst tonight!
We could a-pick'd a bit, eh Johnnie?
  We've got the appetite!
Seein' all that food there
  Makes yer 'ungry, that it do!
We ain't 'ad no dinner-parties lately,
  Johnnie! me and you!

Oh! Johnnie! look at that old gal,
  With only 'arf a gown,
The h'ice she's swaller'd must 'ave cost,
  Ah! well nigh 'arf a crown.
She's 'avin 'arf a quartern now,
  And wants it, that she do,
When I've eaten too much h'ice myself,
  I've 'ad that feelin' too!
Oh! Johnnie! they've pulled down the blind,
  I call it nasty mean.
They're all ashamed that's wot they is,
  Ashamed o' bein' seen
A-eatin' all that food like that,
  'Tain't decent, that it 'ain't!
We wouldn't pull no blinds down
  If we'd 'arf o' their complaint!
So come along, let's orf it, Johnnie,
  Orf it to the Strand,
Now don't yer go a-cryin' Johnnie,
  'Ere give me your 'and.
'Ungry, Johnnie, so am I. We'll get a brown or two
  A-callin' 'Keb or Kerridge, Captin'!'
Johnnie! me and you!

When Father Laid the Carpet on the Stairs
By Nelson Jackson (1911)

We all stood round attentive, father's orders for to
  take,
  And not a word was whispered, such a fuss did father
    make,
Although with smothered chuckles all our little ribs
  did ache,
  When father laid the carpet on the stairs.
First one of us he sent away to purchase carpet tacks,
  Another one for carpet thread, and one to bring
    bees-wax;
And one to find the hammer, and the gimlet, and the
  axe —
  When father laid the carpet on the stairs.

Then father grabbed the carpet and he took it to the
  top,
  The roll was rather heavy and so father let it drop,
But the carpet slithered down, it didn't seem to want to
  stop,
  And father slithered with it down the stairs.
Then father rubbed his funny bone, and father rubbed
  his knee,
  And if anyone was laughing, father glared around to
    see.
And though we were nearly throttled still we bottled
  up our glee,
  When father laid the carpet on the stairs.

Then father tried unrolling it, and climbing bit by bit,
  He got it right up to the top and stooped to make it
    fit,
Then perhaps it was an accident, or perhaps to show
  his grit,
  He tobogganed on his waistcoat down the stairs.
We all of us enjoyed it, it was bliss without alloy —
  Although to show our mirth we were naturally coy.
And mother went behind the pantry door to hide her
  joy —
  When the carpet laid poor father on the stairs.

After superhuman struggles, father got the carpet
  spread,
  He tried to drive a tack in, but he hit his thumb
    instead,
He dropped the hammer with a grunt, and oh! the
  things he said,
  When father laid the carpet on the stairs.
Then father used some language that is not in common
  use,
  And the hammer and the tacks and things he
    covered with abuse,
And father, he consigned the stairs and carpet to the
  Deuce,
  So mother laid the carpet on the stairs.

The Other Department, Please
By Worton David, Bert Lee & Harry Fragson (1912)
Performed by Harry Fragson

I promised the wife the other day
  A yard of lace I'd bring
From one of those Department Stores
  Where they sell ev'rything:
So if you've got an hour or two
  Or three or four to spare,
I'll tell you just exactly
  All the things that happened there:

I went to Counter Number One,
  The shopman said 'How do?
It's been a lovely day today,
  What can I do for you?'
I said 'I want a yard of lace
  To match this for the wife.'

'All right' said he — 'now here you see
  An easy chair — and china ware —
Some pictures rare — a bob the pair —
  And here I've got — a baby's cot —
It's made for one, but holds a lot,
  I think you'll find it meets the case,
But if you're only wanting lace
  The *other* department, if you please,
Straight on and up the stairs.'

So up the stairs I went at once,
  The shopman said 'How do?
It's been a lovely day today,
  What can I do for you?'
I said 'I want a yard of lace
  To match this for the wife.'

'All right' said he — 'now here you see
  Some bowler hats — and choice cravats —
Some shirts galore — at one and four,
  With tails we charge you sixpence more —
And lots and lots of ties with spots —
  And sailor's knots, with purple dots,
But if it's *lace* that you require,
  You'll have to mount a little higher,
The *other* department, if you please,
  Straight on and up the stairs.

So up the stairs I went again,
  The shopman said 'How do?
It's been a lovely day today,
  What can I do for you?'
I said 'I want a yard of lace
  To match this for the wife.'

'All right' said he — now here you see
  Upon this floor — we've books galore;
Now here's a book — that's worth a look —
  'All men are liars' by Doctor Cook;
Smyth Pigott's book, 'Why woman sins,'
  A sequel to 'The Heavenly Twins,'
Another here — 'What Winston did,'
  Appropriately bound in 'Kid:'
But if it's *lace* you want to buy
  I'm much afraid you'll have to try
The *other* department, if you please,
  Straight on and up the stairs.

So up the stairs I went again,
  The shopman said 'How do?
It's been a lovely day today,
  What can I do for you?'
I said 'I want a yard of lace
  To match this for the wife.'

'All right' said he — now here you see
  Some marmalade — of ev'ry shade —
A lovely cheese — that walks with ease —
  Creates a breeze — and warbles glees —
We've ham and lamb — and pots of jam —
  And potted meat from Uncle Sam;

And pickled pork, that's learnt to talk,
  And eggs — God bless the Duke of York!
But if it's *lace* you've come to get,
  You'll have to travel higher yet,
The *other* department, if you please,
  Straight on and up the stairs.

So up the stairs I went again,
  The shopman said 'How do?
It's been a lovely day today,
  What can I do for you?
I said 'I want a yard of lace
  To match this for the wife.'

'All right' said he — 'now here you see
  Some ladies' socks — with fancy clocks —
They're simply prime — they never chime,
  But when it rains you see the time —
We've blouses rare — beyond compare —
  They're rather bare — just here and there —
But as they let in lots of air,
  We've christened them 'Maud Allan' wear:
But if it's *lace* you're anxious for,
  You'll find it on the *bottom* floor,
The *other* department, if you please,
  Straight on and *down* the stairs.

Then down the stairs I went again,
  I found the place at last;
The shopman murmured 'What's for you?'
  My heart was beating fast:
I said 'I want a yard of lace
  To match this for the wife,
I've never had a search like this
  Before in all my life;'

Then as a smile spread over his face,
  I handed to him that sample of lace:
'I want a yard like that, sir,' I cried,
  But he with clarion voice replied,
'I'm sorry, sir, to put you about,
  But that kind of lace, sir, I've just *sold out* —
I've just sold out — I've just sold out —
  I've just sold out.'

The Kid
By Tom Kilfoy (1914)

There's a battleship that's swinging to her anchors
    somewhere North,
  There's a sailor's 'kit' at auction. You'll agree,
They'll fetch *ten times their value,* just for memory of
    the 'Kid',

Who was working out his penance, in that ship upon
    the sea.
He was ragged, he was dirty, and he'd not been
    overfed,
  But he didn't fear the judge nor yet the cop.

He'd been pinched for playing banker with some
    others of his tribe,
    And his legs were just too short to beat the 'slop.'
The judge gave him the option. *He* hadn't much to
    lose.
    'The Prison or the Navy? you can choose.'
So the Kid, he chose the Navy. Jail was not for such as
    he,
    And he went to work his penance, in a ship upon the
    sea.
He was washed and fed, and clobbered, and they made
    the beggar work,
    But he slogged and worried through it, with a smile.
With the hose the jaunty froze him, and he was kicked
    from here to there,
    And his life was simply hell just for a while.
Yet he stuck it like a good 'un; he was never known to
    grouse,
    And he learned to fence, and fight, and wash his
    neck;
And he kept his record cleaner than the sturdiest A.B.
    He was working out his penance in that ship upon
    the sea.
They sent him out to China, where he studied Pagan
    ways,
    And he learned a lot of things he didn't know.
Still he always had a feeling of respect for woman-
    kind,
    And he rung down in their presence to dead slow.
He slugged a crowd of Dagos once for bullying a girl.
    They knifed him till his soul was all but free.
In the sick bay he was mended, tho' he's not the man
    he was;
    But he's working out his penance in that ship upon
    the sea.

When, one night, the storm was raging, all the hatches
    battened down,
    Above the crash of waves, and winds that roared,
Rang the Bosun's 'pipe' and order, rapped out, just
    like a knife
    'Hands! Man the Whaler! Quick! Man overboard!!'
We'd scarce obeyed the order, when The Kid shot o'er
    the side.
    He'd a line around his waist, his arms were free.
He meant to save that jaunty, tho' 'twas one he hated
    most.
    He was working out his penance, in that ship upon
    the sea.
The lifebelt flared, we watched it and we paid the line
    out slow.
    The searchlights found him, fighting inch by inch;
And we cheered and yelled, like blazes, when we saw
    he'd got his man,
    And we rove a stronger line on to the winch.
The whaler fought towards them. He was very nearly
    done.
    The boys all grabbed to save him, just as he
Pushed the jaunty to our gun'le; then he chucked it up,
    poor Kid.
    He'd worked out *all* his penance, in that ship upon
    the sea.
There's a battleship that's swinging to her anchors
    somewhere North.
    There's a sailor's kit at auction. You'll agree,
They'll fetch *twenty times their value* just for memory of
    The Kid
    Who was working out his penance, in that ship upon
    the sea.

Up and Down the Strand
By Sam Walsh (1915)

Shove me off the pavement, push me in the dirt,
    Draw your dainty skirts away, fear they come to
    hurt.
Hurry past and leave me here, holding out my hand,
    Selling matches in the rain, up and down the Strand.
Lord, there isn't no romance, in a case like mine.
    I've had no inglorious fall through womenfolk or
    wine.
No bloomin' awful lurid past, no betrayin' of a trust,
    To make me stand here in the rain a-beggin' of a
    crust.

I was simply born to this, same as thousands more,
    I am one of them what's called the underserving
    poor.
Selling matches in the Strand to anyone I can.
    Yet, God help me now and then I'd like to be a man.
In the Army shelter where I gets my dole
    Of bread and soup, by God, I'd like to smash the
    bloomin' bowl
And fling it in their faces and make a blazin' stir,
    And wake the manhood up in me. Yes, two a penny
    sir.

But I haven't got the brains, no, nor yet the heart.
  I have been, and always shall be, in the blooming
      cart.
Standing in the puddles, wond'ring what you'll give,
  Fearing very much to die, and loathing it to live.

Shove me off the pavement, push me in the dirt,
  Draw your dainty skirts away, fear they come to
      hurt.
Hurry past and leave me here, holding out my hand,
  Selling matches in the rain, up and down the Strand.

Periodicals

By Greatrex Newman, Graham Squiers & Fred Cecil (1916)
Performed by Tom Clare

Have you noticed what parts *Periodicals* play
  In these *Times?*
A sweet girl, for instance, can't keep long away
  From the *Mirror,* —
She owns the *Wide World* as along she will sail,
  Her best frock, — the *Pink 'Un,* — turns other girls
      pale,
Of course she is hoping that her *Daily Mail*
  Will *Observer.*
Now the *Modern Man* sometimes will ask her to say —
  'Yes' or 'No';
If she *Answers* 'Yes,' — and he *Windsor,* next day —
  Financial News;
But the *Bystander* notices after a year,
  He gets tired of *Home Chat,* and his club is his
      Sphere,
He *Telegraphs* home — 'I am working late dear,' —
  The Storyteller!

Of course later on, there will doubtless appear:
  Little Folks.
His boasting is *Graphic,* and all who are near
  Get the *P.I.P.*
And at night there's a *War Cry,* papa you will guess,
  Looking just like a — *Sketch* in his — well — evening
      dress,
Walks round the room trying in vain to suppress *Home
  Notes.*
Later on their ambition in life is to be
  In the *Smart Set,* and you'll often hear *News of the
      Worlds* that they see
From the *Tatler:* but the *Truth* is, these *Tit Bits* soon
  fade right away,
Such *Ideas* have vanished, their *Cassells* decay,
  They leave all *Town Topics,* and end up their day
In *Country Life.*

The Reflections of a Penny

By Valentine & T. C. Sterndale Bennett (1916)
Performed by Dorothy Varick

I was sitting in my armchair in my room the other day,
  And I drew from out my pocket, casually,
'Mid a handful of loose silver — a penny old and worn
  And it seemed to catch my eye immediately.
It was only just a penny, slightly battered, slightly
      bent,
  And the date on it was almost worn away,
But I dreamed that as I gazed at it, it spoke its history,
  And this is what it seemed to me to say:
'What do you know of this world for all your thirty
      years of life?
  What do you know of its trials or its tears?
Why, I've seen full ten times more of life in just one
      single day,
  Than you have seen in all your thirty years!
I have wakened 'mid a crowd of gold and silver in
      Park Lane,

At one, I've help'd to buy some typist's grub,
I've been thrown out to a news-boy for the special four
      o'clock
  And spent the night down in an East-End pub!
I've carried folks for twice their proper distance on a
      'bus,
  Through me, couples spoon for hours in the park,
I've been dropped sometimes in streets and held the
      traffic up for hours,
  And been mistaken for a half-crown after dark!
I've been thankfully accepted by a West-End flower-
      girl.
  I've been hugged by little urchins in the street,
I've been given to a chauffeur as a tip — and then I've
      heard
  Language that I couldn't well repeat!

Some people say I should be proud, but yet, you know,
  I'm not!
  I often hear some beggar make request,
And although my owner's got his pocket stuffed quite
  full of cash,
  He chooses *me* in preference to the rest.
If ever I'm in church, and they are passing the plate,
  It's *I* who am dropped in immediately
While Scotchmen I have known have often shed a
  silent tear
  At the moment they have had to part with me!
On some cold and bitter day outside an East-End
  pastry-cook's,
  I have often known just what it means to stand,
While my tiny ragged owner gazes in with wistful eyes.
  Clutching me within his little grimy hand.

P'r'aps I don't feel proud to know I only mean one
  small meat pie,
  Or a sticky jammy tart maybe — but when
I see his little hungry face just lighten up with joy,
  Well — I'm rather glad that I'm a penny then!
Yes! I'm only just a penny in my suit of dingy brown,
  But my colour doesn't fret me in the least,
And it never troubles me, although they laugh at me
  up West,
  For I guess I've got some real good pals down East.
And one reflection comforts me as through the world I
  roam
  That although a humble penny I may be,
I can say what some of your banknotes and quids can
  never say,
  That all the world has shaken hands with me!'

Charm
By Lawrence Vane (1922)

Here we go! Oh, dear. You know it isn't all sunshine
being a widow. I've been a widow these 5 years come
Michaelmas Tuesday. I have to go about so much
alone. Nasty dark lanes, too! And it doesn't do for us
girls to wander about unprotected. You never know!
You never know when you may get the glad eye or the
postman's knock!
  I'm looking for a little unfurnished cottage and a
man. A little nest for two.

That's the aim of all us girls — a little nest for two.
  But how do we get it? How do we get it?
By charm!
  They say we have two million girls too many,
Quite the wildest thing I ever read.
  For, when we speak of girls, we separate the pearls
From the plain unlucky ones who never wed.
  And when we've got the pearl and plain divided,
Well may you knit your eyebrows in alarm,
  Take a chance with any, but you'll find we've not too
  many
Girls that have that quality of charm.
  What is it that holds men like a magnet?
What makes you play the devil with us girls?

What is that net that few of you escape from?
Tinker, tailor, soldier, sailor, dukes and earls —
  What is it makes some little child attractive?
Awake or when asleep in perfect calm —
  I ask you all who love just such a youngster,
It's charm, just charm.
  Now I don't like to talk about myself, girls,
The fact remains I do attract the boys!
  True my figure's vile, but the men do stare, and
  smile
Students speak of me as 'some big noise.'
  If I sit between some pretty girls at dinner,
The men, you'd be surprised, are such a tease!
  My face is not my label, no, but underneath the table
It's *my* hand, girls, that always gets the squeeze!
  What is it that holds men like a magnet?
What makes you play the devil with us girls?
  What is that net that few of you escape from?
Tinker, tailor, viscounts, dukes and earls —
  Love? 'tis often mere infatuation,
Pretty looks alone may do much harm.
  What made my husband leave me for another?
Charm, just charm!

The Madman's Will
By Peter Cheyney & Harold Arpthorp (1925)
Performed by Albert Whelan

In a work-house ward that was cold and bare,
  The doctor sat on a creaking chair,

By the side of a dying madman's bed.
  'He can't last much longer,' the doctor said.

But nobody cares if a pauper lives,
    And nobody cares when a pauper's dead.
The old man sighed, the doctor rose.
    And bent his head o'er the ricketty bed,
To catch the weak words one by one —
    To smile — as the dying madman said:—
'Beneath my pillow when I am gone —
    Search — hidden there you will find it still!'
'Find what, old madman?' the doctor asked,
    And the old man said, as he died, 'My Will.'
How they all laughed at the splendid jest —
    A pauper madman to leave a will.
And they straightened him out for his final rest,
    In the lonely graveyard over the hill,
And the doctor searched for the paper and found
    The red taped parchment — untied it with zest,
Whilst the others laughingly gathered round
    To hear the cream of the madman's jest.
Then the doctor with mocking solemnity said,
    'Silence, my friends,' and the Will he read.
'I leave to the children the green fields,
    The fresh country lanes for their play,
The stories of fairies and dragons,
    The sweet smell of heather and hay.
I leave to young maidens romantic
    The dreaming which all maidens do.
And the wish that some day in the future
    Their happiest dreams will come true.
To youth I leave all youth's ambition,
    Desire, love, impetuous hate.

And to youth with years I leave wisdom,
    And the hope that it comes not too late.
I leave to the lovers the gloaming,
    The time when all troubles are old,
When true love, hand in hand, goes a-roaming
    To the heart of the sunset of gold
To the mother I leave children's voices
    And curly heads close on her breast,
The soft whispered prayer that rejoices
    Her heart as she puts them to rest.
I leave to old people sweet memories,
    And smiles that endure to the last,
With never a fear for the future,
    And not a regret for the past.
I die without earthly possessions,
    Without the last word of a friend,
To you all I leave good cheer and friendship
    That lasts through all time to the end.
I leave to the wide world my blessing
    In the hope that the long years will find
That my wishes shall grow like a flower,
    And bring God's good peace to mankind.'
The ward doctor laid down the parchment,
    His smile had gone — turned into pain.
The faces around laughed no longer,
    But grew grave with regret that was vain.
'No wonder that he looks so happy,
    Whilst we who derided are sad,
For the things he has left are the best things in life
    I wonder if he *was* mad?'

Auction of Life

By George Arthurs & Gil Roy (1928)
Performed by Fred Lewis

Life is like a game of Auction Bridge,
    You shuffle and you deal!
But whether you happen to cut high or low,
    You soon will discover, as through life you go,
Some men do the calling, while others say 'No!'
    And pass!
You meet a young lady whose features are fair,
    And you think, as partners, you'll make a fine pair,
So you fall in love and you quickly declare
    'Two Hearts!'
Then you press your suit, oh, life's simply grand,
    She leads — to a jeweller's shop in the Strand,
And then every time she exposes her hand,
    'Diamonds!'
You quickly get married, 'mid cheering and grins.
    And you feel like Dummy when that phase begins.
But eighteen months after the doctor says 'Twins!'
    You're doubled!

But soon the love game gets a bit slow,
    You miss your nights out with the boys, don't you
        know.
Your partner declares you've revoked when you go
    To Clubs
Then somebody else trumps your trick on the sly,
    He plays his cards well and she bids you good-bye.
Then, full of remorse, you go to her and cry
    'Fresh deal!'
But all will come right and the rubber you'll gain
    If you will play fair. Have no fear of chicane,
When you kiss and make up, then you obtain
    'Grand Slam!'
So scorn all conventions and never play small,
    When you keep the score and the game is Love all,
And honours you'll gain when you die, and the call
    Is a *Spade!*

The Scot's Lament

By Kitty Kennedy Allen & Kennedy Allen (1929)
Performed by Will Fyffe

I'm a Scot and I'm married, two things I can't help,
   I'm married — but I have no wife —
For she bolted and left me — but that's nothing new,
   It happens sa often in life.
So I journeyed ta London, for that's where she'd gone
   With her lover to hide her disgrace.
And though London's a big town I swore I'd not rest
   Till I'd searched every street in the place.
And I tramped — how I tramped — weary mile upon
   mile,
   Till exhausted and ready ta drop.

I would not give in, so I climbed on a bus,
   And took a front seat on the top.
We came to a halt in a brightly lit square
   To my joy, there ma lassie I spied,
Looking weary and worn, but thank heaven — *alone* —
   From my heart, 'Maggie, Maggie,' I cried.
She gasped with delight as I rose from ma seat,
   But a harrowing thought made me wince,
I couldna get off — for I'd just paid ma fare,
   And I've never caught sight of her since.

Soliloquy of a Tramp

By Gerald Morrison (1932)
Performed by Chesney Allen

Why am I sittin' on this 'ere seat,
   Feelin' so discontent?
'Cos I'm 'ungry and weary, and fed up with life —
   I'm broke — yus — I ain't got a cent.
I've walked and I've walked, till me boots is wore out,
   With no breakfast, no dinner nor tea.
And 'atred and bitterness fills me w'ole soul,
   Why the 'ell do they stare at me?
Yus, I'm fed up with life, and wish I wos dead,
   But nobody seems to take 'eed.
Why, I'd barter me soul, and swear black was white,
   If I could sit down to a FEED!
Just look at them swells in their fine motey cars —
   'undreds in every street,
They chokes you with dust, or they splash you with
   mud,
   From the top of yer 'ead to yer feet.
They never goes 'ungry — they wastes enough food
   To feed dozens of kids ev'ry day.
If they had to work for their bit o' grub —
   Well, God 'elp 'em, that's wot *I* say.
And you bows and you scrapes and you takes off yer 'at

To the Duchess, the Duke and the h'Earl.
Then you reads all about their carryings on,
   In the papers all over the world!
They're always in some kind o' trouble or mess,
   Or else their digestion is gorn,
I've never been troubled in that kind o' way,
   No, never — not since I was born!
Still, when all's said and done, they carn't have it all,
   There's something that we all can share,
The right to live in this funny old world,
   And to breathe the Almighty's fresh air.
I've 'ealth and I've strength, and I goes where I likes,
   And I don't want no h'ancestral 'alls.
So between you and me, this funny old life
   Ain't quite so bad, after all!
Keep joggin' along with a jolly old song,
   You carn't do much 'arm, and you carn't go far
   wrong.
When we've finished with life, and we've passed
   through death's door —
   Well, we're all the *same* then, both the rich *and* the
   poor!

The Old School Tie

By Kenneth & George Western (1934)

Rah, Rah, Rah Rah Rah, Rah, Rah, Rah Rah Rah,
   Hello cads, we're going to sing you a song.
Rah Rah Rah, Rah Rah Rah, Rah, Rah, Rah Rah Rah,

About the old school,
Hooray, Rah!
   Listen you fellas, now look here you chaps,

Let's think of the old school today,
   Of Eton and Harrow and Borstal as well.
Three cheers, follow up and hooray.
   Let's wear that pullover we won at Narkover,
Let's all walk about in small caps,
   And let every mug be a tribute to Rugby,
And bravo, bravissimo, chaps.
   Any old Alsatians here?
There's one or two old Dalmatians, George.
   Really?
Spotted around!
   A cannibal chief sat and sharpened his knives,
Wearing his old school tie.
   Solomon slept with his five hundred wives,
Wearing his old school tie.
   Two hundred and fifty a side it was,
Was it really?
   Yes, that hot weather.
H'm it was warm.
   Very close, almost touching really.
Lloyd George often spoke of his school so they say,
   But now he's a platinum blonde in his way,
He sits up in bed looking like Frances Day,
   Wearing his old school tie.
Toujours la Polytechnic!
   Of course.
Cochran sat down in a gallery queue,
   Wearing his old school tie.
Moses was found in the bullrushes too,
   Wearing his old school tie.
The Royal Garden Party was the smartest for years,
   Jimmy Thomas arrived and they gave him three
     cheers,

He turned up in evening dress, top hat and spurs,
   Wearing his old school tie,
Sic transit Gloria Swanson,
   Oh yes?
Don't forget Marlborough, remember St. Pauls,
   And Dulwich and Hamlet and Stowe,
And Wormwood and Dartmoor and Pentonville too,
   And Dr. Barnado's,
Say there!
   Oh up the Scrubs!
Let's talk about batting and physics and Latin,
   And Classics we took in our stride,
And famous school fellows like Laurel and Hardy,
   And Crippen and Jekyll and Hyde,
But you're forgetting the Shell, you hounds,
   And the Remove, you know.
There's a man in the moon so astrologers say,
   Wearing his old school tie.
They're going to make Hitler the Queen of the May,
   Wearing his old school tie.
At the debts talks when Montague Norman came in,
   They said Oxford or Cambridge? And so with a
     grin,
He lifted his beaver and under his chin,
   He was wearing his old school tie.
Pro bono public house-o.
   Really?
Gandhi's disciples all kicked up a din,
   'Cos Gandhi said 'If we can fight we can win,'
Then his loin cloth fell off but he wasn't run in,
   He was wearing his old school tie.
Rah Rah Rah, Rah Rah, Rah, Rah, Rah, Rah Rah Rah.
   Good hunting cads.

Shootin' and Huntin' and Fishin'
By Ronald Frankau (1934)

I belong, or, at least, I pretend to,
   To the fellows who do what is done,
And we live without reason
   From season to season
With saddle, and fish rod, and gun.

Shootin' and huntin' and fishin'
   Keep us employed on and off,
And we've always use of
   A club most exclus-ove
In case we should want to play golf.
   When we dine at the very best places
And the food isn't right, there's a fuss,
   Though if for tripe some old duchess is wishin',
And Quaglino himself should bring the odd dish in,

As long as there's shootin' and huntin' and fishin'
What does it matter to us?

Shootin' and huntin' and fishin'
   And tent pegging, too, is quite fair.
Though we would be sooner
   Pig-sticking near Poonah
We can't always get over there.
   For politics or politicians
We don't care a proverbial cuss,
   If John Simon is cheerin' and Baldwin is hootin'
'Cause Winston again has to suffer a bootin',
   As long as there's fishin' and huntin' and shootin'
What does it matter to us?

Photographers snap us at dinners,
    But what we all really prefer
Is when they come and raid us
    In plus-fours or waders
Or top-boots *avec* crop and a spur.

Shootin' and huntin' and fishin'
    Give us our greatest rewards,
But we're thrilled to the marrow
    When Eton and Harrow
Fight the good fight out at Lord's.
    And we always visit the boat-race,
Gener'lly chart'ring a bus,
    But though Cambridge wins again, groanin' and
        gruntin',
And the Oxford crew takes to canoein' and puntin',
    As long as there's fishin' and shootin' and huntin'
What does it matter to us?

Shootin' and huntin' and fishin'
    Keep us busy; if they're not enough
We play country-house cricket
    And bowl at the wicket,
Or some of that body-line stuff;
    But if one of our batsmen is injured
Nobody kicks up a fuss,
    Though someone is hit on a pad 'gainst his wishin',
Whether it's that shin or whether it's this shin,
    As long as there's huntin' and shootin' and fishin'
What does it matter to us?

Almost weekly the nice illustrateds
    Into our privacy pry,
We look awfully hearty
    When throwing a party,
But better still castin' a fly.

Shootin' and huntin' and fishin'
    Are good, but to make all serene
We take a lunch bask-ot
    To jolly old Ascot
In order to say we have been.
    We also watch boxing on pictures,
Lest we should be missing the bus;
    Though whether Max Baer keeps grimacin' or
        stuntin'
Till Carnera in rage knocks his jolly old front in,
    As long as we've fishin' and shootin' and huntin'
What does it matter to us?

Shootin' and huntin' and fishin'
    Raise a thirst, and on whisky we thrive;
We don't care an iota
    For pegs that are *chota*,
But barra pegs keep us alive.
    We never break up any meetings,
We can drink without causing a fuss,
    And though Fascists and Communists keep on
        recruitin'
From Walthamstow, Colney Hatch, and Upper
        Tootin',
    As long as there's fishin' and huntin' and shootin'
What does it matter to us?

Shootin' and huntin' and fishin'
    And occasionally, too, we've a 'blind',
And storm Piccadilly
    To look at a filly,
But only to look at her, mind.
    And we sometimes fly over to Paris,
But not for *les femmes* and *la fuss*.
    Should we find some French ladies we're bravely
        confrontin'
And it's perfectly obvious 'Zey only want one t'ing,'
    So long as there's shootin' and fishin' and huntin'
What does it matter to us?

Shootin' and huntin' and fishin'
    Are not always enough for our Pa-s,
And sometimes we're yearning
    Our bread to be earning
By selling insurance or cars.
    And though we're not keen to start working,
If it's outdoors we don't care a cuss,
    Though we may take up poultry — to try to make
        pennies
And don't know which the cock is — nor yet which the
        hen is,
    So long as there's badminton, billiards, and tennis
What does it matter to us?

Bunger-Up O' Rat-'Oles
By Jack Warner (1940)

Now I reely ought ta tell yer abart the job I've got.
  To look at me you wouldn't think it true.
Now I don't look like a feller who 'as to be 'ard 'arted;
  Well I'm not.
But this is what I have ter do.

I'm a bloke wot bungs up rat-'oles, I am reely,
  I'm a rat-'ole bunger upper too and all.
And when I speak of rat-'oles I don't mean babies
  rattles,

I mean 'oles wot's bored by rats right thru' the wall.
Now I've 'ad and 'eard some narrow squeaks in my
  time,
  Though I don't look brave or very fond of strife
Still, all the time there's rat-'oles, there'll be bungers-
  up of rat-'oles,
  So it looks as though I've got a job for life!

The Twirp
By Robert Rutherford & Norman Long (1942)

Chesney Chirp said to his father 'You're a Twirp
  A Twirp, that's what you are,' said he,
To which his dad replied, 'I see so I'm a Twirp,
  And I conclude a Twirp, my lad is something rude?'
'I don't know that,' replied his son,
  'But whatever a Twirp is, you are one!'
At which his father with a frown,
  Turned Cuthbert Clarendon's trousers down.

That evening in the pub Jim Chirp asked one and all,
  'What is a Twirp?' But all he learned, 'midst laughter
  hoarse
Was, 'You're a Twirp yourself of course.'
  Next day the local librarian
Was called on by an anxious man
  Who said to him, 'Can you tell me just what a
  Twirp's supposed to be?'
The gent replied, 'Stay where you are whilst I consult
  Britannica'
  And later came back with a grin and said,
'I fear it isn't in,
  But though the word is not defined I'm sure it

cannot be refined.'
Off to the British Museum Jim hied,
  And once again the question plied
'What is a Twirp? You ought to know.'
  The aged assistants in a row
Let out a howl that broke the gloom and echoed
  through the Mummy Room:
  They turned up Hebrew, Latin, Greek
But not of Twirps did any speak:
  'The origin's obscure,' said they
'And obscene too, Ha-ha Hey-hey!'

Said James, 'It's very plain to me
  Whatever else a Twirp may be
It's something that makes people laugh
  And laughter's what we want — Not Half!
So on the Music Halls went Chirp,
  And billed himself, 'The Perfect Twirp';
And packed with Twirps his patter runs,
  And everywhere he goes great guns;
Three hundred pounds a week earns Jim
  And that's not bad for a Twirp like him.

Pity the Boy who's grown out of his Clothes
By Harry Hemsley (1943)

Pity the boy who's grown out of his clothes,
  My clothes do not fit me at all
I was once very small, now I'm well in the cart
  'Cos I've started to grow very tall.
My elbows commence to stick out of my sleeves
  And my shoes they are pinching my toes;
My pants shrink above me and nobody loves me
  I'm the boy who's grown out of his clothes.
It's jolly rough luck I think you'll agree
  To have to wear clothes not intended for me,

Such as Aunty's pyjamas, pulled in at the waist,
  Without any turnups, she says 'It's bad taste'
And all just because I am growing so fast,
  And suits that once fitted they somehow don't last
And new suits need coupons, and then there's the tax,
  So now I am wearing my Grandma's old slacks.
Grandma's, not Grandad's, as wide as a sack
  Too tight in the front and too big at the back,
And feeling a draught every time the wind blows
  Pity the boy who's grown out of his clothes.

The Grand Old Girls of Britain

By David Jenkins (1944)
Performed by Suzette Tarri

You can talk about your monuments,
   Your bits of ancient Rome;
But there's a sight more stirring
   You can see right here at home.
It's the grand old girls of Britain
   Who are somewhat past their prime,
They'll never get their medals
   Tho' they earn them all the time.
The grand old girls of Britain —
   They're marching every day
With shopping bag equipment,
   They tread the pavement way;
With footsteps rather weary
   And shoulders rather bowed.
They toddle down the Broadway
   To join the queueing crowd.
The tired old girls of Britain;
   They're wearing out their legs,
Through trudging back and forward
   So as not to miss the eggs;
They scorn your five-bob peaches,
   Your posh ten guinea hats,
But they'll climb up half a mountain
   For a bit of cooking fat.
The cute old girls of Britain;
   They're mighty hard to beat,
They're smart as Mister Sherlock Holmes
   At finding stuff to eat;

They gaze behind the counter,
   Their eyes are old but keen,
They know that what they're looking for
   Is very seldom seen.
The great old girls of Britain,
   When the war is really won,
Will get their compensations
   And their little bit of fun.
When the tradesmen call for orders,
   She'll say: 'Blimey so it's you!
Well, try the tradesmen's entrance
   And form a blinking queue!'
The tired old girls of Britain,
   With rheumatics in their joints;
Through tramping round from shop to shop,
   Getting value for their points;
They spurn your fancy pine-apples,
   Your peaches and all that;
But they'll climb up half-a-mountain
   For a bit of cooking fat.
So when you youngsters of today
   Are in the prime of life;
And feeling fit and fine
   In spite of all the years of strife;
You'll owe it to the mothers
   Who stood there in the queue;
They didn't get things for themselves,
   They got them just for you.

Pull Together

By Nosmo King & Ernest Longstaffe (1949)

Every single Briton, who is worthy of the name
   Is naturally proud of his Country and its fame —
But do we all, I wonder, strive with heart and will
   To help her in her troubles and make her greater
     still.

When difficulties threaten us and things don't look so
     bright,
   You'll hear folks say 'Don't worry, we'll muddle
     through all right.'
But why should this great country always have to
   'muddle through'?
   Have you ever stopped to think maybe it is up to me
     and you?

If we'd only trust each other more, and sometimes try
     to see
   The other fellow's point of view, how much easier it
     would be;
For those who have to govern in these very trying
     days,
   When they need co-operation in so very many ways.

If we'd show our sportsmanship: give credit where it's
     due —
   Not letting petty jealousies distort our point of view,
And blind us to the debt we owe to that great man,
     whose name
   As champion in the cause of peace is crowned with
     world wide fame.

If Loyalty and Brotherhood were never needed more,
  Think of the talks of comradeship that reached us
    from the war:
When Prince and Navvy fraternised, their
  understanding to increase:
    So natural! in Wartime! So why not now in Peace?

We're members of one family, our interests are the
    same:
  Prosperity is certain — if we only play the game!
Team spirit! — Faith! — Mutual Trust! — Nothing
  more or less
  Are needed now to make our Country certain of
    success.

At cricket and at football we have learnt what team
    work means —
  From Wembley or the Oval — to the humble village
    greens.

It's 'team work' that is needed now to keep our
    Country great,
  For a Nation cannot prosper on a policy of Hate.

So let's all pull together and let the pull be strong
  Let's be genuinely proud to help the ship of State
    along,
In the cause of Peace and Justice let us one and all
    unite,
  And let our slogan ever be 'For God, for King, and
    Right.'

Optional Verse
Class hatred — Oh so senseless, could be put upon the
    shelf,
  If only he that preached it, would be honest with
    himself
And admit it's a delusion, used for poisoning the mind
  By dishonest agitators with an alien axe to grind.

Thanks Johnny
By Beecher Stevens & Harry Stogden (1951)
Performed by Jack Watson

I was feeling pretty low one day —
  A really miserable cuss.
You know — when you've nothing to say
  And everything's a fuss.
I'd scoffed at my breakfast with my head in the news
  And grunted out answers to all my wife's views.
I'd banged the doors as I busied about
  And finally banged myself out.
I got to the gate — without looking back
  And then was greeted with 'GOOD MORNING,
    UNCLE JACK!'
'N' there all beaming and large as life
  Was Johnny, the Orphan Kid, with a large pocket
    knife.
'Johnny! I snapp'd — what have you got there?'
  And I fixed poor Johnny with an awful stare.
'I've got a sword — and it's a beauty —
  I'm looking after Auntie — while you go on duty,'
You know — that kid, with his great big smile

Just knocked the bottom out of me for a while,
Why? Well — here was a kid with no mum or dad,
  And nothing, really, to make him glad.
Yet, there he was all happy and gay —
  (Quite frankly, I was about to turn him away.)
I stopp'd in my tracks and turned my head
  But suddenly, I smiled instead.
The first that morning — in fact for many a day
  To think young Johnny had shown me the way.
I looked at him and he continued to grin,
  Why, not to smile now seemed a sin.
So soothingly I said — 'Johnny — take care with that
    knife'
  Then I looked back home, waved — and smiled to
    my wife
I went on my way feeling full of joy
  Why the heck can't we always be like that boy?
Carefree — yet thoughtful most of the while —
  Thanks Johnny for making me smile.

PART TWO

WRITERS AND COMPOSERS 1897 — 1946

The writers and composers listed in Part II are shown in traditional form with the name of the author first and the musical arranger second. Many of them are familiar names as the essential source of material for the leading performers in Part I (and many of the additional "star" links are shown in the text in Part II). But what splendid, striking names these words-and-music partnerships had: Ella Wheeler Wilcox and D'Auvergne Bernard; Elphinstone Thorpe and Wolseley Charles; F.Chatterton Hennequin and Blanche Garston Murray; R.R.Pecorini and F.Harper Shove; J.Harrington Weeks and Harold Arpthorp — one wonders how many, if not all, owed something to poetic licence in their names as well as in their work!

Their significance in the history of the monologue goes much wider, however, than their own style and personality, or even the star performers with whom they were associated. For much of their work achieved its greatest exposure far away from the halls — in clubs, at Masonic evenings and, above all, in family gatherings. For the monologue first flourished in days when every self-respecting family indulged in "At Home" musical evenings. For those who could not play a musical instrument, or sing without causing offence, the dramatic recitation solved a problem.

Thus grew up a demand for published material which was intended for domestic consumption with family and friends, as well as, hopefully, for professional performances. Sheet music for monologues would often appear with the name and picture of the artist to whom sole performing rights had been sold, followed by the suggestion, "This monologue may be performed freely anywhere except theatres and music halls." Writers provided the wider audience with a wealth of material in which a high moral tone generally predominated. There was also a strong theme of patriotism which — to the modern eye at least — can be seen as bordering on the xenophobic. As we have already seen, Milton Hayes' *The Whitest Man I Know* might be regarded as offensive in the nineteen eighties. Yet to exclude it would not only be to miss the point of Billy Bennett's 1927 riposte, *The Tightest Man I Know*; more significantly, such monologues are part of our social history, painting a picture of British life in the first half of the twentieth century.

Certainly, the first two monologues in Part II, which were performed by Mel B.Spurr, reflect the earnest tones of the late Victorian era. Spurr was also a regular performer of *Laugh and the World Laughs With You*, which has become a standard British motto and so established its author in the public mind that "Don't Ella Wheeler Wilcox me" was used in popular parlance to mean "Don't preach at me".

The Last Token (1898) is another example of the moral monologue, but the "humorous twist" appears at the start of the Edwardian era. *The Man with the Single Hair* (which was performed among others by the present editor's mother in concert party) used the tried and trusted music hall technique of the "unlikely story". This process was developed further with "tall tales" of which *The 11.69 Express* and *The Lighthouse Keeper's Story* are prime examples.

A Dickens Monologue is interesting in bringing together the main characteristics of Bransby Williams' act. Yet the regular performer listed for this routine is George Phillips and he may well be one of those who — much to William's disgust — cashed in on his success. In the year in which this piece was published, 1910, there were sixteen different Dickensian "acts" working, while in 1896 there had been one — Williams himself. Bransby Williams was actually accused by the Aldwych management of copying Seymour Hicks as Scrooge and, on another occasion, when appearing in a "flying matinee" at the seaside, was asked not to use his Dickens characters, as they were performed there daily.

The monologues included for the period between 1911 and the outbreak of the First World War are a representative sample of the rapidly developing publishing activities of Reynolds and Company (who specialised in this field and who were responsible for almost all the items in Parts I and II). Publishing contracts in those days, long before most writers and musicians had agents, were exceedingly informal. Teddy Bond, the General Manager of Reynolds, would usually drink at the Blue Posts pub in Piccadilly and, it was rumoured, those who bought him a drink were soon seen in print. Reynolds would usually arrange for the musical accompanist, so that some of the words-and-music partnerships never actually met. Cuthbert Clarke was Reynold's chief composer and, because of his status as a West End theatre conductor, might receive a fee of three to five guineas and even a small royalty. Others, like the concert party pianists Blanche Garston Murray and Phyllis Norman Parker, were less well rewarded since their musical commitment was often little more than "vamping". Typically, at the time, writers would receive two guineas and a small royalty.

Writers' work pre-1941 can already be seen as falling into several standard patterns. *The Charge of the Night Brigade* was one of the first of the poetic parodies. The theme in *Bill* of "man's best friend" was soon followed by many others. *What Will the Child Become* introduced the political message: its attack on Poor Law guardians reflected the growing pressure for reform after the Royal Commission Report of 1909. *Reward of the Great* was a return to religion in almost hymn-like form.

The continuing demand for humorous material is reflected in the tongue-in-cheek patriotism of *The Hinglishman,* while *A Clean Sweep* marked the emergence of a new generation of comedy writers. Its author, Greatrex Newman, has enjoyed almost seventy years as a writer (and his contemporary work is sampled in depth in Part III). In 1913, he wrote *A Clean Sweep* for Bransby Williams, using a format made popular by Charles J.Winter (other examples of Newman's early work are *Uncle George* and *Periodicals* in Part I).

The Waster reflects a time when the "remittance man" actually existed and, seemingly, was always bound for a sticky end. *An East End Saturday Night* and *The Man Who Stayed at Home* show the versatility of writers of the day — in this case, F.Raymond Coulson's genuine Cockney pathos is followed by a light-hearted piece which could easily have found its way into *Punch. The Steam Roller Man's Story* is another tall tale, while *Answered* is one more moral injunction from Ella Wheeler Wilcox.

With *The Scrapper and the Nut*, we are introduced to the first of five wartime pieces by F. Chatterton Hennequin. The Hoxton bully is a traditional figure, but his unlikely comradeship with the Belgravia toff reflects changing social values in wartime. Mention of the "Nut" has an especially sad contemporary ring. It had been given wide currency by the disabled matinee idol, Basil Hallam, in his song *Gilbert the Filbert (The Kernel of the Nuts)* shortly before the white feather campaign drove him to his death on the Western Front.

Hennequin's other wartime monologues and Rupert Hazell's *The 'Oxton 'Ero* introduce us to a wide range of British servicemen — not all of them ideal for propaganda purposes. 'Erbert, A.B. is a true stiff upper lip type, but *Alf*, the conscientious objector, the looting *Pincher D.C.M.* and the defeatist *Cheerful Charlie* were daring compositions: Lawrence Eastwood's *The Answer of the Anzacs* and Sam Walsh's *The Mercantile Marine,* for example, show that patriotic feelings were running high.

Supplementing all this military fare was a strong element of "business as usual". Wartime theatre audiences wanted a dash of escapism in the music halls as well as in revue and musical comedy. Some writers managed to combine all these worlds. While in uniform, Rex Newman found time to write a burlesque one-man pantomime for Bransby Williams in "The Passing Show of 1914" at the Palace Theatre, in which the impersonations centred round Fred Emney Senior as Cinderella, George Graves as the Baron and G.P.Huntley as the Fairy Queen. He also wrote another homely wartime piece — *Broom and Co.* — for Bransby Williams.

The musical collaboration which produced *Broom & Co* is an interesting example of the way in which the amateur and the professional worlds intermingled. Fred Cecil, fifteen years older than the young Rex Newman, was a Birmingham estate agent. Rex recalls him "living with his two unmarried sisters and keeping a harpsichord in his bath". His music provided the backing for several early Newman monologues and the composers would "sit there and kid ourselves we were Gilbert and Sullivan".

Rex Newman went on to achieve extraordinary success as a writer and producer for concert party, revue and musical comedy. Wounded during wartime service and awarded the O.B.E., he was well qualified to give a sharper, cutting edge to the post-war satirical monologue in *What Did You Do in the Great War, Daddy?* But his work mainly relied on a gentle, enduring English humour. Indeed, when he was contributing songs like *The King Who Wanted Jam For Tea* for Stanley Holloway in the Co-Optimists, *Punch* magazine said that the new W.S.Gilbert had arrived. His musical collaborator in the Co-Optimists was Wolseley ("Harry") Charles and they also worked together in monologues for Bransby Williams such as *My Love Affairs.* Rex Newman wrote most of his monologues alone, but did from time to time collaborate with others. His most eminent collaborator (as in the case of *A Tattoo Tragedy)* was Clifford Grey, who had achieved instant fame in writing the words for the biggest romantic hit of the 1914—1918 war, *If You Were The Only Girl in The World* (which he composed on the back of an envelope, by candlelight, during a Zeppelin raid on the East Coast).

The other three remaining pieces from the wartime selection were all written in peacetime vein. *The Gardener's Story* was another tall tale which utilised the musical talents of the London pianist, Herbert Townsend. As his repeated entries show, collaborating with a wide range of writers, Townsend became one of the most prolific composers in this field during the next thirty years.

Many of these pieces were intended for Masonic entertainers. This was a relatively lucrative business and performers for Masonic nights were mainly billed as "Humorist" or "Society Entertainers" with material to match. *The Gardener's Story* is a good example of the former, while the Wild West drama of *Phil Blood's Leap* made it ideal for the latter. So, too, did the Cockney sentimentality of *A Little Guttersnipe.* This piece is, however, a rare example of the authors' work:

Tommy Sterndale-Bennett was a distinguished musician and composer (whose daughter Joan has done much to recreate Victorian music hall at the Players' Theatre); his working partner, Valentine (in private life F.Clifford Harris), wrote a few pieces for Dorothy Varick (see Part I), but normally collaborated with J.W.Tate whose marriages, first to Lottie Collins and later to Clarice Mayne, both music hall singers, led to his deep involvement in music hall. Within a year of publishing *The Little Guttersnipe* the Valentine/Tate combination produced *A Bachelor Gay* and, with Harold Fraser-Simpson, the rest of the score for the enormously successful "Maid of the Mountains".

The ex-serviceman's mental anguish in the post-war period is reflected in both *Afterwards* and *The Duet*. But as the twenties progressed, we see the monologue revert to traditional patterns. *The Cabman's Railway Yarn* and *Thrilling Stories* are timeless tall tales. Bransby Williams performed Rex Newman's *My Love Affairs* in 1921, reminding us of his continuing activities and of that of his writers. In 1923, Charles J. Winter (certainly the most successful of the "dedicated" Williams writers) produced a new version of the surprise ending by a constant series of surprises in *Sally's Ups and Downs*. More novelty came in the child impressions of *Girls (According to a Fourteen-Year-Old Boy)* and *Supplanted*. So, too, was the irreverence of youth as reflected in *Our Grandparents' Yarns*.

From time to time, wartime echoes re-appeared as in the roadsweeper's *When You Figger It Out* and H.M.Burnaby's bitter ending to *Jimmy Johnson*. But, in general, the main monologue output reflected traditional themes, even if, as in *Lizette, Queen of the Apaches*, the exotic Parisian background had a contemporary ring as the West End became enamoured by Apache routines in cabaret, revue and musical comedy. The timeless battle of the sexes was reflected in monologues like *Aren't Men Funny*, *Old Flames* (with its bits of business in pulling out the seemingly endless photographs of loved ones), *The Girl at the Ball*, *He Did* and the fascination of the cad in *Two Men*.

Traditional monologue characters and forms still abounded. This was typified by the "Burlington Bertie" tramp re-created by Will Deller in *'Arf A Cigar;* the stiff upper lip in *Square Deal Sanderson*; the Cockney character in *When the Road's Hup it's Hup;* the Shakespearean parody in *Wheels* of "All the world's a stage" and, towards the end of the decade, the enthusiasms for fractured Italian in *My Leetle Rosa* and *Penny for Da Monk*.

As we have seen, the skill and personality of Gracie Fields and Stanley Holloway made the thirties a time when the song monologue had enormous success, not only on the halls, but with the wide public available through recordings and with the new nationwide radio audience. The more traditional material in Part II was also directed to these same outlets. Writers like Percy Edgar (an elocutionist and "Uncle Percy" in the early days of the B.B.C. in Birmingham) and musicians such as Ernest Longstaffe were both on the B.B.C. staff. They, and many freelance writers, found the insatiable demand for radio material provided a valuable commercial outlet for their work. In the samples of their thirties monologues, however, it is clear that, for many writers, the traditions of the halls still prevailed and the broad areas of subject matter are almost identical with those in the twenties.

Thus, *Memories of Waterloo* is one more tall tale. *Suicide, The Sufferer* and *The Man with the Swollen Head* all come under the heading of comedy, albeit with a slightly macabre touch in the first two items. *Tommy Out East* is one of several contemporary touches — in this case the drawbacks of peacetime soldiering. It makes an interesting contrast with the wartime reminder *Road to La Bassée*. *The Old Barnstormer* is another contemporary piece — in this case a reminder of the way in which the cinema was beginning to affect all forms of live entertainment. *Sam's Parrot* is a direct result of the growing success of the Holloway song monologues (although Stanley Holloway has disclaimed any knowledge of this particular piece which was obviously intended to cash in on *Old Sam's* popularity). Its author, V.F.Stevens, was originally a packer for Reynolds and Company who rose to take over the business shortly before its demise.

The Mab Davis child impressions *When I'm Cross* and *What's It For?* and the moral tone of *The Touch of the Master's Hand* bring us back to traditional monologue fare. Indeed, the moral message seemed to reach a crescendo in the last years before the Second World War through Nosmo King's string of earnest injunctions with their revealing titles: *The Killjoy, Loyalty, Providence, The Human Touch* and *Goodbye and God Bless You*. At the same time, the usual monologue variations are evident in *Bill's Trombone* with its Lancashire lion-taming humour; the Cockney cheer in *Lor Lumme, You'd Never Believe It*; the philosophy in sporting guise of *Life is like a Game of Football*; a return to the Wild West in *Frisco Sam, Bad Man*; a cynical old girls' reunion in *Nell* and a reminder of a collector's passion of the day, *Cigarette Cards*.

"Business as usual" seems also to have applied at the outbreak of the 1939–1945 War, with *Me and My Pipe, The Glutton* and *If You'll Pardon My Saying So*, but patriotic fervour is soon in evidence in *The Voyage of the Saucy Jane, My England, The Civilians, Dawn Patrol* and *Merchant Navy*. Of the immediate post-war pieces, *Legs* and *Timmy's Sacrifice* might have been written at any time during the half-century or so of the "monologue proper". Nosmo King's other post-war piece, *Thank You*, a tribute to the architects of victory, is almost the swan song of dramatic recitation, as the end of the war saw the final death throes of live music hall and the dramatic monologue, happily to be replaced by the developments in comedy song monologue that we shall see in Part III.

The Lesson of the Watermill
By Sarah Doudney & Bond Andrews (1897)
Performed by Mel. B. Spurr

Listen to the watermill,
  All the livelong day,
How the creaking of the wheel
  Wears the hours away.
Languidly the water glides,
  Useless on and still,
Never coming back again
  To that watermill.
And the proverb haunts my mind,
  Like a spell that's cast
The mill will never grind
  With the water that has passed.
Take the lesson to yourselves,
  Loving hearts and true.
Golden years are fleeting by.
  Youth is fleeting too.
Try to make the most of life,
  Lose no honest way,
Time will never bring again
  Chances passed away.
Leave no tender word unsaid.
  Love while life shall last,
The mill will never grind
  With the water that has passed.

Work while yet the daylight shines,
  Man of strength and will,
Never does the streamlet glide
  Useless by the mill.
Wait not till tomorrow's sun
  Beams upon your way,
All that you can call your own
  Lies in this to-day.
Power, intellect and strength,
  May not, cannot last,
The mill will never grind
  With the water that has passed.
Oh! the wasted hours of life,
  That have drifted by.
Oh! the good we might have done,
  Lost without a sigh.
Love that we might once have saved
  With but a single word,
Thoughts conceived, but never penned,
  Perishing unheard.
Take this lesson to your heart,
  Take, oh hold it fast,
The mill will never grind
  With the water that has passed.

What is a Gentleman?
By Mrs W. P. O'Donoghue & Bond Andrews (1897)
Performed by Mel. B. Spurr

What is a gentleman? Is it a thing
  Decked with a scarfpin, a chain and a ring?
Dressed in a suit of immaculate style,
  Sporting an eye-glass, a lisp, and a smile?
Talking of operas, concerts, and balls,
  Evening assemblies and afternoon calls?
Sunning himself at 'At Homes' and Bazaars —
  Whistling Mazurkas and smoking cigars?
What is a gentleman? Say, is it one
  Boasting of conquests, and deeds he has done?
One who, unblushingly, glories to speak
  Things that should call up a flush to his cheek.
One who, while railing at actions unjust,
  Robs some pure heart of its innocent trust.
Scorns to steal money, or jewels, or wealth,
  Yet deems it no crime to take honour by stealth!
What is a gentleman? Is it not one
  Knowing, instinctively, what he should shun?
Speaking no word that could injure or pain,
  Spreading no scandal, and deep'ning no stain.

One who knows how to put each at his ease,
  Striving consistently always to please.
One who can tell, by a glance at your cheek,
  When to be silent, and when he should speak?
What is a gentleman? Is it not one
  Working out all that is rightly begun
Living in uprightness, loving his God,
  Leaving no stain on the path he has trod.
Caring not whether his coat may be old,
  Prizing sincerity far above gold,
Recking not whether his hand may be hard,
  Stretching it boldly to grasp its reward?
What is a gentleman? Say, is it birth
  Makes a man noble, or adds to his worth?
Is there a family tree to be had
  Shady enough to conceal what is bad?
Show me the man who has God for his guide,
  Nothing to blush for and nothing to hide,
Be he a noble, or be he in trade —
  He is the gentleman *Nature* has made!

The Last Token

By W. A. Eaton & Bond Andrews (1898)

A holiday in Rome — the azure sky
  Was all unflecked by the clouds as if the eye
Of the Eternal looked from Heaven's high dome
  On the great city, proud, Imperial Rome!
The Coliseum was crowded, row on row
  A sea of human faces all aglow
With mad excitement for the day would be
  A rare occasion of wild revelry.
For there were gladiator fights and shows
  Of manly strength and as a fitting close
To the diversions of that joyous time
  A band of Christians, whose most heinous crime
Was preaching a new doctrine, were to be
  Thrown to the lions that all the crowd might see
How little the strange God, to whom they prayed,
  Cared if his followers were stoned or flayed.
The sports are over and the setting sun
  Is hurrying towards the West as if to shun
The sickening sight. A sudden hush upon the people
    fell,
  And then uprose a fierce and savage yell.
See where they come, that faithful little band,
  Chanting a hymn about their Fatherland:
The Heaven of which they speak with so much joy,
  That home of happiness without alloy!
See yonder maiden with the saint-like face
  And form of beauty, full of fire and grace,
She lifts her head as if she were a queen.
  No trace of fear in her actions seen.
Now come the lions growling with rage,
  Hungry and glad to leave their tight-barred cage.
See yonder royal beast with flowing mane
  Lashing his side and roaring with disdain,
Gazing around upon the yelling crowd,
  Answering their shouts by growlings long and loud.
The maiden stands as statue-like as death,
  The crowd in terror gaze with bated breath.
While as she stands, there falls just by her feet
  A lovely rose, still filled with perfume sweet.
Upward she gazes with wide-open eyes,
  Ah well she knows who flung the dainty prize.
'Tis he, her lover, who had vainly tried
  To win her from the faith for which she died.
He worshipped Venus, Bacchus, and the train
  Of heathen gods who do their votaries chain
To sinful pleasures, making virtue nought.
  She was a Christian, and had often sought
To stir his heart with love of Him who died,

But he had laughed at her most earnest prayer,
  And tossed a goblet in the sunny air,
  And said 'We live and die, then take our fill
Of pleasure now, and let them groan that will.
  Why should we waste our youth in solemn fast,
If we are buried just like dogs at last?
  Nay, drive this Christian nonsense from your head
And be my own, and then when we are wed
  We will worship Venus and the God of Love.
Give me your hand, say Yes, my gentle dove.'
  And as she told him she must confess
Her faith in Christ though martyrdom no less
  Was the reward of all who worshipped Him,
Of all who dared to chant their holy hymn.
  And now she was to prove her faith by death.
The lions were close, she almost felt their breath
  Upon her cheek. She stood with anguish dumb,
And strained her eyes to see if he had come
  To watch her die. The rose had fallen there,
She stooped and placed it in her raven hair.
  Then looked again and saw her lover's face,
And arms held down as if he would embrace
  Her even now. A moment, and she turned
From her set purpose. Then new ardour burned
  Within her breast and she stood proud and calm,
As if she knew the lions could do no harm.
  And then uprose the Christians' holy hymn.
The sickening sight now makes the senses swim.
  And we will draw a veil o'er the sad scene.
Night in the Coliseum — the crowd has gone —
  One being wanders in that scene forlorn.
He stands upon the place where she had died.
  And breathes the name of Christ the crucified.
And stooping down, among the martyred dead,
  He finds a rose now dyed a deeper red.
Some fragments of a dress he knew was hers,
  He places in his breast and new life stirs
Within his heart, and as he leaves the place
  With head bowed low, with slow and solemn pace.
He softly murmurs as he homeward goes:
  'Jesus, be Thou my guide till life shall close.'
But was he coward? Did he hide away?
  Not many weeks, on a great festal day,
Another band of Christians stood to die,
  Lifting their glorious hymn of triumph high.
Where she had stood he boldly takes his stand,
  A withered rose clasped in his strong right hand.

The Man with the Single Hair

By Robert Ganthony & Arthur H. Wood (1902)
Performed by Mel. B. Spurr

He was not bald: for on his shining cranium
  Remained one hair, it's colour pink geranium.
Oh, how he idolised that single hair
  That, last of loved ones, grew luxuriant there.
He counted it each morning: fondly viewed it
  This way and that way: carefully shampooed it.
Brushed it, combed it, scented it and oiled it,
  Dared scarcely put his hat on lest he spoiled it.
In evening dress, arrayed for swell society,
  He'd part it in the middle for variety.
Often he'd curl it, train it o'er his brow
  In navy fashion, as our middies now.
Omitting nothing, with devoted care,
  He'd pet his hirsute pride, his single hair.

But sad to tell!
  Ah bitter was the blow!
There came a day —
  A day of direst woe —
When in his soup it fell! He quickly spied it,
  Then rescued it, and on his napkin dried it,
His only hair. His pet, his flowing tress,
  Chill was his forehead, deep his heart's distress.
'I'm bald at last,' he wailed, in bitter grief,
  'My only hair has fallen like a leaf.
What ho! A taxidermist,' shouted he,
  'I'll have it stuffed, for all mankind to see.
And when, within its case of glass installed,
  The world shall see I was not *always* bald.'

A Tragedy in One Act

By Victor Marsh & Walter Shephard (1904)

The moon shone through the grimy window pane
  Athwart the dusk that gathered in the room.
The day was over, twilight on the wane
  And all seemed wrapped in dark and dismal gloom
Except within the gas light's flickery flare
  Which weakly shed its sickly radiance down
Upon a somewhat strange fantastic chair
  Where sat a beardless youth whose eyes so brown
Seemed starting from their sockets as in fear.
  He clutched the chair with hands both white and
    bony
With head thrown back with throat exposed and bare.
  His whole frame shook and quaked with agony.
Horror! Is this some dreaded den of torture where
  suffer those who sin against the State?

Is this some youthful and rebellious courtier who
  now in pain his crimes must expiate?
I see the dreaded operator near
  As if to seize his victim in his wrath,
To glory in the agony of fear,
  That flecks the victim's lips and chin with froth.
I see the beads of sweat upon the brow,
  The mute appeal within that poor youth's eyes,
As his tormentor pounces on him now,
  For his escape no earthly chance now lies.
I see the glint of steel — a bright blade flash —
  Oh! horrid sight that makes my marrow freeze —
But stop! From out the chair he makes a dash, —
  Pays twopence for his first shave. Next please.

Laugh And The World Laughs With You

By Ella Wheeler Willcox & D'Auvergne Bernard (1904)
Performed by Mel. B. Spurr

Laugh and the world laughs with you.
  Weep, and you weep alone:
For this stolid old earth
  Has need of your mirth,
It has troubles enough of its own.
  Sing, and the hills will echo it:
Sigh, and it's lost on the air;
  For they want full measure

Of all your pleasure,
  But nobody wants your care,
Feast, and your halls are crowded,
  Fast, and they'll pass you by;
Succeed and give,
  And they'll let you live,
But fail — and they'll let you die.

The 11.69 Express
By Ronald Bagnall & William S. Robinson (1906)

You want a railway story while you wait for the
London train,
  It's a story I've never told yet, so I'll tell it to you
  again.
I was only a guard at the time, sir, on the London and
Smash'em Line
  But I shan't forget the mishap to the eleven sixty
  nine.
'Twas a terrible foggy night, sir, and a day I shan't
forget
  The fog was a kind of Scotch mist, sir, and the train
  it was somehow wet!
The train ran upon the line, sir, and the line ran along
the ground
  The engine was full of steam, sir, and the wheels
  were going round;
What *made* the wheels go round and round it's more
than I can say,
  But the signal was dead against us, so we went the
  other way.
We were going a mile a minute, when I stepped out on
the line,
  And the driver said we were due, sir, at eleven sixty-
  nine.
So I got back into the van, sir, and swallowed a bottle
of Bass;
  While we waited two hours, or more, sir, for a luggage
  train to pass.
When all of a sudden I heard, sir, the sound of a
mighty crash
  We could hear the shrieks of survivors, and I
  thought of their ready cash.
So after I'd finished my pipe, sir, I strolled out on to
the line.
  And gazed on the wretched wreckage of the eleven
  sixty-nine.
For the coaches were all in a heap, sir, though why — I
cannot tell.
  And the passengers lying around us, were none of
  'em looking well.
They slept their last sleep on the sleepers, we could
hear the sleepers snore.

It's a sight I've never seen, sir, and shall never see —
before.
For the line was a mass of hats, sir, and blouses all over
the place
  Whilst one of the passenger's noses was in the middle
  of his face
We could hear the hiss of the engine and the moans of
the living souls;
  I thought of the missus at home, sir, and collared
  some of the coals!
I shall *never* forget the sight, sir, though I can't
remember it now.
  But with my tattered banner, I wiped a tear from my
  brow.
I picked my way through the wreckage and got to the
heart of the smash,
  I busied myself with the injured, and helped myself
  to the cash.
For I wanted the money badly, 'cos my rent was in
arrears,
  And mother-in-law had come, sir, on a visit for sixty
  years.
Then I saw a sweet young lady in a mashed potato
state,
  And her final words were, 'Doctor, is my hat on
  straight?'
We stumbled across the stoker, and I thought that he
was dead:
  For his body and legs were missing and we couldn't
  find his head;
I forget what happened next, sir, I remember it all
quite well.
  The crashing of heavy timber all a-tumbling as it
  fell.
The doctors and the looters were round us by the
score,
  And the police were an hour late, sir, as they've
  often been before.
Then two of us lifted the engine and placed it upon the
line
  But here's your down train up, sir, the eleven sixty-
  nine.

The Lighthouse Keeper's Story
By Arthur Helliar & Cuthbert Clarke (1909)

You want to hear of the bravest deed ever done on the
land or sea?

I rather think I can tell yer *that* for it appears 'twas
done by *me*.

Mel B. Spurr, one of the many performers of the 'standard' *Laugh and the World Laughs with You*

Nelson Jackson, a leading exponent of both comic and dramatic monologues during the First World War

No. 130.

THE SCRAPPER AND THE NUT.

Composed by

PHYLLIS NORMAN PARKER

Written and Performed by

F. CHATTERTON HENNEQUIN

Also Performed by

NELSON JACKSON

It was when I was lighthouse keeper, a year or two
    back, not more.
  The lighthouse was built on a rock, sir, 'arf a mile
    pretty near from the shore.
A storm for a month had been raging, no boat could
    approach as we knew,
  And the steamer wot should 'ave brought vittles was
    more than nine weeks overdue.
For days we'd been living on biscuits — they was all as
    there was left to eat.
  On Sundays we fried 'em in lamp-oil, we did it by
    way of a treat.
But that give out arter a bit, sir, so we 'as to partake of
    'em 'rore'.
  Still the lamp was the wust of the bisness, we couldn't
    light up any more.
We'd only one small box o' matches and I took 'em
    above in the lamp,
  And 'eld 'em afore the reflector, till my arm fairly
    ached with the cramp.
They didn't make much of a flare, sir, well, I 'ardly
    expected they would,
  But I had this 'ere great consolation as I'd done all as
    any man could.
I soon finished up all the matches — there was nuffing
    more left I could do,
  So I turns in my 'ammick being sleepy and was off in
    a minute or two.
Soon I dreamt that I sat at a banquet with some nobs in
    a West End hotel,
  They was 'anding round liver and bacon, fried fish,
    tripe and onions as well.
A waiter asked me if I'd 'ave some, and I'd just stuck
    my fork in a lump,
  When I almost fell out of my 'ammick for there come
    a most 'orrible bump!
I knew what it was in a moment, I could tell pretty well
    by the force,
  It was one o' them big ocean liners wot 'ad got a bit
    out of 'er course.
There was dozens more come after that, sir, they
    cannoned us all thro' the night,
  I tell yer I wasn't 'arf glad, sir, when I see it begin to
    get light.
I thought p'r'aps as some very likely might keep up the
    game all the day,
  So I 'ung out a board with 'Wet paint' on, which I
    fancied might keep 'em away.
Being woke up all night by them vessels was enough to
    make anyone mad,
  And the langwidge the crews used was 'orrid, and
    the skipper's was ten times as bad.
So I calls to my mate what was dozing and tells 'im
    some oil must be got,

'There's a shop arf a mile off,' 'e answers, 'shall yer
    swim there or fly there or what?'
'I shall fly there!' I says, 'or I'll try to, just 'ark while I
    tell you my plan,
  You must fasten me on to a rocket and aim it as
    straight as you can.
I must take one as well to come back with, for they
    mightn't p'r'aps 'ave one on land,
  But them ships knockin' bits off our lighthouse is a
    thing as I'm hanged if I'll stand.'
So he fastens me on very careful, I'd a can in my 'and
    for the oil,
  And the wind was a-'owlin' and screamin' and the
    water was all of a boil.
'Now remember,' I says afore startin', 'I'm a-risking my
    life I'll admit,
  But a Briton ne'er shrinks from his duty and that
    lamp there tonight must be lit!'
Them words was scarce out of my mouth, sir, when I
    'ears a loud kind of whizz,
  And away thro' the air I was soarin', and a rummy
    sensation it is!
My mate 'e 'ad once been a gunner, and 'is aim was
    surprisingly true,
  I missed the shop-door I'll admit sir, but bang thro'
    the window I flew.
But the face of the man wot was serving was the thing
    as you ought to have seen,
  When I landed full length on the counter and arskes
    for some best paraffin.
He took me at first for a h'angel till 'e saw as I 'adn't no
    wings,
  And noticed a 'am disappearing with a loaf and some
    pickles and things.
To bring a long tale to a h'end sir, I returned the same
    way as I came,
  'Twas a coastguard as touched off the rocket and I
    can't say a lot for 'is aim.
But my mate who was up in the tower sees me coming
    and 'eld out 'is net,
  I'd 'ave missed by a yard if 'e 'adn't and might a got
    'orribly wet.
And talking o' wet, sir, reminds me as I'm dry enough
    now thro' and thro',
  Wot's that you says, 'Will I join yer.' Well, thankee,
    don't mind if I do.
Good 'ealth sir, it's lucky I met you for there's men 'ere
    by dozens as tries
  To get gents to stand 'em a drink, sir, by tellin' 'em
    'orrible lies.

A Dickens Monologue

By George Phillips & W. R. Simmons (1910)

On a winter's night when wind and rain rage with a
  sullen roar,
    With a pipe, a book, a blazing fire, — what does a
    man want more?
The firelight gleams on rows of books. What shall I
  read to-night?
    Shall fancy roam in musty tome or a modern novel
    light?
Books well known, books unknown, books of immortal
  fame,
    Books whose fame is Empire-wide, bearing an
    honoured name.
Novels, poets, classics, modern wits and ancient
  sages —
    But I take one lettered 'Copperfield' and turn its
    well loved pages.
Through Canterbury's sleepy streets in fancy now I
  roam
    To an ivy-covered, gabled house, 'tis Agnes
    Wickfield's home.
I climb the wide oak staircase and opening wide a
  door,
    There a pale-faced, red-haired clerk I see, stroking
    his lantern jaw.
Then from his seat at the high oak desk the slimy
  creature slides,
    And rubbing his hands with vicious glee, towards me
    slowly glides.
He greets me with effusion, but his handshake makes
  me creep.
    He's a very 'umble person — his name Uriah Heep.

IMPERSONATION OF URIAH HEEP
'David Copperfield'

Yes, Master Copperfield, I am working late, but I'm
  not doing office work.
    Oh no, Master Copperfield, I'm improving my legal
    knowledge by reading through 'Tidd's Practice.'
Oh! what a writer Mr. Tidd is, Master Copperfield.
    I'm a very 'umble person, Master Copperfield,
    And I learnt my 'umility in a very 'umble school.
Father and me was brought up at a Foundation School
  for boys,
    And they taught us to eat 'umble pie with an
    appetite.
Where's my father now? At present he's a partaker of
  glory, Master Copperfield,
    But only in a very 'umble way, you know.

Must you be going now? You don't know 'ow grateful I
  am
    To you for 'onouring our 'umble roof. Goodbye,
    Master Copperfield. Good-bye.

Curse him, the puppy!
    Little does he know that I've got old Wickfield under
    my thumb,
And when I've crushed him I'll marry Agnes in spite
  of you,
    David Copperfield — Curse you!

Oh! you've come back — for your gloves and stick.
    Here they are. Good-bye once more and may Gawd
    bless you.

The firelight fades from the sad, sad page of a book we
  all know well,
    Where the master's pen has written the tale of Little
    Nell.
A storm-torn sky, a night-bird's cry, a glimpse of a
  struggling moon —
    In a churchyard still, on a lonely hill, I walk in the
    gathering gloom
On a new-made grave, 'neath a yew-tree's shade, a poor
  old man is kneeling.
    He came at dawn, he was there at noon, now night is
    on him stealing,
A gentle madness holds his brain, he knows not care or
  sorrow
    With a child-like faith he murmurs, 'She'll come
    a-gain tomorrow.'

IMPERSONATION OF GRANDFATHER
'Old Curiosity Shop'

Sh! Softly — she's asleep in there my Nelly. Sh! We
  must not wake her,
    Though I should be glad to see her eyes again — to
    see her smile —
There's a smile on her face now, but it's fixed and
  changeless.
    I would have it come and go, but that will be in
    God's good time.
See here, her little shoes — she kept them to remind
  her of our last long journey together.
    Her little feet were bare upon the ground;
They told me afterwards how the rough stones had cut
  and bruised them —

But she never told me that, no. God bless her! and
  I've remembered since,
She walked behind that I might not see how lame she
  was.
  She's sleeping soundly, and no wonder. Angel hands
  have strewn the ground deep with snow,
That the lightest footstep may seem lighter yet,
  And the very birds are dead, that may not wake her.
She used to feed them, sir. They never flew away from
  her.
  How is it that the shutters are all up, and the folk are
  nearly all in black today?
They say my Nelly's dead, but, no! She'll come again
  tomorrow.
  In the destroyer's steps there rise up new creations,
  which defy his power,
And his dark path becomes a way of light to heav'n
  She'll — come — again — tomorrow.'

And once again the scene is changed, in Paris now I
  stand,
  While shrieks of hate and blood lust rings thro' the
  desolated land.
Alone the death-cart rumbles, with its load of living
  dead,
  To where Madame La Guillotine up-rears her
  ghastly head.
There Carton gladly gives his life for the freedom of
  his friend,
  And thus his wasted, ill-spent days, haste to a noble
  end.
A little world of love he sees in England fair and free.

And the knitting women, counting, murmur softly,
  'Twenty Three.'

IMPERSONATION OF SYDNEY CARTON
'A Tale of Two Cities'

Goodbye, Lucie, goodbye, Life. Lead on, my gaoler!
  Few are so weary of life's load as I am.
The world in which I have done so little, and wasted so
  much, fades fast from me.
  And in its stead I see the lives of those for whom I
  lay down my life,
Peaceful, useful, prosperous and happy in that
  England which I shall behold.
  I see that child who lay upon her bosom, and who
  bore my name,
A man, winning his way up the path of life which once
  was mine.
  I see him winning it so well that my name is made
  illustrious by the light of his.
I see the blots I threw upon it faded away.
  I see him foremost of just judges and honoured men,
  bringing a boy of my name.
With a forehead that I know, and golden hair to this
  place,
  Then fair to look upon, and I hear him tell the child
  my story in a tender and a faltering voice.
It is a far, far better thing that I do, than I have ever
  done,
  It is a far, far better rest that I go to than I have ever
  known.

The Girl at the Station
By Dorothy Scull & Alfred H. West (1911)

I can't believe you're goin'
  When I see you standin' there
To think this time tomorrow, Bill —
  You'll be miles away from here.
Well, I ain't the one to stop yer,
  But you must bear in mind,
There's another sort of courage, Bill,
  In us wot stays be'ind!
Oh! no! I ain't cryin',
  I got a 'orrid cold.
It's yer old Gawblimy uniform
  Makes you look so strong and bold.

Why! I can see you killin' Germans,
  Jest you give it to 'em 'ot.
Yes, Bill! It's a 'orrid cold, a 'orrid cold I got.
  In fact a perfect noosance!
An' now the train's agoin' to start,
  An' though I loves yer dearly, Bill,
Don't you think I'll break my 'eart.
  No! good-bye old boy,
Gawd bless you!
  Yes! I'll write and you'll write too.
Good-bye — Lor! Yes! I loves yer.
  Gawd! 'e's gone. Wot shall I do?

The Charge of the Night Brigade

By Elphinstone Thorpe & Wolseley Charles (1911)

Down the steps, down the steps,
  Down the steps blundered —
Right down the area steps, policeman six hundred.
  'Come down; don't be afraid,
Missus is out,' cook said.
  Right down the area steps
Strode six hundred.
  'There now, try that,' she said,
Was he at all dismayed?
  No! though the bobby knew
Someone was plundered.
  His not to make reply
'I can't eat rabbit-pie,'
  His but to have a try,
Down at the table sat, policeman six hundred.
  Rabbit to *right* of him,
Cold beef to *left* of him,
  Pork pie in *front* of him, (all of it plundered).
What is there left to tell
  Beef, pork and rabbit fell
Into the jaws of, — into the mouth of — well —,
  Policeman six hundred.
Flashed his good weapon bare,
  Flashed as it turned in air,
Sabr'ing the pork-pie there,

Slicing the cold beef,
While cook stood and wondered.
  Never a word he spoke,
Right thro' the crust he broke,
  Pie-crust and rabbit reeled from his master stroke,
Shattered and sundered.
  Then he sat up again,
Sat up, and pondered.
  Pocket to right of him —
Pocket to left of him —
  Pocket behind him —
All were nigh sundered.
  Stuffed like a shrapnel shell
Why? Well they heard the bell,
  Then he who fed so well
Crept off with bated breath
  Carrying, sad to tell,
All that was left of it,
  Left by six hundred.
When can the memory fade
  Of the grand meal he made,
While the cook wondered?
  Honour the kitchen jade!
Honour the meal he made!
  Noble six hundred.

Bill

By F. Chatterton Hennequin & Blanche Garston Murray (1911)

He was always big and clumsy and his voice is deep
    and gruff,
  But he has got the kindest heart, although his coat is
    rough —
He isn't much to look upon, except maybe his eyes,
  And they are just the softest brown and more than
    human wise.
Oh they sold me a pup when I bought my pal,
  With a dozen lines or so of pedigree,
But the friendly little hail of your sympathetic tail,
  Shows your breeding and your true gentility.
You were not exactly steady — no, your youth was
    very wild,
  Though I nursed you thro' distemper, your
    behaviour made me wild.
Your ways were not respectable, your habits they were
    sad —
  Your morals — don't you wink at me — were most
    uncommon bad.

But in every kind of weather, both in sunshine and in
    rain,
  He was content to stick by me in common loss or
    gain.
I've tramped along this road of life until I couldn't
    stand,
  I've woke to find him close beside, and felt him lick
    my hand.
There were women said they loved me, so they did a
    little while,
  There are friends who when they met me have
    forgotten how to smile.
I never let it worry me although they pass me by,
  For Bill's a friend, whose love will end, when he lies
    down to die.
Don't tell me that you're growing old, for all your
    muzzle's grey,
  I couldn't do without my pal, to cheer me on the
    way.

So just you take it easy Bill, there's only you and me —
  When one is gone the other will be lonely, don't you
    see.
Most all the parson taught me I've forgotten but I
  know,
  There was something 'bout a mansion, where the
    tired people go,
A place of rest for such as us, away from grief and
  sin —

But if they don't admit you, Bill, well I'm not going
  in —
Oh they sold me a pup when I bought you my pal,
  With a dozen lines or so of pedigree,
But the friendly little hail of your sympathetic tail,
  Shows your breeding and your gentility.

What Will the Child Become?
By Parker Nichols (1912)

The Child!
  What will he become? A serious matter truly
To a father of an only one, and perhaps, but not
  unduly,
  To one with children nine to ten, tho' in cases such
    you say,
Bright future's visions loom obscure thro' troubles of
  today.
  In a certain town a wise man dwelt, philosopher and
    sage,
Who told your future, read your past, just then
  Society's rage,
  Phrenology! Psychology! In these fertile fields of
    science —
He wandered plucking golden fruit, and incidentally
  his clients.
  To him went a parent fond, took with him his son.
Laid down a golden fee and said, 'What may the child
  become?'
  The man of mystery took the coin, spun it in the
    air —
Bit it, put it in his vest, and motioned to a chair.
  He wandered round that youngster's head, paused
    on a monstrous bump
The father softly murmured — 'The fender made that
  lump.'
  The wise man frowned, made no reply, but started
    off anew,
Till a piping voice said, 'Daddy, must I have hair drill
  too?'
  At last the sage was satisfied and in manner most
    concise,
He took the parent on one side and gave him this
  advice:—
  'When even's sun is setting low, an hour before the
    gloom,
Place a bible and a sovereign and an apple in a room.
  Thither lead the child and leave him for an hour,
To see which potent agent has proved of greater
  power.

  For if he eat the apple it is a certain sign,
That comforts close at hand form his especial line.
  'Midst Nature's fruits he should be placed, coal, iron,
    corn or such.
As miller, miner, farmer, smith he may accomplish
  much.
  Should he read the bible, a scholar he should be.
Writer, teacher, poet, preacher, or Professor like me!'
  But should he grasp the sovereign — beware, my
    friend, for then —
He holds for weal or woe the power to rule his
  fellowmen.
  Financier or banker, buyer, seller he may be,
Or money-lender, with interest running to Eternity.
  For each can be of evil use — the sovereign most of
    all.'
The Bible can be misapplied, and the apple caused our
  fall.
  Homeward went the parent — in the room he placed
    the youth
With a sovereign and an apple and the Book that
  stands for Truth.
  And in an hour that simple child, when father took a
    look —
Had eaten the apple, pocketed the gold and was sitting
  on the Book.
  And as the parent stood amazed, out spoke this
    precious kid. —
'I'd like another apple pa, also another quid!'
  The child — What did he become? How fared this
    noble youth?
Who was filled with greed and avarice, and who sat
  upon the truth.
  The world alas! holds out rewards for such you must
    allow,
What did the child become?
  Well — he's a poor-law guardian — now!

Reward of the Great
By F. Raymond Coulson & Robert M. Angus (1913)

You in obscurity thirsting for fame,
  Think of the bitters the famous have quaffed.
Mighty Napoleon in exile and shame,
  Plato, the wise man, who never once laughed.
Wolsey brought down for base scullions to mock,
  Chatterton under the suicide's pall.
For Charles, the great King, and brave Raleigh — the
    block,
  And Calvary Cross for the greatest of all!
The axe of the heads-man for Mary, the Queen,
  For Joan of Arc martyrdom — flames raging hot,
For Antoinette's beauty the red guillotine,
  For Lincoln and Garfield the murderer's shot.

For Coriolanus the villainous thrust —
  Death's dagger stained black with ingratitude's gall.
St. John by base treachery laid in the dust,
  And Calvary Cross for the greatest of all!
Citizens lowly who yearn to be great,
  Glory, the goddess, has dust on her wings.
Pause in your bitter arraignment of fate,
  Gaze on the guerdons of Captains and Kings.
The rack for Galileo — torture and strife,
  For Cranmer the stake, cruel death for St. Paul,
For Socrates hemlock, for Caesar the knife,
  And Calvary Cross for the greatest of all!

The Hinglishman
By F. Raymond Coulson & Leslie Harris (1913)

The Hinglishman jumped hout of bed one morn,
  An 'e ses to 'iself ses 'e —
'Thank Gord, I'm a Hinglishman bred an' born,
  An' there's no foreign make abart me.
There's the same British blood in my 'art an' my 'ead
  Wot in Nelson an' Wellington ran.'
A picter of Nelson 'ung over 'is bed,
  An' 'e looked at it (printed in Sweden) an' said,
'Thank Gord I'm a Hinglishman.'
  So 'e combed 'is 'air wiv 'is comb, (made in France),
An' 'e put on 'is French silk scarf;
  In the glarss (made in Austria) takin' a glance,
Saw 'is physog an' gave a loud larf.
  'Har! Har!' 'e ses to 'iself, 'ole cock —
You was built on the werry best plan.'
  ('Ere 'e looked at the time by the German clock),
'Thank Gord I'm a Hinglishman.'
  So 'e put on 'is watch (it was Swiss) an' 'is chain
(German silver) 'I feels quite a treat'
  'E ses to 'iself — 'But I'm gettin' a pain
In my innards for somethin' to eat.'
  So 'e went darn to brekfust, an' sat in 'is chair
(A chair wot was made in Japan)

An 'e ses to 'is missis 'Selina my dear,
I'm starved; but, har, har! a fine spread you've got 'ere,
  Thank Gord I'm a Hinglishman.'
On the toast (which was made of American wheat)
  An' the butter (prime Dutch) 'e begun,
Then 'e tackled a slice of Australian meat
  An' two eggs (laid in France) nicely done,
Wiv a rasher (American) all of 'em fried
  In a werry bright German-made pan;
Then some tea (grown in China) 'e soon stowed inside,
  Wiv Austrian sugar, an' said, full of pride,
'Thank Gord I'm a Hinglishman!'
  Yus, the Hinglishman's blood is all foreign made
An' so is 'is muscle an' bone —
  If the parts wot was genuine Hinglish was weighed,
Wy, there's scarcely a harnce of 'is own!
  Dutch, French, American, German, Chinee —
On a real cosmopolitan plan 'e's built.
  If a man's wot 'e eats, don't yer see?
We're furriners! that's wot we are — you an' me —
  An' I larfs wen a cove to 'iself, ses 'e —
'Thank Gord I'm a Hinglishman.'

A Clean Sweep
By Greatrex Newman & Fred Cecil (1913)
Performed by Bransby Williams

I've 'ad lots o' jobs, — some was good, some was
  bad, —

But the one as I counts the most strange,
Was once when I went to a millionaire's 'ouse

To sweep out the chimneys an' range.
They wanted it doin' at night, rather late,
  When the fires weren't in use, arter tea, —
So I goes ter the place, an' I strolls up the drive,
  About eight o'clock it 'ud be.
When I gets ter the hentrance I sees two fat blokes
  Dressed in gold, an' I 'ears one say:
''Er Ladyship 'as bin hexpectin' Yer Grace,
  Will Yer Grace kindly foller this way?'
Well I looks round ter see who 'e means by 'Yer
    Grace,'
  But there weren't no one there, 'ceptin' me, —
So I think p'r'aps 'Yer Grace' is the *French* word fer
    'sweep,'
  So I follers the bloke just ter see.
Then a lady, all larfin', comes out of a room,
  An' ses: as she looks at me clothes, —
'Why really, I shouldn't 'a' knowed yer, Yer Grace,
  If it weren't fer that wart on yer nose!'
Then she opens a door, an' I sees a big room
  Full o' folks all dressed up in strange things, —
Some was soldiers, some nurses, some sailors, some
    cooks,
  An' sev'ral was hangels wi' wings.
Well, then the band stopped, an' the dancers sat down,
  An' a fat gent comes up on me right,
An' 'e puts sev'ral coins in me fist, as 'e ses:
  'There's the ten pounds I borrowed last night.'
Then a lady comes up, an' ses: 'Really, Yer Grace
  I've larfed till me sides are quite sore,'
So I ses: 'Get some Zam Buk, an' rub 'em wi' that!'
  An' everyone near give a roar.
Then one ses: 'Why weren't you at the hopera last
    night?
  'Ad yer bin playin' polo or goff?'

I ses: 'No, I'd bin playin' at *bathin' the kids,*
  'Cause the missus 'ad took a night off!'
Well then us 'ad supper, — it weren't arf a spread, —
  The best feed I've 'ad in me life! —
An' everyone larfed, an' sed: 'Isn't 'e fine!'
  When the *blankmange* slipped orf o' me knife.
An' they didn't arf roar when I upset me glass
  Down a girl who was dressed all in white, —
But it didn't show much, fer I dusted 'er frock
  Wi' me sleeve, an' me serviorite.
Then the lady as I 'ad fust met in the 'all,
  Who the others all called 'The Dookess,'
She 'ands me a lovely gold watch, an' she ses:
  'That's the prize for the best fancy dress,'
Arter supper us went ter the ballroom,
  An' I tried a dance as they called '*Pass-de-Quart,*'
But I soon chucked it up, 'cause me old 'ob-nail boots
  In the ladies' frocks kep' gettin' caught.
Then the Dookess, 'er ses: 'Your *finance* 'as just come,'
  An' a young gal in low hevenin' dress,
Comes straight up to me, — an' starts larfin', and ses:
  'Well Percy, you do look a mess!'
Then she ses: 'I 'ave just got that ten thousand pounds
  That was lef' me last year by me aunt, —
So now we'll get married next month, shall we dear?'
  I ses: 'No *love*, — hus bloomin' well *shan't.*'
So she ses: 'Why what *reason* is there for delay?
  The pater no longer forbids,' —
I ses: 'There's *ten* reasons!' — 'What are they?' she ses
  I hanswers: '*One* wife an' *nine* kids!'
Then she ses: 'What a bounder you are for a joke,
  And you always so serious keep:—
Now come Percy love — 'I ses: 'Eh! Look 'ere miss,
  I *ain't* "Percy love" — *I'm the sweep!'*

The Waster

By F. Chatterton Hennequin & Blanche Garston Murray (1913)

I'm a thousand miles up country,
  And I'm frozen to the bone,
While my brothers sleep in London,
  And my very name disown.
It's a name that's simply rotten
  In the old land and the new,
Through the whole condemned Dominion,
  I'm a wrong 'un through and through.
A shoddy sort of failure,
  Eh? A Waster! Yes, I know.
A kind of social leper
  So I'm rotting in the snow.

I'm not asking for your pity,
  You can save your little prayers,
I'm a brand beyond redemption,
  In a land where no one cares.
I was shipped without a blessing,
  In a hurry, so to speak,
And the things I left behind me
  Were forgotten in a week;
For the gods that built me crooked,
  Had a sense of humour left,
And the devil made me callous
  Of the good I was bereft.

In the gambling dens of 'Frisco,
    In the drinking halls of sin,
I've a sort of social entree
    That will always pass me in.
Oh, they know me for a rotter,
    From the Yukon to the Clyde,
And many a friendly push I get,
    As down to Hell I slide.
Sometimes inside this cursed cold,
    That grips me to the heart,
I'll pass my checks like some foul rat
    That dies his kin apart
And ne'er a soul will understand,
    The depth of my despair,
And never one within this land,
    Will either grieve or care.

But on my black and wasted years,
    Across the world's disdain,
I know of ONE whose tears will fall,
    With grief for me in vain.
And there you see my punishment,
    The shame that I must bear,
The love I never can escape,
    A crown of thorns to wear,
A shoddy sort of failure, eh?
    A Waster! Yes, I know.
A kind of social leper,
    So I'm rotting in the snow.
I'm not asking for your pity,
    You can save your little prayers,
I'm a brand beyond redemption,
    In a land where no one cares.

An East End Saturday Night
By F. Raymond Coulson & Robert M. Angus (1914)

Saterday nite in Bethnal Green,
    Naptha lamps a-flarin'
Along the gutters for nearly a mile,
    And men and wimmen blarin'.
Men and wimmen with kippers and whelks,
    Taters, an' beans an' marrers,
Nearly a mile in Bethnal Green
    Nothin' but costers' barrers.
Saterday crowds in Bethnal Green
    Sunday dinners a-buyin',
Some without the money to buy,
    Lookin' an' longin' an' sighin'.
Kids wot 'aven't bin washed for years
    Moppin' up 'a 'penny ices,
Mothers o' famerlies gittin' their meat,
    An' batin the butcher's prices.
Pub's an' fried fish shops all full,
    Wives in blazin' rages,
'Usbands up to the same old game,
    Blewin' the whole week's wages.
Fat old wimmen o' sixteen stone,
    Simperin', drunk and leery,
Little gals leadin' their fathers 'ome,
    Staggerin', boozed and bleary.
Pickpockets, blokes on the kinchin' lay,
    Fellers and gals amashin',
Twig young 'Arry acrost the way
    Givin' his tart a thrashin'.
An' twig that pale little barefooted kid —
    Looks as ef she was dyin' —
Sobbin' as ef she'd break 'er 'art. —
    Wonder wot set her cryin'?

Foller that barefooted kid of eight
    Into a lonely turnin'.
Foller 'er up to a fust-floor back,
    Where a taller candle's burnin'.
Father's awaitin' there for 'er,
    An' don't 'e welcome 'er? — Rather!
That little kid's bin out ter beg
    For money — for drink — for father!
'Only tuppence? Wy, dash yer eyes,'
    (There's a look on 'is mug like killin'),
'I told yer not to show yer face
    Until you'd copp'd a shillin'.'
Father ups with 'is 'eavy fist,
    Swears as 'e'll smash and blind 'er.
An' out she dashes, that terrified kid,
    With that 'orrible face behind 'er.
Out she dashes, an' runs, an' runs,
    Pantin', with tears a-flowin',
Out throo the crowd in Bethnal Green —
    Too frightened to look where she's goin'.
There's a roar in 'er ears like the roar of the sea,
    There's a buzzin', an' whirlin', an' hummin', —
Ere's the larst bus comin' up Bethnal Green;
    But that kid don't see it comin'!
Yells, an' shrieks, an' a surgin' crowd,
    Larst bus stops in a hurry.
— 'Lift 'er on to the stretcher, Jim,
    Orl rite, mum, don't you worry;
A doctor won't be no good to 'er,
    Gord bless yer, she's gorn to clover!' —
Saterday nite in Bethnal Green, An' another kid run
    over.

The Man who stayed at Home

By F. Raymond Coulson & George Wells (1914)

Mister Brown, of Turnham Green,
   View'd all bikes with baleful glare,
He was never, never seen
   Scorching off to anywhere.
'Oft a fall upon the head
   Dislocates the vertebrae,
So I'll ride no bike,' he said.
   'Home's the safest place for me!'
Mister Brown of Turnham Green,
   Never motor'd out of town,
Flashing through the sylvan scene,
   Cutting laggard chickens down;
Never went to hunt the deer,
   Never after grouse would roam.
'No,' he cried, 'I'm safest here,
   So I'd rather stay at home.'
Mister Brown of Turnham Green,
   Never in the summer took
Tourist trips; he'd never been
   'On the Continong' with Cook.

'Fogs and rocks and tempests grim
   Menace ships that cross the foam,
And,' he cried, 'I cannot swim,
   So I'm better off at home!'
Mister Brown, of Turnham Green,
   Didn't care for sport at all;
Knew a fellow who had been
   Crippled by a cricket ball.
Knew a man who, catching trout,
   Caught a cold, and — R.I.P.
'Ah,' said Brown, 'beyond a doubt
   Home, sweet home's the place for me!'
So from home at Turnham Green
   Brown was never coax'd away;
Never in a train was seen,
   Off to spend a happy day.
Shunning risk in ev'ry shape,
   There he sipp'd his quiet cup.
But, alas! a gas escape
   One bright morning blew him up.

The Steam Roller Man's Story

By Harry J. Rowland & George Hay (1914)

(Spoken) The road in which I live is *up* as usual and we have a steam-roller endeavouring to put it *down*. Yesterday I chanced to pause for a moment to look at it. The gentleman in charge of the roller seized the opportunity for a few minutes rest and conversation. Carefully checking his iron steed in its wild career, he leisurely climbed down and addressed me thusly:—

'G' morning — 'blige with a match, sir?
   Thanks! Mind if I take a few more?
It's always a bit of a job, sir,
   To get this 'ere bacca to draw.
I can tell by the smell of your pipe, sir,
   As you knows the right sort to smoke.
Thank y', sir, — I should smoke this myself sir,
   If I wasn't so 'orrible broke.
Engineering jobs ain't what they was, sir,
   In the days — but I ain't goin' to brag,
When in front of me roller I'd always
   A man, sir, to carry a flag.
One day the task was entrusted
   To a flag-man, the name o' Jeff.

Careless bloke, sir, but 'ard working,
   And all right except 'e was deaf.
One day we wos working as usual,
   When I 'eard, sir, a sort of a grunt.
Then we jolted a bit and I looks, sir,
   But I couldn't see old Jeff in front.
Then I thought of his being deaf, sir,
   And I trembled just like a leaf,
For I guessed, sir, 'e'd been extra careless
   And somehow 'ad got under-neaf.
He lay in the road — I thought dead, sir,
   But 'e moved, — I was thankful for that.
But bless you, sir, I was a-staggered
   When I see as I'd rolled him out flat.
Yes, sir, flattened him out like a pan-cake,
   All thin like, you understand
As broad as a dozen like you sir,
   But only as thick as your hand.
At first, sir, 'e seemed a bit stunned like,
   And 'e laid in the road there and grinned,
So I helped him up, then started home, sir,
   Lor'! I did 'ave a job with the wind.

For the breeze kept a-catching him broad-side,
　And taking him up like a kite,
And I 'ad to 'old on like grim death, sir,
　To stop him from taking flight.
His family at 'ome they was knocked, sir,
　And you should 'ave 'eard his wife,
Said she'd sooner go 'ome to her mother
　Than live with a freak all her life.
But they took him, sir, into the parlour
　And propped 'im against the wall,
An' they wanted to put 'im to bed, sir,
　But they couldn't think how to at all.
Then I thought of folding him up, sir,
　I 'ad to think everything out,
And next morning we got a hot iron, sir,
　And ironed his creases out.
And we watched him get thinner for months, sir,
　As each evening around him we sat.
You see, sir, 'e lived on flat fish sir,
　And even his voice was flat.
Well, I worried myself wot to do, sir,
　But it wasn't no good to talk,

At last, sir, an idea it struck me
　And next day I takes Jeff for a walk.
And we walks down the road to the yard, sir,
　Where the roller had always stood,
And Jeff props himself up on his thin end, sir,
　And stays like it as well as 'e could.
We knew it was kill or cure, sir,
　So I shakes 'ands, sir, and says good-bye,
And as I climbed on to the engine
　I wiped, sir, a tear from my eye.
Then I starts her right over Jeff, sir,
　And the very next thing I see
Was the roller 'ad rolled out Jeff, sir,
　To the shape as 'e used to be.
Pleased? I should just think 'e wos, sir,
　Tho' some of our blokes was annoyed.
Jeff sir? 'E's carryin' a flag, sir.
　Along o' the unemployed.
He got the sack when they stopped our flags,
　But 'e's well as 'e's ever bin,
You can take my word that it's true, sir,
　The word, sir, of Truthful Jim.'

Answered
By Ella Wheeler Wilcox & George Hay (1914)

Good-bye — yes, I am going.
　Sudden? Well, you are right.
But a startling truth came home to me
　With sudden force last night
What is it? Shall I tell you? —
　Nay, that is why I go.
I am running away from the battlefield,
　Turning my back on the foe.
Riddles? You think me cruel!
　Have you not been most kind?
Why, when you question me like that,
　What answer can I find?
You fear you failed to amuse me,
　Your husband's friend and guest.
Whom he bade you entertain and please —
　Well, you have done your best,
Then why, you ask, am I going!
　A friend of mine abroad,

Whose theories I have been acting upon,
　Has proven himself a fraud.
You have heard me quote from Plato
　A thousand times, no doubt;
Well, I have discovered he did not know
　What he was talking about.
You think I am speaking strangely?
　You cannot understand?
Well, let me look down into your eyes,
　And let me take your hand.
I am running away from danger —
　I am flying before I fall;
I am going because with heart and soul
　I love you — That is all.
There, now, you are white with anger.
　I knew it would be so.
You should not question a man too close
　When he tells you he must go.

The Scrapper and the Nut
By F. Chatterton Hennequin & Phyllis Norman Parker (1915)
Performed by Nelson Jackson

By his Christian name the 'Scrapper,' you may very
　fairly guess

He was a most unholy terror and a bully more or
　less,

In the neighbourhood of Hoxton where he lived but
    did not work,
  Things that were clean and decent he much
    preferred to shirk.
But hidden in his brutal mind, *was* something that was
    good,
  For when his country needed him, he did as all men
    should;
And though he'd never learned to work, he tried his
    awkward best,
  Until the Sergeant counted him a soldier with the
    rest.
Now the 'Nut' in nowise differed from the others of his
    kind,
  For his socks and ties were perfect and his manners
    most refined,
His silk neckwear was immaculate, by dainty pins
    secured,
  His mother called him 'Cecil,' and his nails were
    manicured.
And underneath his wellbrushed hair, perhaps he
    owned a brain,
  Though he hated mental exercise, and thinking gave
    him pain.
He was fairly hot at tennis, and at most sports you
    could name,
  So when he too was needed, well, he had to play the
    game.
Now, call it chance or what you like, I hold it
    something more,
  These two enlisted side by side, and loathed each
    other sore,
For 'East is East and West is West', as Kipling truly
    says,
  And Hoxton and Belgravia are different in their
    ways.
So it happened in the canteen, Cecil's temper to annoy,
  The 'Scapper' called him 'Lizzie' and his 'mother's
    only joy,'

Then the 'Nut' put down his paper, as he languidly
    arose,
  And smote the astonished 'Scrapper' most severely
    on the nose.
The 'Scrapper', give him credit, could have killed him
    on the spot,
  And knowing what he might have done, he waited
    and did not.
For something woke inside him, as he scratched his
    puzzled head,
  And 'Love-a-duck, I'll take it back', was all the
    Scrapper said.
And from that time, these opposites have seldom
    disagreed,
  But try to help each other, in their ever present
    need.
For death close by their elbow, in the slaughter pen of
    strife,
  Has taught them both the meaning of the riddle we
    call 'life.'
Day after day they struggle, while the 'Scrapper'
    laughs at fate,
  And the 'Nut' is keen as mustard in his very muddy
    state,
And when each grim day's work is done, they lie down
    side by side,
  And not yet is the bullet cast, that can these two
    divide.
Oh Private 'East' and Private 'West,' may both come
    home again,
  But if you live or if you die, the debt will still
    remain,
For 'tis of you and such of you, in days beyond your
    ken,
  Our children's children will repeat; *you, both of you,
    were men!*

'Erbert, A.B.

By F. Chatterton Hennequin & Percy Watson (1915)

Now I ain't proud, I never 'old wiv lookin' down on
    folks
  'Ose education ain't first class like some more
    favoured blokes.
I pity's them for what they miss they wasn't brought up
    right
  To never 'ave no savvy fair nor mix wiv the Helite.

But one thing hiritates me and drives me horff my
    chump
  A chap wot drops 'is Haitches gives me the bloomin'
    'ump.
But once I had a shipmate not so very long ago,
  A finer man was never shipp'd from Portsmouth to
    the 'Oe,

'Is manner wiv the ladies was a thing to dream about,
  Tho' when it came to Haspirates 'e always left 'em
    out.
Once we was with two nice young girls, real 'igh class
    extra jam.
  When in the midst of supper 'e says ' 'Orace 'ave
    some 'am.'
On one occasion off Spithead a princess come on
    board,
  Wiv duchesses and h'admirals and 'is nibs the First
    Sea Lord.
She patted guns and looked at things as pleased as she
    could be,
  Till a gust of wind took hoff 'er 'at and blew it out to
    sea.
Then 'Erbert put 'is spoke in and 'e put the lid on fair,
  'E says, 'Never mind yer 'at miss, you just 'old on to
    yer 'air.'
But soon we 'ad our 'ands full with something different
    quite,
  When we caught the Deutchers napping and they 'ad
    to stand and fight.
We sank one blessed cruiser and the sea was black
    around,
  Wiv struggling 'uman creatures wiv the wounded
    and the drowned.
When we launched our boats and 'Erbert went to save
    them from their fate;
  'E says, 'Now then 'Orace 'urry, never mind their
    'ymn of 'ate.'
And then from their 'ead quarters some German
    h'airships came
  To drop their bombs on friend and foe — a dirty
    wicked game —

Poor 'Erbert's boat went under but we launched
    another quick
  And pulled away like demons, till I thought my back
    would rick.
And when we got quite close to them my word I give a
    yelp,
  For I knew that it was 'Erbert when some-one
    shouted ' 'Elp.'
'E'd saved a German 'ambone who was pretty nearly
    drown'd,
  And 'Erbert 'e was wounded as we very quickly
    found.
We got 'im to the sick bay but the doctor shook is 'ead,
  And I 'eard 'im say beneath 'is breath, 'It's a marvel 'e
    ain't dead.'
When the chaplain asks 'im gently, 'Is there 'ope?' 'E
    answers, 'None'
  Then 'Erbert gives a sort of smile and whispers,
    ' 'Ow's the 'Un?'
We said the 'Un was mending and 'e whispers, 'That's
    all right,'
  And so low we 'ardly 'eard 'im it was something like
    a fright,
'If I've killed a lot of 'umans, well I saved one life
    to-day
  Will they know it where I'm going sir, is it 'Ell or
    'Eaven, eh?'
Then the Chaplain says, 'It's 'Eaven man' and turned 'is
    'ead aside,
  But the Haitch he dropp'd on purpose went with
    'Erbert when 'e died.

Broom An' Co.

By Greatrex Newman & Fred Cecil (1915)
Performed by Bransby Williams

This meetin' of the partners in the firm of Broom
    an' Co.,
  Is 'eld because the cash in 'and 'as run exceedin'
    low, —
In fact the firm is stoney broke, they've neither crumb
    not crust,
  They've tried to raise the wind — but found they've
    only raised the dust.
Ten years ago a crossin' sweeper easy earned 'is keep,
  But now — wi' naught but motor cars — there's only
    smells to sweep.
Besides, it's no use me an' you a-breakin' of our 'earts,

We can't compete against them swagger Corporation
    carts.
The truth is mate, we're past it, — yes, we'll 'ave to
    shut up shop,
  We're growin' old, — why both of us is nearly bald
    on top.
When you was young an' trim an' smart, why then
    you'd almost brains, —
  You was a marvel then at fetchin' fag-ends out
    o' drains,
An' if a stray cigar stump should be chucked down by a
    gent,

You dashed off with your 'ead down like a blood
    'ound on the scent.
I'll bet you ain't forgot the day you found that shillin'?
    No — the share'olders got dividends that night
        from Broom an' Co.
Sometimes our luck 'as bin right in, an' sometimes —
    well, it ain't,
    But you've kep' always cheerful though — no
        grousin', nor complaint.
An' when at times I've 'ad the 'ump, an' felt fed-up or
    ill,
    You've seemed to kind o' smile at me, an' whisper
        'stick it Bill.'

For years you've swep' that crossin' — rain or sunshine
    — every day,
    You've never wanted over-time nor struck for 'igher
        pay;
While ev'ry *Sunday* mornin' you was always to be
    found,
    In a churchyard, gently sweepin', round a little
        raised up mound:
An' while you've quietly swept about, I've sent to
    'Eaven a prayer —
    That *we* might pass them Golden Gates — an' sweep
        a crossin' there.

The Answer of the Anzacs
By Lawrence Eastwood & Edgar Rooksby (1916)

There was once a mother Lion,
    And she stood on Dover cliffs,
Where the water wags and washes,
    Where the salt the Sea-Horse sniffs.
And she growled: 'The clouds look angry,
    They'll burst in storm today —
And all my cubs are distant,
    Twelve thousand miles away.'
And mother stood there all alone,
    And mother *meant* to stay,
Though all her cubs were distant,
    Twelve thousand miles away.
Then rose a mighty eagle,
    And it screeched at Dover cliffs,
Where the water wags and washes,
    Where the salt the Sea-Horse sniffs.
'I'll break you, mother lion,
    Though you're mighty proud today,
Don't count upon your cubs, my dear,
    Kids don't turn out that way.'

Still mother faced the storm alone,
    For *that* was mother's way.
But her cubs were calling to her —
    Twelve thousand miles away.
Then hove in sight a mighty fleet,
    That made for Dover cliffs —
Where the water wags and washes,
    Where the salt the Sea-Horse sniffs.
And from that mighty fleet there sprang
    The 'Anzacs' in array —
A hundred thousand cubs
    From twelve thousand miles away.
And mother locked them to her breast,
    Then thundered 'cross the bay —
'My cubs are all around me,
    They're by my side today;
You've blundered, master eagle,
    And your blunder's deep and vast;
For mother England's mighty cubs
    Will bring you down — *at last*!'

The Gardener's Story
By E. A. Searson & Herbert Townsend (1916)

A small lemon please, thank you kindly.
    Nothing in it? no thank you, not me.
I'm a tote, though I wasn't, not always.
    I used to drink frequent and free.
I don't say it boastful, that's silly,
    But I did use to do the job brown.
And when I at last gave up the tiddley,
    There was more than one pub that shut down.

My job? I'm a Gardener when working,
    I'm resting just now, so to speak,
But if the missus ain't better by Monday,
    Someone must do something next week.
I took a dislike to the Gardening
    Thro' a 'orrid experience I ad',
Which came as a shock to the system
    And was very near driving me mad.

I'd been taking my lotion too freely
  Yes, matters were getting quite warm.
And as I'd run thro' the whole of my ready,
  I made up my mind to reform.
So I drank what was left in the bottle
  And the gentleman's garden I seeks,
Where my odd job of digging and 'oeing
  'Ad been waiting for three or four weeks.
I'd been digging for several minutes,
  And was taking a rest for a term.
When casting my eyes on the ground sir
  I suddenly spotted a worm.
I've seen a few worms sir, while gardening
  And digging and 'oeing the beds
But this one it fair took the biscuit,
  And I'm blowed if it hadn't two 'eads.
If I catch that I thought it's a fortune
  'E'd fetch goodness knows what at a sale
So I let go the fork I was 'olding
  And made a quick grab at his tail.
As I grasped it, it seemed to grow bigger
  It was thick as my fore-arm I found.
Then before I 'ad time for much thinking
  The worm went 'eads first in the ground.
I clung like grim death to the reptile,
  With my fingers I took a firm 'old,
But its strength, it was simply enormous,
  It pulled me right down in the mould.
But I wouldn't let go, that's my spirit,
  I 'eld on for all I was worth
So we started to go down together
  Right into the bowels of the earth.
There were many more worms I kept seeing
  All colours, blue, yellow and pink.
Yes, talk about back to the land sir,
  It was all right for me, I don't think.
And the worst of it was that the climate
  As our way we continued to force

Got warmer and warmer and warmer
  As it naturally would do, of course.
We got lower and still it got 'otter
  In my fright I thought suddenly well,
By the temperature and the direction
  We're going to, there I couldn't tell
I'd 'ave given my 'and to get back sir,
  As I thought of my 'ome with a tear
I was almost releasing my 'old sir,
  When I struck on a brilliant idea.
For a saying I'd many times 'eard of,
  In my brain began sudden to burn
A true and a simple old proverb,
  If you tread on a worm it'll turn.
And at once I resolved I'd tread on 'im,
  And I prayed that my nerve mightn't fail,
It worn't easy to tread on 'im, gov'ner,
  And me 'anging on to 'is tail
Still I swung my feet over my shoulders,
  While I still kept a grip on 'is nibs,
And I poised my 'ob-nails for a moment
  Then dropped 'em bang on to 'is ribs.
And the trick worked as right as a trivet
  'E suddenly slackened 'is pace,
And to my great relief, the next minute
  Completely went right about face.
And 'e made for the surface like lightning
  Through the same path we'd made the descent,
And the sweat, it poured off me like rain, sir,
  At the terrible rate that we went.
I shrieked in my terror, I did, sir,
  Though of sense I was nearly bereft,
And I soon recognised the direction
  We made straight for the garden we'd left.
We burst thro' the old garden border
  Made a blooming great 'ole in the 'edge,
Smash'd the cucumber frame all to pieces,
  And the same evening I signed the pledge.

Conscientious Alf

By F. Chatterton Hennequin & Phyllis Norman Parker (1916)

He's a little pale-faced skinny cove that doesn't weigh
  ten stone,
  And he used to have a conscience, now his fist is full
  of bone.
He's got a punch like Jimmy Wilde and Billy Wells in
  one,
  You just say 'How's your conscience Alf?' and then
  you'll see some fun.
He used to preach against all wars, and violence and
  such,

Outside the pubs on Saturdays but no one listened
  much,
Till one fine day he fell in love, then war broke out on
  top,
  And his life was not worth living, for his girl says
  'Shut up shop!
You go and put on khaki quick and give your tongue a
  rest.'
  And Alf, whose mind was artful, says, 'Eliza, I'll
  attest!'

And so he did in Group sixteen, without a single
squeal,
  Then spat upon his two and nine, 'What ho! when I
  appeal!'
When Group sixteen was cited, oh! he went up like a
bird,
  And laid his case before them, such a case was never
  heard.
He told them how he loved them all, his heart was soft
and kind,
  Until the blessed chairman's eyes, with tears was
  nearly blind.
Mousetraps he says was sinful, flypapers made him
squirm,
  And he'd never fished for tiddlers, 'cause he couldn't
  hurt a worm.
The whole tribunal sat and sobbed, the sitting was
dissolved.
  And from Military service, Alf was then and there
  absolved.
So home he went to Liza, full of joy, but not for long,
  For he found her with a Naval chap, and going very
  strong!
Then Alf felt something go off Pop! He barked just
like a dog,

He fell upon that sailor bloke and downed him like
a log.
The air was full of hymns of hate, they made Eliza
cough,
  And six coppers and a fireman had to pull young
  Alfred off.
They strapped Jack on an ambulance, and as they bore
him past,
  I heard him say, 'God bless old Tirps, the fleet's
  come out at last!'
Then Alf's Eliza grabbed his ear, her face was one
broad grin,
  'Now where's that blessed conscience Alf? You've
  done the old thing in.
You join the London Scottish, say you're Mac, and
wear a kilt,
  And if you find your knees are cold, I'll lend you
  mother's quilt!'
So Alf goes back and tells 'em straight, 'I thought my
'eart was kind,
  But now it ain't, you sign me on! I've changed my
  blooming mind!'

Pincher D.C.M.

By F. Chatterton Hennequin & Cuthbert Clarke (1916)

The British soldier 'as 'is faults, 'e's 'uman like the rest,
  'E 'as the little weaknesses that's common to the best.
'E's 'asty in 'is language, but you wouldn't call 'im
mean,
  'E's fairly open-'anded and I think you'd say 'e's
  clean.
'E's respectful to the women folk, wherever 'e may
roam
  And 'e don't 'urt little children, 'e's too fond of 'em at
  'ome.
'E likes 'is bit of grousing, but 'e's straight and 'e can
shoot,
  And there's one thing you can bet on, 'e doesn't burn
  or loot.
Now of course there *is* exceptions, there's bound to be
you know,
  When you come to take an army of a million men or
  so.
I know one who's got a medal, and 'e well deserves it
too.
  Tho' 'is principles was rotten, but I leaves 'is case to
  you.
'E 'adn't got no shame at all, 'e ses, 'What o! the loot!

Bits and things dropped in a 'urry, we shall find
  when we're en route.'
So we tried 'ard to convince 'im and 'e 'ad three scraps
that night
  Because we named 'im 'Pincher' and it suited 'im all
  right.
When we got on active service, oh 'e 'ad a shocking
blow
  For the orders about looting was most plainly N.O.
  — no.
And 'e couldn't eat his 'bully' when he passed things on
the road
  For 'e got the 'ump with thinking of the things 'e
  might 'ave stowed.
But at Mons 'e turned quite cheerful, and I 'eard the
blighter say —
  'There's no 'arm now in looting, where the folks
  have gone away.
For you see it stands to reason all the things they leave
behind
  Will be collared by the Germans without asking Do
  you mind?'

But 'e didn't get much looting, we was moving night
    and day
  With 'ardly time to eat or sleep and fighting all the
    way.
Till one evening spent and weary, we 'ad a spell of
    rest.
  In a village called Le — something — and then
    Pincher did 'is best.
First 'e started on a chateau, just to see what 'e could
    find
  And 'e found most every blessed thing the owner'd
    left behind.
When 'e 'ad to leave the chandelier it nearly broke 'is
    'eart.
  And 'e'd a took the grand pianner if 'e'd 'ad an 'orse
    and cart!
You ought to 'ave seen 'im loaded with whatever 'e
    could bring,
  'E was full of clocks and vases all tied up with bits of
    string.
'E got a marble statue of a girl without her clothes,
  And a bust of Julius Caesar that 'e'd dropped and
    broke its nose.
There was spoons in ev'ry pocket all mixed up with
    bric-a-brac,

And half a dozen 'earthrugs, rolled up careful on 'is
    back.
When 'e come into the café, we was looting on our plan,
  I ses, 'Love a duck, it's Pickford been and lost 'is
    bloomin' van.'
We was just a-going to ask 'im where the dickens 'e 'ad
    been,
  When a coal-box 'it us sudden, and the roof came
    tumbling in.
All the bottles fell on Pincher, and it fairly made 'im
    squint
  When the lady with no clothes on 'ad a bath in cream
    de mint.
Then a bullet knocked me over, and I couldn't laugh
    no more,
  When 'e dropped 'is precious 'earthrugs just to lift
    me from the floor.
For tho' 'e knew 'e'd lose the lot, 'e stuck to me like
    glue
  An' when 'e got me in the lines, so 'elp me bob, it's
    true,
'E'd got three bullets in 'im, 'e could 'ardly stand or
    see,
  And the only loot left on 'im was 'is trousers, shirt
    and me!

A Little Guttersnipe
By Valentine & T. C. Sterndale-Bennett (1916)

It is quite a simple story of an ordinary type
  And the hero of it's only just a little gutter-snipe
There's not very much about it that's particularly new
  But he told it me exactly as I'm going to tell it to
    you.
I fancy it is quite a year or more since it took place
  But it's left behind a memory that nothing can efface.
And I know that he'll remember it when years have
    passed away
  How the Fresh Air Fund once took him to the
    country for a day.
'Blimey Guv'nor I remember it, it was a 'eavenly day
  We went down to Eppin' Forest in the country miles
    away.
The trees they was in 'undreds, my word they was a
    sight.
  All growin' thick like coppers dahn our street on
    Sunday night!
There was birds, they weren't in cages, they just flew
    about on wings
  And butterflies and bumblebees, sort o' coloured
    flies wot stings

There was little sheep wiv woolly coats a-'oppin' round
    and round
  Wot 'ad got no labels stuck on 'em at one and four a
    pound.
But the flowers 'swelp me, guv'nor, they fairly giv me
    fits
  The colours, why they beat me muvver's Sunday 'at
    to bits.
They let me pick 'em, decent o' the owner I must say
  But p'r'aps he knew I doesn't get an outin' ev'ry day.
Would I like to go down there again — why guvnor, if
    I could
  I'd sell papers for a solid week for nuffin' — that I
    would.
I'd promise to pick no flowers at all, for I eggspect
  If we did it sort o' regular the owner might object.
I'd even walk there all the way, I wouldn't want no
    train
  If I only thought them Fresh Air blokes would take
    me there again!'
One little shilling does it — and I think you'd be
    content

To hand it over gladly if you know just what it
    meant,
For if you could see the joy that it can make or it has
    made,
    Well I reckon you would think yourself a thousand
       times repaid.
It only means a drink or a cigar to you perhaps,

But it means a touch of Heaven to these little ragged
    chaps,
Just an hour or two of brightness in their misery and
    strife,
    Just a glimpse of God's own sunshine in some little
      East End life.

Cheerful Charlie

By F. Chatterton Hennequin & Phyllis Norman Parker (1916)

AUTHOR'S NOTE Mr. Hennequin acknowledges with
pleasure that the idea for this Monologue was
personally suggested to him by a fellow author
Mr. Bertram Burleigh who had already written and
published a story entitled 'The Pessimist.'

We called him Cheerful Charlie, a pessimistic chap,
    Who never saw no good in life, but only black
      mishap.
On sunny days he shook his head and said it smelt like
    rain,
    He'd eat and drink enough for two, then say it
      caused him pain.
He looked just like a funeral, the day that he was wed
    And whispered in his best man's ear, 'I might as well
      be dead.'
When war broke out he gave a sigh and said, 'They'll
    soon get here
    And we shall live on sauerkraut and dirty lager
      beer;
And if they fail, well what's the odds them Russians,
    mark my word,
    Will turn on us and scoop the lot, we can't win, it's
      absurd.
If I enlist it won't help things, I know that ALL IS
    LOST;
    Most likely we'll be submarined before we get
      acrost.'
But when we fell back, gave him his due, he didn't say
    a word,
    And all the time when things went wrong his voice
      was never heard.
He took his whack and did his bit and always helped a
    pal,
    And oftentimes he's closed their eyes as tender as a
      gal.
But when we got the upper hand and things were
    going strong

    I'm blest if he don't start afresh and say, 'It can't last
      long.'
He grumbled through three victories and cursed at 60
    Hill,
    Because he said he came away from home and never
      made no will.
He says, 'Each hour may be your last and mine too,
    don't forget it!'
    Then someone hit him with a spade and said, 'Lor
      Lumme! let it!'
We had to take some big Redoubt, we knew the day
    before,
    And Charlie says, 'It's suicide, the regiment is no
      more!'
But he was first inside their trench and laying
    Germans out,
    When in we tumbled after him, just as he got his
      clout.
They carried him to hospital and took away one arm;
    And pinned a medal on his breast to keep the beggar
      calm.
The Colonel says, 'Cheer up my man, we've got them
    fairly beat!'
    Then Charlie gives a mournful smile, and says, 'Ho
      yes! but where's the Fleet?'
So he's gone back home to Blighty but he's left a blank
    behind,
    For we took no stock of his poison gas when we knew
      his heart was kind.
But in his favorite little pub he turned the beer all sour
    With the dismal tales of 'orrors that he tells them by
      the hour.
The potman's gone and drowned himself, the
    barmaid's off her chump,
    And ever blessed soul he knows has got the
      blooming hump!

The 'Oxton 'Ero
By Rupert Hazell & Jan Hurst (1917)

'Ere, 'eard the latest? I'm a hero just because I strafed
    some Huns
    And they're goin' to D.C.M. me 'cause they say I
        saved some guns.
Yus and I'm a noble patriot so the Colonel says — it's
    right,
    Patriot — why I joined the Army cos I loves to have
        a fight.
'Ere it's a rummy sort of feeling, this 'ere 'ero business
    is,
    Why they treats me like a Baron and they fusses
        rahnd my Liz:
It's a funny world, now ain't it, I remember fightin'
    once
    Fifteen policemen down at 'Oxton an' all I got was
        eighteen months.
Yus and now I'm paid to fight like and I puts eight
    Germans out,
    Gets a bullet in me shoulder and me features
        knocked about.
Ladies comes into my ward and brings me fags and
    'ugs me wife,
    Asks me if I'll sign their albums. Oh! my uncle what
        a life.
Yus, an' as soon as I gets better, up they comes wiv
    motor-cars,
    Brings me sweets and brings me 'bacca, yus an'
        fifteen-inch cigars.
An' they spreads me out on cushions wiv a big fur rug
    on top,
    Me on cushions like a necklace in a Bond Street
        jew'ler's shop.

Why they fights to take me out to tea and dinner every
    day,
    So I 'as a little bit wiv each, it's easier that way.
And once when I gets back and couldn't eat nurse says,
    'You must!'
    And she tempted me wiv rabbit-pie — well I 'ad to
        'ide the crust.
But there's only one thing spoils it and upsets me 'appy
    life,
    Between ourselves — it's like this 'ere I've got a
        jealous wife.
There's a gal wot's allus 'angin rahnd, (of course I
    knows it's wrong)
    And Liz says when she says good-bye she 'olds me
        'and too long.
I think she's rather gorn on me, they calls her 'Lady
    Rose',
    'Cos just before she gets to me she powders up her
        nose.
But the missus needn't care about this little bit of fluff,
    I'll bet old Liz could give her points at makin'
        currant duff.
Well, I suppose I'd better get along, there's quite a big
    affair
    At arf-past five at our Tahn 'All I've got to meet the
        Mayor,
They're givin' me a watch and chain, and after that I
    goes
    To 'ave a bit of dinner (mum's the word) with Lady
        Rose.

Phil Blood's Leap
By Robert Buchanan & Cuthbert Clarke (1918)

We were seeking gold in the Texan hold, and we'd had
    a blaze of luck,
    More rich and rare the stuff ran there at every foot
        we struck;
Like men gone wild we t'ild and t'ild and never
    seemed to tire,
    The hot sun beamed and our faces streamed with the
        sweat of mad desire.
I was Captain then of the mining men, and I had a
    precious life,
    For a wilder set I never met at derringer and knife;

Nigh every day there was some new fray, a bullet in
    some one's brain,
    And the cussedest brute to stab and to shoot was an
        Imp of Sin from Maine:
Phil Blood, well, he was six foot three, with a squint to
    make you skeer'd,
    Sour as the drink in Bitter Chink, with carroty hair
        and beard.
With anything white he'd drink or he'd fight in fair or
    open fray,
    But to murder and kill was his wicked will,

If an Injun came his way.
We'd just struck our bit of luck, and were wild as
 raving men,
 When who should stray to our camp one day but
 Black Panther, the Cheyenne.
So I took the Panther into camp and the critter was
 well content,
And off with him, on the hunting tramp, ere long our
 hunters went.
 And I reckon that day and the next, we didn't want
 for food:
And only one in the camp look vext — that Imp of Sin
 — Phil Blood.
 Well, one fine day we a-resting lay at noontide by
 the creek,
The red sun blazed, and we felt half dazed, too tired to
 stir or speak.
 When, back just then came our hunting men, with
 the Panther at their head.
Full of his fun was everyone, and the Panther's eyes
 were red,
 And he skipped about with a grin and a shout, for
 he'd had a drop that day.
And he twisted and twirled, and squeal'd and shirl'd in
 the foolish Injun way.
 With an ugly glare, Phil Blood lay there, with only
 his knife in his belt,
And I saw his bloodshot eyeballs stare, and I knew how
 fierce he felt!
 When the Indian dances with grinning glances
 around Phil as he lies,
With his painted skin and his monkey grin — and leers
 into his eyes.
 And before I knew what I should do, Phil Blood was
 on his feet,
And the Injun could trace the hate in his face, and his
 heart began to beat.
 And 'Git out o' the way,' he heard them say, 'for he
 means to have your life.'
But before he could fly at the warning cry, he saw the
 flash of the knife.
 'Run Panther, run!' cried everyone, and the Panther
 turned his back,
With a wicked glare like a wounded hare,
 Phil Blood sprang on his track.
 Now the spot of ground where our luck was found
 was a queerish place, you'll mark,
Jest under the jags of the mountain crags and the
 precipices dark;
 Far up on high, close to the sky, the two crags leant
 together,
Leaving a gap, like an open trap, with a gleam of
 golden weather.
 If a man should pop in that trap on the top he'd
 never rest arm or leg

Till neck and crop to bottom he'd drop and smash on
 the stones like an egg!
 'Come back, you cuss! come back to us, and let the
 Injun be!'
I called aloud, while the men in a crowd stood gazing
 at them and me.
 But up they went, and my shots were spent, and at
 last they disappeared,
One minute more, and we gave a roar, for the Injun
 had leapt and cleared!
 For breath at the brink — but — a white man shrink,
 when a red had passed so neat?
I knew Phil Blood too well to think he'd turn his back
 dead beat!
 He takes one run, leaps up in the sun, and bounds
 from the slippery ledge,
And he clears the hole, but — God help his soul! —
 just touches the t'other edge!
 The edge he touches, then sinks, and clutches the
 rock — our eyes grow dim —
I turn away — what's that they say? — He's hanging on
 to the brim!
 And as soon as a man could run, I ran the way I'd
 seen them flee,
And I came mad-eyed to the chasm's side, and what do
 you think I see?
 I saw him glare, and dangle in air, for the empty
 hole he trod,
Help'd by a pair of hands up there — the Injun's, yes,
 by God!
 I held my breath so nigh to death, Phil Blood swung
 hand and limb,
And it seemed to us all that down he'd fall, with the
 Panther after him;
 But the Injun at length put out his strength and
 another minute past,
Then safe and sound to the solid ground he drew Phil
 Blood at last!
 What did Phil do? Well, I watched the two, and I
 saw Phil Blood turn back,
Bend over the brink and take a blink right down the
 chasm black,
 Then stooping low for a moment or so, having
 drawn his bowie bright,
He chucked it down the gulf with a frown, then
 whistled and slunk from sight.
 And after that day he changed his play, and kept a
 civiler tongue,
And whenever an Injun came that way, his contrary
 head he hung;
 But whenever he heard the lying word, 'It's a lie!'
 Phil Blood would groan;
'A snake is a snake make no mistake! But an Injun's
 flesh and bone!'

The Mercantile Marine
By Sam Walsh & Daisy McGeoch (1918)

I think perhaps 'tis possible that some of us forget
  In reckoning up the gratitude we owe
That there's another fighting fellow to whom we owe a
    debt,
  A gentleman that's not so much on show.
He's dressed in Navy Blue, and he wears a badge, 'tis
    true,
  But a gold lace decoration isn't seen.
But he'll go it 'hell for leather' in the dirtiest kind of
    weather,
  In the service of the Mercantile Marine!
His aim is sure and steady and his eye alert and keen,
  On the periscope that chases in his wake.
He'll thrash across the ocean past the skulking
    submarine,
  Through mine-strewn fields of terror, for our sake.

He's the goods train of the ocean, he's the Santa Claus
    of war,
  He's the arm on which we nationally lean.
He's the best part of a sportsman, of a soldier, of a tar,
  He's the Service of the Mercantile Marine.
So shout the songs of allies, the battle-hymn of France,
    America, Belgium and Japan.
Britain and her Colonies and all the other chaps —
  Heroes and sportsmen to a man.
And when the glory of the war and the history of its
    fame,
  Is written plain for all men to be seen.
Not the least who shall be honoured for upholding
    Britain's name,
  Is the Laddie of the Mercantile Marine.

What did you do in the Great War, Daddy?
By Greatrex Newman & Tom Clare (1919)
Performed by Tom Clare

Take my head on your shoulder, Daddy,
  Tell me the tale once more.
I've often asked you to tell me, Daddy,
  What you did in the Great, Great War.

What did you do in the Great War, Bertie?
  'I,' said the young man from the grocery store,
'Took no coupons from the woman next door
  Whose husband was on the tribunal.
All single girls got butter fresh and lumps of sugar
    large,
  The married ones, I gave them all a half an ounce of
    lard,
And that's what I did in the Great War, Daddy.'

What did you do in the Great War, Maria?
  'I,' said the maiden aunt with zeal,
'Tried to knit a pair of socks
  But couldn't turn the wheel,
So I changed it into a hearthrug.
  I knitted chest protectors and warm body belts
    galore
Embroidering them in coloured silks with roses round
    the door,
  And that's what I did in the Great War, Daddy.'

What did you do in the Great War, Frederick?
  'I,' said the special, 'from ten to four
Guarded the local reservoir
  And saw that no one drank it.
When small boys got impertinent, I soon pressed the
    stopper
  And frightened them by threatening to whistle for a
    copper,
And that's what I did in the Great War, Daddy.'

What did you do in the Great War, Muriel?
  'I,' said the land girl, 'rose at six,
I fed the cows and milked the chicks,
  I was a farmer's boy.
I said goodbye to crepe de chines and pretty low-
    necked blouses
  And wore an old, thick, flannel shirt and an ugly
    pair of — braces,
And that's what I did in the Great War, Daddy.'

What did you do in the Great War, Bill?
  'I,' said the man who made munitions
Paid real cash for those chips and fishions
  (Pass me the asparagus).

Me and my missus went in shops and bought each
    thing they sold us
  I changed me shirt each week and bought two pianos
    with the bonus,
And that's what I did in the Great War, Daddy.'

What did you do in the Great War, Jane?
  'I,' said the lady with voice pathetic,
'Sang songs without giving an anaesthetic,
  I sang to soldiers, I sang to wounded Tommies,
With their beds all in a row.

We do not want to lose you, but we think you ought
    to go,
And that's what I did in the Great War, Daddy.'

And all the profiteers,
  Who had been so long in clover
Fell a-sighing and a-sobbing
  When they heard the war was over.
For they'd all made their bit
  In the Great War, Daddy.

Afterwards
By Leonard Pounds & Cuthbert Clarke (1919)

Now the God of War has ceased to rule,
  And I'm back at my desk again.
The saddle gives place to a well-worn stool,
  And the rifle makes way for the pen.
The tick of the clock on the office wall
  Displaces the big guns' roar,
The 'phone-bell has ousted the trumpet-call,
  A soldier am I no more.
The past few years now appear a dream;
  An illusion vast and grand,
The maxims' rattle and shrapnel's scream
  Just echoes of Slumberland.
As I lie abed in the early morn
  I wake from sleep profound,
As without on the wind, most clearly borne,
  I imagine I hear this sound:—
Even that call, which I used to hate
  The command to get out of bed
Inspires regret, and a yearning great
  For the life that is past and dead.
I turn with a sigh to resume my sleep,
  But as soon as I doze once more,
My heart gives a throb, and from bed I leap
  At the sound of this call of yore:
'All you who are able, come off to the stable,
  And water your horses and give them some corn.'
I return to bed for an hour or so,
  And at eight I rise at last,
Then again, as I down to breakfast go,
  Comes that phantom trumpet blast:—
'Come to the cook-house door, boys, come to the cook-
    house door.'

When I reach the office so grim and bare,
  And a start at work have made,
  I long to 'slope arms' with a ruler there,
And the paste-pot's a hand grenade.
  Inside the ledger I next will look,
But no figures I seem to see,
  The only entry inside the book
Reads 'Kit inspection at 3.'
  And the almanac, I do declare,
Reveals itself to me
  As a charge-sheet shewing just why I'm there
'Awarded life-long C.B.'
  As the charwoman passes the manager's lair,
With a slov'nly gait,
  I'm impelled to shout 'March to attention there!'
Or 'Keep that back up straight!'
  I collect my thoughts with a weary smile,
And endeavour to settle down
  To examining bills on a rusty file,
And I conjure a 'business' frown.
  Here, 'mid the City traffic's row,
How I miss my dear old 'gee'!
  I wonder who grooms and rides him now —
Does he wonder what's happened to me?
  My body is here, but my soul's afar;
It exists in the stormy past.
  The faces of comrades remain with me
And will do until the last.
  When discharge from the Army of Life comes round
And Death stands guard at the door,
  I shall hear 'Lights out' distinctly sound,
As it did in the world-wide war.

The Duet
By Ella Wheeler Wilcox & George Hay (1920)

I was smoking a cigarette; Maud, my wife, and the
    tenor McKey

Were singing together a blithe duet.

And days it were better I should forget came suddenly
    back to me.
    Days when life seemed a gay masque ball,
And to love and be loved as the sum of it all.
    As they sang together the whole scene fled,
The room's rich hangings, the sweet home air,
    Stately Maud, with her proud blonde head,
And I seemed to see in her place instead
    A wealth of blue-black hair,
And a face, ah! your face — yours, Lisette,
    A face it were wiser I should forget.
We were back — well, no matter when or where,
    But you remember, I know, Lisette,
I saw you, dainty and debonair,
    With the very same look that you used to wear
In the days I should forget.
    And your lips, as red as the vintage we quaffed,
Were pearl-edged bumpers of wine when you laughed.
    Two small slippers with big rosettes
Peeped out under your kilt-skirt there,

While we sat smoking our cigarettes.
(Oh, I shall be dust when my heart forgets!).
    And singing that self-same air;
And between the verses for interlude
    I kissed your throat, and your shoulders nude.
You were so full of a subtle fire,
    You were so warm and so sweet, Lisette;
You were everything men admire,
    And there were no fetters to make us tire;
For you were — a pretty grisette.
    But you loved, as only such natures can,
With a love that makes heaven or hell for a man.
    They have ceased singing that old duet,
Stately Maud and the tenor McKey.
    'You are burning your coat with your cigarette,
And *qu'avez vous*, dearest, your lids are wet,'
    Maud says, as she leans o'er me.
And I smile, and lie to her, husband-wise,
    'Oh, it is nothing but smoke in my eyes.'

The Cabman's Railway Yarn
By E. A. Searson & Herbert Townsend (1920)

Here, keb, sir, d'you want a four-wheeler?
    You don't? No, exactly of course,
No one does, they never want me sir,
    And they don't want the keb or the 'orse.
Take you down the Strand for a bob sir?
    Patronise the old firm Billy Webb,
Here make it half a thick 'un guv'nor!
    And I'll give you the 'orse and the keb.
Nothing doing? Orl right keep your 'air on,
    Yer needn't get ratty and shout,
Don't slang an unfortunate bounder
    Who's down, and who's very near out.
Time was when I wasn't a cabby.
    I was once on the railway, a fact,
And I might have been general manager,
    If it hadn't have been I got sacked.
It was back in the time of the strike sir,
    My line was 'it 'ard sir, you see,
And men were so scarce in those times sir,
    Why, they even thought something of me.
And day after day they got shorter
    And shorter of workers, and so
They bunged me on the train sir, one evening,
    To take her to Bexhill you know.
Well, it wasn't for me to make trouble,
    Though it didn't seem right I must say,
I'd never before *been* to Bexhill,
    And I 'ad no idea of the way.

Still I got a shove-off at eight-thirty,
    And things for a time went on fine,
Till they pulled me up sudden at Willesden,
    And said I was on the wrong line.
So I was, it was no good to argue,
    But it wasn't my fault you'll admit,
Still I went back and looked for my line, sir,
    And discovered it after a bit.
To a porter I says, 'I want Bexhill!
    Which way do I take this 'ere train?'
He says, 'Straight on until you reach Clapham,
    Then if you're in doubt ask again.'
I cheered up and pushed on a bit further,
    But I somehow seemed all of a maze,
For in front I could see the lines parted
    And branched off in different ways.
My stoker, Bill Jones, hollers quickly,
    'The left hand for Clapham, hold tight!'
But I knew what a liar Bill Jones was,
    So I pulled her head round to the right.
Bill 'ad spoke the truth for a wonder,
    As I found out before very long,
For an hour after, when I reached Ilford,
    I knew very well something was wrong.
It's a mystery to me how I got there,
    But the night was as dark as could be,
And you couldn't 'ave blamed any driver,
    Let alone a poor novice like me.

Well we turned round the train and went back, sir,
  The Inspector he showed us a light,
He said, 'Straight on until you reach Stratford,
  And then bear a bit to the right.
Keep off the down line if you can mate,
  I'm telling you plainly, because
I hope with good luck by twelve thirty,
  You'll get back to wherever you was.'
Well I carefully followed directions,
  Got through London without any slip
And glad enough too, for the passengers
  By now were beginning to chip.
I felt a bit doubtful at Barnet,
  But I ran through the station quite fast,
And I felt very proud two hours after,
  When I saw Clapham Junction at last.
Then I give 'er 'er 'ead, and we moved some,
  Bill stoked up the furnace with care,

And I said, 'If we keep on the metals
  By seven we ought to be there.'
And the men in each signal box shouted,
  And waved some red flags at us too,
I 'ollers back, 'Are we down-hearted?'
  And Bill 'e calls out, 'Toodle oo!'
At last there looms out a big station,
  And lights on the water I saw,
I says, 'Bill, I believe we 'ave got there,'
  But Bill only murmurs, 'O lor!'
We ran to the end of the station,
  Where the book-stall man's busy at work;
We came up with a bump on the buffers,
  Which brought the train up with a jerk.
You'd have thought there'd been a mishap, sir,
  The passengers swarmed out in a group,
Was it Bexhill? No, matey, Victoria!
  We'd been bloomin' well looping the loop.

Thrilling Stories
By Reuben More & Herbert Townsend (1920)

I'll relate some thrilling stories,
  Told down at the Old Ship Inn,
By a sea-dog who has travelled,
  By the name of Mack'rel Jim.
'Once,' said he, 'on board the Eggshell,
  We were wrecked off Monkey Brand,
Sinking fast, but from the funnel,
  I jump'd ten miles on to land.
Then I heard the shouts of "Save me, save, oh save me
    from the wreck."
  Let those women perish, never!
Back I jump'd upon the deck.
  One by one I safely fired them from our cannon to
    the shore,
Crowds were cheering, but I told them that there
    would be no encore.
  People gave me watches, money, with excitement
    most intense,
Talk of wealth, well altogether, two bob short of
    eighteen pence.'
  Landlord, just fill up Jim's tankard, (this you'll
    nightly overhear)
'Want another yarn?' says Jimmy, 'Right you are,' then
    drinks his beer.
  'Once upon a desert island, I was stationed for a
    time,
Stationed, — tho' there was no station, —
  Picking chloride out of lime.
Animals, you ask? Well rather, snakes of all kinds in
    your bed,

Tigers there with double bodies, — some with only
    just a head.
One dark night (it made me shudder) came a most
    unearthly growl.
  Looking up I saw a lion, out upon its nightly prowl.
Then it sprang and soon devoured me, —
  But my senses did not roam,
With a knife I ripped it open —
  Had it stuffed and brought it home.
Hand my mug Bill; here's good health boys — 'nother?
    thanks, I'll try a beer.
  How's the clock? It wants five minutes — time for
    one more yarn to hear.
I shall ne'er forget the night boys, up at Jarrow on the
    Tyne.
  From the railway station platform — fell a woman
    on the line.
On the track I in a moment sprang as people
    shrieked with fright,
  Round the bend the Scotch Express was dashing
    madly into sight.
Quickly then I knelt beside her, — to the metals
    holding fast,
  The train it rattled o'er my body, — like a
    switchback thundering past.
The girl was saved, — but that reminds me, once I
    heard the cry of 'Fire,'
  A New York building 'sixty stories' — flames were
    leaping 'liar' — higher —

A child up at the attic window, — cried for help, each
   heart stood still.
   Fiendish flames in all directions, — who will risk
      their life? — "I will."
Through the blinding smoke I mounted, — upward
   with determined face —
   Seized the child, then from the window — sprang
      midst yells into space,
At blinding speed we dashed to earth, ten miles a
   second I suppose,

The awful rate gave me a chill, I stopped midway to
   blow my nose.
Then the child screamed out — 'where's mamma? left
   behind to burn — to die!'
   'No,' said I, 'She shall not perish! — I'll return my
      child, don't cry.'
Back I went and left the infant — floating on the fiery
   breeze —
   Saved the mother, — bet your life — what?' 'Come
      along now — Time, gents, please!'

My Love Affairs

By Greatrex Newman & Wolseley Charles (1921)
Performed by Bransby Williams

Through falling in love I've had lots of surprises
   I've flirted with girls of all sorts, shapes and sizes;
My first love affair was a bad one I'm told,
   I think at the time I was eighteen *months* old —
And *she* was the baby next door, such a pet,
   We went out each day in the same bassinette —
Till one Sunday morning when down in the park,
   She sucked all the paint off my new Noah's Ark, —
So then, very coldly, I bade her adieu,
   And took back my presents, — and some of hers too.
The years rolled along, but I stayed fancy free,
   Until I met Rose, it was down by the sea, —
Her beauty ensnared me, and swift as a flash,
   I formed for that maiden a wonderful 'pash'.
I think I was just over eight, or p'raps nine,
   And scorning all warning of women and wine
I spent all my savings, while she led me on,
   Until all my fourpence was squandered and gone:—
Then quickly she left me, that false, fickle jade,
   And stole both my heart and my bucket and spade.
The next one concerned was a damsel named Kate,
   At last, now I thought, I have met my true mate,
'Twas no boy and girl sort of friendship I mean,
   For when I met Kate I was nearly — *thirteen*.
The course of true love though can never run smooth,
   Her mother soon showed that *she* did not approve.
And though Kate had sworn that to me she would
   cling,

Well — *back came my solid gold nine-penny ring!*
Next Daisy enslaved me, that girl I adored —
   Until my affections were captured by Maud,
And Maud had two sisters, named Elsie and Claire,
   I couldn't choose which — so I courted the pair;
All these, and lots more, I attempted to win,
   Both tall ones, and short ones, and thick ones and
      thin —
I worshipped them all and would gladly have wed,
   But each chose some *other* young bounder instead.
I went to their weddings, then screwed up my pluck,
   And sent just a clock or a cruet, for luck.
Ah well, such is life, and left out in the cold,
   I soon settled down as a bachelor bold. —
Till one day *she* came, and in blissful content
   I then started learning what love really meant. —
We planned for our wedding, how happy those hours,
   The birds gaily sang to the trees and the flowers,
The breeze whispered joy, but that never came,
   I found I'd a rival, and he made a claim.
The days turned to night, and made Winter of Spring,
   The flowers drooped their heads, and the birds
      ceased to sing —
The breeze said 'good-bye' with its tenderest breath —
   My rival had won, and his name — it was — Death.

Our Grandparents' Yarns

By Leonard Pounds & Cuthbert Clarke (1921)
Performed by Dorothy Varick

Now our grandparents sit in their easy chairs,
   With wrinkled-up brows 'neath their silver hairs

Comparing our latter-day ways with theirs
   And shaking their heads the while.

Their assertions will all of them go to show
  How pure were the people of long ago.
    That mankind then knew no guile.
The yarns that our grandparents spin!
  In their day it seems the world was free of sin!
Boys all loved to go to school,
  Where they never broke a rule,
    Or inserted in the master's chair a pin!
It appears that all young men,
  Never stayed out after ten,
    And no maiden bared her shoulders at the play!
They possessed no vice or taints —
  Just a crowd of earthly saints
Were the folks of our grandparents' day!
  Hear our grannies avow, with a wry grimace,
That slang on their tongues never found a place,
  And never a maid would her lips disgrace
By cigarette held between.
  In quarrels all men a soft answer chose,
Instead of proceeding by violent blows,
  To alter the contour of someone's nose,
To vent a revengeful spleen!
  The yarns that our grandparents spin!
In their day it seems the world was free of sin!
  Ev'ry lawyer just would be,
And would ne'er accept a fee

If a client's case perchance he failed to win!
Calves and ankles were not shown;
  Tittle-tattle wasn't known;
And from church umbrellas never went astray.
  This conclusion we derive —
All too good to be alive
  Were the folks of our grandparents' day.
Our credulity strains at its leashes tight
  When we gather that cabmen were all polite;
That every post office pen would write:
  And that little boys all said 'please'.
To his elders each junior raised his hat,
  No person played billiards, or games like that!
One doubts if a dog ever chased a cat,
  Or a mouse ever stole the cheese!
The yarns that our grandparents spin!
  In their day it seems the world was free of sin!
They will laud up to the sky
  Deeds performed in days gone by,
But decry our own with supercilious grin.
  Though we smile at tales like these.
We grow older, by degrees,
  And grandparents *we* may be some future day:
And when we're toothless, bent, and lame,
  We shall say the very same
Things as all of our grandparents say.

When You Figger It Out!
By R. R. Pecorini & F. Harper Shove (1921)

I do 'ave a time when you figger it out,
  A-pushin' dead leaves and a-muckin' about
In the gutters and streets. Yus there isn't much doubt,
  I do 'ave a time when you figger it out.
I remember the days long ago when in luck,
  There wasn't much need to be pushin' o' muck,
I didn't wear fusty old corduroy breeks,
  An' I'd got some good colour in these poor old
    cheeks.
I was straight, I was tall, an' I 'adn't a care,
  An' I took such a pride in the clothes that I'd wear.
Eh! many's the time why I'd shave ev'ry day,
  And grease me old forelock the fash'nable way.
I'd put on swell duds, an' set out for the park,
  A-bent on a-sparkin' by way of a lark.
I was *'IT'* I can tell you! Gals loved me some-how:
  But lumme! who loves sich a poor old cuss now?
I married. Why, blow me! I'd nearly forgot,
  It seems as 'twere back somewhere round the year dot.
She's gone now. God bless her, she left me a boy.
  A cute little beggar, a bundle of joy.

He loved his old dad, too. Ah! bless him! 'Tis true: —
  You knows 'ow *your* boy thinks the world about you!
But he's gone too — My 'Arry, a-missin' they said,
  Then about a year after, 'Reported as dead.'
Aye! he died, did my boy, an' he couldn't be found
  Tho' his mates, so they told me, searched all around
On the field where 'e fell when they made the attack.
  But one day they found 'im and carried 'im back.
Yus! He's up at the Abbey, and the great folk they say,
  Kneel and mourn for my 'ero while I work my way
Through the muck and the litter! They call 'im
  'Unknown,'
  But God let *me* know him — My 'Arry! My own!
I made my way up there a-dressed in my best,
  Just to see where my boy's been a-laid out to rest,
An' it seems kind of helpin' me on with my job,
  Abrushin' an' pushin' to earn a few bob.
I do 'ave a time when you figger it out
  A-pushin' dead leaves and a-muckin' about
In the gutters and streets. Yus there isn't much doubt,
  I've 'ad a time when you figger it out.

Girls! (according to a 14-year-old boy)
By Dorothy Turner & Ernest Longstaffe (1922)
Performed by Dorothy Varick

Ugh! Don't ask *me* what I think about girls —
  I'm fed up with the whole blinkin' crowd.
Sisters and cousins and aunts and such things
  Ought never have been allowed.
I've got some of each, an' I give you my word
  There's not one in the whole blinkin' lot
That can talk to a chap for a minute on end
  Without spoutin' some silly rot.
The niff of face powder all over the house,
  Is enough to turn anyone sick.
But when they expect me to kiss 'em Good-night
  I guess it's a trifle too thick.
An' look at the rum sort of clothes that they wear —
  All neenong, and gores, and that stuff
Called crepe-de-thingummy, that falls into bits
  If you handle 'em just a bit rough.
I'm hustled and ordered from pillar to post
  I can't call my soul my own,
It's 'Freddie do this' or the other old thing —
  Wish they'd jolly well leave me alone,
But if ever I'm wanting a button sewn on
  Or the school badge put on me straw hat,
They've gone to a cooking or ambulance class
  Or some new fangled piffle like that.
They'll yell like the deuce at a beetle or mouse
  And to see a dead cat makes 'em faint,
But it licks me completely the nerve that they've got

To make a chap feel what he ain't.
Why they'll talk to a fellow who's won the V.C.
  As if he'd done nothing at all,
And a chap who can run up his century, sure,
  Must answer to *their* beck and call.
And crumbs — as for honour, they haven't a spark,
  For if ever I do nick a fag,
Or get in the pantry to sample the tuck,
  It's odds on that someone'll lag.
The conceit of them, too — why they reckon sure
   thing,
  They'll be marrying heroes and earls
But it ain't much good grousing about 'em I s'pose
  They couldn't help being born girls.
There's only one blessing as far as I know
  For a chap who's got sisters like me,
When ever some Johnny comes foolin' around
  And wants to spoon on the Q.T.
He'll tip me a bob to keep out of the way,
  Ugh, as if I should bother my head
To look through a keyhole, I'm only too glad
  To be off to the pictures instead.
I must keep me eyes open, if they spot me here now
  They're sure to start making a song
'Bout being untidy, or washing me neck,
  So I think p'r'aps I'll hop it — so long!

Jimmy Johnson
By H. M. Burnaby (1922)

He was Mr. Jimmy Johnson, and he earned a weekly
  wage,
  And his life was eventful as a squirrel's in a cage.
He was only one of many, who've forgotten how to
  feel,.
  He was something in the City, and he helped to turn
  a wheel.
He possessed a wife and kiddies, living somewhere
  Brixton way,
  And he drew his humble pittance, weekly, every
  Saturday,
And the bit of grub on Sundays that it managed to
  contrive,
  Provided the incentive to go on — to keep alive.
And that was why he added rows of figures nice and
  neat,

He was Mr. Jimmy Johnson — life was sweet.
Then somewhere a bugle sounded, and he kissed his
  pen good-bye.
  His stool he kicked from under him — no time to
  wonder why,
He embraced his wife and kiddies, and he told 'em not
  to pine,
  He was Private Jimmy Johnson, number 12129.
He liked it when they asked him if he minded forming
  fours,
  He presented arms 'by numbers' to the sergeant's
  loud applause.
He bought a little toothbrush — and a tin of 'Soldiers
  friend',
  They said with luck he might become a soldier in
  the end.

He didn't quite appreciate the stuff he'd got to eat,
  But he was Private Johnson — life was Sweet.
Then Jimmy Johnson found himself up in the firing
  line,
  Where he learned the art of warfare — number
  12129.
The sergeant came and told him they were going to
  attack,
  Then he got that sinking feeling, but he bravely kept
  it back.
They reinforced his courage with the regulation rum,
  And he trusted to the Fates, to steer him clear of
  'Kingdom Come.'
Stranger figures loomed about him, minds with but
  one single thought,
  So he dealt with the obstruction, in the way that he'd
  been taught.
'Twas in self-defence he did it — quite an ordinary
  feat,

But he was Private Johnson — life was Sweet.
He is Mr. Jimmy Johnson, and he's got an empty
  sleeve,
  And he's smiling very bravely — while he's trying to
  believe
He was something in the Army, now he's broken on
  the wheel,
  Once again he's one of many who've forgotten how
  to feel,
Forgotten by the stay-at-homes — who not so long ago,
  Said they didn't want to lose him, but they thought
  he ought to go.
And he's holding on tenaciously, and hoping p'raps
  some day,
  He will find the silver lining, when the clouds have
  rolled away.
You can see them all around you, some sell matches in
  the street,
  There are many Jimmy Johnsons — *is* life sweet?

Supplanted

By Iris Potter & Cuthbert Clarke (1923)

We've got a nasty ickle baby come to live with us,
  I fink it really isn't fair the way they make a fuss
About a fing what's got no sense and hardly any hair,
  And isn't half so pretty as my ickle Teddy Bear.
What is the use of baby? Well! I really cannot see,
  But mummie finks it's awful nice and loves it
  better'n me.
I've been so very lonely since that nasty baby came,
  I'm sure that fings will never, never, never be the
  same.
Why! When it cries they always run to cuddle it and
  see
  If anyfink's the matter, or perhaps it wants its tea!
They spoil it somefink awful and don't care 'bout me at
  all,
  I'd like to frow dat baby right across our garden
  wall.

The uvver day I stuck a pin in baby's arm to see
  If sawdust twickled out of it, but baby squealed at
  me!
It never lets me play with it just like my dollies do,
  And when it sleeps I have to be so quiet and sleeping
  too!
I mustn't shout or make a noise, or play upon the stair,
  I'd like to punch that baby — if I only dare!
My nursie says that baby's put my nose all out of joint!
  It doesn't feel no different, though it's wobbly at the
  point,
But den my nose was always small and rather hard to
  blow,
  I cannot see what baby's done until it starts to grow.
And if it grows all crooked I'll just tell you what I'll do
  I'll pray to God for baby's nose to grow all crooked
  too!

Sally's Ups and Downs

By Charles J. Winter (1923)

I met a dear old friend of mine today,
  A chap I hadn't run across for ages:
Of course we talked about the good old times
  And all that had occurred at different stages.

I asked about his mother and his dad,
  And all his friends with whom I had been pally,
And then I said, 'one thing I'd like to know
  If you can tell what's happened to dear old Sally?'

He laughed, then shrugged his shoulders, then he
  sighed
  And said, 'I'm sure I don't remember quite all,
She's had so many curious ups and downs,
  But still, I'll try to give a full recital.
Well, first you must know that her old uncle died,
  He was fond of her, that you can tell,
For he left her a good sum of cash at the bank,
  And he left her the business as well.'
Said I, 'Well that was a good thing!'
  'Oh not *very* good, for the business went wrong,
Till of all her wealth she was bereft;
  And when she'd paid up and got everything square,
She just had *one* sovereign left.'
  'Oh dear,' said I, 'that was too bad.'
'Oh not *very* bad, for this sovereign I'm told,
  She'd invested with great enterprise
In a lottery ticket, and heard later on
  That this ticket had won first prize.'
Said I, 'What a slice of good luck!'
  'No, it wasn't a slice of *good luck*,' said my friend,
'It turned out an unfortunate job;
  For being hard up, this same ticket she'd sold
Just a few days before — *for five bob.*'
  'Well,' said I, 'that was bad luck indeed.'
'Well not *quite* so bad, for the man who had won —
  Out of sympathy, so it was said —
Came to see her, got chummy, and then fell in love,

And after a time they got wed.'
'Come,' said I, 'that was good after all.'
  'Well not quite *so good* for this fellow it seems
Led a terrible dissolute life.
  He spent all the money, then started to drink,
And came home and browbeat his wife.'
  Said I, 'Well that was rotten luck!'
'Oh not *quite* so bad for he died in a month,
  And although all his cash he'd got through
He wasn't quite broke, for he left her the house,
  All crammed with old furniture too.'
'Come, come, that was not bad,' said I.
  'Oh well it *was* bad in the end,' said my pal,
With a curious kind of grin,
  'For a thunderstorm came and the house it got
    struck,
And the whole of the roof fell right in.'
  'Great Scott,' said I, 'that was bad luck.'
'Oh not *very* bad, for an old chest got smashed,
  And lay all in bits on the ground.
And there in a secret drawer open to view
  Were bank-notes quite ten thousand pound.'
Said I, 'Well her luck turned at last!'
  'I'm not sure' said he, 'but she banked all the cash,
For somehow she felt that she must.
  And I'm wondering what's going to be the next
    move,
For I've just heard that the bank has gone *bust.*'

Lizette, Queen of the Apaches
By Percy Edgar, Leslie Paget & Cyril Carlton (1924)

Oft as I sit alone at night and gaze in the embers' glow,
  A wistful face comes back to me from out of the long
    ago.
Lizette, Queen of the Apaches!
  'Twas over in Paris first we met in those Quartier
    Latin days,
Ah, those happy days of struggle and fun,
  It was jolly companions every one.
Even now there's a mist before my gaze,
  When I think of those dear old student days;
She crept to my door a tragic mite,
  One eve when the snow lay deep and white,
She seemed all big eyes and golden head,
  'Some bread to eat,' was what she said.
My first impulse was to ring my bell
  For the police, but I loved them none too well.
Then those pleading eyes brought me 'neath their
    sway,
  And she crept in my home and my heart to stay.

They were happy years we together knew,
  Till unnoticed, the child to a woman grew.
She was mixture of mother, sister, child,
  With a touch of the tigress too when wild.
And a love that I was too blind to see,
  Yet it had its beginning and its end in me.
To me she was comrade, nothing more,
  The woman in her I hardly saw
Till a blackguard sneer struck the jarring note
  And I choked back the lie in the coward throat.
Too late! A curse on that hated word,
  For I knew next morning she'd overheard.
She left me a note but all it said was,
  'Adieu mon ami.' Lizette had fled.
Three years passed on and I found myself
  With a dare-devil English chum,
We were seeing life in the underworld,
  In a low Parisian slum.
'Twas a spice of danger tempted us,

For grim death was always nigh,
And for strangers who sought Apacheland
  Discovery meant to *die*.
'Twas a Cabaret called 'The Café of Death.'
  Well named if there's ever one been.
By some she-desperado kept, we'd heard.
  Tho' the Apaches, they called her *Queen*.
Danté himself could scarce describe
  The frequenters of that place.
Every nameless crime of the human kind
  Was stamped on each vicious face,
The room was hot, or the wine was drugged,
  For Heaven alone knows why —
  Suddenly Hell itself broke loose —
And they pointed at me whilst '*Spy!*
  Spy!' burst from every throat!
Standing back to back were we.
  It was death to us both remaining there
And death to us both to flee.
  Came a sudden stir in the ring of knives

And a woman reached my side,
  In the gruff *patois* of Apacheland.
'*Stand back you dogs,*' she cried!
  She was supple and lithe as a panther,
I saw two bright eyes gleam
  Through the mask she wore, and that silver voice,
Was I mad, or in a dream?
  '*Stand back, Canaille, your Queen commands!*'
See! At me a knife-thrust sped,
  But a woman throws herself between,
And she caught the blow instead!
  The police break in, of course too late,
Mad with grief I hold her head,
  '*Bon soir, mon ami, you know me, yes?*'
Then a sigh — and *Lizette was dead!*
La Reine des Apaches, La Reine des Apaches
Save a wealth of love to myself bequeathed,
  With sin and crime is her memory wreathed,
But a woman, if ever a woman breathed —
  Was Lizette, La Reine des Apaches.

Aren't Men Funny?

By Dion Lane & Hilda Bertram (1924)

When I was quite a little girl my mother used to say:—
  'Aren't men funny?'
Now I'm grown up I say the same thing twenty times a
    day,
  'Aren't men funny?'
They're as full of contradictions as an egg is full of
    meat.
  They're shy, they're hot, they're cold, they're sour
    and yet they're sweet;
They're one big great conundrum; and so I'll just
    repeat
  'Aren't men funny?'
They'll gaze into their sweetheart's eyes (not knowing
    love is blind)
  Aren't men funny?
And use up all the words of love in 'Nuttall's' they can
    find,
  Aren't men funny?
They'll kiss her sixteen times an hour; her lips, her
    eyes, her cheek,
  But, when they're wed, she, feeling 'down,' one little
    kiss would seek,
He'll say, 'But dear old girl, you know, I kissed you
    twice last week'.
  Aren't men funny? *Stingy!*
He'll rule the land with iron hand, and yet his baby's
    'boss,'

Aren't men funny?
He'll *die* for *his* opinions, if his wife gives hers, he's
    cross,
  Aren't men funny?
He says, 'I love the girl who's made of real sterling
    stuff,
  With commonsense and brains; if she's got those,
    well, that's enough.'
And yet he'll go and marry some young giggling bit of
    fluff;—
  Aren't men funny? *They're all alike!*
They say it's man's prerogative to grumble and to
    grouse,
  Aren't men funny?
The dinner's cold; a button's off; all's wrong about the
    house, —
  Aren't men funny?
They'll storm and tear, (p'raps even *swear*,) declare
    they will not stay.
  They'll dash off to the 'Pictures,' or perhaps go to a
    play,
Bring home a box of chocolates, and kiss our tears
    away, —
  Aren't men funny? *They all do it!*
They're woman's greatest blessing, tho' they cause *most*
    of her troubles,
  Aren't men funny?

They don't like 'soft soap' yet you'll find them always
    'blowing bubbles,'
    Aren't men funny?
They'll shed their blood like water to defend their
    native soil;
    Wounds they simply glory in, from nothing they
    recoil, —
At *home* they have a fit if on their neck they have a
    boil,
    Aren't men funny? *Look out for squalls!*
But still, with all their little ways, and though we still
    must ask

    Aren't men funny?
We cannot do without them, tho' often they're 'a task,'
    Aren't men funny?
We women do our level best, at all times, to impress
    them,
    Tease them, scold them, flatter them, and sometimes
    caress them:—
Deep in our heart of hearts we say, (and mean it
    too) God bless them, *but*
    Aren't men funny? *I ask you.*

Old Flames
By W. S. Frank & Frank S. Wilcock (1924)

N.B. *During the introduction* the artist pulls a handful of photos from his pocket and refers to them as required by the monologue.

Of photos I've here quite a charming collection
    Of girls I have loved with a passing affection.
Full many a maid in my time I have kissed,
    For things that are sweet I could never resist,
And many a maiden of bashful fifteen,
    I've thought quite divine till another I've seen.
My darling Babette I shall never forget,
    She wept on my shirt front and made it all wet.
Quite charming was Grace all excepting her face,
    And her nose which kept 'Roman' all over the place.
And then there was Kitty whose teeth were so pretty,
    She used so much Odol her kisses were gritty.
While darling Pandora with hair like Aurora,
    Spent a small fortune on Boots' Hair Restorer.
And beautiful Betty I kissed on the jetty,
    Nose like a radish and hair like spaghetti.
I leave Isabella to some other fellow,
    Her ribs stick out just like a broken umbrella.

Amelia, Ophelia and haughty Cordelia,
    To some might appeal but they didn't appeal 'ere.
    (Help!)
And here's darling Lulu, I might have wed you Lou,
    But when I met you Lou we hadn't a sou Lou!
And Eleanor who lived just next door,
    Her face was her fortune, but oh! she was poor.
There's sweet little Minnie who hails from New
    Guinea,
    I called her banana for she was so skinny.
In her garden so green I met charming Eileen,
    She'd scores of cucumbers but never a bean.
Bewitching Vanessa, so pretty, God bless her,
    She broke it all off when she fell off the dresser.
And here is the last of this charming collection
    Of girls I have loved with a passing affection,
The best of the bunch, well now who can it be?
    That tip-tilted nose seems familiar to me;
Those cherry-like lips, now I'll swear on my life,
    I'll give 'em a kiss, and why not?
She's my wife!

Square Deal Sanderson
By Frank A. Terry (1925)

They called him Square-deal Sanderson, down Fallen
    River way,
    A poker face, with eyes of steel, and when he made
    gun-play,
His draw was just like lightning, that made men catch
    their breath,
    And fall, or leap back out of range beyond that
    belching death.

He didn't always shoot to kill: he'd give his gun a
    twist,
    And ere you'd touched your trigger he'd got you
    through the wrist.
You never saw him stunting: but off the trail one day
    I heard some shots, and, peeping through, saw
    Sanderson at play.

He'd been firing at a tree-trunk on which he'd cut a
knot;
  And by the look of things I guess he'd got it ev'ry
  shot.
He'd call round once or twice a year, then hit the trail
again;
  From North to South, from East to West, his tracks
  were ever plain.
He never picked a quarrel; he never owed a sou;
  Square-deal was his name, and he was square deal
  through and through.
Animals adored him: a man once kicked a dog;
  Sanderson's left arm shot out and felled him like a
  log.
I shan't forget the night in Jackson's Poker Dive,
  And the look upon his face when he saw Bully
  Deane arrive.
Now, Bully was a 'two gun' man, a killer, real darned
bad;
  He'd cheat at cards and cheat you at the 'draw' if
  you'd be had.
Well, Square-deal flashed a roll of notes, and Bully saw
the pile,
  And said, 'Say, stranger, what d'yer say to poker for
  a while?'
They played, and Bully lost at first — it always was the
same,
  Until the stakes grew higher, then he played another
  game.
Square-deal said, 'Well, I'll play these,' and Deane
discarded one,
  Then as he dealt another, like a shot out of a gun
Square-deal knifed his hand and card right through
  the table-top.
  His gun flashed out: 'You cur,' he said, 'You see I've
  got the drop:
You've got three aces in your hand; the joker's at the
back;
  The other card my knife's gone through was dealt
  beneath the pack.
I've waited for you, Bully Deane, and got you fixed at
last:
  And now we'll have a little chat about your dirty
  past:
About the girl you lured from home, from a husband
clean and white,
  Who left her unprotected while he went to France to
  fight.
You told her lies about him, until at last she fell.
  She fled with you one night, and then you made her
  life a hell.
You clubbed her, kicked her, starved her, you played
the Devil's game.

Her husband found her dying, and learnt about her
shame.
And when he followed after you you waited in his
track,
  You didn't fight him like a man, you shot him in the
  back.
That youngster was my brother, the woman was his
wife.
  I've waited now for three long years, and sworn to
  have your life.
I ought to shoot you like a dog, I guess I've got the
right,
  But you're going to get a square deal from
  Sanderson to-night.
Now keep your left hand on the board, I'm going to
sheathe my gun,
  And then you're going to start for yours the minute I
  say "one"!'
Square-deal drew his hand back slow, and let his iron
drop,
  Then brought it back to touch the bully's 'cross the
  table top.
Then quickly changing hands he got the knife into his
right,
  'That makes us both left-handed, and the fairest way
  to fight.
And, furthermore, you're going to get a start in case
you whine,
  I'll give you to the table edge before I start for mine.
Now draw your hand back slowly, then dive quick for
your gun.'
  The Bully's hand went slowly back, and Square-deal
  shouted 'One'.
Then like a flash of lightning that rends the clouds
apart
  Square-deal's hand swept back and shot the bully
  through the heart.
His head fell on the table; his left hand hit the floor;
  His gun was in its holster — he hadn't time to draw.
Then Square-deal lifted up his eyes towards the ceiling
there,
  And murmured: 'Brother, Sonny Boy, I reckon
  that's all square.'

OPTIONAL FINISH
Then standing up, he sheathed his iron, not looking
  left or right,
  With head erect and shoulders squared he walked
  into the night.

'Arf a Cigar
By Martyn Herbert & Herberte Jordan (1925)
Performed by Will Deller

I've found a cigar, leastways, 'arf a cigar,
   Well it's only a stump, still it's there.
Not a bad sort o' find when you're down on your luck;
   It'll last twenty minutes, wiv care.
Things 'as bin pretty bad, an' I'm very near broke,
   I've not 'ad a smoke all the day.
It don't run to cigars, so 'ere's jolly good luck
   To the chap as threw this one away.
I shan't 'arf cause a stir as I stroll in the Park,
   (I shall probably sleep there tonight.)
'Obnobbin' wiv some o' the swells as I know,
   Well, that is, I know 'em by sight.

It gives you ideas when you're smokin' cigars,
   I shan't lunch at Lockhart's to-day
I shall dine with Duke 'Umphrey, an' kid I'm a torf,
   Like the chap as threw this one away.
Very likely the feller as threw this away
   'As troubles enough of his own;
A position to keep up, a 'alf dozen kids,
   An' a wife as won't let 'im alone.
So I dare say I'm 'appier, when all's said an' done,
   Wiv me shag an' me dirty ole clay.
You can 'ave your cigars, but I wouldn't changes places
   Wiv the chap as threw this one away.

The Girl at the Ball
By George Logan & Wyn Gladwyn (1926)

There are old-fashioned fogies who talk about 'Cupid',
   And 'love at first sight', it's ridiculous, stupid!
Yet, while memory lasts, I shall always recall
   Just a girl whom I met — quite by chance — at a ball.
The purest of accidents brought us together,
   We talked about commonplace things — and the weather;
But somehow she — well — she was different, that's all!
   Oh! the wonderful eyes of that girl at the ball.
Such a shy little maid, neither pert nor designing,
   But oh! she had eyes that just couldn't help shining!
They say there were other girls, beautiful — tall,
   But they passed me unnoticed, that night at the ball.
'Twas many years later I learnt the full story,
   My heart holds her image and crowns it with glory,
For she'd made a sacrifice some might think small,
   Oh! the sad, wistful eyes of that girl at the ball!

First a father hardpressed, then a rash speculation,
   A whisper of scandal that spelt ruination,
The creditor off'ring to settle it all
   For the hand of the girl whom I met at the ball.
I knew that she loved me, though no word was spoken,
   'Twas there in her eyes; but her poor heart was broken.
We parted — a banal 'Good-night!' that was all! —
   And I dreamt of the eyes of that girl at the ball!
Ah, that night was the first and the last time I met her,
   I light my cigar and I say, 'I'll forget her!'
But each ring of smoke, be it ever so small,
   Frames the face of the girl whom I met at the ball.
Sometimes by the fireside I watch the flames leaping,
   And out of each flame I see two brown eyes peeping;
I know it's all nonsense, and yet — after all —
   How they haunt me, those eyes of that girl at the ball!

When the Road's (H)Up it's (H)Up
By Ernest Longstaffe (1926)

Where ever there's a busy spot you'll find me,
   A-working in the middle of the street,
With traffic all around me and behind me,
   I marks a spot, then rails it nice and neat;
But first I lights a fire an' gets it glowin'
   To warm meself, an' cook a bit o' grub.

Then builds a hut for shelter when it's blowin',
   That's situated 'andy for the pub.
I digs an 'ole that goes down to Australia,
   Then mixes pints of earth with quarts of slops.
To try an' move me on would be failure,
   For 'ere I am, an' when I'm 'ere, I stops.

When the road's h'up, it's h'up:
  And the reason doesn't bother me:
True, the taxi-drivers swear,
  While policemen tear their 'air,
An' ask 'ow long I think I'm goin' to be?
  But *I* don't know, and *you* don't know:
So I ain't a-goin' to tax me brain:
  For it's ten to one,
When the job is done.
  It'll all come up again (not 'arf)
It'll all come up again.
  I'd often longed to 'ave a bit of money
To rent a plot for cabbages and beans:
  With p'r'aps a hive of bees to give me 'oney,
Though never seemed to 'ave the private means.
  But *these* 'ere h'operations is h'extensive,
That means I'll h'occupy this spot for life,

I think I'll make a will (though it's h'expensive)
An' see if I can leave it to the wife.
  I'm goin' to 'ave the wireless h'installated,
That's if I find I 'ear it thro' the din,
  Then in me leisure I'll get eddicated,
So don't disturb me when I'm list'ning in.
  When the road's h'up, it's h'up:
An' I'm goin' to live me life in peace.
  When we've finished with the drains,
There's the gas an' water mains:
  So it's just the same as 'avin' it on lease.
For *I* don't know, an' *you* don't know,
  But the answer's pat an' plain,
That it's ten to one
  If the job *gets* done,
It'll *all* come h'up again, (trust *me*)
  It'll *all* come h'up again.

He Did

By Greatrex Newman & Alice Pardoe (1926)

Cupid sat upon a sunbeam
  Looking very deep in thought.
With his little bow and arrow
  He was out in search of sport.
Soon he spied a youth and a maiden,
  By a rose-bush partly hid,
And although he hated hurting
  Those who might be merely flirting,
Though he knew 'twas disconcerting,
  Still — *he did.*
To that youth and that maiden
  All the world became so fair,
And the birds all started singing
  In the lilac-scented air.
And he asked her — might he kiss her?
  He would do as she should bid; —
And although she said she couldn't
  Ever let him, and she wouldn't —

Most improper, and she shouldn't —
  Still — *she did.*
Then he told her that he loved her,
  In a voice of joy and pride,
And he asked her would she wed him?
  Would she be his blushing bride?
And the maiden cast her eyes down,
  And remained in silence long.
Do you think the story ended
  In the way that fate intended?
And that Cupid murmured 'Splendid!'
  No — *you're wrong.*
For the maiden then admitted
  One small fact that she had hid,
That her *husband* might not let her —
  And she told the youth he'd better
Go away and soon forget her —
  And *he did.*

Wheels

By J. Harrington Weeks & Harold Arpthorp (1926)

All the world's a wheel!
  And all the people in it always wheels.
They have their punctures and their pleasant times,
  And in this life the wheel plays many parts.
There's first the infant riding in his pram
  With nurse attached, the pretty little lamb,

With joy he chortles or with temper squeals —
  On Wheels.
And then a child of six, a budding 'sport!'
  His little scooter is his only thought;
He flies along — the utmost pleasure feels
  On Wheels.

When ten, or there abouts he thinks it great,
  Upon one foot to fix a roller skate.
No other joy to him so much appeals —
  As Wheels.
Then pa buys him one of the best of bikes
  On it he goes — most anywhere he likes
And school he'll dodge — neglected are his meals
  For Wheels.
And then his motorbike with neat side-car next,
  It takes him swiftly, near and far,
With pretty flappers happy hours he steals,
  On Wheels.
Then a real car — a bus that fast he drives,
  And poor pedestrians scared out of their lives,
Ducks, dogs and porkers take madly to their heels —
  Some Wheels!

Perhaps he crashes in that self-same car
  And lying prone he sees, aye, many a star.
The ambulance arrives and with him deals —
  More Wheels!
Years roll along, and grey-haired now is he;
  Gouty, and grown devoid of energy,
In bath-chair sat his form a rug conceals,
  Still Wheels.
A solemn silence falls, he sleeps that last long sleep,
  And round his bier the shadows creep,
Thro' the stilled air the sound of church bells steals,
  And to his rest he goes,
On Wheels.

My Leetle Rosa
By Ernest Longstaffe (1927)

Yesterday I went into the flower shop and I ask-a the man,
  'How mooch you want for-a one red-a rose in da window?'
The flower-a man, he look-a and he say, 'Two-a shilling each.'
  Then I say, 'I canna pay-a so mooch, mak' a leetle cheap.'
The flower-a man he say, 'No cheaper — they're two-a shilling each.'
  I go outside and look-a in da window at the nice-a red-a rose,
And pretty soon a young-a lady come (a beautiful young-a lady)
  And she say-a, 'Oh the pretty red-a rose — How mooch?'
The flower-a man he smile and say-a, 'Six-a pence each.'
  The lady she buy-a one-a red-a rose, and she go away.
I go-a once-a more to da flower-man, I say, 'Scusa me — Signor,
  How mooch you want for one-a red-a rose in da window?'
The flower-a-man, he say, 'I tell you before, they're two-a shilling each.'
  I say, 'Mak' a little cheaper of me Signor, mak' a leetle cheap?'
The flower-a man he say, 'No cheaper — two-a shilling each.
  What-a for you want-a red-a red-a rose?'
I say, 'I tell-a you what for I want-a the red-a red-a rose.

I had a leetle girl-a once, and she was just like-a dis (so high)
And because she look-a like dis-a flower, we call-a her 'Rosa'.
  We were so happy together — me, da mamma and-a da leetle Rosa.
But one day-a da mamma she die. Signor.
  I bury her quite away in da country and-a leetle Rosa and-a me were left alone.
How I love-a that child. She was such a sweet leetle-a child
  And every night when I come-a home from da work
I go da hill-a top. And I say-a, 'Hello Rosa'
  And she say-a from da window up-a high, 'Hello Papa'
And-a every night Signor, I go that-a way.
  But one night just-a like-a always I say, 'Hello Rosa.'
But there was no 'Hello Papa.'
  She was-a no-a there Signor — she was dead.
I bury my leetle Rosa by da mamma
  And I have been all alone.
Signor, I just-a want-a red-a red-a rose
  To put on da grave of my leetle-a Rosa.
That is all — Signor that is all.
  Scusa me. Signor to take-a so mooch of your time.
Scusa me, Signor, what you say?
  The whole bunch-a for nothing?
The whole bunch-a for me for nothing?
  Thank-a you (Gratzia) Thank-a you (Gratzia)
Signor, thank-a you.'

Two Men
By George Arthurs & Cuthbert Clarke (1928)

I know a man who's bold and bad,
  His actions make his people sad.
But he's so tall and handsome, he
  Can always get a smile from me.
But oh, he's bad, so people say,
  He turns the night-time into day,
But how he thrills me when he flirts,
  And kisses me until it hurts.
He's always chasing skirts!
  He drinks and smokes, tells risky jokes,
They say he's crooked, but, well, I don't know!
  He's devil-may-care, but I declare
He's got a voice that sets me all aglow.
  He gambles, too, I know it's true,
For what is love but just a game of chance?
  The things he's said make me turn red,
But oh, by Golly, how that man can dance!
  He's bad, they say, but all the same,
He's handsome, tall and slim.
  And I've got a happy feeling, 'cause
One day I mean to marry him!

I know a man who's awful good,
He always does the things he should.
  He never smokes, he never swears,
But how he puffs when climbing stairs!
  He's always home at half-past eight,
For dinner he is never late,
  But he's so fat and looks so weird
Since he has grown a mottled beard,
  A thing I've always feared!
He loves to preach, and wants to teach
  All people how to eat and drink and live,
But he's out-size, has fishy eyes,
  Or that much I would probably forgive.
He flirts? Not he! He's fond of tea,
  We've never had a quarrel or a tiff,
His mind is strong, he's never wrong,
  But goodness me! That fellow bores me stiff!
He's good, they say, but all the same
  He's ugly, fat and grim.
Still I've got a happy feeling, 'cause
  Tomorrow I'm *divorcing* him!

Penny for Da Monk
By Martyn Herbert & Louise MacBean (1929)

Ain't got no fader, ain't got no moder,
  Ain't got a friend in da world, no sister
    or broder.
Dat's why I'm lonesome, dat's why I'm blue
  Only da monkey to love me, dat's why I say to you:
Give-a me a penny for da monk', you make-a me
    'appy,
  'Cos da monk' he verra beeg-a friend of mine.
Ain't got any money for an organ for to play,
  Only got-a da leetle monk', so dat is why I say:
Give-a me a penny for da monk', he verra hungry,
  An' he's all I got, you see.
S'pose you feelin' sorry an' you give-a da monk' a
    penny,
  Den da monk', he give-a da penny back to me.
He make-a me 'appy, he make-a me smile,
  He make-a me angry as well, just once in a while.
He see da banana, he pinch dem an' run.
  I scold him an' den I forgiven him,
'Cos da monkey he give me one.
  (As though speaking to monkey inside coat)
Oh ho, Pietro, you ready for show-a da treeck?
  Oh you feel-a da cold?
Il poverino, he verra cold, he verra hungry
  An' I no getta da money for to buy-a da banana.

Both my broder, dey make-a da money.
  Antonio, he play-a da organ.
Giovanni, he make-a da ice-cream,
  Make-a da hokey-pokey, verra nice.
Ride-a da tricycle, ring-a da bell,
  'Stop me an' buy one.'
Me, I only got-a leetle monk'.
  Never mind,
Amico da mio, you show-a da treeck,
  Make-a da smile, make-a da money.
Den one day, may-be,
  We take-a da beeg ship back to Italie,
Caro Napoli, where da sun shine,
  An' da skies are blue all-a da time.
Give-a me a penny for da monk', you make-a me
    'appy,
  'Cos da monk', he verra beeg-a friend of mine.
Ain't got any money for an organ for to play.
  Only got da leetle monk', so dat is why I say:
'Give-a me a penny for da monk'; he verra hungry,
  An' he's all I got, you see.
S'pose you feelin' sorry, an' you give-a da monk' a
    penny,
  Den da monk', he give-a da penny back to me.'

Memories of Waterloo
By Cyril Percival & Cuthbert Clarke (1930)

What's that you called me? 'Old Timer' —
   I'm not goin' to say it ain't true —
Don't mind if I do 'ave a pint sir,
   Though it ain't like the old time brew.
'Ere's my best respects for yer 'ealth, sir,
   I always drops in 'ere for two —
'Cause this 'ere pub's called 'Dook o' Wellington',
   Which reminds me of Waterloo.
Do I remember it? Not arf!
   I don't see no call for surprise —
I may be just going on ninety,
   My 'ead's clear when memories do rise.
I served with the Dook from the start, sir,
   A youngster just bursting with pride,
I can see it as clear as today, sir,
   When the Dook and I took our first ride.
'Ow the guards envied me on that day, sir,
   Down the line standing by the Dook's side —
And they all tried 'ard to be chosen
   For behind the Dook to ride.
Together we faced many dangers,
   But always we won our way through,
I remember that charge through the snowdrift
   On the journey to Waterloo.
We've been through 'ail and fog, sir,
   And nights dark enough for a spook,

With the guard behind a-cheering
   For my pluck and the Iron Dook.
We've dashed down the line at a run, sir,
   Without any fear for the worst,
And sometimes we worked at such pressure
   The Dook 'as been fit to burst.
We fought many battles together,
   But nothing we ever went through
Could compare with the records we made, sir,
   From the coast to Waterloo.
Times 'ave changed since them days, sir,
   With aeroplanes, motors, and so
When the old dook was finished, it broke my 'eart
   And they told me that I'd have to go.
There's a new dook about so they tell me,
   Just an idea to keep up the name —
They can say what they like 'bout the new 'un,
   But believe me, the old dook was game!
What's that, sir, where are me medals?
   Don't chip in — the story you'll spoil,
I was just going to say that they're thinking
   Of runnin' the new dook on oil!
'Oo's a liar? — I never said soldier! —
   I've a pension — I'm not kiddin' you —
The old 'Iron Dook' was my engine
   What I drove to and from Waterloo!!

Suicide
By Roy Clegg & Harold Clegg-Walker (1931)

Now I am a fellow who's lived —
   I've lived and I've loved and I've lost,
I loved a fair damsel who didn't love me,
   So my fate to the winds must be tossed.
She laughed when I tried to be serious,
   Her pretty heels trampled my heart,
The future means nothing, so now I must die,
   But the question is — how do I start?
To jump in a river and drown
   Is a good plan, or so I've been told.
But if some poor simpleton does fish you out,
   You get such a terrible cold.
To turn on the gas and be smothered
   Is one way, but you never can tell
If someone will biff in and spoil the whole thing,
   And just curse you for making a smell.
To hang by the neck on one's braces
   Is sometimes considered the thing,

But I fear mine would hardly stand up to the strain,
   For already they're tied up with string.
I like the idea of revolvers,
   I'd prefer to be shot than to hang,
But ever since childhood I've always been scared
   Of things that go off with a bang.
I once had a vague sort of notion
   Of leaping beneath an express,
But one has to consider one's fellows, you know,
   The chappies who clear up the mess.
Still the Underground might offer scope,
   One could sit down upon a live rail,
But that involves trespassing — what a disgrace
   If the corpse had to serve time in jail.
Now Keatings kills bugs, moths and beetles,
   In that case it ought to kill me.
The butler must make me some sandwiches, James!
   No. Dash it! he's gone out to tea.

Never mind though, there must be some way,
   Such as hurling yourself from a cliff,
Even then you might find that you'd only been
      stunned,
   And you'd wake up most frightfully stiff.
I've given up thinking of razors,
   I've tried and I'm wondering yet

How these fellows who do it can cut their own throats,
   It's a thing that's beyond my Gillette.
No, really, I'm finding that this sort of thing's
   Not as easily done as it's said.
So I think I'll pop off for the week-end or so —
   And perhaps shoot some rabbits instead.

The Man with the Swollen Head
By Alec Kendall & Cuthbert Clarke (1931)

It takes all sorts to make a world.
   And it's full of all sorts no doubt.
There are men *and men* but of all the men
   There's one we can well do without.
The man with the swollen head, that's him,
   With that satisfied atmosphere,
Full of himself and inwardly thinks
   The world's all right, *I'm here.*
You know the man, you've seen the type,
   As a rule his own praises he sings.
Put him on horseback he'll ride to hell,
   When he feels the strength of his wings.
You needn't look far to find him,
   You can soon pick him out from the rest,
He thinks all the pavement and part of the street
   Are essential to show off his chest.
The man with the swollen head,
   The fellow who *will* put on airs,
Face made of brass, full of bombast and gas,
   Born lucky and vacant upstairs.
He's a world in himself so he thinks,
   Right off the beaten track,
His hat goes on with a shoehorn,
   And his shirt buttons up at the back.
He likes to hear himself talking,
   What *he* did and what *he* can do,

Admits the world was made in *six* days,
   But *he* could have made it in *two.*
He and himself, alone they stand,
   Aloof midst the mighty throng.
How was the world made without him?
   When he dies, will it all go wrong?
The man with the swollen head,
   A cheap picture lavishly framed.
Sympathize with him, poor devil,
   He's more to be pitied than blamed.
It isn't his fault — it's his parents,
   It's with them we should feel annoyed.
They should have drowned *him* not the *others,*
   He's the one they should have destroyed!
Still, we all have our faults, why worry.
   We each have our lives to live.
Here below, there's few of us *perfect.*
   So it's best to forget and forgive.
We pass this way but once, that's all:
   What does it matter who's who?
Jack'll be as good as his master
   When we stand in the final queue.
And when Gabriel sounds his trumpet
   And the names of the good ones are read,
Let's hope there'll be room for us as well as the
   Man with the swollen head.

Tommy out East
By Alan Sanders & Henry Cheel (1932)

I am baked and I am thirsty, in this blarsted burnin'
      sun,
   For the sand's got in my system, and it's damned
      near spoilt my gun.
But our blue-eyed baby captain, who is learnin' 'ard to
      swear,
   Says we're 'oldin' up the Empire, though we're far
      from Leicester Square.

I believes him when 'e says it, but at times I wish I
      knew
   That a little 'ome I thinks of, in the Dials — where I
      grew,
Were just a trifle nearer, so that I could go and see
   What my mother is a-doin' — if she's thinkin' 'long 'o
      me.

For it's marchin', and it's fightin' and it's 'ard I give my
    word
  To keep yer face a-smilin' when they've given yer
    'the bird',
But when murky day is over, and we gets the
    'LIGHTS OUT' clear,
  I can 'ear the call of London, and I dream I'm tastin'
    beer.
I've got a gal in Shoreditch — 'ere's 'er photo next me
    'eart —
  And Gawd, I wonder if she's gone and left me in the
    cart.
For this waitin' game don't suit 'er; she says all soldiers
    flirt,
  Just as if she couldn't trust me with another bit o'
    skirt!

The rosy East ain't rosy like them writers 'ave you
    think.
  And if you should 'ave a 'beano', well, they shoves
    yer into 'clink'.
With the Temples and Pagodas all a-roastin' in the
    sun,
  You can 'ave the blinkin' blindin' East — give me
    'Ampstead 'Eath for fun!
Oh, we're 'oldin' up the Empire, though we're distant
    from the smoke,
  And the sun beats down in glory, 'nuff to burn up
    any bloke.
But it's night-time when I feels as if I'd copped out
    unawares
  'Cos my 'eart's in Seven Dials, in my 'ome up many
    stairs!

The Old Barnstormer
By Frank Wood & Cuthbert Clarke (1933)

Don't wake me up, for I'm dreaming to-night
  Of the good old days long since taken flight.
We were either play-acting or running a booth
  With animals, freaks, and our motto — 'The Truth!'
Walk up! Walk up! Walk up and see
  The horse's head where his tail ought to be.
Yes, that was the old Barnstormers' cry
  In the good old days long since gone by.
The unselfish days when each of us shared
  The good with the bad and nobody cared.
When luck was out and little to eat,
  The ground for a bed, the sky for a sheet.
Walk up! Walk up! Walk up and see
  The Horse's head where his tail ought to be.
How the people laughed when his 'rudder' they saw
  In the manger while there was his head on the floor.
Walk up and see the Giddy Giraffe,
  With a neck ten foot long that'll make you 'laff',
And all that he lives on is one meal a day,
  'Cos a little with him goes a blooming long way.
Walk up! and see the famous freak,
  'The Bearded Lady' from Cripple Creek.
There's only two nights to gaze on this freak,
  He's got to go back to his wife next week.
The Human Ostrich, a funny galloot,
  Swallowed swords and chewed glass like a kid eating
    fruit.
Then he had to lay off, for the silly great goat
  Had some kippers and got a bone stuck in his throat.
Jugo, the Juggler, who juggled with knives,
  And scared all the audience out of their lives.

His wife on the stage, and he in the pit,
  While ev'ryone marvelled why she wasn't hit.
He'd throw at her head and he once got so near,
  By the eighth of an inch a big knife grazed her ear.
And a navvy somewhere in the back seats roared
  'I'm blowed if 'e ain't gone and missed 'er, the fraud!'
Walk up! Walk up and take a good view
  Of the old spotted leopard from Wongapaloo!
He can change all his spots and without any bother,
  When he's tired of one spot he sits on another.
Here walk up and see the performing flea,
  He was born in Brighton in seventy-three.
To the people what went there to spend a week-end,
  He was known to the crowd as a bosom friend.
I shall never forget our old play-acting crowd,
  We'd tramped fifty miles and though poor we were
    proud.
We arrived at a village and there we could see
  The sun in the distance as bright as could be;
I cried, 'Cheer up, laddies, and on with the show,
  Yon sunset provides us a welcoming glow.'
Then a yokel cried, 'That be no sunset, ole Squire,
  Vor that be the bloomin *theatre* on fire.'
Walk up! Walk up! what glorious times —
  No velvet curtains with headlights and limes —
None of your talkies and music that's canned
  A drum and a whistle that did for a band.
When the curtain falls and a voice calls me
  To a place be it colder or warmer
I hope I shall hear Walk up and see
  The last of an old barnstormer!

A Tattoo Tragedy

By Greatrex Newman, Clifford Grey & Fred Cecil (1933)

Her name was Ermyntrude,
    In a circus she tattooed —
A girl who had designs on ev'ry man;
    Until she traced a heart
On the arm of Joseph Smart,
    She won him — and they furnished her plain van.
Of course she left the show
    The day she married Joe,
The tattoo needle she would 'need' no more,
    But Joseph, foolish youth,
Soon learned the dreadful truth.
    The 'Bearded Lady' was his *ma-in-law!*
All day about the place
    He could see that hairy face,
He couldn't dodge it even in the street.
    It made him use an oath
To see that stringy growth,
    That harvest festival of shredded wheat!
Each day he longed to get
    A present from Gillette,
And hand it to the mother of his bride.
    'Twas obvious of course
She'd swallowed some poor horse,
    And left the tail to dangle just outside.
Joe's bearded ma-in-law
    Out-whiskered Bernard Shaw,
And sometimes drove poor Joseph on the 'binge';
    He staggered home one night
At four a.m. — quite 'tight' —
    So Ermyntrude, his wife, planned her revenge.
Up to his side she crept
    And while he soundly slept
Undid his coat and shirt in manner weird.
    Then when his chest was nude
Upon it she tattooed
    Her Mother's face, the Lady avec Beard!

Joe woke at half past nine
    And saw the dread design,
It stared out through his little Aertex vest.
    A horrible surprise,
Could he believe his eyes?
    The face he hated, grinning from his chest!
He straightway signed the pledge
    And lived on fruit and veg',
He thought that he was 'seeing things', poor youth.
    But even when T.T.
That fungus'd face he'd see,
    Until at last there dawned the tattooed truth!
He left his wife, of course,
    And sued for a divorce,
And as the neighbours kept asking why?
    He roamed from Shepherd's Bush
To Ashby-de-la-*Zush,*
    From far-off Peckham Vale to Maida Rye.
In deep despair at last
    He bought a mustard plast',
And plonked it on his chest without delay.
    That plaster burned and burned.
To tear it off he yearned,
    But hoped it would singe the beard away.
The mustard was so strong
    He left it on too long.
And while he peeled it off, his chest was sore.
    So blistered was the skin,
It made a *double chin,*
    The beard looked *twice the size it was before!*
Poor Joe went raving mad,
    His end came swift and sad,
That tattooed picture must remain he knew;
    Resigned, he softly sighed.
Then whispered as he died:
    'Thank Heav'n it's not a *talking* picture too!'

The Sufferer

By L. E. Baggaley & Edwin John (1934)

Now hospitals aren't cheerful places,
    Not even the best, you'll agree:
But the one that fair gives you the horrors
    Is that at St. Earaches-on-Sea.
It says o'er the gate 'English Martyrs,'
    A name that inspires a doubt,
It's appropriate, though, because many go in,
    But very few live to come out.
A cousin of mine, name of Arnold,

Who went there for treatment last year,
Says the bloomin' place very nigh killed him,
    And it all came about like this 'ere.
He lay there one day in a dark dreary ward,
    Its name was the 'Angel of Death.'
They'd all got such names, nice and sociable like,
    When you saw 'em you fair caught yer breath.
Now Arnold was not feeling robust,
    His face was a nice shade of green,

He'd a mouth like a dustbin, and felt a bit raw
  Around where his appendix had been.
A sour-faced Sister then entered
  And said 'You're to come right away,
Operation it's got to be done o'er again.'
  The patient looked up and said 'Eh?'
She retorted 'It's no good being stupid,
  Them forceps has got to be found,
They must be inside you, so Doctor Scull says,
  And that's where they are, I'll be bound.'
Our Arnold was always obliging,
  'Twas a way that he'd had all his life.
So he pulled on his slippers and followed her out,
  And was shortly put under the knife.
The next day a towel and bandage were missed,
  And Arnold was opened once more.
By then he began to get slightly annoyed,

Life for him seemed to be one big bore.
The staff of 'The Martyrs' all laughed and agreed
  That the series of mishaps was rummy
The Matron remarked 'When we slit him again,
  We'd best fit a 'zip' on his tummy.'
The climax arrived on a Tuesday
  When they all gathered round him to gloat
And Matron said 'Come on, you're wanted,
  For Doctor Shroud's lost his white coat.'
At that Arnold's patience fair failed him,
  'Oh has he,' said he, 'where's my hat?
I don't mind a bandage or forceps and such,
  But a jacket — I'm not wearing that.
An instrument-shelf and a cupboard I've been
  Since I came in but three days ago.
But at being a cloakroom gratuitous like
  I'm drawing the line — cheerio!'

Sam's Parrot

By V. F. Stevens & Lauri Bowen (1934)

Optional introduction: Ladies and Gentlemen, I'm sure quite a lot of you must have heard about Sam Small, and of his various escapades. He is represented as being a very wide awake person, but in reality he is just as open to being 'caught' as anyone else, and this little monologue deals with an occasion on which 'Owd Sam' was anything but wide awake.

Na tha's 'eard of owd Sam, well, that very same chap
  Were out walking one day for a stroll
'E were padding down t' high street just casual like,
  On his way to sign on for the dole.
After passing three tripe shops 'e 'appened to come
  To a place 'e'd not noticed afore,
'Twere a shop where they sold diff'rent live stock and
    pets —
  A kind of menagerie store.
'E stood garping in th' window at pups, slugs and
    birds,
  All int'rested like as could be,
When a voice near at 'and seemed to shriek in his ear
  'Eeh, Lad, Ah knaws summat 'bout thee.'
  'E were that surprised, an' t' shopman inside,
Having noticed how Sam had turned pale,
  Come outside to see if owd Sam wanted owt,
'E were keen like on making a sale.
  Sam said 'No lad, there's nowt theer that I want to
    buy.'
And then went as red as a carrot,

'But that theer thing's champion — by gum, I'd
    like 'e.'
And the shopkeeper yelled *'What! That parrot?*
  But no lad, tha reely could not afford 'e
Unless tha can spare fifteen quid,
  An' even at that price I'd lose on the deal,
She cost more'n that, that she did.'
  Owd Sam were crestfallen, but then an idea
Must have entered the shopkeeper's head.
  'Theer's only one thing tha can do, lad, says 'e,
Take two of 'er eggs 'ome instead.
  They're two bob apiece, an' all tha's to do,
Is to just shove 'em under a hen,
  An' tha'll 'ave a parrot like *that* in a month,
Aye they're bound to be 'atched out by then.'
  Well, Sam dubs up brass and goes 'ome with th' eggs.
As pleased wi 'imself as could be
  And the Parrot's last words seemed to ring in his
    ears
'Eeh, Lad, Ah knows summat 'bout thee.'
  Now it must 'ave been fully six months after that,
When Sam went down t' High Street once more.
  An' 'appening to pass by that very same shop,
'E 'eard someone calling from t'door
  'Eeh Lad,' said the voice, *'but ah knows about thee.'*
Said Sam, 'Aye but tha's out of *luck!*
  'Cos Ah knows summat 'bout *thee* too, owd lass,
Thy bloomin' 'usband's a duck!'

The Road to La Bassée

By Bernard Newman & Harold Arpthorp (1934)

I went across to France again, and walked about the
    line,
    The trenches have been all filled in — the country's
        looking fine.
The folks gave me a welcome, and lots to eat and
    drink,
    Saying ''Allo, Tommee, back again? 'Ow do you? In
        ze pink?'
And then I walked about again, and mooched about
    the line;
    You'd never think there'd been a war, the country's
        looking fine.
But the one thing that amazed me most shocked me, I
    should say
    There's buses running now from Bethune to La Bassée!
I sat at Shrapnel Corner and I tried to take it in,
    It all seemed much too quiet, I missed the war-time
        din.
I felt inclined to bob down quick — Jerry sniper in
    that trench!
    A minnie coming over! God what a hellish stench!
Then I pulled myself together, and walked on to
    La Folette —
    And the cows were calmly grazing on the front line
        parapet.
And the kids were playing marbles by the old
    Estaminet —
    Fancy kiddies playing marbles on the road to
        La Bassée!
You'd never think there'd been a war, the country's
    looking fine —
    I had a job in places picking out the old front line.
You'd never think there'd been a war — ah, yet you
    would, I know,
    You can't forget those rows of headstones every mile
        or so.
But down by Tunnel Trench I saw a sight that made
    me start,
    For there, at Tourbieres crossroads — a gaudy ice-
        cream cart!
It was hot, and I was dusty, but somehow I couldn't
    stay —
    Ices didn't seem quite decent on the road to
        La Bassée.
Some of the sights seemed more than strange as I kept
marching on.
    The Somme's a blooming garden, *and there are houses
        in Peronne.*
The sight of dear old Arras almost made me give three
    cheers;
    And there's kiddies now in Plugstreet, and *mamselles*
        in Armentiers.
But nothing that I saw out there so seemed to beat the
    band
    As those buses running smoothly over what was No
        Man's Land.
You'd just as soon expect them from the Bank to
    Mandalay
    As to see those buses running from Bethune to
        La Bassée.
Then I got into a bus myself, and rode for all the way,
    Yes, I rode inside a bus from Bethune to La Bassée.
Through Beuvry and through Annequin, and then by
    Cambrin Tower —
    The journey used to take four years, but now it's half
        an hour.
Four years to half an hour — the best speedup I've
    met.
    Four years? Aye, longer still for some — they
        haven't got there yet.
Then up came the conductor chap, *'Vos billets s'il vous
    plait.'*
    Fancy asking for your tickets on the road to
        La Bassée.
And I wondered what *they'd* think of it — those mates
    of mine who died —
    They never got to La Bassée, though God knows
        how they tried.
I thought back to the moments when their number
    came around,
    And now those buses rattling over sacred, holy
        ground
Yes, I wondered what *they'd* think of it, those mates of
    mine who died.
    Of those buses rattling over the old pave close
        beside.
'Carry on! That's *why* we died!' I could almost hear
    them say,
    'To keep those buses *always* running from Bethune to
        La Bassée!'

When I'm Cross

By Mab Davis (1934)

My mother says when I am cross
    As I *am* now and then,

It's better not to talk at all,
    But count inside, to ten.

'Cos, if you do it slowly
  Just like this: *one, two, three, four!*
By the time you've finished,
  You're not angry anymore!
It sounds all right, but then somehow,
  It doesn't work with me,
And when I've counted up to ten
  I'm *cross* as I can be.
And so I've found another way,
  I whisper very low,
And so that no one else can hear
  The *rudest* words I know:
Bother, bloomin', hang and drat,
  Female, blazes, beast and cat.
Golly, blinkin', pig and mug,
  Spit and stomach, bosh and slug.
When I've said all these I find
  I can feel quite good and kind.
Aunt Jane comes to stay with us,
  She's awfully tall and thin.
She always makes me very cross,
  As soon as she comes in.
Because she says 'Now *don't* do that'
  And '*Don't* make such a noise'
She says, 'Be seen and never heard's
  The rule for little boys.'
She tells me not to slam the door,
  And not to tease the cat,
And '*Don't* speak with your mouth full, child'
  And silly things like that.
I often feel I'd like to throw
  An inkpot at her head.

But then I'd get in such a row,
  And so I say instead:—
Bother, bloomin', hang and drat,
  Female, blazes, beast and cat,
Golly, blinkin', pig and mug,
  Spit and stomach, bosh and slug,
Then I say it all again,
  Out loud I say 'Yes, Aunt Jane.'
I know you won't believe it,
  But I've *seen* it, — and it's *real!*
My Mummy's bought a baby girl
  Imagine how I feel.
It's not a nice one, either
  'Cos it's ugly, and it's bald.
It's not the leastest bit of good,
  It won't come when it's called.
If she'd only bought a puppy
  Well, that wouldn't be half bad!
But to go and waste her pennies
  On a *baby* — makes me mad!
When I first heard about it
  I hid down in the shed
At the bottom of the garden,
  And right out loud I said:—
Bother, bloomin', hang and drat,
  Female, blazes, beast and cat,
Golly, blinkin', pig and mug,
  Spit and stomach, bosh and slug.
I said another one as well,
  I'd better spell this: H E L!

What's It For?
By Mab Davis (1935)

The world seems crammed full, fit to bust
  With things I mustn't do!
I wonder they don't cage boys up,
  Like lions at the Zoo.
And if they did I shouldn't care,
  If I was a lion I'd *roar,*
While, as it is, if I just sniff!
  Well, what are noses *for?*
Yesterday I got so mad,
  I *had* to tease our cat,
I pulled her tail, and made her squawk
  Right out loud — like *that!*
And then they sent me straight to bed,
  You bet I slammed the door
Well, anyway, the cat is mine,
  And what are cat's tails *for?*

They said to me 'Now, be quiet, do,
  While grandpa has his doze,'
I never made a bit of noise,
  But *he* did — with his nose.
So I just splashed some ink at him,
  To teach him not to snore!
So then there was *another* row,
  Well, what are bald heads *for?*
I had a great big apple,
  I bought it for a penny,
They said 'Give little sister some,
  Because she hasn't any'
And so I gave her all the pips,
  The maggots and the core,
And then they said 'You greedy boy!'
  Well, what are sisters *for?*

I'm always asking questions,
   The sort that start with 'Why?'
I want to know how hens lay eggs
   And how the birds can fly?
I want to know 'bout 'babies' —
   There's one called 'twins' next door,
I b'lieve it's got a head both ends!
   I wonder what that's *for*?

Oh dear! I dunno what to do —
   I've scribbled on the wall,
I've been and let the hens all loose,
   I've made holes in my ball.
I've turned on all the bathroom taps,
   It's running on the floor,
And everybody's *cross* with me!
   But — I *dunno* what for!!

The Touch of the Master's Hand
By Myra Brooks Welch & Ernest Longstaffe (1936)

'Twas battered and scarred and the auctioneer
   Thought it scarcely worth his while,
To waste much time on the old violin
   But held it up with a smile.
'What am I bidden good folks,' he cried,
   'Who'll start the bidding for me?
A guinea, a guinea, then two, only two?
   Two guineas, and who'll make it three?
Three guineas once, Three guineas twice,
   Going for three?' But *no!*
From the room far back a grey haired man
   Came forward and picked up the bow,
Then wiping the dust from the old violin
   And tightening the loose strings.
He played a melody pure and sweet,
   As a carolling angel sings.
The music ceased and the auctioneer
   In a voice that was quiet and low,
Said, 'What am I bid for the old violin?'
   And then held it up with the bow.

'A thousand guineas, and who'll make it two,
   Two thousand, and who'll make it three?
Three thousand once, three thousand twice;
   And going and gone,' said he.
The people cheered but some of them cried,
   'We do not quite understand
What changed it's worth?'
   Swift came the reply 'The touch of a master's hand.'
And many a man with life out of tune,
   And battered and scarred with sin,
Is auctioned cheap to a thoughtless crowd
   Much like the old violin.
A 'mess of pottage,' a glass of wine.
   A game, and he travels on.
He is 'going once,' he's 'going twice,'
   He's 'going' and almost 'gone;'
But the Master comes and the foolish crowd
   Can never quite understand,
The worth of a soul and the change that's wrought,
   By the touch of the Master's hand.

The Killjoy
By Nosmo King & Ernest Longstaffe (1937)

The Killjoy died and passed along
   To that peaceful happy State:
He'd often pictured in his dreams
   And stood before the gate.
He tried to pass the portals,
   When a quiet voice said, 'Stay!
What did you do on earth my friend
   And who are you anyway?'
The Killjoy in astonishment
   Said, 'Surely you know me
And all the splendid things I've done
   To help humanity?
To administer the law
   I did my duty in a way

That made me feared by every
   Common sinner in my day.
I did my very best to ban
   All Sunday games, and then
I closed the public houses
   To the working man at ten.
Music Halls and Theatres
   I abhorred, and in 'Revue'
The shameful human female form
   I hid from public view.
Lovers in the open parks
   A pretty price they paid —
They were most severely dealt with
   By the Purity Brigade —

Prolific lyricist F. Chatterton Hennequin, seen here in character as *'Erbert, A.B.*

Vernon Watson, who chose Nosmo King as his stage name so that his name would be up in lights anywhere that smoking was forbidden

And should a good man fall from grace
  And dare to misbehave,
Relentlessly I'd hound him down:
  Aye even to the grave.'
The voice cried, 'Stop: I've heard enough:
  It's very plain to see
You haven't judged your fellow men
  By standards set by me,
But by your own small, narrow soul —
  Oh, how could you succeed?
Self-righteousness your watchword,
  Intolerance your creed!
You've been sadly misinformed
  That fact is very clear,
Only those who've radiated joy
  Can ever enter here.
But you have lived to kill that joy,
  You must reap just what you sow

Besides the laughter here would shock you,
  You'll be happier *below*.'
The Killjoy trembled like a leaf
  And said, 'Am I awake?
I cannot dwell with murderers
  There must be some mistake.'
'There's no mistake,' the voice replied.
  'It's just your point of view —
Perhaps you've never stopped to think
  They might object to you!
You've quite a lot in common
  Though you both play different roles,
They only kill men's bodies,
  But *you* destroy their souls.'
And so the Killjoy joined his friends,
  Who'd kept for him a seat
With all the other Killjoys —
  Just to make their Hell complete.

Loyalty
By Gloria Storm, Nosmo King & Ernest Longstaffe (1937)

Never believe the worst of a man
  When once you have seen his best,
Of any loyalty worth the name
  This is the surest test.
Gossip is ready at every turn,
  Your faith and trust to slay,
But the loyal soul is deaf to doubt,
  Whatever the world may say.
Whatever you hear on others' lips,
  Don't let it soil your own;
Let your faith still stronger be,
  While the seed of slander's sown;

Keep the image before your eyes,
  Of the friend who's a friend to you:
And stand by that friend through thick and thin
  Whatever the world may do.
Never believe the worst of a man,
  When your own soul sees the best;
All that matters is what *you* know
  Not what the others have *guessed*
And if all that *you* know is straight and fine
  And has brought you friendship's joys.
Be proud to treasure the truth that's yours,
  Whatever the world destroys.

Providence
By Ernest R. Heale, Nosmo King & Ernest Longstaffe (1938)

Have you ever been broke, just to the wide
  With just what you stand up in, and nothing beside?
Living on scraps for best part of a week,
  When you can't get 'em and know where to seek.
I've been like that on a cold winter's night
  When the streets were deserted with nothing in sight
But a slow moving Bobby, whose job is to see
  That the public's protected from fellows like me.
Who get put inside to answer the Court
  Why they're wandering round with no means of
    support.

It always strikes me as a queer sort of joke,
  To pick on a man just because he is broke.
Do they think he enjoys wand'ring round in the rain,
  Soaked thro' to the skin with a dull aching pain,
Thro' his stomach forgetting its last decent meal,
  Just praying for the time when it's too numb to feel.
Life isn't worth much when you get to that state
  Or just waiting to die with nowhere to wait —
I remember the time, it's a long while ago,
  When I stood on a bridge, with the river below.
The last food I'd had was two days before

And I never expected I'd need any more —
That night was the worst that ever I've known,
  With a dirty wet fog that chilled to the bone.
I set my teeth hard, and I set down my heel,
  On the rail that my hands were too perish'd to feel,
When a snivelling pup came out of the fog
  And whimpered at me — just a scrap of a dog.
Bedraggled and dirty like me, just a wreck,
  With a sad little face on his poor scraggy neck.
A few seconds more and I would have died
  But he just licked my hand and I sat down and cried.
And I covered the poor little chap with my coat
  And I carried him off with a lump in my throat.
I took him along to the one place I knew
  Where they'd give him a bed and a biscuit or two.
They didn't feel keen on taking him in
  But the sergeant in charge gave a bit of a grin
When I told him the dog could do with a meal
  'I'll fix *him* up, but how do *you* feel?'
It may be, perhaps, that the Sergeant had seen
  The state I was in, I wasn't too clean,

The hunger and cold that I'd suffered all day
  Exhausted my limits — I fainted away.
Well, they fed me and slept me, and gave me two bob,
  And the following day they found me a job.
I've worked ever since and put a bit by,
  I'm comfortable now and I don't want to die.
I've a nice little house in a quiet little street,
  With a decent sized garden that's always kept neat,
I've worked there a lot when I've had time to spare,
  And I'm so proud of one little corner that's there.
With the pick of the flowers round a little old stone
  That stands in a corner, all on its own.
It bears an inscription — not very grand —
  The letters are crooked, but you'll understand —
That I wasn't too steady, I couldn't quite see
  At the time that I carved it — quite recently.
Here are the words that I carved on the stone:
  'Here lies my friend — when I was alone,
Hopeless and friendless, just lost in a fog,
  God saved my life — with the help of a dog.'

Common Sense

By A. Hickman-Smith, Nosmo King & Ernest Longstaffe (1938)

When trouble looms around you and danger lies
    ahead;
  When your faith is almost shattered and your hopes
    are nearly dead,
There is always something left you — and it's not a
    mere pretence,
  View your difficulties calmly — and use your
    common sense.
When there's talk of strife and danger and rumours fill
    the air,
  When the facts are so distorted, that your views
    become unfair,
When mere trifles get so magnified until they seem
    immense,
  Just forget your party politics — and use your
    common sense.
Other folks have got their troubles and they've got
    their point of view;
  And it's not in human nature —, all to think the same
    as you.
Try to see things from *their* angle, — listen in to their
    defence,
  And you'll come to agreement, — if you use your
    common sense.

Though we're given brains and judgment — quite a
    few of us I guess
  Let others do our thinking — and with borrowed
    views impress
Many other thoughtless people — who as a
    consequence,
  Believe the things they wouldn't — if they'd used
    their common sense.
Life is far from easy, tempers frayed and feelings sore;
  Because the world is suffering from an aftermath of
    war.
Rationing, controls and queues have grown to be
    immense!
  When they surely could be lessened — if we used
    our common sense.
Now the clouds have all departed — and there's
    brightness in the air,
  And once again instead of strife — there's gladness
    everywhere,
Now the gloom of yesterday has gone — the feeling of
    suspense,
  It is because when things looked hopeless —
    SOMEONE USED HIS COMMON SENSE!

Bill's Trombone

By Edwin John (1938)

When Bill were late from work one night he hadn't
come to harm
  But when he did arrive he carried parcel under
th' arm.
'What's that?' said owd Bill's missus in a somewhat
doubtful tone.
  'I bought it secondhand,' said Bill wi' pride, 'it's a
trombone!'
That properly set missus off, but Bill didn't dispute
her,
  He just ate tea and went upstairs and took his
trombone tutor.
First blast he gave cracked window pane and it were
such a row
  The neighbours thought as somebody were torturin'
a cow!
And policeman on his beat outside turned pale and
phoned up station,
  And streets away folk bunged up ears, there was
some consternation!
As weeks went by his tone improved and neighbours
got immune,
  And now and then they even thought they
recognised a tune.
A circus come to town one day wi' band trombonist ill,
And manager were in a sweat until he heard of Bill.
He found him in the 'Dog and Duck' and offered him
a job,
  Wi' loan of fancy uniform as well as fee five bob.
That night in tent Bill looked a treat and music
sounded grand,
  Especially when Bill were playin' same tune as the
band!
All Wigan folks was there enn block, Bill's missus were
that proud,
  She said, 'Bah Gum! I never knew our Bill could
blow that loud!'
The star turn of the show were then a furrin' looking
chap
  Climbed into cage o' roarin' lions and didn't care a
rap!
At least he didn't care until the biggest lion made bold
  To sock him one in t'lug wi' paw and laid the beggar
cold!
Then this ferocious animile walked straightway out of
cage

And glared around the circus ring lashin' his tail wi'
rage.
There weren't no rush for doors or owt, and all was
still as still,
  For t' folks was petrified wi' fear, all exceptin' owd
Bill.
He climbed down from his seat in t' band and walked
into the ring,
  And putting trombone next lion's ear, he blew like
anything!
At this the creature gave a roar, but owd Bill didn't
flinch,
  He blew another mighty blast and never gave an
inch.
This made the lion blink a bit, he thought as Bill were
spoofin',
  And then he let off such a roar as nearly fetched the
roof in!
Bill looked the lion up and down and said, 'All right,
you gump,'
  Then took trombone and blew a noise resemblin' t'
last trump!
He blew trombone clean inside-out, and spellbound
folks all saw
  T' lion put tail betwixt his legs and touch forelock
wi' paw.
He gave a coo like little dove, his face were drawn and
sad,
  As owd Bill shoved him back in t' cage, and people
cheered like mad!
And as he stood in t' circus ring before the cheerin'
masses,
  He found himself kissed on both cheeks by buxom
circus lasses!
'Look here, me lad,' said missus, when she got Bill
home that night,
  'Dunna thee play wi' lions no more thee gave me
such a fright!
'I'll tell thee what,' she added, 'I've ne'er heard of such
a thing
  As kissin' them there hussies in a public circus ring!'
Bill said he wouldn't play no more as his trombone
were burst —
  The runnin' cost were far too high in keepin' down
his thirst!

Lor Lumme! You'd never believe it

By H. M. Burnaby & Herbert Townsend (1938)

'Ow do, ev'ry one — Missis Crowe is the name.

A respectable woman, I 'opes you're the same;

Now my old man retired from 'is bizness last year,
　So I goes out charin' yerss, that's why I'm 'ere.
I've a regular round, *and* the things as I've seen,
　Take the people I *do* for, at Number Sixteen!
All this 'ere central 'eatin', armchairs made o' steel,
　Lor lumme! you'd never believe it!
They sleeps in twin beds, they're a swindle I'd say;
　Ain't no twin in the family — yet — anyway,
They've a son, drives a motor, it goes whizzin' by,
　All covered with mottoes, fair catches yer eye,
There's one on the front of it, sez 'Jump or die!'
　Lor lumme! you'd never believe it!
Yerss! an' wots more, they're noodist, they've ladies an'
　　gents,
　In their bit o' back garden, no clothes, no pretence,
I know, 'cos I once had a garp through the fence
　Lor lumme! you'd never believe it!
There's them couple o' corfdrops, wot's took 'Mon
　　Repos'
　They only moved in there a few days ago,
Now *she* went out charin' one time, same as me;
　While *'e* used to be a bricklayer, yer see,
Touched lucky, they did, which you don't as a rule,
　'Avin' got 'em all right in a big football pool.
They sits down to breakfast, in full h'evening dress.
　Lor lumme! you'd never believe it!
Big six course dinners, she puts on at night;
　'E kicks, 'cos there ain't tripe and onions, that's right.
She dresses 'im up, like a posh country squire,
　An' keeps talkin' of tutors she's goin' to 'ire;
Cos 'e *will* drop 'is haitches, and spit in the fire.
　Lor lumme! you'd never believe it!
Card parties! such luck you'd never conceive,
　Ev'ry thing that they touch turns to gold I believe,
And it will, while 'er old man's an ace up 'is sleeve.
　Lor lumme! you'd never believe it!
Now old Mother Finch, where I goes, at 'The Firs'
　She's a packet, and so is that daughter of 'ers,
When the two of 'em starts, they fair makes the place
　　buzz,
　Wot one doesn't think of, the other one does,
'Arf-a-crown *and* me dinner I gets, if yer please,
　And last Thursday I clicks, for some nice bread and
　　cheese.
All 'oity toity', as poor as church mice.
　Lor lumme! you'd never believe it!
They've bin lookin' so 'ard for a 'usbind for years,
　That they've both gorn and sent theirselves
　　crosseyed, poor dears,
'Ere! she giv' me a 'at once, a 'at's, wot she said,
　It was more like a 'ouse, and as 'eavy as lead,
Like a blinkin' great bee-hive stuck upon me 'ead.
　Lor lumme! you'd never believe it!
And one day she sez, with 'er eyes all aglow,

'Ere's lingerie *you'll* find it useful I know,'
And there's me, give up red flannelette, years ago.
　Lord lumme! you'd never believe it!
Now the ol' Missus 'Obson, at flat number three,
　Between me and you, she's a nice cup o' tea,
Lor! the things she ain't bin, and the things she ain't
　　done,
　From wot I can see, that old girl *is* a 'one',
She's a bit of a mystery, no shadder o' doubt,
　Where 'er money comes from, I can't just make out.
Ev'rything's posh like, an' all up to date.
　Lor lumme! you'd never believe it!
Yet if anyone knocks at the door of the flat,
　She goes all 'ot an' bothered, and yells out 'Oo's
　　that?'
There's orniments, all 'idden up, more or less,
　Knives, forks, an' spoons, well you can't 'elp but
　　guess,
'Cos some is marked Lyons and some L.M.S.
　Lor lumme! you'd never believe it!
She gits watched by the Tecs at the big stores in town;
　'I'm just pickin' up bargains,' she'll say with a frown.
They say, 'We'll pick *you* up, if you don't put 'em
　　down.'
　Lor lumme! you'd never believe it!
But, I knows a backroom, where the sun's peepin'
　　through
　Up three flights o' stairs, the address, is West Two,
One o' my Reg'lars, she's just eighty four,
　Yerss, I've known 'er for years, so I *knocks* on the
　　door,
And I 'ears a 'Come in', in a voice soft an' low,
　And an old lady's step, as is falterin' an' slow.
All alone with 'er mem'ries, of days past an' gorn.
　Lor lumme! you'd never believe it!
Yerss, *she* give me my first job, as maid, at the Hall
　I've the picture in front o' me, 'angs on the wall,
There's 'er 'usbind, the General, 'e won a V.C.,
　There's the 'orses, an' 'ounds, 'neath the old chestnut
　　tree,
And then came the smash up, then Napoo, Fi*nee*.
　Lor lumme! you'd never believe it!
But I'd trudge up them stairs if they measured a mile,
　Just so me and My Lady can chat for a while,
And me payment is 'andsome, just 'er *thanks*, and 'er
　　smile.
　That's right though you'd never believe it!

Life is like a Game of Football

By Alec Kendall & A. W. Parry (1938)

Life is a game of football,
　　We each have a place in the team,
Whether amateur or professional,
　　For points we plot and scheme.
We're born just like a wee ball,
　　And soon we're taught the pace,
Right from the day we enter the fray
　　We're kicked all over the place.
We all begin as amateurs
　　From then on it's ding dong,
Through penalties, fouls and scrimmages,
　　We dribble our way along,
We get in many tight corners,
　　And emerge with many a scar,
To find ourselves offside, maybe,
　　In the net or over the bar.

Oft-times we get reverses
　　Go half-back and full-back too,
Though at half-time we may be losing
　　We charge forward to win our way thro'.
The going at times may be heavy
　　But the goal for which we aim,
Is well worth all the tackling,
　　So we keep on playing the game.
We have our last kick in the Final
　　The season draws to a close,
The game is done, have we lost or won?
　　When the referee's whistle blows?
Into which league shall we enter?
　　How's the score with you and I?
Will it be relegation? Or the play-ground in the sky?

Frisco Sam — Bad Man

By Warren Hastings & Herberte Jordan (1938)

*Say! Folks, you ever seen a rip-snortin', gun-totin' rattlesnake
with boots on? Wall, Strangers, you're lookin' at one here
right now. Yes Sir! You're a' lookin' at pizen dynamite an'
fork lightenin' what's liable to blow-up at any split second.
Wow!* (Suddenly draws gun from belt, jumps in air and
lands with feet wide apart, head thrust forward in
menacing attitude, scowling face, guns levelled. After
keeping this posture for a few seconds slowly relaxes,
and returns guns to belt).
*Say! Folks, you wanter know who I am? I'll tell you who I
am. I'll say I'm Frisco Sam — Bad Man.*

Why, Strangers, you know me,
　　Frisco Sam from Sanfransee,
Alabam or Tennessee —
　　That's me!
I'll say I'm goldarn tough.
　　I'll say I'm all-fired rough.
No guy can't call my bluff — 'S'enough!
　　Say, when I'm on the spree.
Hell's gates jest *yearn* for me.
　　There's sure some jubilee — Believe me!
When I get riled an' sore,
　　Jest watch me snort, an' roar,
An' shoot strangers by the score — or more
　　When Sheriffs see me — Say!
You watch 'em fade away,
　　Or kneel right down an' pray — Hey!

I've shot so many men,
　　Eighteen-hundred an' ten.
I stopped a-countin' then Amen.
　　I runs my own graveyard,
Epitaphs by the yard.
　　Grave-diggers working hard, sure, pard.

*Wall, folks, I allus believes in givin' a corpse a real
comfortable, elegant, slap-up funeral. So I bin a' writin' a few
obituary epitaphs fer them bone-headed critters what had a
slight misunderstandin' with me, and in consequence has
passed away sudden — with their boots on. I allow I ain't no
high-falutin', fancy, pen-pushin' poet, but I done my best, an'
I reckon I've pre-dooced one or two epitaphs such as any
reg'lar corpse oughter be proud of. Just get this one fer a start
— (Produces small book from hip pocket).*

The bones what's buried here below, belonged to Silas
　　Carr.
　　If he hadn't a' drunk Frisco's drink by mistake, he
　　　wouldn't be where 'e are.
Here's another —
　　Reposin' here in this cold clay, lies all what's mortal
　　　of Reuben Gray.
He put so much whisky an' rum away, that his pickled
　　remains won't ever decay.
　　I'm mighty proud of that there effort, Strangers.
Here's another —

Here lies the body of One-Eyed Pete. He died while
  standin' on his feet,
He was took sudden while on the bust. Ashes to ashes
  an' dust to dust.
And another —
Under this sod lies 'Killer' Dan, who died thro'
  ignorance
  He might a' bin chawin' terbaccer yet, but his gun
  got caught in his pants.

Dan was sure hot on the draw — but he was unlucky.
There's only two kinds of people where I come from — the
Quick an' the Dead.
Here's the last one, an' I guess William K. Shakespeare
couldn't a' done no better —

Here lies the karkis of Two-Gun Jake. Shed no salt
  tears mother.
  He sure was a four-flushing low down snake an' so
  was his goldarn brother.

The burg where I hail from is known as Paradise City. The
place ain't very big. The population is allus bein' redooced
so rapid that it ain't never had time to grow. There's only 18
buildings in Paradise City — 17 saloons an' one
undertaker's. The undertaker is the richest man in the
country. Strangers, believe me, that place is so allfired tough
that rattlesnakes eat outer yer hand in the street. Shootin' is
continuous day an' night, an' the noise is such that you can't
hear yerself speak. The boys allus talks to each other in the
deaf an' dumb language. An' when I've said that I guess I've
sure said a mouthful.
Now, Folks, you all know who I am here below.

I ain't no fancy movie star
  I ain't no cowboy lar-de-dar
But when I'm down at Casey's Bar,
  I guess I'm the whole darn show — an' I oughter
  know!

Nell
By George Arthurs & Cuthbert Clarke (1939)

Nell was my friend at college,
  The best friend I ever had,
We shared each other's secrets,
  She laughed when I was sad;
And I did the same with Nellie,
  We were a loyal pair,
And we vowed that ever after
  All things in life we'd share.
We parted, met, then once more
  We parted for a while,
But yesterday we met again,
  She kissed me, with a smile,
Then murmured, 'Phyllis! Dearest!
  Oh, aren't you looking well!
I do believe you're slimmer!'
  A darling girl is Nell!

We asked the usual questions,
  You know how women chat,
'Do say who made that gown, dear?'
  And 'Oh, that lovely hat!'
Then in a tiny tearoom,
  Exchanging hopes and fears,
We talked of what had happened
  Within the last few years.
And when at last she left me,
  It was to say good-bye,
A tear fell when she kissed me,
  I—I had to cry;
With sympathetic glances,
  We each arranged our furs,
When she went back to *my* husband,
  And I went back to *her's!*

Cigarette Cards
By Margaret Howe & Cyril Baker (1939)

If you should smoke a cigarette, in train or tram or
  bus,
  And total strangers that you meet start talking,
  please don't fuss.
Though it's not strictly British and you hate it from
  the start,

Don't get the answer ready, 'I'm a stranger in this
  part'.
For they haven't murky motives, like the blokes in
  novelettes,
  They only want the cards you've got inside your
  cigarettes.

Now if knitting is a mystery and your wife's two purl
  one plain,
    Keeps on driving you quite crazy, very soon they
    can explain.
Both the double clove-hitched reef stitch and the Shark
  tooth cable twine,
    If you'll only take the trouble to read series number
    nine.
Though you've followed Mr. Middleton, your rose
  trees have got blight,
    And your hollyhocks insist on shrinking quite two
    feet per night.
Quickly number three will settle that, or turn to
  number four,
    If you want to know the way to get back tools you've
    lent next door.
They've the stones unturned in Parliament since Julius
  Caesar came,
    And each single 'avenue explored' you'll find them
    all by name,
Also pictures of that famous 'fence' each member sits
  with glee.
    You can find them all, with footnotes, done in series
    thirty three.
Your pet goldfish may have typhoid and it sadly flaps
  its fins,
    And you've looked for help in Whitaker and asked
    for Godfrey Winn's,

But if you want really sound advice on how to treat
  your pets,
    You just simply can't get better than from cards in
    cigarettes.
If you're keeping ducks or chickens, they will tell you
  how to spot
    Any green-eared red minorca from a pink-eyed
    wyandotte
They've got staggers, and they're starving — Heavens
  knows just what they need
    But the only other card you've got's about canary
    seed.
Golf by self-tuition's easy, that's if you complete your
  set.
    The old Colonel's badly bunkered and I think he's
    still there yet.
He's cursed the course, the Cabinet, and giv'n the
  caddy hell,
    'Cause the poor kid said, 'Gosh! Guv'ner, you need
    number eight as well'.
For the total annual sneezes brought on by the
  common cold
    Or how to find a train that runs to Potash-on-the-
    Wold,
How to tell high tide in Leap Year or to play
  Tom-Tom Duets,
    You'll find all with diagrams on the cards in
    cigarettes.

The Human Touch
By E. J. Gargery, Nosmo King & Ernest Longstaffe (1939)

In this wonder-world of progress in which we live
  today,
    We find what intellect can do with lifeless earth and
    clay.
We see how man can utilize, from Nature's mystic
  store,
    The forces lying dormant there and never used
    before.
And when inventions multiply, and science does so
  much,
    We rather tend to minimise the vital *Human Touch*.
We've attained the age of iron, of machinery, of force.
    We've reached the point where *Robots* do the work of
    man and horse.
We've found the means of harnessing the ingredients
  of our sphere,
    And made them do the jobs *men* did, before
    machines were here
For in our workmanship today in music, art and such,

The medium of a soulless tool oft kills the *Human
  Touch*.
We had our lesson in the war, of where it all might
  lead,
    When scientist and chemist worked to meet the
    nation's need.
The slaughter of a million men, by gas, by steel, by
  gun.
    Taught the awe-struck sons of earth what mind and
    brains had done;
But midst the welter and the blood, with faltering
  hands, we'd clutch
    That clear, white, shining, radiant touch, the heroic
    Human Touch.
There's surely something very wrong when Christian
  men employ
    Their brains and power and knowledge, merely to
    destroy:
One day these great inventions that benefit so few,

May claim Poetic Justice by destroying me and you.
And should that day come, be assured we couldn't
    hope for much,
    For we lose our very birthright, when we lose the
    Human Touch.
So in this age of progress in which we have our place,
    If we would seek the mainspring of the glory of our
    race.

Then it's deeper than the working and the probing of
    the mind,
    And it's loftier than the products of the genius of our
    kind!
The *Human Touch* the touch Divine upon the earthy
    clod
    That takes the vileness out of man and brings him
    nearer God.

Good-Bye and God Bless You
By Nosmo King & Ernest Longstaffe (1939)

I love the Anglo Saxon speech
    With its direct appeal:
It takes a hold, and seems somehow
    To sound so very real.
I don't object that men should air
    The Gallic they have paid for
With 'Au revoir,' 'Bon soir Cherie,'
    For that's what French was made for.
But when a crony takes your hand
    In parting to address you,
He drops all foreign words and says,
    'Good-bye, old chap, God bless you.'
It seems to me a sacred phrase
    With reverence impassioned,
Handed down from righteous days,
    Quaintly, yet nobly fashioned.
Into the porches of the ear
    It steals with subtle unction,
And in your heart of hearts appears
    To work its gracious function.

And all day long with pleasing song
    It lingers to caress you,
I'm sure no human heart goes wrong
    That's told 'Good-bye — God bless you.'
I love the words — perhaps because
    When I was leaving mother,
To join the others over there
    We looked at one another,
I saw then in her dear old eyes
    The love she couldn't tell me,
A love eternal as the skies
    Whatever fate befell me.
She put her arms around my neck
    To soothe the pain of leaving,
And though her heart was nigh to break
    She spoke no word of grieving —
She said, 'I will not cry my dear
    For fear it should distress you,'
And with her parting kiss she smiled
    And said, 'Good-bye — God bless you.'

Me and My Pipe
Clifford Grey, Bert Lee & Ernest Longstaffe (1940)

We sit by the fireside in my easy chair,
    Just watching the shadows that play here and there.
We've only a cottage upon the hill side,
    But it's home and it's shelter so we're satisfied.
Me and my pipe, my pipe and me,
    Old pals together content as can be,
Some sigh for wealth, some want a name,
    But my ounce of 'Baccy' is worth all your fame.
When others start nagging and cannot agree,
    I smile at my pipe and my pipe smiles at me.
Easily pleased with a pipe you say.
    Maybe I am but I'm built that way.
For he comforts me with his soothing weed,
    Tho' my old pal costs a bit more to feed,

I've got to pay, and I gladly do.
    It takes more than a Budget to part us two.
Folks tell me mine is a lonely life,
    Instead of a pipe, I need a wife,
For a pipe goes out, I say with a grin,
    Well so do wives you can't keep 'em in.
Folks shake their heads, and they often say,
    'He doesn't like girls, he's not built that way.'
That's what they think, but they don't know,
    There was someone once in the long ago
As fair as a summer rose was she:
    And one brief summer she bloomed for me.
The golden sunshine lit love's flame,
    But she droop'd and died when winter came.

Me and my pipe, my pipe and me,
 Old pals together content as can be,
Some sigh for wealth, some want a name,
 But my ounce of 'Baccy' is worth all your fame.
When others start nagging and cannot agree,
 I smile at my pipe, and my pipe smiles at me.
And now, as I sit in my lonely den

Through the hazy smoke-clouds once again,
 I see my rose of the long ago,
 And she smiles at me, for she seems to know
That I've found a pal who is staunch and true,
 Who'll comfort me when the day is through,
And that's why my pipe is a pal to me,
 He brings back a fragrant memory.

The Glutton
By L. E. Baggaley & Herbert Townsend (1940)

Seven hundred years odd come next August,
 Skegness had a bit of a shock,
When a great crowd of fellers on horses
 Were seen gathered under the clock.
At first it were thought t'were an outing,
 Till somebody spotted King John,
Who were hiding away from the barons,
 On account of a row that were on.
In those days there weren't any pierrots,
 At least they weren't properly known,
So if visitors wanted enjoyment
 It had to be fun of their own.
Now the King, he were one for a frolic,
 So after a gallon of beer
He announced he were going mixed bathing,
 Wi' a lass he'd got off with on t' pier.
He borrowed a tandem from t' garage,
 And Mabel said, 'Let's be off, Jack.'
So they started, and she took the front half,
 While King took it easy at back.
In less than an hour sea were sighted,
 Tide weren't as far out as they'd thought,
And Mabel soon popped on her costume,
 While John donn'd an old crown he'd brought.
They splashed and cut all sorts of capers,
 Not taking much notice of tide,
Till King, who were getting a thirst on,
 Commenced out of t' water to stride.
When he came to look round for his raiment,
 T'were a most tragic moment for John,
For t'were all washed away — save his trousers.
 Aye, even his scout belt were gone!
'Well, ain't that annoying,' said Monarch,
 'I'm sure I can't walk thro' the town

And appear before crowds of me subjects
 In a pair of grey flannels and crown!
We mun walk along sands to some village,
 I'm certain 'twould be more discreet,
And then, when it's dark, we'll go inland
 And happen get summat to eat!'
So off they trudged, maid in wet costume —
 And King in his flannels much smirched —
He were feeling annoyed, cos a seagull
 Had lit on his crown and sat perched.
At last when a pub were reached safely
 And a nice fire were warming their feet,
The King asked, 'Hast got any lampreys? —
 Then bring us two surfeits — toot sweet.'
Now John, he were partial to lampreys
 And had soon finished his little pile
And were helping the lass wi' her plateful
 An' laughing and chatting the while
He'd forgot for a time that his armour
 Were every bit swep' out to sea,
And the piece round his middle — like corsets
 Had it's use when he'd had a big tea!
And lampreys are prone to expansion,
 (Which means when they're eaten — they swell.)
And John muttered, 'Ich dien' — or summat like that,
 Which meant he weren't feeling too well.
Landlord were just saying to swineherd,
 'Nay lad, that's no fly, it's a hop!'
When there came from direction of t'parlour,
 The sound of a very loud 'POP.'
The host took one look round the portal,
 Then shut it wi' never a word.
In fact he said nowt till he'd drunk half a pint
 To the health of King Henry The Third!

The Voyage of the 'Saucy Jane'
By Val L. Regan & Herberte Jordan (1941)

This is the tale of the 'Saucy Jane,'
 Who sailed out to the lightship and then back again;

For years she had wallowed her way round the bay
 With trippers, and babies, and lovers each day.

Till a maggot, deep hid in a maniac's brain,
  Stirred; and lashed him to visions of lunatic gain.
Then the laughter was hushed as the war clouds drew
  near,
  And the 'Saucy Jane' brooded alone at her pier.
Her sleek sides grew rusty, her paint drab and grey,
  Her engines stood silent as day after day,
The great ships of war; sisters under the skin
  Hurried past the backwater she lay rotting in.
While her skipper, as grizzled and old as was she,
  Fumed and groaned as he heard the guns thudding
    at sea.
Then a whisper was heard going round and around,
  Much too good to be true; yet the whisper gained
    ground,
Till the skipper climbed up on the bridge once again,
  And with tears in his voice said, 'We're off, Saucy Jane!
Then the old ship moved off with a creak and a quiver,
  To join the strange fleet that had come down the
    river.
There were tug-boats and barges of curious smell,
  There were sleek motor-boats, paddle steamers as
    well,
River launches and wherries and sailing craft too,
  And each boat had an equally curious crew.
On that shore of the Channel where once had been
  France,
  Stood the men who had struggled thro' Death's
    crimson dance;
While the skies overhead rained a murderous hate

And it seemed as though help would arrive much
  too late;
Till that curious fleet with the curious crew,
  Into sight and the bomb-spattered battle zone drew,
With the 'Saucy Jane' puffing black smoke in a cloud
  While her skipper steered, cursing and swearing
    aloud.
By guess and by God, they were hoisted aboard,
  And the old 'Saucy Jane' her defiance now roared,
While down in her vitals a strange stokehole gang
  Shovelled coal mixed with blood while they sweated
    and sang.
As the bullets whizzed round and the shrapnel fell fast
  Till a sickening crash robbed old 'Jane' of her mast;
Then a wounded Jock shouted, 'Ah'll bet ye ma kilt
  That the auld girl will mak' it — *This tub was Clyde*
    built!'
The old ship floundered on in a last burst of pride;
  Then help was around her and boats at her side
But the old 'Saucy Jane,' with a strange kind of grace;
  Gave a sigh as she welcomed the sea's cold embrace;
Just as if she had known she was needed no more.
  She slid to her rest, on the soft ocean floor.
In the years still to come, when the story's complete,
  On the long scroll of honour, that curious fleet,
That ragtag and bob tail of vessels and crews,
  Will have earned a renown that *no* ship would
    refuse;
And more honour and glory no vessel will gain
  Than that valiant lady *'The Old Saucy Jane!'*

If You'll Pardon My Saying So
By Warren Hastings & Herberte Jordan (1941)

Spoken. 'Watkins, the perfect family butler, addresses
the young master who is still abed'

A lady to see you, Mr. Archibald, sir.
  The matter appears to be pressing.
Luncheon was served quite an hour ago,
  I did not awaken you, sir, as you know.
There are times, sir, when sleep is a blessing.
  I have here some ice, sir, to place on your head,
And also a whisky and 'polly'.
  I don't know what time you retired to bed,
But the party sir, must have been jolly,
  If you'll pardon my saying so.
The lady in question a-waiting below,
  Is accompanied, sir, by her mother,
And also a prize-fighting gentleman, sir,
  A pugnacious character one might infer,

Whom the lady describes as her brother.
  The elderly female is quite commonplace,
A most vulgar person, I fear, sir,
  Who shouts in a nerve wracking falsetto voice,
And her language is painful to hear, sir,
  If you'll pardon my saying so.
The prize-fighter person is burning with hate.
  He refers to you, sir, as a 'twister.'
He threatens to alter the shape of your 'clock,'
  To break you in half, sir, and knock off your 'block,'
Unless you do right by his sister.
  The young lady says, sir, with trembling lips,
That you made her a promise of marriage.
  She wants to know why she should eat fish and chips,

While you, sir, ride by in your carriage,
  If you'll pardon my saying so.
Sir John has a dreadful attack of the gout,
  He is fuming to beat all creation.
My lady, your mother, is up in the air.
  She is having hysterics, and tearing her hair,
And borders on nervous prostration.

Would you wish me to pack your portmanteau at
  once,
And look up the times of the trains, sir?
  Or perhaps you would rather I brought you a drink,
And a pistol to blow out your brains, sir.
  If you'll pardon my saying so.

My England
By Arthur Victor & Ernest Longstaffe (1941)

Old England is a country of fields an' 'edges green,
  Of little streams an' little woods, the prettiest you've
    seen.
It's a tanner to the country on the bus outside your
    door
  You, the missus and the kids — what could a bloke
    ask more?
An' I want to keep it just like *that!*
  Yes, I want to keep it just like *that!*
Old England ain't a country what's ruled by Gestapos.
  By blokes dressed up in uniforms and goodness only
    knows.
You sees a copper now an' then but if you ain't on the
    twist,
  They treats you matey an' polite, there ain't no
    mailed fist
An' I want to keep it just like *that!*
  Yes, I want to keep it just like *that!*

Old England ain't a country of Heils and raise yer arm
  An' you can 'ave a pint at night and never do no
    'arm,
An' if you 'as a drop too much an' runs the guv'ment
    down,
  There ain't no concentration camps around an
    English town,
An' I'm going to keep it just like *that!*
  Yes I'm going to keep it just like *that!*
This England's full of freedom for blokes like me an'
    you,
  Make no mistake we treasure it an' are fighting for it
    too.
I don't allow nobody for to dictate fings to me,
  Excepting p'raps the missus — still that's 'ow it ort to
    be,
An' I mean to keep it just like *that!*
  Yes, *I mean to keep it Just Like That!*

The Civilians
By Nosmo King, Percy Nash & Ernest Longstaffe (1941)

The British fighting forces are a pattern to the world,
  They command respect and honour where'er our
    flag's unfurl'd,
Their courage and tenacity, they've proved in
    countless ways,
  And never more heroically than in these stirring
    days.
But courage isn't only found beneath a uniform,
  Our wonderful civilians too have stood up to the
    storm.
These civilian men and women who have reached the
    very height,
  Of loyalty and courage in the front line of the fight.
Cheerfully and bravely they have answered to the call.
  Their fame will live for evermore for God has
    blessed them all.

And when the devastation and the smoke has cleared
    away,
  There'll remain a figure standing in the glory of the
    day.
On its brow a crown of laurels, and a smile upon its
    face
  'Tis the emblem of the people, of a never beaten race
The people of a country who have stood up unafraid
  To face the fearful carnage and the terror of the
    raid,
So let us all with grateful hearts each night and ev'ry
    morn,
  Fall on our knees and thank our God, that we are
    British born.

Dawn Patrol
By Warren Hastings & Herberte Jordan (1942)

I had a brother dressed in blue,
  An airman young and fine.
At dawn beside his Hurricane
  I took his hand in mine.

He said with a smile I knew so well,
  'Just off for a spot of fun.'
I placed his hand in the Hand of God,
  And he flew toward the sun.

Merchant Navy
By V. F. Stevens & S. Brown (1943)

Charlie's said good-bye to Nell,
  Jim's got his seaboots to pack,
Shorty and Pete stroll down the street,
  Arm in arm with Jack,
They've finished their spell of shore leave
  They've had their round of sport,
And the sea blue glint in their fearless squint
  Tells that their ship's leaving port.
No braid adorns their reefer, no flash, no stripes, no
  pips
  But a tiny 'M.N.' denotes they're the men who go
  down to the sea in ships.
Out where the convoys muster on the wide eternal
  blue
  'Midst mine, torpedo, bomb and shell, they've got a
  job to do,
A job for nerves of tempered steel, and hearts that
  ne'er will slack,
  For where they're bound no peace is found, either
  going or coming back.
Oh it's peep thru' those glasses, Shorty, and mark well
  what I say,

Up there, in the heavens J.U.87's and blimey they're
  headed this way.
So get Charlie out o' the galley, tell the doctor he'd
  better stand by,
  Clamp down your tin hat, you're bound to need that,
  especially when stuff starts to fly
There goes Action stations for Merchant Navy Man
  too,
  And the heliograph's ray from the battleships say,
  The convoy must get through
With the escort's guns a-spewing and the carrier's
  brood in flight,
  Scorched by the breath of sudden death, these men
  know how to fight.
Fight thru' the hell of battle on the seas o'er which they
  ride,
  And the U Boats spoil is a patch of oil left on the
  place where they died.
Gentlemen! Here is a toast and keep their memory
  green.
  Up on your feet, and drink it neat!
The Mercantile Marine!

Legs
By Warren Hastings (1945)

Legs — Legs — Legs.
  See 'em on the tables, see 'em on the chairs,
See 'em on the parlour maid walking up the stairs,
  See 'em on the horses, see 'em on the dogs,
See 'em on the pussy-cats, see 'em on the frogs.
  See 'em when they're mutton, see 'em when they're
  pork,
See 'em when they're wooden, see 'em when they're
  cork,
  See 'em on the elephant, see 'em on the flea,

And on lovely people same as you and me.
  See 'em on a camel, see 'em on a crow,
See 'em at the theatre dancing in a row.
  See 'em on the soldiers as they march in step,
See 'em on the jitter-bugs full of gin-and-pep,
  See 'em on a Scotsman, see 'em on a Greek,
See 'em in silk stockings, beautiful and sleek.
  No matter what you call 'em pins, or props, or pegs,
Limbs, or shanks, or spindles — they're Legs — Legs
  — Legs!

Timmy's Sacrifice

By William H. Dawes, Nosmo King & Herbert Townsend (1946)

One evening ev'ry year the local Mayor was wont to
  meet
  The children of the city at their annual Christmas
    treat;
And so that none should hunger at this season of Good
  Will,
  The board was spread with Yuletide fare that all
    might eat their fill.
A mighty Christmas tree was placed at one end of the
  hall,
  It's glitt'ring branches laden down with lovely gifts
    for all.
'But with so many guests to satisfy,' His Worship
  smiled,
  'There can be but one gift — and only one — for
    every child.'
So one by one each childish heart was fill'd with happy
  joy,
  And sounds of 'Ooh!' and 'Ah!' were heard as each
    received his toy.
One little chap called Tim seemed dazed at this
  display;
  'Twas plain to see that presents very rarely came his
    way.
His clothes, tho' tidy, bore the mark of many a patched
  up tear,
  Sign of a loving widowed mother's never-failing
    care.
'Tis now his turn to take a gift — O, what a glad
  surprise!
  A box of soldiers! Timmy's joy was written in his
    eyes.

He stretched his hands out eagerly — and then, we saw
  him pause;
  One wistful look, and then he spoke — and oh, the
    loud guffaws
That echoed round the room as, shyly, timidly, he
  said,
  'Please sir, I'd like a dolly for a little girl, instead.'
The jeering sniggers of the rest made Timmy blush
  with shame;
  'He wants a dolly!' someone sneered, another:
    'What's her name?'
The kindly Mayor said, 'Oh, but why a doll, my little
  son?
  The soldiers for a lad like you are surely much more
    fun?'
'It's for my little sister, sir, she's ill, and — oh, I know
  She's longing for a little doll because she told me so.
You said one present for each child, and so I'd raver,
  sir,
  Give back the sojers and I'll take a doll instead — for
    her.'
As Timmy finished speaking, not a single sound was
  heard,
  Glances were averted and many eyes were blurred.
Sarcastic sneers and sniggers faded in a trice,
  For Timmy's story told a tale of great self-sacrifice.
And when the children, homeward bound, went filing
  thro' the door,
  A lovely doll — and soldiers, too — young Timmy
    proudly bore.

Thank You!

By Margaret Hodgkinson, Nosmo King & Herbert Townsend (1946)

In this glorious hour of victory, when the world at last
  is free,
  Free for ever from the shackles of a hateful tyranny;
When the long, dark night of anguish and of dread has
  passed away
  And there dawns the radiant promise of a new and
    better day;
In the midst of our rejoicing, let us pause awhile, and
  think
  Of those to whom we owe so much, who brought us
    from the brink

Of disaster and destruction to the final shining goal,
  Who saved this land from conquest — aye, saved its
    very soul,
Let us think of them today, and of our overwhelming
  debt,
  And say a simple 'thank you' lest we all too soon
    forget!
First then, THANK YOU, Royal Navy, for the service
  that is yours,
  Of keeping safe, inviolate, our sacred British shores;
We thank you for Tarranto, Matapan and Narvik Bay,

For the conquest of the U-boat — for the Bismarck,
  the Graf Spee
And we THANK YOU Merchant Seamen, you of
  finest mettle bred,
  For your superhuman task in keeping Britain armed
  and fed,
We THANK YOU British Army, for your grand
  immortal work,
  From that hour of tragic glory on the beaches of
  Dunkirk,
Till the day when, four years later, with your allies
  you were hurled
  To storm a fortress continent and liberate the world.
We THANK YOU Royal Air Force — who can count
  our debt to you?
  From that 'finest hour' when we were saved by your
  immortal 'few'
Until as lords and conquerors of the air, we saw you
  rise
  And sweep your way to overwhelming victory in the
  skies.
We THANK YOU 'Monty', Eisenhower, McArthur
  and the rest,
  Our leaders in the field, whose names fill ev'ry
  British chest
And over all, for ever shining in undying fame.
  We THANK YOU Winston Churchill — blest for
  ever be your name!
Our brothers of the Commonwealth, who loyal proved
  and true,
  Who gave your all to serve the Mother-land — we
  THANK YOU, too;

We THANK YOU, gallant Allies, who have striven at
  our side,
  Whose sons, with ours, have won the day, with our
  sons fought — and died
We THANK the Women of this land, with heartfelt
  proud 'well done!'
  The factory lass, farm hand, the nurse, the girl
  behind the gun,
We THANK those brave civilians, who, thro' terror,
  loss and grief,
  Endured unto the end with fortitude beyond belief,
And let us now remember too, with mingled pride and
  pain,
  In silent grateful homage, the unnumbered
  thousands slain!
They died for us that we might see this day — their
  blood was shed;
  Sorrowfully, yet proudly, we salute our honoured
  dead,
And in their ranks one dear loved name stands forth
  for ever blest,
  Son of a brave and mighty race, the noblest and the
  best;
Through all these years, deep shrined in ev'ry British
  heart he's dwelt,
  With grateful hearts we bless and thank him,
  Franklin Roosevelt.
But more than all, with humble hearts, we cry on
  bended knee,
  Thanks be to Thee, Almighty God, Who gave us
  Victory!

PART THREE

PERFORMERS AND WRITERS 1938 — 1981

As we saw in Part II, the 1939-1945 war marked the end of the dramatic monologue along with the death of live music hall. In the post-war period, it has been replaced by the comedy song monologue, initially through radio and recordings and latterly in intimate revue.

This development has been associated with a group of performers who wrote much (and in some cases all) of their own material. The writer makes no apology if his post-war selection extends the musical monologue to what might also be described as comic songs or burlesque ballads. The main factor in making these final choices has been to identify material which is in the comedy song monologue style: in which the words are more important than the music, and in which the personality of the performer is as intimately identified with his material as was ever Bransby Williams, Billy Bennett, Stanley Holloway or Gracie Fields.

Cyril Fletcher comes into this category with his popular *Dreamin' of Thee* and the five examples of 'Odd Odes' which follow it. Once more, Greatrex Newman appears in the monologue story: it was he who discovered Cyril Fletcher at a Sunday night concert at the Prince of Wales Theatre, London, in the late thirties. Cyril was reciting *The Highwayman* with a comedy encore. He was studying elocution at the Guildhall School of Music, but his father hoped that Cyril would work as an insurance clerk rather than risk the hazards of a theatrical profession. Despite this parental frown, Rex Newman was able to put him into his 'Fol de Rols' seaside concert party at the White Rock Pavilion, Hastings.

Rex recalled that one of his retired concert party comedians, Leslie Hollwood, had used a recitation about a love-sick Tommy which he thought might be suitable for Cyril Fletcher. For a long time it was difficult to trace the author, who — somewhat surprisingly — turned out to be the thriller writer Edgar Wallace: he had written the piece while a war correspondent in the Boer War.

It was included when the Fol de Rols went on the air for a six week BBC season at the end of the summer, and Cyril's version of *Dreamin' of Thee* firmly established him 'on the air'. The 'Odd Odes' followed from Cyril Fletcher's own pen and, over forty years later, this performer's continuing mastery of the spoken word is demonstrated in BBC-TV's 'That's Life'.

It was also BBC radio that marked the start of Arthur Askey's big personal following associated with his catch-phrases 'Hello, Playmates' and 'I Thang Yew' in 'Bandwaggon'. This was soon supplemented by a highly successful recording career and the items included in Part III for Arthur Askey, listed in order of recording date, span the last forty years. But Big-Hearted Arthur had served a long apprenticeship in show business before his first recording and radio success. Originally a clerk in the local education office in Liverpool, he spent the first ten years of his show business career in seaside concert parties which, in the winter, he combined with Masonic entertainment, cabaret and music hall appearances.

Like Cyril Fletcher, Arthur Askey drew on his own writing skills, but he was also fortunate in finding a number of writers and composers whose work was tailor-made for his style and personality. Of these, chief credit must go to Kenneth Blain, a fellow Merseyside comedian. He wrote and composed *The Bee Song*, but sold the performing rights to Arthur Askey for two guineas for one concert party season. There would be many subsequent payments as the song became Arthur's main meal ticket. Blain followed this with several animal songs, of which *Chirrup* and *The Moth* are typical examples. Although printed in song form, these numbers essentially drew on the same standard musical background, placing stronger emphasis on the words than on the music. This monologue format is even more pronounced in *The Seaside Band*.

Robert Rutherford and Frank Wilcock, long-standing writers and composers of monologues, contributed singly or together to the build-up of Arthur Askey's career with non-animal subjects such as *All to Specification* and *The Flu Germ*. One of their classic pieces, *The Villain Still Pursued Her*, also brought a vivid reminder of burlesque drama in Arthur Askey's long-playing record revival in 1976 (a splendid summary of his career entitled 'Before Your Very Eyes', released by Decca Argo, ZDA 173).

The song-writing team of Barbara Gordon, Basil Thomas and Robert Gordon also added to the list of 'Askey animals'. They were later to write the score of one of Arthur's biggest musical comedy successes — 'The Kid from Stratford' in 1948.

Arthur would add his own contributions to all his song-writers' efforts and, to vary the schoolboy humour of his 'Insectivorous' and 'Wee Beastie' songs, he would frequently ad lib between verses. A good example of this is in his performance of *The Worm*. After the first verse-ending of 'Squiggle, squiggle, squiggle, squirm, squirm, squirm', Arthur would add, 'Pretty, isn't it? Any questions?' After the second, he added, 'Ada, put it down. You don't know where it's been.' After the third, 'New readers begin here. This would have suited Eartha Kitt.' And finally, in getting in the last word, 'My assistant will now pass among you with copies for sale.'

Arthur Askey's own writing and composing skills are evident in other examples of his animal songs, including *The Seagull* and *The Ant. The Seagull* used a simple musical arrangement which provided the backing of several similar pieces (demonstrating yet again that the words rather than the music were the chief ingredient). *The Ant* was one such derivative piece for which the words were written by Dan Leno Jr., the son of the great music hall comedian.

Although Arthur Askey has been blessed with exceptional performing longevity, Stanley Holloway has the unique distinction of having appeared in Variety before the First World War and in the Royal Variety Command Performance in 1981. As we saw in Part I, in the process he became Britain's outstanding comic monologuist and his continued success is illustrated by his work in this field during the last forty years.

Indeed, he may be said to have personally initiated the death knell of the dramatic monologue with the sketch *Pukka Sahib*, originally written by Reginald Purdell for one of the Savage Club's Saturday night entertainments. Stanley suggested it as a possible item to his co-star and closest friend, Leslie Henson, for the 1940 revue, 'Up and Doing'.

Based on the Milton Hayes recitation of *The Green Eye of the Little Yellow God*, the sketch involved Stanley as a serious monologuist in full evening dress, hounded to distraction by Leslie Henson and Cyril Ritchard as two Indian army officers. From their vantage point in the stage box, they interrupted throughout and constantly sought to make Stanley 'dry' or smile. As he has recalled,

'If they had succeeded, the monologue would have lost all credibility and it was one of the hardest jobs of my life to resist the leg-pulling of that sophisticated artist Cyril Ritchard and my beloved, gravelly-voiced friend, Leslie Henson.'

The *George Lashwood Monologue* was written by Frank Eyton for another revue at the Saville Theatre 'Fine and Dandy' in 1942. It was performed by Stanley as a tribute to Lashwood, who had died only a few weeks earlier. In recreating his turn, Stanley came on in a frock coat and top hat, and performed the decline and fall of a 'swell' whose bogus aristocratic pretensions are revealed when he describes his schooldays at Harrow *College* instead of Harrow *School*.

After his great success in 'My Fair Lady', Stanley was persuaded in the mid-fifties to revive the monologues of his youth in a series of recordings. *The Street Watchman's Story* had been the opening recitation in Bransby Williams' act. Unlike Williams' many tear-jerking pieces, the words are full of humour and were perfectly suited to Stanley's resounding Cockney impression. *Evings' Dorg 'Ospital* and *On Strike* were two more Cockney pieces written by Charles Pond in 1906. It must have been regarded as mildly daring at that time to expose the activities of those who looked after the pets of the well-to-do, such as Evings (the Cockney rendition of Evans). That piece has a timeless appeal to dog-lovers, and there is a strangely contemporary flavour to *On Strike*, with its account of an early demarcation dispute. Whether its implicit male chauvinism is in keeping with modern thinking is more open to question.

Sweeney Todd, The Battle of Hastings and *Magna Charter* were all published in the mid-thirties to meet the ever-growing demand for the song monologue. Stanley did not perform them at that time, and indeed, the two Marriott Edgar compositions, *The Battle of Hastings* and *Magna Charter*, were intended for the author's own use. However, Stanley derived particular satisfaction from the 1975 recordings for two reasons: first, because he had suggested the repeated use of "Arold on 'is 'orse with 'is 'awk in 'is 'and' in *The Battle of Hastings*, and second, because *Magna Charter* contained one of his favourite monologue endings.

Albert's Reunion and *The Parson of Puddle* were also recorded in 1975. The modern 'Albert' piece was based on a draft which the musical comedy performer, Stanley Lupino, had prepared between the wars, and Stanley Holloway later re-wrote it with its modern references to 'Born Free' for his appearance on the BBC's 'Parkinson' show in 1978. At the same time, Rex Newman was revising *The Parson of Puddle* for publication. Stanley had originally recorded it forty years earlier, using his 'clergyman' voice. In the fresh 1975 recording he combined it with *Albert's Reunion, Magna Charter* and *The Battle of Hastings*, under an overall title he especially relished, 'Life in the Old Dog Yet' (Argo ZDA 170).*

* In 1980, EMI's long-playing record ONCM 533 'Stanley Holloway: More Monologues and Songs' containing several of the items in Part I was released to mark Stanley's ninetieth year.

Joyce Grenfell, alas, is no longer with us. Yet the recollection of her unique monologue performing style is, happily, maintained in many recordings. These date from her emergence first as a writer, and then as a performer, with the BBC during the last war. Initially, she made her mark with a form of pure monologue — 'making up people' and telling stories about them in a style which was much influenced by his childhood memories of a family friend, the brilliant American impressionist, Ruth Draper.

With the post-war blossoming of intimate revue, Joyce Grenfell built up a repertoire of immensely believable characters reflecting her own Anglo-American background: the Society Hostess, Shirl's Girl-Friend, the American Tourist and many more. She also, in partnership with Richard Adinsell, produced a range of song monologues which — for the purposes of this book — allows us to concentrate on those items whose poetic form, charm and sophistication ushered in a new monologue era.

Oh, Mr du Maurier in fact links almost directly with the birth of the monologue in the Victorian age, when attractive literary ladies were drawn by the artist George du Maurier for 'Punch'. This piece, with words by Joyce Grenfell and a lilting melody by Richard Adinsell, was used in Noel Coward's revue 'Sigh No More' in 1945. In the same show, Joyce Grenfell showed her versatility with a Cockney version of the master's own composition *The End of the News*.

The words for *Maud* were written by Joyce Grenfell's cousin, Nicholas Phipps, who is better known to the general public as the moustachioed Guards type of a thousand bit parts in British films. His parody of *Come into the Garden, Maud* was used to create — if such a contradiction is possible — the song monologue duet which Joyce Grenfell performed with the ideally-cast harassed, earnest figure of Julian Orchard in 'Penny Plain' in 1951.

Three Brothers was another Grenfell/Adinsell composition for revue. Its compassion for the spinster and her relatives is echoed again in *Stately as a Galleon* with the perfectly observed set of characters (and the music) of Old Time Dancing. It too was written for revue, and achieved even wider popularity with a 1964 recording. The last five Grenfell items selected were all written for theatrical performances and mostly used in the one-woman show 'Joyce Grenfell Requests the Pleasure of your Company' and in 'Joyce Grenfell: A Miscellany'. They were included in her own selection from thirty-six years of stage work in the book of songs and sketches entitled 'Stately as a Galleon' published by Futura in 1978. They make a fitting tribute to Joyce Grenfell's skill as a writer and performer, especially if one follows the advice she gave in the Foreword to that book:

'My hope is that as you read you will invent and hear for yourself the sounds each character makes. In reading a monologue, as in hearing it in the theatre, or on radio, half the work needed to complete the performance comes from the reader/audience. It is a joint exercise for two imaginations, yours and mine, meeting and making a whole.'

Michael Flanders, too, is sadly missed. In partnership with Donald Swann he provided comedy material of exceptional wit and sophistication for a whole string of West End revues from 'Oranges and Lemons' in 1948 to 'Fresh Airs' in 1956.

Then, on 31st January, 1956, greatly daring, the Flanders and Swann team opened in 'At the Drop of a Hat' for a two-week run at the New Lindsey Theatre. The audience, Donald Swann has revealed, consisted of the Dartington Hall Summer School of Music mailing list and all those critics who, it was rightly assumed, would have few competing theatrical attractions on New Year's Eve. The rest, as they say, is history: 'At the Drop of a Hat' was succeeded by 'At the Drop of Another Hat' and these shows were to run — almost without a break — for the next ten years in London and every part of the British Isles, and throughout the United States, Canada, Australia and New Zealand.

In the process, the Flanders and Swann partnership raised the comedy song monologue to its highest art form. Technically, it could be argued that they worked out their material in duet form. But their work was complementary rather than in unison. The bearded Michael Flanders, long established as a professional broadcaster, brought a sharp incisive mind to the production and delivery of the words and an energy which made light of his permanent confinement to a wheel-chair. At the piano, the bespectacled Donald Swann — apart from utilising his skills as a pianist and classical composer — was more of an appreciative audience and butt for the Flanders humour than fellow narrator.

It was Michael Flanders who aptly summed up the *raison d'être* of their compositions, when, at the start of their show, he would remark:

'I must say, travelling round this country, things have come to a pretty underpass here in England. It's small wonder that satire squats hoof-in-mouth under every bush. The purpose of satire it has been rightly said, is to strip off the veneer of comforting illusion and easy half-truths. Our job, as I see it, is to put it back again.'

'At the Drop of a Hat' followed this precept faithfully, though sometimes with a sharp cutting edge. Thus *A Transport of Delight*, while a rollicking, open-road piece, also gets in a dig at the road hog bus driver. *The Gnu* and *The Hippopotamus*, on the other hand, are two of a long line of innocent animal tales whose popularity has spread far and wide. The music hall choral joys of 'Mud, mud, glorious mud' in *The Hippopotamus* have so far been translated into eighteen languages. *Have Some Madeira, M'Dear* also displays its music hall antecedents as (almost) straight Victorian melodrama.

Design for Living is part of what seems at times almost a Flanders and Swann fixation with housing. In introducing it, Michael Flanders would wheel himself to centre stage and pronounce, rather grandly, 'I live in Kensington — naturally. He (pointing at the shy, blinking — almost under the piano — figure of Donald Swann) claims to live in South Chelsea (long pause) — Battersea!'

At the start of 'At the Drop of Another Hat' in 1963, the same theme was taken up once again. 'Donald's moved since we last met. He used to live in Prince of Wales Drive, Battersea, but since he became a great star he thought it wasn't really very suitable and he now lives in Albert Bridge Road, Battersea — getting on for Clapham Common. Not that it matters where you live south of the river now, because, as you know, under the new London plan they're lumping all these areas together — they're going to call them Brighton.'

At the end of this patter, Michael Flanders would move smoothly into the problems of domestic upheaval and so to *The Gas Man Cometh*. *The Bedstead Man* in the same show was probably inspired by walks on the Sussex Downs when Michael Flanders and Donald Swann were at school at Lancing together. The obvious irony of *A Song of Patriotic Prejudice* cannot disguise its Englishness and Michael Flanders was inclined to suggest it as the natural (and National) English anthem.

In the Bath was constantly developed by the revue technique of changing the names to those of contemporary figures in the last verse. Similarly, the 1980 date shown against *The Wart Hog* and *The Wom Pom* reflect the continuing popularity of the Flanders and Swann animals. In that year, these items were included in a long-playing record (EMI ONCR 527) entitled 'The Bestiary of Flanders and Swann'. In some entertaining sleeve notes, Charles Fox related these pieces to the whole animal literary heritage, citing, among others, John Donne's elephant, Blake's tiger and the whole imaginary world of Lear's toeless pobble, to which may be added the Flanders and Swann *Wom Pom*.

Certainly part of Michael Flanders' own enthusiasm for the animal song was what he saw as a continuation of Aesop's Fables. More practically, *The Wom Pom* was introduced as new material while playing on Broadway and provided a natural show-stopping finale.

It is tempting, therefore, to leave the Flanders and Swann selections there, but the writer cannot resist, by way of a footnote, that variation of the old English folk song and a timeless warning to all governments, *There's a Hole in my Budget*. The main characters are part of a long historical tradition in which the Prime Minister and the Chancellor of the day are described as dancing round the stage in ever-increasing inflationary circles. When the piece was first performed in 'Airs on a Shoe String' in 1953, it 'starred' Winston Churchill and Rab Butler. With the new faces at Nos. 10 and 11 Downing Street over the intervening years, so the appropriate cast changes were written in until, in *The Songs of Michael Flanders and Donald Swann* (Elm Tree 1978), Donald Swann rewrote the piece to refer to Jim and 'Eyebrows' Denis. The latest Margaret and Geoffrey version brings us bang up to date.

So, too, does the 1981 selection of the work of Rex Newman. As we have seen, his career as a writer of monologues now stretches for almost seventy years from the world of Bransby Williams before the First World War to the new updated pieces originally written for his own concert party, the famous Fol de Rols. Some, like *Turn Again, Whittington* remind us of Rex's great success in a musical comedy collaboration with Clifford Grey (as in the case of 'Mr Whittington' for Jack Buchanan and 'Mr Cinders' for Bobby Howes).

Overall, these monologues show both their traditional links as in *The Big Tale of Hoo Flung Mud* (a parody of *The Pigtail of Li Fang Fu*), and the contemporary flavour of pieces such as *It Pays To Advertise*. In between, they reveal the wit and humour that have made Rex Newman one of the most popular and well-respected men in the theatrical profession.

They need little by way of explanation, offering the chance for any performer to show their real and continuing attraction. Gentle reader — as our Victorian literary predecessors would write — why not you?

Dreamin' of Thee

By Edgar Wallace & Ernest Longstaffe (1938)
Performed by Cyril Fletcher

Dreamin' of thee! Dreamin' of thee! Sittin' with my
elbow on my knee,
I orter be a-polishin' the meat dish an' the can —
I orter draw the groceries, for I'm an ord'ly man,
But wot are bloomin' rations, an' wots a pot or pan,
When I'm dreamin' O my darlin' love of thee.
Dreamin' of thee! Dreamin' of thee! Firin' at the rifle
range I be,
I've missed a fust class targit — an' I've missed the
'ill behind,
I nearly shot a marker once! (which wasn't very kind)
The orficer he swears at me — but really I don't mind,
I am dreamin' O my darlin' one of thee.
Dreamin' of thee! Dreamin' of thee! Me, as was
smart as smart cud be!
My kit is all untidy — an' it's inches thick in dust,
An' my rifle's fouled an' filthy, an' my baynit's red
with rust,
They've tried to find a reason but I've seen 'em further
fust.
An' they never guess I'm dreamin' dear of thee.
Dreamin' of thee! Dreamin' of thee! They can't make
out wot's comin' over me.

The fellows think I'm barmy, an' the Major thinks
it's drink,
The Sergeant thought it laziness, so shoved me in the
clink!
The Colonel called it thoughtlessness, so gave me
time to think,
An' to dream again my darlin' one of thee.
Dreamin' of thee! Dreamin' of thee! Wot's two hours
sentry go to me?
A-sittin' in a sentry box a-thinkin' of your eyes,
The ord'ly officer come along an' took me by
surprise.
'E said as I was sleepin' an' the usual orfice lies,
When I was only dreamin' love of thee.
Dreamin' of thee! Dreamin' of thee! Wond'rin' what
they're goin' ter do ter me —
Oh when I'm in the Ord'ly Room I know I'll cop it
'ot,
I'll be 'auled before the C.O., p'raps git sentenced to be
shot
But whether I git punishment, or whether I do not,
They can't prevent me dreamin' love of thee.

Theophelus and his Operation

By Cyril Fletcher (1939)

My friend Theophelus Carnation
Would talk about his operation
And gazed upon with much delight
The scar of his appendicite!
The surgeon had so neatly put
A row of stitches sewn with gut
But Theophelus with half a swirl
Loved ev'ry stitch, both plain and purl.
One day as he sat in his tub
He gave his favourite spot a rub,
To his surprized delight he found
The catgut made a Kreisler sound
And so next day he bought a bow
And started playing 'Sweet and Low'

And in a week could play the air
Of 'Deep Purple' and 'The Maiden's Prayer'.
The B.B.C. soon got to hear
And called for Theo to appear
And said that he and his incision
Must both appear on Television.
He learned the new swing music gait
He'd drop a stitch to syncopate
And his Dance Band became the new sensation,
'Theophelus and his Operation.'
Theophelus got quite wealthy soon
Each stitch in time would play its tune
Although he grew a trifle gummy
Through rubbing resin on his tummy.

The Fan

By Cyril Fletcher (1939)

This is a tale of Eliza Tweet
Who strolled one night along the street,

Picking with dainty finger tips
A fourp'ny plaice and two of chips

Wrapped in a sheet of news which seemed
  To have pictures which were most refeened.
When suddenly in such a flutter
  She threw her chips out in the gutter
For on that greasy paper there
  Was the answer to her maiden's prayer.
For underneath her piece of plaice
  Was Cyril Fletcher's smiling face
But where the vinegar had trickled
  His features were a trifle pickled.
But Eliza loved it just the same
  And put it in a photo frame
And now at bedtime has to pause
  'Cos Cyril's on her chest of drawers.

She turns his face round to the wall
  While she takes off her where-with-all
And dons her nightie neat and plain
  And shyly turns him round again
And then she murmurs, 'G'night Duck',
  And kisses where a chip has stuck,
Which mars his classic lips so chaste
  And gives them such a funny taste
And then she tells him she'll be true
  And swears he answers 'Thankin' you',
Then jumps in bed to take her rest
  With Cyril clutched against her breast
And whispers, 'Now I hope to be
  Dreamin' O' my love of thee.'

The Mermaid
By Cyril Fletcher (1939)

On Hastings Beach some time ago
  A Boatman by the name of Joe,
Looked up and in amazement saw
  A mermaid washed up on the shore.

His eyes bulged as, without delay,
  She rose and, shaking off some spray,
Proceeded to remove her tail
  And put same in a nearby pail.

Joe was astounded — rubbed his eyes
  The mermaid then to his surprise
Said in a foreign voice 'Ah, oui
  M'sieur, I do not like ze sea'.

And where before her tail had been
  A pair of shapely limbs were seen
And Joe said 'Gosh! this is a case'
  And couldn't look her in the face.

She said to Joe 'Let's get away,
  I'm sick of seeing waves and spray
Like jelly bobbling up and down,
  M'sieur let's go and see ze town.'

Joe's blushes met his ginger hair
  'Cos mermaids have no clothes to wear.
He muttered 'I shall get it strong
  If the Watch Committee come along.'

Quite a few people stopped to smirk,
  A newsboy shouted out, 'Nice work.'
Some more collected — quite a jam
  And watched them board a Tram.

The tram conductor watched them come
  Then said to Joe ''ere! nark it chum.
Bring 'er on 'ere — you've got a sauce,
  If she's Godiva, fetch an 'orse.'

Joe said to him quiet as can be,
  'She's just a mermaid from the sea,'
And the tram-man said 'Oh! Yes, Old Bean
  And what are you — the Fairy Queen?'

A policeman quickly hove in view
  Took out his book, said 'What's to do'
And the mermaid laughed and said, 'I guess
  I love your English policemen, yes'.

Sad to relate this copper brave
  Fell for her charms, became her slave
And she left poor Joseph in the lurch
  And married the cop in Hastings Church.

All that was left then was Joe's pail
  Containing her discarded tail.
And he, sore at being left so flat,
  Gave it to the lodger's cat.

Song of the Fletchers
By Cyril Fletcher (1940)

We are very select in this studio
  And our blood is as blue as the sea
Each noddle contains its full quota of brains
  There's no sap in our family tree.

Yes, I'm one of the Fletchers of Frinton
  And I'm terribly proud of the fact,
For the Fletchers elsewhere make our family despair
  For their lack of discretion and tact.

After having some port, they will lick at the cork
  And make scrunchy noises with their pickled pork
And stab stout-hearted waitresses' rears with a fork —
  I'm glad I'm a Fletcher of Frinton.

Oh! I'm one of the Fletchers of Frinton,
  We've no use for the Fletchers of Fife,
They remove chewing gum with their fingers and
    thumb
  And eat garden peas with a knife.

The Fletchers of Folkestone are never at ease
  They wipe sticky hands on their elbows and knees
And knock out their pipes on the side of the cheese.
  So, I'm glad I'm a Fletcher of Frinton.

Tra-la-la Tra-la-la

The Fletchers of Finchley are fearless,
  As into a battle they fling
But when one removes his waistcoat it proves
  That his trousers are kept up with string.

Oh! I'm one of the Fletchers of Frinton
  Not one of the Fletchers of Fleet
Who sit on the stairs, at social affairs
  Discussing the corns on their feet.

On the river at Henley — Great Scott! What a crew
  Not blazers and straw hats like other folks do,
They turn up in bowlers and body belts too.
I'm glad I'm a Fletcher of Frinton.

Then just look at the Fletchers of Feltham
  When the siren commences to wail,
There's no breeding at all, they just squat in the hall,
  Eating winkles and shrimps from a pail — so low!

We stay in our shelters with wine ruby red,
  But the Fletchers of Feltham, you'll find them
    instead
With a barrel of beer underneath Grandma's bed.
So, I'm glad I'm a Fletcher,
  Yes frightfully Fletcher,
I'm glad I'm a Fletcher of Frinton.

Ode of the Fletcher
By Cyril Fletcher (1940)

This is the history, somewhat wild,
  Of such a sweet and handsome child,
From which you'll never guess I betcher
  'Twas Cyril 'Dreaming of Thee' Fletcher.

The stork it seemed just dumped him down
  Beneath a whelk stall in Camden Town
And he weened himself in Blackwall Tunnel
  By sucking brown ale through a funnel.

Oft times he'd cast aside his dummy
  And hitching his binder round his tummy
Proclaim in accents loud and true
  Such cute remarks as 'Thanking you'.

Tho' people wondered more and more
  Just what the heck he thanked them for
And when at school amused them all
  By writing rude rhymes on a wall.

But later upon the concert stage
  His oddest odes became the rage
And BBC officials spoke,
  'We must have a basin of this bloke,'
But told him when he first began,
  ''Ere, keep the party clean, old man.'

But as the public ear he gained,
  His rhymes got really most refained.
He told them an ode, he thought a gem,
  Made girls believe he dreamed of them,

Now when he does a wireless show
  And starts off with 'Thanks ever so'
A million damsels sigh with bliss,
  'It's Cyril, oh, we must hear this'.

The Bee Song

By Kenneth Blain (1938)
Performed by Arthur Askey

Oh what a wonderful thing to be,
  A healthy grown up busy busy bee,
Whiling away all the passing hours,
  Pinching all the pollen from the cauliflow'rs,
I'd like to be a busy little bee,
  Being just as busy as a bee can be
Flying round the garden brightest ever seen,
  Taking back the honey to the dear old queen.

Chorus
Bz bz bz bz, honey bee, honey bee.
  Bz if you like but don't sting me,
Bz bz bz bz, honey bee, honey bee,
  Bz if you like but don't sting me.

Oh what a wonderful thing to be,
  A healthy grown up busy busy bee,
Toying with the tulips, tasting ev'ry type,
  Building up the honey-comb that looks like tripe.
I'd like to be a busy little bee,
  Being just as busy as a bee can be,
Flying all around in the wild hedgerows,
  Stinging all the cows upon the parson's nose.

Oh what a wonderful thing to be,
  A healthy grown up busy busy bee,
Visiting the picnics quite a little tease,
  Raising little lumps upon the maidens' knees,
I'd like to be a busy little bee
  Being just as busy as a bee can be,
Flirting with the butterfly strong upon the wing,
  Whooppee! O death where is thy sting?

Oh what a wonderful thing to be,
  A nice obedient busy busy bee,
To be a good bee one must contrive,
  For bees in a beehive must beehive,
But maybe I wouldn't be a bee,
  Bees are all right when alive you see
But when bees die you really should see 'em,
  Pinned on a card in a dirty museum.

Chirrup

By Kenneth Blain (1938)
Performed by Arthur Askey

I wish I were a tiny bird a-soaring in the sky,
  I'd stretch my wings and other things and fly and fly
  and fly,
Oh I should be a shy little bird,
  A sly little bird, a c'y little bird,
A really 'do or die' little bird,
  What lives up in the sky,
Chirrup, Chirrup, Chirrup, Chirrup, sweet, sweet,
  sweet, cuck-oo
  Chirrup, Chirrup, Chirrup, Chirrup, sweet, sweet,
  sweet, cuck-oo.

I wish I were a tiny bird, the same bird as before,
  I'd soar and soar and soar and soar, until my tail was
  sore,
Oh I should be such a silly little bird,
  Willy nilly little bird, Piccadilly little bird,
A sort of 'come and kiss me Willie' little bird,
  What lives up in the sky,
Chirrup, Chirrup etc.

I wish I were a tiny bird, a H'ostrich or a H'eagle,
  I'd flirt with Tom and Fred and John, and give them
  all the needle,
Oh I should be a wooing little bird, trouble brewing
  little bird,
  Nothing doing little bird,
A sort of 'married man's ruin' little bird
  I'd knock them all sky high
Chirrup, Chirrup etc.

I wish I were a tiny bird, a sparrow or a starling,
  With cunning zest, I'd feather my nest, and be an old
  man's darling,
Oh I should be a spooney little bird,
  A crooney little bird, 'milk and hooney' little bird,
A 'Die soon and leave me all your money' little bird
  Gee whiz, my hat, hoch aye,
Chirrup, Chirrup etc.

I wish I were a tiny bird, I'd sing thro' sun and fog,
  I'd lightly trip from twig to twig and back from twog
  to twog,
Oh I should be a chronic little bird,
  Cyclonic little bird, carry-on-ic little bird,
A 'Let's have another gin and tonic' little bird,
  What lives up in the sky.
Chirrup, Chirrup etc.

All to Specification

By Robert Rutherford & Frank Wilcock (1939)
Performed by Arthur Askey

For months and months I searched both near and far,
  To find a house — you know how scarce they are:
But glory be, I got one t'other day,
  I bought it from an Agent who was giving it away:
Five thousand pounds — that's all, just as it stands —
  Two bedrooms and a place to wash your hands:

It's a lovely little villa and we've christened it
  'The Shack' —
  And it's — all to specification:
When we go out we always hope it's there when we get
  back — all to specification
  The Station is two minutes walk I heard the Agent
  tell,
I missed the train first morning and I found out very
  well —
  It's half an hour at least and then you've got to run
  like Hell —
And it's — all to specification!

I noticed we'd a most unpleasant smell:
  I sent off for the builder, Mr. Snell:
I asked, 'Is it the drains?' He rubbed his chin:
  He said, 'It can't be drains 'cos I forgot to put them
  in.'
Said he, 'That's rather awkward for you isn't it, but
  still —
  To make it right I'll knock you three-and-ninepence
  off the bill':

It's a lovely little villa and we have a lot of fun —
  And it's — all to specification:
It's nice to sit and hear them eating soup next door but
  one — all to specification:
  The bathroom's rather small but it has all that we
  require,

The plug-hole's always bunged up so I poke it with a
  wire:
  We've got two taps but that which says 'hot water' is a
  liar —
And it's — all to specification!

The small repairs I do myself of course:
  I've sawn the tops and bottoms off the doors:
They used to stick but now they shut all right —
  But what a draught — it blew the missus out of bed
  last night:
The roof let water in at first, it fairly made me wince,
  But it got blown off last Thursday and we've never
  seen it since:

It's a lovely little villa and it's called 'The Shack' you
  see —
  And it's — all to specification!
It should be called 'The Ruins' 'cos it's darn-well
  ruined me — all to specification!
  Our garden's like the wilderness where Israelites
  were led,
I told the wife I'd buy some sheep and in reply she
  said —
  'The place is always flooded, you should buy some
  swans instead.'
And it's — all to specification!

The gable-end fell down today and messed things up a
  bit,
  A bricklayer came round — he said, 'I know the
  cause of it —
Them bricks ain't got no mortar on — they've stuck
  'em up with spit.'
  There's no place like Home, and it's — all to
  specification!

The Worm

By ? Woodward & Arthur Askey (1939)

I am a sweet little wriggling worm,
  Covered with mud from head to stern,
Passing the time from night till morn
  Leaving little casts in the middle of the lawn,
Just an ordinary little worm,
  Squiggle, squiggle, squiggle, squirm, squirm,
  squirm.

I'm such a dear little Iggly worm,
  One of the sort that rarely turn,
I'd rather be out in a storm or a blizzard
  Than filling empty spaces in a blackbird's gizzard,
Just an ordinary little worm,
  Squiggle, squiggle, squiggle, squirm, squirm,
  squirm.

I was out wriggling through the dew
   When a gardener's spade cut me in two — ugh!
I felt so silly, it made me laugh,
   Saying, 'Good night' to my better half.
Just two ordinary little worms,
   Squiggle, squiggle, squiggle, squirm, squirm,
      squirm.

I'm such a sleek little wriggling worm,
   Haven't any hair, so I don't need a perm,
But some day it will be my fate,
   Sitting on a pin, as a small boy's bait,
That's the end of every little worm,
   Squiggle, squiggle, squiggle, squirm, squirm,
      squirm.

The Seagull
By Arthur Askey (1940)

I'm a silly seagull flying in the sky
   Ever, ever, ever, ever, ever so high.
Two big wings and a large yellow beak,
   Feathers on my chassis, oh I do look chic.
Flying very high, flying very low,
   You can never catch me, oh dear no.
Happy at the seaside, never having words,
   Happier in Bond Street with the other birds.
Just a silly seagull, that's all —
   Fly away Peter, fly away Paul.

I'm a silly seagull flying in the sky
   Ever, ever, ever, ever, ever so high
Following the big ships when they're on a cruise,
   Peeping through the portholes and getting lovely
      views.
Flying very high, flying very low,
   You can never catch me, oh dear no.
When the weather's stormy, passengers look gray,
   Then we get excited 'cos dinner's on the way.

Just a silly seagull, that's all —
   Fly away Peter, fly away Paul.

I'm a silly seagull flying in the sky
   Ever, ever, ever, ever, ever so high.
Tho' I cannot sing like the birdies in the park,
   Don't think I'm a sissy 'cos I often have a lark.
Flying very high, flying very low,
   You can never catch me, oh dear no.
Flying round a liner — racing neck and neck
   Then our favourite pastime, playing hit the deck.
Just a silly seagull — that's all —
   Fly away Peter, fly away Paul.

When we see somebody we like
   We're as sweet as treacle;
When we see somebody we hate
   Pop — goes the seagull.
Just a silly seagull, that's all —
   Fly away Peter, fly away Paul.

The Budgerigar
By Barbara Gordon, Basil Thomas & Robert Gordon (1941)
Performed by Arthur Askey

Tra la la la, I'm a budgerigar,
   I chatter and chirrup and tweet.
In the language of birds,
   I use very rude words,
And ev'ryone murmurs 'How sweet!'
   If something upsets me I fly in a rage,
Then it takes them an hour to clean out my cage.
   With a titty fallol and thanks ever so ta;
Hip hip hoorah, I'm a budgerigar.

Tra la la la, I'm a budgerigar.
   They're trying to teach me to speak.
I rehearse day and night
   But it doesn't sound right,
'Cos I haven't a roof to my beak.
   Though some of my feathers have not been the same
Since I once got mixed up in a badminton game;
   With a titty fallol and thanks ever so ta;
Hip hip hoorah, I'm a budgerigar.

Tra la la la, I'm a budgerigar,
  But I have been left in the lurch.
I'm divorced from my mate,
  Now I sit here in state,
All alone on my rod, pole or perch.
  The ladies don't like me,
I'm left high and dry,
  But even my best friends will not tell me why.
With a titty fallol and thanks ever so ta;
  Hip hip hoorah, I'm a budgerigar.

Tra la la la, I'm a budgerigar.
  My list of long words is immense.
I repeat with great ease
  What is said by M.P.'s;
Such a pity it doesn't make sense.
  I once cracked a joke that made ev'ryone shriek,
But Vic Oliver pinched it the following week.
  With a titty fallol and thanks ever so ta;
Hip hip hoorah, I'm a budgerigar.

The Pixie
By Barbara Gordon, Basil Thomas & Robert Gordon (1941)
Performed by Arthur Askey

I'm a little pixie, dancing in the glen;
  Sitting down and standing up and sitting down
    again.
Dainty as a snowflake, tripping on my toes,
  With little fairy dew-drops dripping off my nose.
All about the woodlands, how I love to roam;
  Any little toad-stool's a gnome from gnome.
Just a little pixie, nimble as can be,
  With a hey nonny nonny and you can't catch me.
Hokus pokus,
  Hiding in a crocus,
Sliding down a moonbeam
  On me little tokus.
Did you ever see such a funny little bloke as me?

I'm a little pixie, dancing in the glen;
  Sitting down and standing up and sitting down
    again.
Once I stole a baby, then I took its place;
  I did feel such a sissy in my nappy and my lace.
They put me in a cradle; they bathed me in the sink,
  They scrubbed me with a loofah, and left me in the
    pink.

Just a little pixie, nimble as can be,
  With a hey nonny nonny and you can't catch me.
Hokus pokus,
  Hiding in a crocus,
Rolling home at midnight,
  Slightly out of focus . . .
Did you ever see such a funny little bloke as me?

I'm a little pixie, dancing in the glen;
  Sitting down and standing up and sitting down
    again.
Getting up to mischief, specially in the Spring.
  Making lots of whoopee inside the Fairy Ring.
Going out to parties, hoping it'll mean,
  A bit of slap and tickle with the Fairy Queen.
Just a little pixie, nimble as can be,
  With a hey nonny nonny and you can't catch me.
Hokus pokus
  Hiding in a crocus,
Haven't paid the landlord;
  Frightened of the brokers.
Did you ever see such a funny little bloke as me?

The Death-Watch Beetle
By Barbara Gordon, Basil Thomas & Robert Gordon (1941)
Performed by Arthur Askey

I'm the Death-Watch Beetle, knock, knock, knock,
  Giving you a leetle shock, shock, shock.
Ev'ry piece of wood I touch is sure to rot,
  In the dining room, the bedroom or the
    you-know-what.

If you've been out to a dinner and you've had a lot to
    drink,
If you hear some funny rumbling it may not be what
    you think,

Two of the longest-lived and most versatile of music hall and concert party artists, Stanley Holloway (*above*) and Arthur Askey (*right*)

'Cos I may be doing Boomps a-daisy underneath the
　　sink.
　　I'm the Death-Watch Beetle, knock, knock, knock.

I'm the Death-Watch Beetle, knock, knock, knock,
　　Giving you a leetle shock, shock, shock.
Walnut or mahogany's the same to me,
　　I had a bite of walking stick today for tea.
I'm also fond of books and once I found one in a
　　drawer,
　　I was almost half way thro' it when I shouted out
　　'Oh Lor,'
'Cause I suddenly remembered that I'd eaten it before!
　　I'm the Death-Watch Beetle, knock, knock, knock.

I'm the Death-Watch Beetle, knock, knock, knock,
　　Giving you a leetle shock, shock, shock.
If you hear a tapping noise that sounds like morse,
　　I'm practising hot breaks inside the rocking horse.
There's not another insect as unpopular as I,
　　You are sure to get the wind up when you hear my
　　little cry,
You phone the undertakers and you kiss yourself
　　good-bye.
　　I'm the Death-Watch Beetle, knock, knock, knock,
The Death-Watch Beetle, sang this song:
　　Doo-dah doo-dah.
Then he raised his hat and he said:
　　'So long.'
Doo-dah doo-dah day.

The Foreign Legion
By Arthur Askey (1941)

See that gang of ruffians come marching o'er the sand.
Out of time and out of step — they haven't got a band.
Fighting with the Arabs and our friends from La Belle
　　France,
If you dare to lag behind, you get kicked in the pants.

Marching with the Foreign Legion.
　　Marching on to who knows where.
Across the hot Sahara — with sand on your tarara,
　　That's the life of every Legionnaire.
Marching on to death or glory
　　Knowing there are none to care:
Just a real Beau Geste — with whiskers on your chest
　　That's the life of the Legionnaire.

It's a hell of a life in the Legion,
　　When you're out in the desert I mean.
This story I'll tell you is clever,
　　It's not only clever — it's clean.

When first I was sent down from Oxford,
　　To London I came for a job.
But I stole all my Grandfather's money,
　　Amounting to seventeen bob.
For six months I lived like a prince, sir,
　　Wine, women and song all day long.
Till I found that I'd only got fourpence,
　　So I cut out the wine and the song.

The women still hovered around me.
　　I thought they were under my spell.
But I found they were after my fourpence,
　　So I gave them a soldier's farewell.

It was then that I thought of the Legion.
　　I joined with the greatest of ease.
I thought perhaps they wouldn't have me,
　　As I suffered from duck's disease.

I chummed up with one they called Stinker,
　　The deepest-dyed villain of all.
He'd had to leave home in a hurry,
　　After writing rude words on a wall.
Our Captain we hated like poison.
　　He had a moustache like a bedsock.
And what the men called him led me to believe
　　That he had been born out of wedlock.

He took us a route march and lost us.
　　An obsolete map they had sold him.
He said 'Listen men, I don't know where to go',
　　So every one of us told him.
After six months of hell I absconded,
　　If captured I well know my fate.
So i just put myself in my diary
　　And palmed myself off as a date.

I landed in England last Tuesday,
　　It wasn't so hard to detect it.
For I'd sand in my whiskers and sand in my hair,
　　And sand where you'd never expect it.
Now here I am back entertaining,
　　Singing songs ancient and new,
Striving and straining to get a good laugh
　　Out of boss-eyed palookas like you.

The Flue Germ
By Robert Rutherford & Arthur Askey (1942)

Oh I ain't no bird and I ain't no bee
  I ain't no wopse and I ain't no flea,
Who the devil am I — wait and see —
  I'm a little flu-germ — can't catch me!

After somebody, I don't care who,
  I've got a lot of dirty work to do,
Better look out — it might be you —
  A-a-a-a-a-atchoo!
Inside — Outside — Someone always cops it;
  Upstairs — Downstairs — In my lady's whats-it:
Sniff-sniff-snuffle-cough — All over town,
  Atchoo! Atchoo! And they all fall down!

Oh I fear no quacks, they can do their stuff,
  They chase me round and they treat me rough,
Then I catch them bending and give them snuff —
  I'm a little flu-germ — Gosh I'm tough!

After somebody, I don't care who,
  I've got a lot of dirty work to do,
You ask your doctor, he'll tell you,
  A-a-a-a-a-atchoo!

First class — third class — Guard and Engine Driver;
  Sailors — Whalers — don't forget the Diver!
Sniff-sniff-snuffle-cough — all round town,
  Atchoo! Atchoo! All fall down.

Oh I'm in the air and I'm in the news,
  I'm in your combs and your socks and shoes,
When I climb in bed I don't care whose —
  I'm a little flu-germ — I thank youse!

After somebody, I don't care who,
  I've got a lot of dirty work to do.
Now then, Playmates, what about you?
  A-a-a-a atchoo!
Lotions — potions — those are what I thrive on,
  Asp'rins — quinine — what I keep alive on,
Sniff-sniff-snuffle-cough — don't be a clown,
  Go to bed at once — or your blinds fall down!

The Ant
By Dan Leno, Junr. (1942)
Performed by Arthur Askey

I'm a little ant, a busy little ant,
  I work fifty times as hard as any elephant.
Watch me as I slither,
  Hither unto thither,
Then back again to hither,
  Till I'm fairly in a dither,
If you've any sluggards,
  Send 'em round to me,
Whoops a daisy! — I'm a crazy,
  A. — N. — T.

I'm a little ant, a greedy little ant,
  If I get much fatter, I shall really have to 'bant'
When you have your pic-nic,
  With the Poly-'tic'-nic,
I saunter round your sandwiches,
  And give the ham a quick lick.
Skating on the butter,
  And swimming in the tea,
Whoops a daisy! — I'm a crazy,
  A. — N. — T.

I'm a little ant, a saucy little ant,
  You would really be surprised, the way I gallivant,
My favourite gallivant, is —
  To visit Country Shanties,
And get into the panties
  Of the Uncles and the A'nties.
I 'specially like the
  Aunties at the BBC.
Whoops a daisy! — I'm a crazy
  A. — N. — T.

I'm a little ant, a universal ant,
  Doesn't matter where you go, you'll find that I'm extant,
Clapham Park to Cuba,
  Margate to Majuba,
I'm a bigger nuisance than
  Old 'Nasty Schiklegruber'
I heard him saying yesterday,
  He wished that he could be
Whoops a daisy! — Just a crazy
  Ant, like me.

I'm a little ant, a busy little ant,
  Toiling all the time until, I have to stop and pant,
Digging miles of passages,
  Running out with 'messages',
Bringing home the bacon,
  And occasionally, 'sassages'
Laying little eggses for
  The goldfish's tea,
Whoops a daisy! — I'm a crazy,
  A. — N. — T.

I'm a little ant, an artful little ant,
  Where the courting couples court, I love to gallivant,
A couple down at Kew,
  I watched them bill and coo,
Then I wandered up her stocking
  As I'd nothing else to do,
He wondered why she slapped his face,
  She didn't notice me,
Whoops a daisy! — I'm a crazy,
  A. — N. — T.

The Seaside Band
By Kenneth Blain (1947)
Performed by Arthur Askey

Once at the seaside feeling very reckless,
  I banged down twopence and I rolled on the pier,
Hadn't gone far when the strains of music
  Floated on the breeze and landed on my ear.
I quickened up my steps for I love nice noises,
  Very soon arrived right opposite the band,
Saw the conductor on a lemonade box,
  With his little baton stuck up in his right hand.
One, two, three, four, off went the cornet,
  Five, six, seven, eight, the fiddlers followed suit,
A man in the corner playing on the piccolo,
  Keeping time with the sole of his boot,
Right behind him a fellow with a trombone,
  Blowing like the deuce
With his cheeks outside
  Working so hard that both his little eyeballs
Left their sockets and stood outside.

High upon a rostrum a drummer very lonely,
  Drums all round like bees in a swarm
Looking very cold and his nose quite scarlet,
  Banging on the cymbals to keep himself warm,
Opposite to him was a man with a toupee,
  Spitting down a reed — what a nasty man!
Sitting next to him was a fellow with a French Horn,
  Full of sole and bitter beer, twopence on the can.

Fellow with a 'Cello, hmph, hmph, hmph, hmph,
  Trying very hard to saw it in two,
His pal with the double base cuddling it fondly,
  Looking like a camel with a dose of 'flu.
The man with the piccolo fed up with the darned
    thing,
  Sick and tired of hearing the same old toot,
Thought he'd like a change so he put it down beside
    him

Then he started messing with a full sized flute.

A man with a bassoon, nothing on his music,
  Sat like a mute, never said a word,
Just as I thought he was going to fall asleep,
  He picked up his bassoon and gave us all the bird.
Then a little man with walrus whiskers,
  (How he got his breath, well I don't know,)
Found he'd got his fungus stuffed down the
    mouthpiece,
  And wondered why he couldn't play his little oboe.

The man with the trombone lost his temper,
  Thought the couldn't hear him and said, 'Here
    goes,'
Took a long breath and blew all his false teeth,
  Right on the bridge of the conductor's nose,
Then the conductor getting very angry,
  Waved his other hand with a rum tum tum,
It caused such a draught that the man with the harp,
  Went clean thro' the air and fell thro' the drum.

Bang bang bang, went the man with the cymbals,
  Tootle-ootle-oot said the flute so gay,
Fiddle and viola screaming like the wind,
  And the cornet broke his promise trying to reach
    top 'A'.
What a pandemonium ev'rybody diff'rent,
  Each with the other was trying to compete,
But strange to relate — it must have been a fluke,
  They all finished dead on the same down beat,
Rule Britannia, they made the echoes ring,
  And I felt sorry when they played,

God Save Our King!

The Moth

By Kenneth Blain (1947)
Performed by Arthur Askey

You can have your birds, you can have your bees,
   But to me they're simply froth
'Cos the thing I'd really like to be,
   Is not a bird or a flower or a bee,
Or a fish or a camel or a jumping flea,
   But a little moth.
Fluttering round a little candle, frightened to go near
   A-singeing of your chassis, and feeling mighty queer
Or bashing out your brains against a chandelier,
   Like a moth, a little moth.

Light and airy, just like a fairy,
   Chewing up yards of cloth,
Just think of the joys and the fun, my boys,
   Enjoyed by the flighty, on it's all righty,
Just had a meal off a lady's nighty,
   Nonstop nibbling moth.

You can have your ham, you can have your lamb,
   You can have your chicken broth,
But the things on which I'd like to dine,
   Are a little bit of fur or crepe-de-chine,
Or some red flannelette from an old maid's spine,
   Like a moth — a little moth.
Bringing up a family, remembering it's due
   To tell them what they 'moth' do and what they
      'mothn't' do,
And to choose what they must chew and what they
      must eschew
   Like a moth — discerning moth.

Light and airy, just like a fairy,
   Chewing up yards of cloth,
But think of the scare of dyspepsia,
   That's caused by fruity — nice and juicy
Left off trousers of a Burton suity,
   To a non stop nibbling moth!

You can shout till you're hoarse on your big gold
      course,
   It arouses all my wrath,
They do nine holes they all get tight,
   But to nestle in a camisole pure and white,
And do eighteen holes in the middle of the night.
   That's a moth — a little moth.
Hating all the nudists — they're very, very rude,
   The bare idea appals one, although I'm not a prude,
Not even just a fig leaf to make you think of food,
   Annoys a moth — a little moth.

Light and airy, just like a fairy,
   Chewing up yards of cloth,
Just think of the joys and the fun, my boys,
   Of a greatly daring, drinking, swearing,
Don't care a damn for bits of camphor
   Non-stop nibbling moth!

When you cry with grief for your poor bad teeth,
   I could laugh my head right off,
For a moth has molars strong and fine,
   Off any old thing a moth can dine,
He could almost eat a pawnbroker's sign,
   Could a moth — a little moth.
Yet upon occasion life could be a curse,
   Imagine for a moment, could anything be worse,
Than being found dead in a scotsman's purse,
   Like a moth — a Gaelic moth.

Light and airy, just like a fairy,
   But think of the end without a friend,
Of a bashed up, smashed up, crushed up,
   Bust up, squashed on the floor,
And finally brushed up,
   'Who the hell wants to be a moth.'

The Villain Still Pursued Her
(Filthy Ferdinand)

By Robert Rutherford & Frank Wilcock (Recorded 1976)
Performed by Arthur Askey

The theatre was crowded from the ceiling to the floor;
   The orchestra had played the overture:
At last the curtain rises on the scene — a lonely
      moor —

And the heroine so innocent and pure:
She thinks that she's alone but soon amid a storm of
      boos
   There emerges from behind a blasted tree

The form of Filthy Ferdinand who tells her she must
    choose
    Between his foul caress and povertee:

The villain still pursued her — yes with ruin she was
    faced:
    Through twenty scenes he followed her, but still the
    maid was chaste:
In Scene the First he lured her to a lonely house he
    knew;
    He muttered 'None can save you now' as the candle
    out he blew,
But the Hero struck a match and shouted 'What's the
    matter wid chew?'
    And Filthy Ferdinand was foiled again!

And the villain still pursued her, yes he chased her
    high and low;
    I don't know what he asked her, but she always
    answered 'NO':
In the Second Scene he caught her and prepared for
    the attack,
    He got her on the table — things were looking very
    black,
But the furniture men turned up just then and took the
    table back —
    And Filthy Ferdinand was foiled again!

And the villain still pursued her, up and down the
    stage he glared,
    And half-way through the show he sent his boots to
    be repaired:
In Scene the Third he caught her all alone in her
    boudoir,
    He said — 'I've chased you long enough, now you'll
    be chaste no more':
But she'd concealed a mousetrap in her flannelette
    pegnoir —
    And Filthy Ferdinand was foiled again!

And the villain still pursued her — to hope she faintly
    clings,
    When she hears a bottle of Guinness being opened
    in the wings:
Scene Four's inside the Barracks and the girl with
    fright is blue,
    A great big Sergeant Major with a fist the size of two,
He turns upon the villain and he says, 'Get in the
    queue' —
    And Filthy Ferdinand is foiled again!

And the villain still pursued her, but her virtue could
    not shake,

Till the gallery got impatient — shouted 'Give the
    lad a break':
Scene Five — he wooed her in a wood, the maiden
    gave a scream,
    The hero on his bicycle appeared upon the scene
He tore the villain's trousers off and exposed his
    wicked scheme —
    And Filthy Ferdinand was foiled again!

And the villain still pursued her, and there's one more
    scene to go,
    And virtue is triumphant — she's as pure as trodden
    snow:
For in the end he chased her to a sugar factoree
    And she pushed him in a big machine to end his
    villain-ee
So any of you people might have had him in your
    tea —
    And Filthy Ferdinand was foiled again —
Foiled again!
    Then they play 'The Queen' and shout
'Pass along there — this way out' —
    And Filthy Ferdinand is foiled again!

EXTRA:
And the villain still pursued her — the maiden's in
    despair:
    She cried 'I am undone' — and some rude person
    shouted 'Where?'
He chased her to the cemetry — the place was dark
    and drear,
    'At larst I've got you in my power' he said with
    fiendish leer,
But a voice behind a tombstone yelled 'You can't do
    that there 'ere':

And the villain still pursued her — there was no one to
    console her,
    His eyes were flashing fire and he was breathing
    gorgonzola:
He tied her to the railway track and gave a cruel
    shout —
    'The ten-fifteen express is due, and there's nobody
    about'
But the Station-master came and cried — 'That ruddy
    train's scrubbed out'.

Pukka Sahib

Sketch by Reginald Purdell (1940)

(Based on *The Green Eye of The Little Yellow God* by Milton Hayes)

Played in 'Up and Doing' at the Saville Theatre, London, 1940-42, with the following cast of Characters:

The Reciter   Stanley Holloway
The Colonel   Leslie Henson
The Major   Cyril Richard

(The Reciter *walks on to the stage and prepares to recite.*)

Reciter: The Green Eye of the Little Yellow God, by Milton Hayes.
There's a green-eyed yellow idol to the north of Kathmandu.
There's a little marble cross below the town;
There's a . . .
The Colonel: (Interrupting from a box.) Have you been there lately?
Reciter: I beg your pardon?
The Major: (From the box.) The Colonel said 'Have you been there lately?'
Reciter: Where?
Both: Kathmandu.
Reciter: No, as a matter of fact I haven't been there for some time.
The Major: What were you there with? Indian Army? Indian Civil?
The Colonel: Or the Fol-de-Rols?
Reciter: Well, to be perfectly frank —
The Major: As a matter of fact I know Kathmandu well. It's a second home to me.
The Colonel: I love every inch of the place. I was only there last year.
The Major: I came through a couple of months ago on my way home. The whole place was changed terribly.
The Colonel: Yes, bad show.
Reciter: That's very interesting. But why are you telling me all this.
The Major: Just to put you right geographically.
The Colonel: You see, the whole place has been changed under a town planning scheme.
The Major: For instance, there's a large public library and public baths combined erected in the square. The Office of Works have moved the idol to the south of Kathmandu.
The Colonel: And the cemetery has been moved and there is now a cinema. Hideous thing.

The Major: So that marble cross you spoke about is now above the town.
Reciter: Perhaps I'd better start again.
Both: But do.
Reciter: The Green Eye of the Little Yellow God, by Milton Hayes.
There's a green-eyed yellow idol to the . . .
The Major: South.
Reciter: South of Kathmandu.
There's a little marble cross . . .
The Colonel: Above.
Reciter: (Dully.) Above the town.
There's a broken-hearted woman tends the grave of Mad Carew.
The Major: Did you know Fanny Shannon?
Reciter: Did I know who?
The Major: Fanny Shannon. You remember General Shannon's eldest girl.
The Colonel: Tim Shannon — damn good scout.
The Major: Yes indeed. You're quite out of order saying she's broken-hearted. She was naturally upset at Carew's death, but she got over it.
The Colonel: Didn't she marry a rich American?
The Major: Yes, they've got three boys at St Paul's.
Reciter: How then shall I describe her?
The Major: Oh — *(Whispers to the Colonel.)* We suggest a comparatively broken-hearted woman.
Recitr: I'd better start again.
Both: But do.
The Major: Only you don't mind if we have a drink?
The Colonel: Splendid idea. *(He rises to go.)*
The Major: Oh, there's no need to go, Colonel. You can get one here. I've got Sabu standing by.
(An Indian Servant enters and salutes.)
The Major: What will you have?
The Colonel: I'll have a chota-peg.
The Major: One chota-peg, and I'll have a Passion Fruit.
(The Indian Servant exits.)
Oh, and Sabu — not too much fruit.
Reciter: May I carry on?
Both: But do.
Reciter: There's a green-eyed yellow idol to the south of Kathmandu.
There's a little marble cross above the town.
There's a comparatively broken-hearted woman tends the grave of Mad Carew and the little god for ever gazes down.

The Colonel: Up, sir, up.

Reciter: (Hastily.) Up. He was known as Mad Carew.

The Major: Oh, ridiculous. The man wasn't mad at all. He was mentally deficient, yes. You couldn't call him absolutely crackers.

Reciter: He was known as Mentally Deficient Carew by the Subs. of Kathmandu.
He was hotter than they felt inclined to tell.

The Colonel: Too much curry powder. Too much Mepharine.

Reciter: (Miserably.) But for all his foolish pranks . . .

The Major: Foolish pranks be damned, sir. You don't call writing rude words on the walls foolish pranks.

Reciter: Well, I didn't know

The Colonel: No, neither did I.

The Major: What, Carew? Horrible habits.

The Colonel: Tell me a couple. *(They whisper.)* No — Government House.

The Major: Government House. I tell you, the Viceroy was livid. In front of Noël Coward, too.

Reciter: He was worshipped in the ranks.
And the Colonel's daughter smiled on him as well . . .
(The Colonel and the Major rise.)

The Major: Now, that's a cad's remark, sir. If you want to know, my brother was engaged to her at the time. I . . . *(He attempts to climb over the box.)*

Reciter: I'm sorry, I didn't know. I apologise.

The Colonel: I should darn well think so. *(To the Major.)* I'd accept his apology.

The Major: Would you? Very well, we don't want a scene.

The Colonel: We needn't look.

The Major: No, turn your back on the blighter. *(He picks up a programme.)* Who is he? *(Announces Reciter's name.)*
Never heard of him. Hippodrome or local theatre, I suppose.

Reciter: She was nearly twenty-one.

The Colonel: (With a roar of derisive laughter.) Twenty-one be damned! She was thirty-nine if she was a day.

The Major: Mind you, she didn't look it. She had everything lifted — or practically everything. All the main essentials.

Reciter: And arrangements had been made to celebrate her birthday with a ball.

The Colonel: Extraordinary. I don't remember that.

The Major: No, I think you were away at the time. It was during the rains. You were up at Rumblechelly-pore — on that sewage commission.

Reciter: He wrote to ask what present she would like from Mentally Deficient Carew. They met next day as he dismissed his squad.

The Colonel: Platoon.

Reciter: As he dismissed his squad.

The Colonel: Platoon.

Reciter: Squad.

The Colonel: The Subaltern commands a platoon.

Reciter: But it must be a squad, it's got to rhyme with yellow God.

The Major: We don't give a hoot what it's got to rhyme with, sir. King's Regulations — it's a platoon.

Reciter: They met next day as he dismissed his platoon. And jokingly she said that nothing else would do
But the green eye of the . . .

The Major: Chocolate-coloured coon . . .

The Colonel: (Roaring with laughter.) Jolly good.

Reciter: (Hysterically.) The night before the dance, Mentally Deficient Carew sat in a trance.

The Major: Sat in a trance — he sat in a blancmange. I remember it well. He was as tight as a tick.

Reciter: And they chafed him as they puffed at their cigars.

The Colonel: Wait a minute. Chafed him? Are you referring to his underwear or his brother officers?

Reciter: His brother officers.

The Major: Then the word is chaffed — or if you come from the North Country — the 'A' is short and it would be chaft.

Reciter: It might interest you to know that I do come from the North Country. I would prefer the word chaft.

The Colonel: Then by all means say chaft.

Reciter: Very well, I will say chaft.

Both: But do.

Reciter: (Lapsing into North Country.) And they chaft him as they puffed at their cigars.
(The Colonel and the Major laugh and applaud.)
(Enter the Indian Servant. He speaks in double-talk Hindustani.)

The Major: Oh, we can't get a drink here. Come on, let's go to the bar. Sorry we've got to go, so we'll leave you poofing and chaffing.

Reciter: Gentlemen, please, Gentlemen, will you please let me continue. Don't you realise this is my livelihood, my business? May I please continue?

Both: But do. *(They both laugh.)*

Reciter: (Going mad.) There's a broken-hearted Idol
To the West of Mad Carew;
There's a cross-eyed yellow woman
Doing all a Cat Can Doo. Ha Ha Ha!
(He screams insanely and rushes from the stage.)

The George Lashwood Monologue

(From *Fine and Dandy*)
By Frank Eyton (1942)
Performed by Stanley Holloway

I've always been a gambler
　Since the day when I was born.
And thus you see me standing here
　A thing of shame and scorn.
At five years old I stole a shilling
　From my Aunt Maria,
And lost it playing pitch and toss
　With bad boys in the choir.
I went to Harrow College
　While a boy still in me teens,
And got in with the gambling set
　And staked beyond me means.
I couldn't pay me card debts
　Which was quite a large amount,
And got sneaked on — to the teacher
　By the winner — a Viscount.
I got the sack from Harrow
　And I had to take the knock,
The scandal made me poor old dad's grey hair
　Turn white with shock.
For months I didn't gamble,
　Got a job and earned me pay,
And gradually me poor old dad's white hair
　Turned back from white to grey.
But I've got the gambling fever
　Deeply rooted in me blood,
And having no cards up me sleeve
　Was soon dragged in the mud.
One night I lost a cool thou'
　And I staggered out a wreck,
And forged another person's name
　On someone else's cheque.

The Police, of course, arrested me
　For this diabolical crime,
And so it was me dad's grey hair
　Turned white a second time.
But now I've served me sentence
　And they've set me free again,
So as I'm out of prison
　I will sing you this refrain:

I'm going away
　I'm going away
I'm leaving my homeland's shore.
　I'm going away
I'm going away
　An exile from England's door.
I've been a fool,
　Poker and pool
Have landed me in the cart,
　Then a forced bill of sale
Landed me up in jail
　And I've broken me parents' hearts.
That's why I'm . . .
　Sailing away to Australia
Across all the land, sea and foam,
　I've been rather a failure
But I'll start again out there.
　Now when I make good in Australia
And find wealth across the foam,
　I shall come back from there.
And they'll make me Lord Mayor
　For the sake of the old folks at home.

Evings' Dorg 'Ospital

By Charles Pond (1906)
Recorded by Stanley Holloway 1957

'Ere, Evings wasn't always in th' dorg trade,
　But wot'd it matter?
Anything that Evings turns 'is 'and to 'e'd make a do of
　it.
　It ain't buyin' or sellin' dorgs what Evings does so
　　well at neither,
It's th' 'ospital under th' shop where Evings gets th'
　brass.

Five an' twenty t' thirty dorgs at seven an' six a week,
It soon mounts up yer know, and no aht-goin's.
　They git nuffin t' eat at Evings's. That's Evings' big
　　secret.
Th' other mornin' Evings was standin' at the door of 'is
　　shop
　Scalin' a bull dorg's teef,
When up drives a carridge an' pair

And aht a lady gets with a little Italian grey 'ound
Which was snarlin' an' snappin' somethin' shockin'.
  Wallop! goes the bulldog dahn the flap into th'
    'ospital.
The lady 'ands 'er dorg t' Evings.
  'Mind 'e don't bite,' she sez.
'Little dorgs never bite me, Mum,' sez Evings.
  Well, I dunno what it is about Evings,
But directly 'e gets 'old of a dorg th' dorg seems t'
    know somethin'
  And never takes 'is eyes orf Evings.
'Is pahr over animals is marv'llous.
  Well, look wot 'e's dun wiv Missus Evings.
'Wot's th' matter with th' little feller?' sez Evings.
  The lady explained as 'ow 'e used t' be able t' eat
    steak
But lately only a very tiny bit of chicken nah and agin.
  'Poor little dear,' sez Evings.
'But wot's the little chappie's name, Mum?'
  'Fido,' sez the lady.
''Ere 'e'll soon be orlright wiv us, Mum,
  That is, if 'e aint gone too fur,' sez Evings.
'Seven 'n' six a week is our usual charge
  But if 'e 'as been in th' 'abit of eatin' chickin . . .'
Well, the lady offer'd t' make it arf a sov'rin a week
  And sez, 'You will be kind to 'im, won't you?'
'Kind t' 'im? Bless you, Mum,' sez Evings,
  'D'you know th' 'ard part of this business is partin'
    with th' little creatures
At th' end of th' week when their time's up?'
  The lady 'ands Evings two luvley cushi'ns,
One for th' day and one for th' night,
  And after a lot of kissin' and cuddlin' the carridge
    drives orf.
Wallop! goes Fido dahn th' flap into th' 'ospital.
  'E gets put on a couple of inches of chain
And a combin' and brushin' wot 'e never fergits.
  And in less than a couple of days 'e's dartin' abaht
And catchin' the little bits of tripe wot they fling rahnd
  As quick as any of 'em.
It was a sight to see 'em as Evings goes dahn wiv th'
    basket,

All their teeth a-glistenin' and their little rudders a-
    goin' like mad.
'E don't 'arf fling it t' 'em and they're on it ev'ry time,
  Just abaht 'arf ahnce a-piece.
But it's when the ladies call for th' dorgs as you ought
    to 'ear Evings.
  When the lady calls for Fido 'e sez, ''E's orlright nah,
    Mum,
But we've 'ad a very anxious time wiv th' little feller.
  Me and th' Missus was up th' 'ole of th' first night
    wiv 'im.
I got a little rest th' second night, but th' Missus she
    stuck to 'im,
  And with th' aid of gentle nursin' and 'is own brave
    little 'eart
We pulled 'im rahnd.'
  And 'e goes t' th' flap and 'e sez, 'Bring little Fido
    up.'
As soon as 'e sees 'is Missus 'e goes nearly mad,
  Right over 'er shoulder, aht into th' street,
Up on to th' coachman's box, dahn agin and back into
    th' shop.
  Th' lady was delighted. 'Oh aint 'e improved,' th'
    lady said.
'Yes, Mum,' sez Evings. 'I think when you gets 'im 'ome
  You'll find as 'ow 'e'll be able t' eat a little bit of
    chickin nah.'
The lady 'ands Evings th' sov'rin.
  O' course Evings aint got no change, but 'e'd send for
    it if the lady wished it.
But the lady wouldn't 'ear of such a thing.
  And said she'd be quite sure t' send Mrs Evings a
    present for 'er great kindness.
Which Evings sez they didn't expect but would be only
    too pleased t' 'ave,
  If it was only aht of rememb'rance of little Fido
'Oo'd endeared 'isself to th' 'earts of all.
  Yeh, and there's many a party wouldn't be nearly so
    snappish
If they 'ad a week at Evings,
  But 'e dursn't trust them.
Dorgs can't talk.

The Street Watchman's Story

By Charles J. Winter (1910)
Recorded by Stanley Holloway 1957

Some chaps gets the fat, and some chaps gets the lean,
  When they start on their journey thro' life,
Some makes pots of money by being M.P.s
  And some gets it by taking a wife.
Some learns a good trade such as Dustman or Sweep,

Which the same I'd have done if I'd knowed,
But the special profession I've drifted to now
  Is 'Minding a 'ole in the road'.
As a rule it's a nice quiet comfortable job.
  But there's times when I've hated the work.

For instance I once had to go Christmas Day
  On a job which I'd tried hard to shirk.
I minded that 'ole, sir, the whole blessed day,
  Till my dinner and teatime had gone,
And my Christmas dinner (if any was left)
  I should have when relieved later on.
At home we'd some friends and we'd got a big goose,
  And I'd ordered a half ton of coal,
Yet here was I sitting at seven P. hem
  A-shivering in front o' my 'ole.
And I thought of them all making merry at home,
  Stuffed with goose from their heads to their toes,
They'd just about leave me a cut off the beak,
  Or the end of the Parson's nose.
And I sat quite despondent and dozed half asleep,
  I was feeling quite humpy and sore,
When from one of the big houses just on my right
  A swell flunkey stepped out through the door.
He came straight to me and he said with a bow,
  Which made his gold lace gleam and shine,
'The Countess's compliments as you're alone
  She'll be pleased if you'll step in and dine.'
Well I very near dropped to the ground with surprise,
  For it wasn't a safe thing to do.
What if thieves came and pinched a great heap of them
    stones,
  Or 'opped off with a drain-pipe or two?
Then I thought of the Countess's kindness of 'eart
  How she'd thought of me lonely outside,
So I scraped the clay off my boots with a spade
  And I follered the flunkey inside.

And there sat the Countess all merry and bright
  With diamonds and jewels all a-glow,
In a silk dress which must have cost nigh twenty
    pound,
  Though there wasn't much of it you know.
Her husband the Viscount was there at her side,
  While the waiters flew round with a whizz,
And in half a jiff I was seated with them
  A-eating and shifting the fizz.
The Viscount he drank to my jolly good health
  As he took from his wine-glass a pull,
I only just nodded — I couldn't say much —
  For my mouth, like my heart, was too full.
When we'd finished, us gents all puts on a cigar,
  And the perfume was simply sublime,
By the bands that was on 'em, why I'll guarantee
  They must have cost fourpence a time.
Then the ladies they starts playing 'Kiss-in-the-ring'
  And the Countess enjoyed the game too,
When she gets in the ring she just turns straight to me
  And she says, 'Mr. Nobbs, I'll have you.'
O, I didn't know which was my 'ead or my 'eels,
  It was like being in Fai-ry-land,
But I threw down my smoke and I wiped my
    moustache,
  Just like this, with the back of my 'and.
She put up her lips looking saucy and sweet,
  And I blush'd as towards her I stole,
I bent forward and then I woke up just in time,
  Or I might have fell clean down the 'ole.

On Strike

By Charles Pond (1906)
Recorded by Stanley Holloway 1957

When I lays dahn my tools I lays 'em dahn,
  I laid 'em dahn seven year ago over a matter of three
    shilling a week.
Now there's people 'oo'll say 'Fancy a man being aht o'
    work seven year over a matter o' three shilling a
    week.'
  People what don't understand the principle of the
    thing,
The principle of a fair living wage and that's wot I'm
    a-standin' aht for.
  And I wouldn't let my old woman work for the
    money she do in the steam laundry,
Only somebody's got to keep the 'ome up.
  It would never do for both ov us to be aht.
She was only a-sayin' to me the other morning as she
    was a-bringing me up my cup o' tea and a bit o'
    toast afore she was goin' aht t' work,

'Why don't you get into Parliament?'
And that's where I ought t' be.
  And the first Act o' Parliament I should pass 'd be
Concerning the hover-crowdin' on the hearly mornin'
    trams.
  A woman can't git t' 'er work, she's got t' walk and
    walk 'ome again.
Now you know there's 'eaps o' fings want haltering in
    this 'ere country,
  But you'll never get nuthin' done so long as they
    won't fink.
Fink! Why, they won't even read.
  Why you can see 'undreds and fahsands goin' out t'
    work wivaht even 'avin' read their mornin' paper.
Why you know the most terrible fings might 'appen
    during th' night,

The most frightful disaster, the most 'orrible
national catostrophe.
Why Bass's Brewery might be burnt t' the grahnd
And a man'd start work in a state of blind
hignorance.
Now I remember th' time when there was a interest
took in politics,
I remember the time at hour political club when you
couldn't get near the bar on a Sunday morning.
And wot do yer find nah? A few bicycles outside and
'arf the trade in the place small lemons.
And that's wot old England's a-driftin' to.
Now the Chancellor of the Hexchequer said the other
day,
'E says — and I quite agree wiv' 'im fer once,
'E says the falling off in the consumption of beer is
halarming.
The falling off in the consumption of beer *is*
halarming.
But there's something more halarming what the
Chancellor of the Hexchequer did not tell you.
And that is this,
That concurrently simultaneous and identical wiv the
fallin' off in the consumption of beer

Is the total and utter disappearance of the
conversational powers of man.
For I defy anyonc to get hup a political hargument on
cocoa.
It can't be done.
Now I'm a paper-'anger be trade I am and wild 'orses
can't drag me from paper-'anging,
The very last time I picked hup my tools seven year
ago
They tried it on wiv me but it didn't come orf,
They didn't know 'oo they was a-dealin' wiv.
I got the money what I arsked afore I started on me
job which was the stripping of a wall.
Well, I 'adn't been a-workin' for a couple of hours
before I comes across an old bell wire in the wall.
I called up the foreman. 'What's the matter wiv you?' 'e
says.
I says, 'Look at this old bell wire in the wall.'
'Pull it aht,' 'e says, 'What?' I says.
'Pull it aht,' 'e says.
I says, 'You'll pardon me, that's plumber's work.' And I
lays down me tools.
And when I lays dahn me tools, I lays 'em dahn.

Sweeney Todd, The Barber

By Bob Weston & Bert Lee (1935)
Recorded by Stanley Holloway 1957

In Fleet Street, that's in London Town,
When King Charlie wore the Crown,
There lived a man of great renown,
It was Sweeney Todd, the Barber.

One shave from him and you'd want no more —
You'd feel his razor sharp
Then tumble wallop through the floor
And wake up playing a harp

— and singing.

Sweeney Todd, the Barber
Ba Goom, he were better than a play,
Sweeney Todd, the Barber
'I'll polish him off,' he used to say.

His clients through the floor would slope,
But he had no fear of the hangman's rope
Dead men can't talk with their mouths full of soap,
Said Sweeney Todd, the Barber.

Now underneath the shop it's true
Where other bodies tumbled through
There lived a little widow who
Loved Sweeney Todd the Barber.

She made her living by selling pies,
Her meat pies were a treat,
Chock full of meat and such a size
'Cos she was getting the meat from

Mr Sweeney Todd, the Barber.
Ba Goom, he were better than a play
Sweeney Todd, the Barber
'I'll polish them off,' he used to say.

And many's the poor young orphan lad
'Ad the first square meal he'd ever had —
A hot meat pie, made out of his Dad
From Sweeney Todd, the Barber.

170

It was Saturday night in old Sweeney Todd's shop
   And his customers sat in a row
While Sweeney behind a screen shaved some poor mug
   And his sweetheart made pies down below.

Though none were aware, it were cut prices there
   They were rolling up in twos and threes,
And his foot was quite sore pressing knob on the floor
   And his voice went from saying 'Next please'.

First a swell took the chair. He said, 'Ha, Ha, my man,
   Just a shave and a perfumed shampoo
For I've just got engaged.' Sweeney just pressed the knob
   And said, 'There now, it's all fallen through.'

Then a bookmaker said, with his mouth full of soap,
   'They're all backing favourites today
So I'll bet I'll go down.' Sweeney said 'So you will,'
   And he did — he went down straight away.

But what rotten luck — the darned trap went and stuck
   For the hinge he'd forgotten to grease:
And a customer there started calling out 'Police'.
   Just as Sweeney was saying 'Next please'.

Yes, he ran to the door and he shouted 'Police'.
   He called 'Police' nine times or ten:
But no policeman arrived and a very good reason —
   The police weren't invented by then.

But up came the brave Bow Street runners — hurray!
   And he had to let many a pie burn
While they dragged him to quad, and next day
     Sweeney Todd
   Was condemned to be switched off at Tyburn.

And there on the gibbet he hangs in chains,
   And they do say a little black crow
Made a sweet little nest in old Sweeney Todd's
     whiskers
   And sang as he swang to and fro.

Sweeney Todd, the Barber
   Ba Goom, he were better than a play:
Sweeney Todd, the Barber
   They buried him underneath the clay.

And old Nick calls him from his grave
   Shouting 'Wake up, Sweeney, I want a shave,'
And Mrs Nick wants a permanent wave
   From Sweeney Todd, The Barber.

The Battle of Hastings
By Marriott Edgar (1937)
Recorded by Stanley Holloway 1975

I'll tell of the Battle of Hastings,
   As happened in days long gone by,
When Duke William became King of England,
   And 'Arold got shot in the eye.

It were this way — one day in October
   The Duke, who were always a toff,
Having no battles on at the moment,
   Had given his lads a day off.

They'd all taken boats to go fishing,
   When some chap in t' Conqueror's ear
Said 'Let's go and put breeze up the Saxons;'
   Said Bill — 'By gum, that's an idea.'

Then turning around to his soldiers,
   He lifted his big Norman voice,
Shouting — 'Hands up who's coming to England.'
   That was swank 'cos they hadn't no choice.

They started away about tea-time —
   The sea was so calm and so still,
And at quarter to ten the next morning
   They arrived at a place called Bexhill.

King 'Arold came up as they landed —
   His face full of venom and 'ate —
He said 'If you've come for Regatta
   You've got here just six weeks too late.'

At this William rose, cool but 'aughty,
   And said — 'Give us none of your cheek;
You'd best have your throne re-upholstered,
   I'll be wanting to use it next week.'

When 'Arold heard this 'ere defiance,
   With rage he turned purple and blue,
And shouted some rude words in Saxon,
   To which William answered — 'And you.'

'Twere a beautiful day for a battle;
  The Normans set off with a will,
And when both sides was duly assembled,
  They tossed for the top of the hill.

King 'Arold he won the advantage,
  On the hill-top he took up his stand,
With his knaves and his cads all around him,
  On his 'orse with his 'awk in his 'and.

The Normans had nowt in their favour,
  Their chance of a victory seemed small,
For the slope of the field were against them,
  And the wind in their faces and all.

The kick-off were sharp at two-thirty,
  And soon as the whistle had went
Both sides started banging each other
  Till the swineherds could hear them in Kent.

The Saxons had best line of forwards,
  Well armed both with buckler and sword —
But the Normans had best combination,
  And when half-time came neither had scored.

So the Duke called his cohorts together
  And said — 'Let's pretend that we're beat,
Once we get Saxons down on the level
  We'll cut off their means of retreat.'

So they ran — and the Saxons ran after,
  Just exactly as William had planned,
Leaving 'Arold alone on the hill-top
  On his 'orse with his 'awk in his 'and.

When the Conqueror saw what had happened,
  A bow and an arrow he drew;
He went right up to 'Arold and shot him.
  He were off-side, but what could they do?

The Normans turned round in a fury,
  And gave back both parry and thrust,
Till the fight were all over bar shouting,
  And you couldn't see Saxons for dust.

And after the battle were over
  They found 'Arold so stately and grand,
Sitting there with an eye-full of arrow
  On his 'orse with his 'awk in his 'and.

Magna Charter
By Marriott Edgar (1937)
Recorded by Stanley Holloway 1975

I'll tell of the Magna Charter
  And were signed at the Barons' command
On Runningmead Island in t' middle of t' Thames
  By King John, as were known as 'Lack Land'.

Some say it were wrong of the Barons
  Their will on the King so to thrust,
But you'll see if you look at both sides of the case
  That they had to do something, or bust.

For John, from the moment they crowned him,
  Started acting so cunning and sly,
Being King, of course, he couldn't do any wrong,
  But, by gum, he'd a proper good try.

He squandered the ratepayer's money,
  All their cattle and corn did he take.
'Til there wasn't a morsel of bread in the land,
  And folk had to manage on cake.

The way he behaved to young Arthur
  Went to show as his feelings was bad;
He tried to get Hubert to poke out his eyes,
  Which is no way to treat a young lad.

It were all right him being a tyrant
  To vassals and folks of that class,
But he tried on his tricks with the Barons an' all,
  And that's where he made a faux pass.

He started bombarding their castles,
  And burning them over their head,
'Til there wasn't enough castles left to go round,
  And they had to sleep six in a bed.

So they went to the King in a body,
  And their spokesman, Fitzwalter by name,
He opened the 'ole in his 'elmet and said,
  Concil-latory like, 'What's the game?'

The King starts to shilly and shally,
  He sits and he haws and he hums,
'Til the Barons in rage started gnashing their teeth,
  And them with no teeth gnashed their gums.

Said Fitz, through the 'ole in his 'elmet,
  'It was you as put us in this plight,'
And the King having nothing to say to this 'ere
  Murmured, 'Leave your address and I'll write.'

This angered the gallant Fitzwalter;
   He stamped on the floor with his foot,
And were starting to give John a rare ticking off,
   When the 'ole in his 'elmet fell shut.

'We'll get him a Magna Charter,'
   Said Fitz when his face he had freed;
Said the Barons, 'That's right and if one's not enough,
   Get a couple and happen they'll breed.'

So they set about making a Charter.
   When at finish they'd got it drawn up,
It looked like a paper on cattle disease,
   Or the entries for t' Waterloo Cup.

Next day, King John, all unsuspecting,
   And having the afternoon free,
To Runningmead Island had taken a boat,
   And were having some shrimps for his tea.

He had just pulled the 'ead off a big 'un,
   And were pinching its tail with his thumb,
When up came a barge load of Barons, who said,
   'We thought you'd be here so we've come.'

When they told him they'd brought Magna Charter,
   The King seemed to go kind of limp,
But minding his manners he took off his hat
   And said, 'Thanks very much, have a shrimp.'

'You'd best sign at once,' said Fitzwalter,
   'If you don't, I'll tell thee for a start
The next coronation will happen quite soon,
   And you won't be there to take part.'

So they spread Charter out on t' tea table,
   And John signed his name like a lamb.
His writing in places was sticky and thick
   Through dipping his pen in the jam.

And it's through that there Magna Charter,
   As were signed by the Barons of old,
That in England to-day we can do what we like,
   So long as we do what we're told.

Albert's Reunion
By Stanley Holloway (1978)

You've heard of Albert Ramsbottom,
   And Mrs Ramsbottom and Dad,
And the trouble the poor Lion went to
   Trying to stomach the lad.

Now after the Lion disgorged him,
   Quite many a day had gone by;
But the Lion just sat there and brooded
   With a far away look in his eye.

The Keepers could nowt do with Lion
   He seemed to be suffering pain,
He seemed to be fretting for summat,
   And the curl went out of his mane.

He looked at his food and ignored it,
   Just gazed far away into space;
When Keepers tried forcible feeding
   They got it all back in their face.

And at Mr and Mrs Ramsbottom's
   The same kind of thing had begun —
And though they tried all sorts of measures,
   They couldn't rouse Albert their son.

Now Mr Ramsbottom got fed up
   With trying to please him in vain,
And said, 'If you don't start to buck up
   I'll take you to Lion again.'

Now instead of the lad getting frightened
   And starting to quake at the knees,
He seemed to be highly delighted
   And shouted, 'Oh, Dad, if you please.'

His father thought he had gone potty,
   His Mother went nearly insane,
But Albert just stood there and bellowed,
   'I want to see Lion again.'

Now Mr and Mrs Ramsbottom
   Decided the best thing to do,
Was to give way to Albert and take him
   Straightaway back to the Zoo.

The moment the Lion saw Albert,
   'Twere the first time for weeks it had stirred;
It moved the left side of its whiskers,
   Then lay on its back and just purred.

And before anybody could stop him,
    Young Albert were stroking its paws;
And whilst the crowd screamed for the Keepers
    The little lad opened its jaws.

The crowd by this time were dumbfounded,
    His Mother was out to the wide,
But they knew by the bumps and the bulges
    That Albert were once more inside.

Then all of a sudden the Lion
    Stood up and let out a roar;
And Albert, all smiling and happy,
    Came out with a thud on the floor.

The crowd by this time were all cheering,
    And Albert stood there looking grand
With his stick with the 'orse's 'ead 'andle
    Clutched in his chubby young hand.

The Lion grew so fond of Albert
    He couldn't be parted from lad;
And so the Zoological Keepers
    Sent round a note to his Dad.

'We regret to say Lion is worried
    And pining for your little man,
So sending you Lion tomorrow,
    Arriving in plain covered van.'

And if you call round any evening,
    I'll tell you just what you will see —
Albert is reading to Lion in bed,
    And what is he reading? *Born Free.*

The Parson of Puddle
By Greatrex Newman (1979)
Performed by Stanley Holloway

In the clean little, green little,
    God-save-the-Queen little,
Parish of Puddle o'er which I preside;
    There dwells a poor lassie
Who's now rather passé,
    There seems to be almost no flesh on her chassis;
And weight-watchers query
    And ask for *her* theory,
For she keeps as thin as a *lath* —
    And I'm bound to admit
I was shocked quite a bit
    When I saw her to-day in her *bath—chair,* and
      noticed a skeleton she;
Oh Lack-a-day! Oh Lack-a-day! Oh Lack-a-day *Me!*

In the free little, spree little,
    Colour-TV little,
Parish of Puddle o'er which I preside;
    We had a school outing
With races and shouting
    With little Girls Guiding and little Boys Scouting;
And when all the teachers
    Were cooling their features
With bottles they'd bought at an *Inn* —
    One said 'Don't you think
You'd like something to drink?'
    I said 'Yes, I should love a large *gin—ger beer* or
      lemonade, if I may?'
Yea Verily! Yea Verily! Yea Verily! *Yea!*

In the brash little, rash little,
    Sausage-and-mash little,
Parish of Puddle o'er which I preside;
    It fell to my duty
To wed a blonde beauty
    To bridegroom in khaki, a Second Leftootey;
And both were delighted
    And got quite excited
When just as a twelve-month had *run* —
    One Sunday in May
On a lovely spring day
    She presented her spouse with a *Sun—day school*
      Hymn Book of Ancient and Mod.;
Odds Bodikins! Odds Bodikins! Odds Bodikins! *Odd!*

In the blank little, swank little,
    Two-pubs-and-bank little,
Parish of Puddle o'er which I preside;
    A spinster named Mary
Once opened a Dairy,
    And as new-laid eggs seemed to be neces*sary* —
She purchased some hens —
    Which she fed in their pens,
But when egg-collecting she *went* —
    She found with dismay
That those birds could not lay,
    For each of those fowls was a *gent—(t)eel* and bashful
      young rooster, you see;
Oh Fiddle-de! Oh Fiddle-de! Oh Fiddle-de! *Dee!*

In the gay little, stray little,
  Hip-hip-Hooray little,
Parish of Puddle o'er which I preside;
  A widow — misguided —
Much gossip provided,
  And some folk heard more of the details than I did;
So, duty compelling

I called at her dwelling
(I meet all my flock when I *can*) —
  As she came to the door
It was plain that she wore
  An assortment of beads and a *fan — tastic* costume
    she'd bought in Bombay;
Hey Nonny No! Hey Nonny No! Hey Nonny No! *Nay!*

Oh Mr. Du Maurier!
By Joyce Grenfell & Richard Adinsell (1945)

I have stood for Mr. Millais, and I've sat for Madox
    Brown;
  I've been graceful for D. G. Rossetti, in a florissy-
    Morissy gown.
I seem to delight each pre-Raphaelite, Mr. Holman
    Hunt takes me to lunch;
  I've been in half-tones by Sir Edward Burne-Jones,
    but I've never appeared in 'Punch'.

Oh, Mr. Du Maurier! Why cannot I be
  One of your wittier women like the lady on page two
    three?
There may be prettier women, plus grande dame
    maybe;
  But they couldn't find one more Du Maurier, or
    more drawier than me.

The Rossettis read me poems at the house in Cheyne
    Walk;
  And Lord Tennyson flattered me lately, in a Lordly-
    Maudly talk.

I seem to incite the writers to write, Mr. Ruskin
    admires my mind;
  Mr. Browning finds I'm like a mystical rhyme,
    Du Maurier only is blind.

Oh, Mr. Du Maurier! I would like to know
  On what your neglect of me hinges, for it hurts my
    vanity so.
I've got the face and the fringes, so I say pianissimo,
  I would sit for you, dear Du Maurier, con amorier
    molto.

Oh, Mr. Du Maurier! Perhaps I'm out of date.
  Time flies when one isn't counting at a beastly
    priestly rate.
The years must have gone on mounting, and now I
    estimate
  That I'm seventy years, dear Du Maurier, what a
    bore-ier too late.

The End of the News
from 'Sigh No More'
By Noel Coward
Performed by Joyce Grenfell

Heigh-ho, Mum's had those pains again,
  Granny's in bed with her varicose veins again,
Ev'ry-one's gay because dear cousin Florrie
  Was run down on Saturday night by a lorry.
We're so glad Elsie's miscarriage
  Occurred on the Wednesday after her marriage.
When Albert fell down all
  The steps of the Town Hall
He got three bad cuts and a bruise,
  We're delighted
To be able to say
  We're unable to pay
Off our debts;

We're excited
Because Percy's got mange and we've run up a bill at
    the vet's.
  Three cheers, Ernie's got boils again
Ev'rything's covered in ointment and oils again
  Now he's had seven, so God's in his heaven
And that is the end of the news.

Heigh-ho, ev'rything's fearful
  We do wish that Vi was a little more cheerful;
The only result of her last operation
  Has been gales of wind at the least provocation.
Now don't laugh, poor Mrs Mason

Was washing some smalls in the lavatory basin
When that old corroded Gas Heater exploded
    And blew her smack into the Mews.
We're in clover Uncle George is in clink
    For refusing to work for the war,
Now it's over Auntie Maud seems to think
    He'll be far better placed than before.
What fun, dear little Sidney
    Produced a spectacular stone in his kidney.
He's had eleven,
    So God's in his heaven
And that is the end of the news.

Heigh-ho, what a catastrophe Grandfather's brain is
    beginning to atrophy,
    Last Sunday night after eating an apple

He made a rude noise in the Methodist Chapel.
    Good egg, dear little Doris
Has just been expelled for assaulting Miss Morris.
    Both of her sisters are covered in blisters
From standing about in the queues.
    We've been done in
By that mortgage foreclosure
    And father went out on a blind;
He got run in
    For indecent exposure
And ever so heavily fined.
    Heigh-ho, Hi-did-dle-did-dle,
Aunt Isabel's shingles have met in the middle.
    She's buried in Devon,
So God's in his heaven
    And that is the end of the news.

Maud

By Nicholas Phipps & Richard Adinsell (1951)
Performed by Joyce Grenfell & Julian Orchard

A Victorian garden on a summer night. French windows at the back, leading to the house. A man in Victorian evening dress enters, and sings.

MAN   Come into the garden, Maud,
           I am here by the gate alone.
           I am here by the gate alone.

MAUD, ravishing in a hooped ball-dress appears at the windows. She answers.

MAUD   Maud won't come into the garden,
             Maud is compelled to state,
             Though you stand for hours
             In among the flowers
             Down by the garden gate.
             Maud won't come into the garden,
             Sing to her as you may,
             Maud says she begs your pardon
             But she wasn't born yesterday.
                                                       She retires

MAN   (*with passion*)
           She is coming my love, my dear,
           She is coming, my life, my fate!
           The red rose cries 'She is near, she is near!'
           And the white rose weeps: 'She is late!'

MAUD re-appears.

MAUD   But Maud's not coming into the garden,
             Thanking you just the same.
             Though she looks so pure
             You can be quite sure
             Maud is on to your little game.
             Maud knows she's being damping,
             (And how damp you already must be)
             But Maudie is now decamping
             To her lovely hot water b.!

MAN   Come into the garden, Maud . . .

MAUD   (*interrupting*)
             Frankly Maud wouldn't dream of coming
                 into the garden,
             Let that be understood,
             When the nights are warm
             She knows the form,
             Maud has read 'Red Riding Hood.'
             Maud didn't need much warning
             She watched you with those pink gins,
             So she bids you a kind good morning —
             And advises two Veganins.

The MAN opens his mouth to start again, but MAUD beats him to it.

MAUD You couldn't really seriously think that Maud
            is going to be such a sucker as to come into
            the garden.
         Flowers set her teeth on edge,
         And she's much too old
         For a stranglehold

In a prickly privet hedge.
Pray stand till your arteries harden,
It won't do the slightest good,
Maudie's NOT coming into that garden —
And you're mad to have thought she would!

Three Brothers
By Joyce Grenfell & Richard Adinsell (1953)

I had three Brothers,
   Harold and Robert and James,
All of them tall and handsome,
   All of them good at games.
And I was allowed to field for them,
   To bowl to them, to score:
I was allowed to slave for them
   For ever and evermore.
Oh, I was allowed to fetch and carry for my Three
      Brothers,
   Jim and Bob and Harry.

All of my brothers,
   Harry and Jim and Bob,
Grew to be good and clever,
   Each of them at his job.
And I was allowed to wait on them,
   To be their slave complete
I was allowed to work for them
   And life for me was sweet,
For I was allowed to fetch and carry for my Three
      Brothers
   Jim and Bob and Harry.

Jim went out to South Africa,
   Bob went out to Ceylon,
Harry went out to New Zealand
   And settled in Wellington.
And the grass grew high on the cricket pitch,
   And the tennis court went to hay,
And the place was too big and too silent
   After they went away.

So I turned it into a Guest House,
   After our parents died,
And I wrote to the boys every Sunday,
   And once a year they replied.
All of them married eventually,
   I wrote to their wives, of course,
And their wives wrote back on postcards —
   Well . . . it might have been very much worse.

And now I have nine nieces,
   Most of them home at school.
I have them all to stay here
   For the holidays as a rule.
And I am allowed to slave for them,
   To do odd jobs galore,
I am allowed to work for them
   And life is sweet once more,
For I am allowed to fetch and carry for the children of
   Jim and Bob and Harry.

Stately as a Galleon
By Joyce Grenfell & Richard Adinsell (1964)

My neighbour, Mrs. Fanshaw, is portly-plump and
      gay,
   She must be over sixty-seven, if she is a day.

You might have thought her life was dull,
   It's one long whirl instead.
I asked her all about it, and this is what she said:

177

I've joined an Olde Thyme Dance Club, the trouble is
that there
    Are too many ladies over, and no gentlemen to
    spare.
It seems a shame, it's not the same,
    But still it has to be,
Some ladies have to dance together,
    One of them is me.

Stately as a galleon, I sail across the floor,
    Doing the Military Two-step, as in the days of yore.
I dance with Mrs. Tiverton; she's light on her feet in
    spite
    Of turning the scale at fourteen stone and being of
    medium height.
    So gay the band,
So giddy the sight,
    Full evening dress is a must,
But the zest goes out of a beautiful waltz
    When you dance it bust to bust.

So, stately as two galleons, we sail across the floor,
    Doing the Valse Valeta as in the days of yore.
The gent is Mrs. Tiverton, I am her lady fair,
    She bows to me ever so nicely and I curtsey to her
    with care.
So gay the band,
    So giddy the sight,
But it's not the same in the end
    For a lady is never a gentleman, though
She may be your bosom friend.

So, stately as a galleon, I sail across the floor,
    Doing the dear old Lancers, as in the days of yore.
I'm led by Mrs. Tiverton, she swings me round and
    round
    And though she manoeuvres me wonderfully well I
    never get off the ground.
So gay the band,
    So giddy the sight,
I try not to get depressed.
    And it's done me a power of good to explode,
And get this lot off my chest.

Rainbow Nights
By Joyce Grenfell & Richard Adinsell (1978)

When we were young, oh *years* ago,
    The Yanks and the Canadians was here.
Me and Gladys had some fun,
    Didn't we, Glad?
We did.
    Now we're married, happily.
Our boys got back at last.
    I married Ken, she married Len,
And both of them is lovely men,
    But all the same just now and then
We like to dream of the past.
    Me and Gladys had some fun, we did,
Didn't we, Glad?
    We did.

Saturday nights at Rainbow Corner!
    Me and Glad would go up West
Through the blackout in the winter
    Dressed up in our best.
It was lovely, wasn't it, Glad?
    'Hiya, Babe!' and 'Hey, Goodlookin'!'
'Come to Poppa!' — 'Say, what's cookin'?'
    Hank and Joe and Red and Slim
Standin' on the corner there, chewin',
    'Hiya, Gorgeous, how'm I doin'?'
Wasn't it lovely, Glad?
    Just to think of it makes you sad.
Wasn't it lovely, Glad?

Lovely times at Rainbow Corner!
    All that food and warmth and lights,
Bubblegum and Coca-cola,
    All the dancin' through the nights.
It was lovely, wasn't it, Glad?
    'Hiya, sweetheart, what a dame!'
'Hiya, honey, what's your name?'
    Hank and Joe and Red and Slim
Standin' on the corner there, lazy.
    'Hiya, dream girl, let's go crazy.'
Wasn't it lovely, Glad?
    Just to think of it makes you sad.
Wasn't it lovely, Glad?

Now we're married girls it's nice
    To think back to the days gone by.
We had lovely outin's then,
    Didn't we, May?
We did.
    We worked in the fact'ry then,
Hard it was and fast,
    But then we used to get away,
And then we'd let ourselves go gay
    And we was rich on all that pay.
It's nice to dream of the past.
    Me and Gladys had some fun, we did.
Didn't we, Glad?
    We did.

Saturday nights at Rainbow Corner!
  Me and May our hair done swank
On our shoulders soft and silky,
  Set for dancin' with a Yank.
It was lovely, wasn't it, Glad?
  'Hiya, Baby, hey, Goodlookin'.'
'Come to Poppa!' — 'Say, what's cookin'?'

Hank and Joe and Red and Slim
Leanin' on the corner there winkin'.
  'Hiya, Marlene, let's get stinkin'' —
Wasn't it lovely, Glad?
  Just to think of it makes you sad.
Wasn't it lovely, Glad?

At the Laundrette
By Joyce Grenfell & Richard Adinsell (1978)

They have chamber music concerts at the Town Hall,
  At the library you can read and read and read,
There are churches and a chapel,
  And societies where they grapple with *all* sorts of
    problems
But they none of them met our need.
  We were hungry for some wider sort of experience,
We were restless and as nervy as could be,
  Then we all of a sudden found fulfilment,
And we found it where you wouldn't of thought it
    would be.

We found fulfilment at the Laundrette,
  Life took on a meaning rich and new.
It's impossible to think when you're standing at the
    sink,
  But down at the Laundrette there is nothing else to
    do.
You can think or you can read or you can natter —
  It doesn't really matter what you do —
And it's such a loverly treat,
  Not to be standing on your feet
At the Laundrette, the loverly Laundrette,
  Oh, we've found fulfilment at the Laundrette.

Glad, here, is absolutely altered —
  Mondays were her misery before.
She would start the day with dread,
  Seeing agony ahead,
But now with the Laundrette she's not worried any
    more.
  She is calm and she is cool and she is grateful,
Her Mondays are not hateful any more,
  She is just a shining ray,
Every minute of the day.

Neither Glad nor me, we
  Don't go to the pub, see,
We like it more at the Laundrette
  And use it more like a club.
It's ever so peaceful and clean there,

  It does you good to be seen there,
You never know who is next to you,
  And you never know who's just been there,
Washing the towels and shirts and sheets,
And socks and frocks, etcetera,
  Used to get worse and worser and worser,
But now it gets betterer and betterer.

We found fulfilment at the Laundrette,
  We've found a wider purpose in our lives.
We have made a little clique,
  And we meet there in the week,
And all through the Laundrette we're becoming better
    wives.
  In these ugly days when everyone is greedy,
We were needy for a sunbeam in our lives.
  And the sunbeam we have found,
As our washing whizzes round,
  Is the Laundrette,
The loverly Laundrette,
  We've found fulfilment at the Laundrette.

The Countess of Coteley

By Joyce Grenfell & Richard Adinsell (1978)

The Countess of Coteley!
  Wife of the Eleventh Earl,
Mother of four fine children,
  Three boys and a girl.
Coteley Park in Sussex,
  Strathrar on the Dee,
Palace Gardens, Kensington,
  Aged thirty-three.

Look at the Countess of Coteley!
  Here you see her when
She was at her zenith and the year was nineteen-ten.

Is she happy, would you guess?
  The answer to that question is, more or less.
For she's never heard of Hitler, and she's never
    thought of war,
  She's got twenty-seven servants, and she could get
    twenty more.
She never sees a paper, and she seldom reads a book,
  She is worshipped by her butler, tolerated by her
    cook.
And her husband treats her nicely, and he's *mostly* on a
    horse,
  While the children are entirely in the nursery of
    course.
So no wonder she is happy — she's got nothing else to
    do.
  O, no wonder she is happy, for she hasn't got a clue,
To the future that is waiting, and the funny things
    she'll do
  About . . . thirty-seven years from now.
When you see her in this flashback it is rather hard to
    guess
  That she'll be a sort of typist in the W.V.S.

She will learn to woo her grocer: she won't have a cook
    to woo,
  But a Czechoslovak cleaner may pop in from twelve
    to two.
Speaking worldlily she'll dwindle. She will change her
    book at Boots,
  And lecture on Make-do-and-Mend to Women's
    Institutes.
She will lose the Earl quite quietly, and her young will
    leave the nest,
  She never knew them very well, so that is for the
    best.
And Coteley, Strathrar, Kensington will vanish with
    the rest
  About . . . thirty-seven years from now.
Now the National Trust has Coteley, which is quite a
    handy dodge,
  And she'll make a flat of part of what was once the
    keeper's lodge.
She will seldom dress for dinner, she will dote on Vera
    Lynn,
  She will take in the *New Statesman*, but she won't be
    taken in.
Here you see her in this flashback looking decorative
    but dumb,
  For she hasn't got an inkling of the jolly days to
    come!
Though the distances she'll travel are incredible to tell,
  And the quandaries she'll cope with will be
    absolutely hell,
She'll emerge in Forty-seven having done it rather
    well!
  Will she be happy, would you guess?
The answer to that question is . . . Y-e-s.

Picture Postcard

By Joyce Grenfell & Richard Adinsell (1978)

Before pin-up girls there were picture-postcard
photographs of actresses on sale, and this lyric is about
a showgirl in the 1914-1918 war. Skindles is the name
of a riverside hotel at Maidenhead where young
officers of the day took their girls. There is a legend
that says no officer in the 'Blues' — the Household
Cavalry — in those days was permitted to marry an
actress.

I'm the picture-postcard that your Uncle Willy kept
  In his wallet, till the very day he died.
I'm the picture-postcard that your Auntie Milly found
  In your Uncle Willy's wallet,
When he dropped it on the ground.
  How your Uncle Willy frowned!
How your Aunt Milly cried!
  (For she was only a bride.)

He lied, of course. He tried of course,
  Denied he'd ever known me.
He sighed, of course, and cried, of course,
  Pretended to disown me.
But I'm the picture-postcard that your Uncle Willy
    kept
  In his wallet till the very day he died.
While awake or while he slept,
  In his wallet ever after,
Till the very day he died.

As a showgirl I played at the Palace
  In the First War, long ago.
And he was a subaltern in the Blues,
  And oh! he loved me so.
But he was already promised
  To the Lady Millicent Platt,
And though it seemed a pity —
  That was that.

We knew at the time it was Kismet;
  It wouldn't have worked, you see,
For they don't marry actresses in the Blues —
  So that was that for me.
But oh! the happiness, oh! the joy;
  Even now the memory kindles,
Then we parted, broken-heartedly,
  One summery Sunday at Skindles.

But I'm the picture-postcard that your Uncle Willy
    kept
  In his wallet till the very day he died.
While awake or while he slept,
  In his wallet ever after. Till the very day,
The very day,
  The very day he died.
Do you wonder how I know?
  Your Auntie Milly told me so.

Dear François
By Joyce Grenfell & Richard Adinsell (1978)

Dear François

Out of the blue I write to you to say that all is well in
London still. I trust your wife is well? — You too? Do
write and tell me all your news. My daughter,
Adrienne, is growing up. She's seventeen today. I
thought you'd like to know — after so long — that all
is well here.

I wish you could see my daughter,
  She's not in the least like me.
She's small and dark and lightly made,
  Not in the least bit English, I'm afraid.
I wish you could see my daughter,
  She's amusing and she's kind.
She's got a lively mind, like you.
  I'm very proud of her.

There's no excuse for writing now,
  I thought I never would.
What's past is past,
  And both of us are happy now,
And so the news is good.
  Perhaps I'm wrong in writing,
But the war's so far away —
  Another world,
But I am grateful for the past today.

I wish you could know my daughter,
  Oh, I'm prejudiced, I agree,
But none the less she does impress
  Everyone else, and so it's not just me.
I felt I must talk about her,
  But it's the middle of the night,
And a foolish time to write.
  I said I never would.

Dear François,
  Have no fear, I will not fail.
This letter will not reach you,
  That I swear.
I write to you every year,
  But none of my letters
Ever catch the mail.

A Transport of Delight (The Omnibus)
By Michael Flanders & Donald Swann (1956)

Some talk of a Lagonda,
　Some like a smart M.G.,
Or for Bonnie Army Lorry
　They'd lay them doon and dee.
Such means of locomotion
　Seem rather dull to us —
The Driver and Conductor
　Of a London Omnibus.

Hold very tight please, ting-ting!

When you are lost in London
　And you don't know where you are,
You'll hear my voice a-calling:
　'Pass further down the car!'
And very soon you'll find yourself
　Inside the Terminus
In a London Transport
　Diesel-engined
Ninety-seven horse-power
　Omnibus!

Along the Queen's great highway
　I drive my merry load
At twenty miles per hour
　In the middle of the road;
We like to drive in convoys —
　We're most gregarious;
The big six-wheeler
　Scarlet-painted
London Transport
　Diesel-engined
Ninety-seven horse-power
　Omnibus!

Earth has not anything to show more fair!
　Mind the stairs! Mind the stairs!
Earth has not anything to show more fair!
　Any more fares? Any more fares?

When cabbies try to pass me,
　Before they overtakes,
I sticks me flippin' hand out
　As I jams on all me brakes!
Them jackal taxi-drivers
　Can only swear and cuss,
Behind that monarch of the road,
　Observer of the Highway Code,
That big six-wheeler
　Scarlet-painted
London Transport
　Diesel-engined
Ninety-seven horse-power
　Omnibus!

I stops when I'm requested
　Although it spoils the ride,
So he can shout: 'Get aht of it!
　We're full right up inside!'

We don't ask much for wages,
　We only want fair shares,
So cut down all the stages,
　And stick up all the fares.
If tickets cost a pound apiece
　Why should you make a fuss?
It's worth it just to ride inside
　That thirty-foot-long by ten-foot-wide,
Inside that monarch of the road,
　Observer of the Highway Code,
That big six-wheeler
　Scarlet-painted
London Transport
　Diesel-engined
Ninety-seven horse-power
　Omnibus!

The Gnu
By Michael Flanders & Donald Swann (1956)

A year ago last Thursday I was strolling in the zoo
　When I met a man who thought he knew the lot;
He was laying down the law about the habits of
　Baboons
　And the number of quills a Porcupine has got.

I asked him: 'What's that creature there?' He
　answered: 'H'it's a H'elk'.
　I might have gone on thinking that was true,
If the animal in question hadn't put that chap to shame
　And remarked: 'I h'aint a H'elk. I'm a G-nu!

I'm a G-nu, I'm a G-nu,
  The g-nicest work of g-nature in the zoo!
I'm a G-nu, how do you do?
  You really ought to k-now w-ho's w-ho.
I'm a G-nu, spelt G.N.U.,
  I'm g-not a Camel or a Kangaroo,
So let me introduce,
  I'm g-neither Man nor Moose,
Oh, g-no, g-no, g-no, I'm a G-nu!'

I had taken furnished lodgings down at Rustington-on-
  Sea
  (Whence I travelled on to Ashton-under-Lyme)
And the second night I stayed there, I was wakened
  from a dream
  Which I'll tell you all about some other time.

Among the hunting trophies on the wall above my
  bed,
  Stuffed and mounted, was a face I thought I knew.
A Bison? An Okapi? Could it be . . . a Hartebeeste?
  Then I seemed to hear a voice: 'I'm a G-nu!

I'm a G-nu, a g-nother G-nu,
  I wish I could g-nash my teeth at you!
I'm a G-nu, how do you do?
  You really ought to k-now w-ho's w-ho.
I'm a G-nu, spelt G.N.U.,
  Call me Bison or Okapi and I'll sue!
G-nor am I in the least
  Like that dreadful Hartebeeste,
Oh, g-no, g-no, g-no, I'm a G-nu!'

The Hippopotamus
By Michael Flanders & Donald Swann (1956)

A bold Hippopotamus was standing one day
  On the banks of the cool Shalimar.
He gazed at the bottom as it peacefully lay
  By the light of the evening star.
Away on a hilltop sat combing her hair
  His fair Hippopotamine maid;
The Hippopotamus was no ignoramus
  And sang her this sweet serenade:

Mud, mud, glorious mud,
  Nothing quite like it for cooling the blood!
So follow me, follow,
  Down to the hollow
And there let us wallow
  In glorious mud!

The fair Hippopotama he aimed to entice
  From her seat on that hilltop above,
As she hadn't got a ma to give her advice,
  Came tiptoeing down to her love.
Like thunder the forest re-echoed the sound
  Of the song that they sang as they met.
His inamorata adjusted her garter
  And lifted her voice in duet:

Mud, mud, glorious mud,
  Nothing quite like it for cooling the blood!
So follow me, follow,
  Down to the hollow
And there let us wallow
  In glorious mud!

Now more Hippopotami began to convene
  On the banks of that river so wide.
I wonder now what am I to say of the scene
  That ensued by the Shalimar side?
They dived all at once with an ear-splitting splosh
  Then rose to the surface again,
A regular army of Hippopotami
  All singing this haunting refrain:

Mud, mud, glorious mud,
  Nothing quite like it for cooling the blood!
So follow me, follow,
  Down to the hollow
And there let us wallow
  In glorious mud!

Have Some Madeira, M'dear
By Michael Flanders & Donald Swann (1956)

She was young! She was pure! She was new! She was
  nice!
  She was fair! She was sweet seventeen!
He was old! He was vile and no stranger to vice!
  He was base! He was bad! He was mean!

He had slyly inveigled her up to his flat
  To see his collection of stamps,
And he said as he hastened to put out the cat,
  The wine, his cigar and the lamps:

'Have some Madeira, m'dear!
  You really have nothing to fear;
I'm not trying to tempt you — it wouldn't be right.
  You shouldn't drink spirits at this time of night;
Have some Madeira, m'dear!
  It's very much nicer than Beer;
I don't care for Sherry, one cannot drink Stout,
  And Port is a wine I can well do without;
It's simply a case of *Chacun à son GOUT!*
  Have some Madeira, m'dear!'

Unaware of the wiles of the snake in the grass,
  Of the fate of the maiden who topes,
She lowered her standards by raising her glass,
  Her courage, her eyes — and his hopes.
She sipped it, she drank it, she drained it, she did;
  He quietly refilled it again
And he said as he secretly carved one more notch
  On the butt of his gold-handled cane:

'Have some Madeira, m'dear!
  I've got a small cask of it here,
And once it's been opened you know it won't keep.
  Do finish it up — it will help you to sleep;
Have some Madeira, m'dear!
  It's really an excellent year;
Now if it were Gin, you'd be wrong to say yes,
  The evil Gin does would be hard to assess
(Besides, it's inclined to affect m' prowess!)
  Have some Madeira, m'dear!'

Then there flashed through her mind what her mother
    had said
  With her antepenultimate breath:
'Oh, my child, should you look on the wine when it's
    red
  Be prepared for a fate worse than death!'
She let go her glass with a shrill little cry.
  Crash, tinkle! It fell to the floor.
When he asked: 'What in heaven . . .?' she made no
    reply,
  Up her mind and a dash for the door.

'Have some Madeira, m'dear!'
  Rang out down the hall loud and clear.
A tremulous cry that was filled with despair,
  As she paused to take breath in the cool midnight
    air;
'Have some Madeira, m'dear!'
  The words seemed to ring in her ear
Until the next morning she woke up in bed,
  With a smile on her lips and an ache in her head —
And a beard in her earhole that tickled and said:
  'Have some Madeira, m'dear!'

Design for Living
By Michael Flanders & Donald Swann (1956)

When I started making money, when I started making
    friends,
  We found a home as soon as we were able to.
We bought this little freehold for about a thousand
    more
  Than the house our little house was once the stable
    to.
With charm, and colour values, wit, and structural
    alteration,
  Now designed for graceful living, it has quite a
    reputation . . .

We're terribly *House and Garden*
  At Number Seven B,
We live in a most amusing mews —
  Ever so very Contemporary!
We're terribly *House and Garden;*

The money that one spends
To make a place that won't disgrace
  Our *House and Garden* friends!

We planned an uninhibited interior decor,
  Curtains made of straw,
We've wall-papered the floor!
  We don't know if we like it, but we're absolutely sure
There's no place like home sweet home.

We're fearfully *Maison Jardin*
  At Number Seven B,
We've rediscovered the Chandelier —
  Ever so very Contemporary!
We're terribly *House and Garden.*
  Now at last we've got the chance,
The garden's full of furniture
  And the house is full of plants!

Oh, it doesn't make for comfort
   But it simply has to be;
You mustn't be left behind The Times
   Furnishing Company!

Have you a home that cries out to your every visitor:
   'Here lives somebody who is Exciting to Know!' No?

Why not . . .
Save little metal bottle-tops and nail them upside down
to the floor? This will give a sensation of walking on
little metal bottle-tops, turned upside down and nailed
to the floor.

Why not . . .
get hold of an ordinary Northumbrian Spoke-shaver's
Coracle, paint it in contrasting stripes of Telephone
Black and White, and hang it up somewhere?

Why not . . .
keep, on some convenient shelving, a little cluster of
clocks; one for each member of the family, each an
individual colour? I like to keep mine twenty minutes
fast, don't you?

Why not . . .
drop in one evening for a Mess of Pottage? *My*
speciality. Just aubergine and carnation petals — but
with a six shilling bottle of *Mule du Pape,* a feast fit for

a king! I'm delirious about our new cooker fitment
with the eye-level grill. This means that without my
having to bend down the hot fat can squirt straight into
my eye!

We're frightfully *House and Garden*
   At Number Seven B,
The walls are patterned with shrunken heads,
   Ever so very Contemporary!
Our search for self-expression
   Leaves us barely time for meals;
One day we're taking Liberty's in,
   The next we're down at Heal's!

With wattle screens and little lamps and motifs here
   and there,
   Mobiles in the air,
Ivy everywhere,
   You mustn't be surprised to find a cactus in the
   chair,
But we call it home sweet home.

Oh, we're terribly *House and Garden*
   As I think we said before,
But though Seven B is madly gay —
   It wouldn't do for every day —
We actually *live* in Seven A,
   In the house next door!

The Gasman Cometh
By Michael Flanders & Donald Swann (1963)

'Twas on a *Monday* morning
   The *Gasman* came to call;
The gas tap wouldn't turn — I wasn't getting gas at all.
   He tore out all the skirting boards
To try and find the main,
   And I had to call a *Carpenter* to put them back again.
Oh, it all makes work for the working man to do!

'Twas on a *Tuesday* morning
   The *Carpenter* came round;
He hammered and he chiselled and he said: 'Look
   what I've found!
   Your joists are full of dry-rot
But I'll put it all to rights.'
   Then he nailed right through a cable and out went
   all the lights.
Oh, it all makes work for the working man to do!

'Twas on a *Wednesday* morning
   The *Electrician* came;
He called me 'Mr. Sanderson' (which isn't quite my
   name).
   He couldn't reach the fuse box
Without standing on the bin
   And his foot went through a window — so I called a
   Glazier in.
Oh, it all makes work for the working man to do!

'Twas on a *Thursday* morning
   The *Glazier* came along,
With his blow-torch and his putty and his merry
   Glazier's song;
   He put another pane in —
It took no time at all —
   But I had to get a *Painter* in to come and paint the
   wall.
Oh, it all makes work for the working man to do!

185

'Twas on a *Friday* morning
  The *Painter* made a start;
With undercoats and overcoats he painted every part,
  Every nook and every cranny,
But I found when he was gone
  He'd painted over the gas tap and I couldn't turn it
    on!

Oh, it all makes work for the working man to do!

On *Saturday* and *Sunday* they do no work at all:
  So 'twas on a *Monday* morning that the *Gasman* came
    to call!

The Bedstead Men
By Michael Flanders & Donald Swann (1963)

When you're walking in the country
  Far from villages or towns,
When you're seven miles from nowhere and beyond,
  In some dark deserted forest
Or a hollow of the Downs,
  You may come across a lonely pool, or pond.
And you'll always find a big, brass, broken bedstead by
    the bank:
  There's one in every loch and mere and fen.
Don't think it's there by accident,
  It's us you have to thank:
The Society of British Bedstead Men.

Oh the hammer ponds of Sussex
  And the dew ponds of the West
Are part of Britain's heritage,
  The part we love the best;
Every eel- and fish- and mill-pond
  Has a beauty all can share . . .
But not unless it's got a big brass broken bedstead
    there!

So we filch them out of attics,
  We beg them from our friends,
We buy them up in auction lots
  With other odds and ends,
Then we drag them 'cross the meadows
  When the moon is in the sky . . .
So watch the wall, my darling, while the Bedstead Men
    go by!

The League of British Bedstead Men
  Is marching through the night,
A desperate and dedicated crew.

Under cover of the hedges,
  Always keeping out of sight,
  For the precious load of Bedsteads must get through!

The Society for Putting
  Broken Bedsteads into Ponds
Has another solemn purpose to fulfil;
  On our coastal sands and beaches
Or where waving willow wands
  Mark the borders of a river, stream or rill,
You'll always find a single laceless left-hand leather
    boot:
  A bootless British river bank's a shock.
We leave them there at midnight;
  You can track a member's route,
By the alternating prints of boot and sock.

Oh the lily ponds of Suffolk
  And the mill-ponds of the West
Are part of Britain's heritage,
  The part we love the best;
Her river banks and sea-shores
  Have a beauty all can share,
Provided there's at least one boot,
  Three treadless tyres,
A half-eaten pork pie,
  Some oil drums,
An old felt hat,
  A lorry load of tarblocks
And a broken bedstead there!

A Song of Patriotic Prejudice
By Michael Flanders & Donald Swann (1963)

The rottenest bits of these islands of ours
  We've left in the hands of three unfriendly powers;
Examine the Irishman, Welshman or Scot,

You'll find he's a stinker as likely as not!
The English, the English, the English are best!
  I wouldn't give tuppence for all of the rest!

186

The Scotsman is mean, as we're all well aware,
  And bony and blotchy and covered with hair;
He eats salty porridge, he works all the day
  And he hasn't got Bishops to show him the way.
The English, the English, the English are best!
  I wouldn't give tuppence for all of the rest!

The Irishman now our contempt is beneath;
  He sleeps in his boots, and he lies in his teeth;
He blows up policemen, or so I have heard,
  And blames it on Cromwell and William the Third.
The English arc noble, the English are nice,
  And worth any other at double the price!

The Welshman's dishonest — he cheats when he can —
  And little and dark, more like monkey than man;
He works underground with a lamp in his hat
  And sings far too loud, far too often, and flat.
The English, the English, the English are best!
  I wouldn't give tuppence for all of the rest!

And crossing the Channel one cannot say much
  For the French or the Spanish, the Danish or Dutch;

The Germans are German, the Russians are Red
  And the Greeks and Italians eat garlic in bed.
The English are moral, the English are good
  And clever and modest and misunderstood.

And all the world over each nation's the same —
  They've simply no notion of Playing the Game;
They argue with Umpires, they cheer when they've
    won,
  And they practice beforehand, which spoils all the
    fun!
The English, the English, the English are best!
  So up with the English and down with the rest!

It's not that they're wicked or naturally bad:
  It's knowing they're *foreign* that makes them so mad!
For the English are all that a nation should be
  And the flower of the English are Donald* and me!
The English, the English, the English are best!
  I wouldn't give tuppence for all of the rest!

* *At this point the singer may substitute the name of the
pianist.*

In the Bath
By Michael Flanders & Donald Swann (1963)

Oh, I find much simple pleasure when I've had a
    tiring day
  In the bath, in the bath!
Where the noise of gentle sponging seems to blend
    with my top A
  In the bath, in the bath!
To the skirl of pipes vibrating in the boiler room
    below,
  I sing a pot-pourri of all the songs I used to know,
And the water thunders in and gurgles down the
    overflow
  In the bath, in the bath!

Then the loathing for my fellows rises steaming from
    my brain
  In the bath, in the bath!
And condenseth to the Milk of Human Kindness once
    again
  In the bath, in the bath!
Oh, the tingling of the scrubbing brush, the flannel's
    soft caress!
  To wield a lordly loofah is a joy I can't express.
How truly it is spoken, one is next to Godliness
  In the bath, in the bath!

Then there comes that dreadful moment when the
    water's running cold
  In the bath, in the bath!
When the soap is lost forever and one's feeling tired
    and old
  In the bath, in the bath!
It's time to pull the plug out, time to mop the
    bathroom floor.
  The towel is in the cupboard, and the cupboard is
    next door!
It's started running hot! Let's have another hour or
    more
  In the bath, in the bath!

I can see the one salvation of the poor old human race
  In the bath, in the bath!
Let the nations of the world all meet together face to
    face
  In the bath, in the bath!
One with Kissinger, Kosygin and all those other chaps,
  Sadat and Chairman Mao, then we'll have some
    peace perhaps —
Provided Harold Wilson gets the end without the taps
  In the bath, in the bath!

The Warthog

By Michael Flanders & Donald Swann (1980)

The jungle was giving a party,
  A post-hibernation ball,
The ballroom was crowded with waltzing gazelles,
  Gorillas and zebras and all.
But who is that animal almost in tears
  Pretending to powder her nose?
A poor little Warthog who sits by herself
  In a pink satin dress with blue bows.
Again she is nobody's choice
  And she sings in a sad little voice:

'No one ever wants to court a Warthog
  Though a Warthog does her best;
I've spent a lot of money for a Warthog,
  I am kiss-proofed, and prettily dressed.
I've lustre-rinsed my hair,
  Dabbed perfume here and there,
My gums were tinted when I brushed my teeth;
  I'm young and in my prime
But a wallflower all the time
  'Cause I'm a Warthog,
Just a Warthog,
  I'm a Warthog underneath.'

Take your partners for a Ladies Excuse Me!

Excited and radiant she runs on the floor
  To join the furore and fuss;
She taps on each shoulder and says, 'Excuse me',
  And each couple replies, 'Excuse us!'
Then having no manners at all
  They sing as they dance round the hall:

'No one ever wants to court a Warthog,
  Though a Warthog does her best;
Her accessories are dazzling for a Warthog,
  She is perfumed and daringly dressed.
We know her these and those
  Are like Brigitte Bardot's,
Her gown is just a scintillating sheath,
  But she somehow fails to please
'Cause everybody sees
  That she's a Warthog,
Just a Warthog,
  She's a Warthog underneath!'

Head hanging, she wanders away from the floor,
  This Warthog whom nobody loves,
Then stops in amazement, for there at the door
  Stands a gentleman Warthog impeccably dressed
In the act of removing his gloves;
  His fine chiselled face seems to frown
As he looks her first up and then down.

'I fancy you must be a sort of Warthog,
  Though for a Warthog you look a mess.
That make-up's far too heavy for a Warthog;
  You could have chosen a more suitable dress.
Did you have to dye your hair?
  If that's perfume, give me air!
I strongly disapprove of scarlet teeth;
  But let us take the floor
'Cause I'm absolutely sure
  That you're a Warthog,
Just a Warthog,
  The sweetest little,
Neatest little,
  Dearest and completest little
Warthog . . . underneath!'

The Wompom

By Michael Flanders & Donald Swann (1980)

You can do such a lot with a Wompom;
  You can use every part of it too;
For work or for pleasure
  It's a triumph, it's a treasure;
Oh, there's nothing that a Wompom cannot do!

Now the thread from the coat of a Wompom
  Has the warmth and resilience of wool;
You need never wash or brush it,
  It's impossible to crush it,
And it shimmers like the finest sort of tulle.

So our clothes are all made from the Wompom —
  Model gowns, sportswear, lingerie —
They are waterproof and plastic,
  Where it's needed they're elastic
And they emphasise the figure as you see.

Hail to thee blithe Wompom,
  Hail to thee O plant,
All providing Wompom,
  Universal Aunt!

You can shave with the rind of a Wompom
  And it acts as a soapless shampoo,
And the root in little doses
  Keeps you free from halitosis —
Oh, there's nothing that a Wompom cannot do!

Now the thick inner shell of a Wompom
  You can mould with the finger and thumb;
Though soft when you began it
  It will set as hard as granite
And it's quite as light as aluminium.

So we make what we like from the Wompom
  And that proves very useful indeed,
From streets full of houses
  To the buttons on your trousers,
With a Wompom you have everything you need.

Gaudeamus Wompom,
  Gladly we salute
Vademecum Wompom,
  Philanthropic fruit!

Oh the thin outer leaf of a Wompom
  Makes the finest Havana cigar,
And its bottom simply bristles
  With unusual looking thistles,
But we haven't yet discovered what they are!

You can do such a lot with a Wompom;
  You can use every part of it too;
For work or for pleasure
  It's a triumph, it's a treasure;
Oh, there's nothing that a Wompom cannot do!

Oh, the flesh in the heart of a Wompom
  Has the flavour of Porterhouse Steak,
And the juice is a liquor
  That will get you higher quicker —
And you're still lit up next morning when you wake!

Wompom, Wompom,
  Let your voices ring,
Wompom, Wompom,
  Evermore we sing!

To record *What is What* in a Wompom
  Needs a book twice as big as *Who's Who;*
I could tell you more and more a-
  Bout this fascinating flora:
You can shape it, you can square it,
  You can drape it, you can wear it,
You can ice it, you can dice it,
  You can pare it, you can slice it . . .
Oh, there's nothing that a Wompom cannot do!

There's a Hole in my Budget
By Michael Flanders & Donald Swann (1953)

There's a hole in my Budget, dear Margaret, dear
  Margaret,
  There's a hole in my Budget, dear P.M., my dear.

Then mend it, dear Geoffrey, dear Geoffrey, dear
  Geoffrey,
  Then mend it, dear Geoffrey, dear Geoffrey, my
  dear.

But how shall I mend it, dear Margaret, dear
  Margaret?
  But how shall I mend it, dear P.M., my dear?

By building up exports, dear Geoffrey, dear Geoffrey,
  By increased production, dear Geoffrey, my dear.

But that means working harder, dear Margaret, dear
  Margaret,
  And the workers must have more incentives, my
  dear.

Then decrease taxation, dear Geoffrey, dear Geoffrey,
  And raise all their wages, dear Geoffrey, my dear.

And where is the money to come from, dear Margaret?
  But where is the money to come from, my dear?

Why out of your Budget, dear Geoffrey, dear
  Geoffrey,
  Out of your Budget, dear Geoffrey, my dear.

But there's a hole in my Budget, dear Margaret, dear
    Margaret,
  There's a hole in my Budget, dear P.M., my dear.

Then mend it, dear Geoffrey, dear Geoffrey, dear
    Geoffrey,
  Then mend it, dear Geoffrey, dear Geoffrey, my
    dear.

But how shall . . .

This song is a dialogue between the Prime Minister and Chancellor of the day. The two performers wander round the stage or room in a slow inflationary spiral.

It Pays To Advertise
By Greatrex Newman (1981)

T.V. 'commercials' advertise
  Dog foods — detergents — pills — pork-pies —
While grateful customers report
  And praise the gorgeous goods they've bought.
With every purchase each is so *delighted*
To tell you on the 'telly' they're invited.

We see a smiling, working HOUSE-WIFE from the Midlands, who pauses while hanging out her snow-white washing — to tell us:

My 'usband's a miner, 'e waerks darn the pit,
  'Is shaerts get real mucky wi' coal-dust an' grit;
'Is vests though are waerse — they get blacker than
    black —
  Each vest 'as a seam of Grade A. Nutty Slack.
But since I've used *SOAPO* for my weekly wash
  'Is shaerts are bright white — 'e looks posher than
    posh —
'E used to look fealthy — 'is shaerts was so daerty —
  But *now* — gets free pints from a *barmaid* called
    Gaertie!
      ('Silver threads among the gold')
Shaerts an' vests are growin' old —
  SOAPO'S waerth it's weight in gold;
'Tuppence-orf' all week it's been —
  SOAPO washes *cleanest clean.*

A friendly YOKEL blows the froth off his tankard, and offers his testimony:

When Oi were a lard —
  A good toime Oi 'ard —
Though mighty poor pay Oi were gettin';
  Whoile sittin' on stoiles
Wi' ole Varmer Goiles
  My whistle were wantin' much wettin'.
So when up Oi grew
  Oi tasted the brew

Of *THINGUMMY'S BEER* — draught an' bottle;
  That beer be the best —
It grows 'air on tha chest —
  So pour more an' more darn tha throttle.

So 'ere's to good cheer —
  Drink *THINGUMMY'S BEER* —
Though 'Temperance' may be tha motto —
  Doan worry bart nowt —
All the 'ops 'ave 'opped out —
  So Sup up! Tha'll never get blotto.

An' allus remember — when tha be *cursed* wi' a *thirst* ·
  Simply say: '*BRING-A-ME* a *THINGUMMY!*'

What is Home without a Mother? A most charming young MOTHER makes this appeal — straight from the heart:

A mother's true love is a pearl beyond price —
  Such tender protection — unselfish advice;
Her children feel safe as she tucks them to sleep —
  Then out on the landing she'll silently creep.
With fervent 'Bless Mummy' they ended their
    prayers —
  She opens a door at the top of the stairs —
And as the sun sets — at the peaceful day's end —
  She sprinkles new *LAVVO* — it's *clean round the bend.*

Twinkle, twinkle little germ,
  LAVVO makes you writhe and squirm;
Sprinkle, sprinkle — then '*Adieu*'
  '*Good-bye*' — '*Farewell*' germs in 'loo'.

A very popular type is the young MAN-ABOUT-TOWN, who talks to his pals at the Club, — but remembers the Government warning:

190

Joyce Grenfell as she appeared in Noel Coward's revue
Sigh No More at the Piccadilly Theatre, 1945

Greatrex Newman, who wrote for Bransby Williams
and Tom Clare and is still writing in 1981

Greatrex Newman's famous Fol-de-Rols Concert Party, 1938: (*back row, l. to r.*) Walter Midgley, Eric Whitley,
Richard Murdoch, Jack Warner, Robin Ford, Arthur Askey; (*centre row*) Gladys Vernon, Peggy Rawlings
(Mrs Richard Murdoch), Gladys Merridew, Thurza Rogers, Elfrida Burgess; (*front row*) Margaret Freeman,
Hilda Burdon, Joan Heath, Nora Whitworth

Down in the bar — we were yarning and joking —
  I started coughing — my chest gave a wheeze —
Chumley said 'What cigarettes are you smoking?
  Cut out the coughing — just try one of these.'
    (Produces large packet: continues a la salesman:)
These are the new filter-filled — called
  PERFECTION —
These *are* perfection — without boast or brag,
These have the all-the-way built-in protection —
  Plus new ingredient — FERTILIZED SHAG!

Generous coupons — enclosed in each packet —
  Wonderful gifts — for the olds and the youngs —
One hundred coupons: — a *silk smoking jacket!*
  Five hundred coupons: — a *new pair of lungs!*
    ('Work, Boys Work')
Smoke boys smoke, have a *PERFECTION*,
  Gives you energy and drive;
With the new gigantic size
  Smoke does *not* get in your eyes —
Smoke *PERFECTION* — and you'll live to twenty-five!

With Their Heads Tucked Underneath Their Arms
By Greatrex Newman (1981)

Shed a tear of sad regret
  For poor Marie Antoinette,
Lady Jane Grey, Anne Boelyn —
  Regal ladies — all 'done in.'
Louis Sixteenth met his fate,
  Robespierre became 'the late,'
Charles the First — likewise despatched, —
  All their 'nappers' were detached:

PARIS: 1793:
Pity Marie Antoinette,
  Understandably upset:
Most unfortunate mistake
  Saying 'Let 'em all eat cake!'
Through the extra cake they ate
  French girls put on so much weight
That they one and all approved
  When her 'loaf' had been removed.

1793:
Poor King Louis X.V.I.
  King of France in days gone by,
Had to bow the regal knee
  And became Ex. V.I.P.
Of all follies he'd his share,
  All except Folies Bergere;
Felt a rather painful jar —
  Tete tucked underneath his *bras.*

1794:
Robespierre soon rose to fame,
  When the Reign of Terror came;
Then the guillotine, you bet,
  Gave more shaves than Blue Gillette.
In those Revolution days
  Pheasants sang the Mayonaisse;
Robespierre was most perplexed
  When they said 'Your neck's the next!'

LONDON: 1536:
Anne Boelyn was quite serene
  As King Henry's second Queen;
When Jane Seymour joined the race
  She came in third — just got a place.
But King Henry had, of course,
  Found a short *cut* — for divorce,
So Queen Anne walked Bloody Tower —
  Minus head — at midnight hower.

1554:
Lady Jane Grey, meek and mild,
  Was a bright, observant child;
Without effort, without fuss,
  Soon passed her Eleven Plus.
When she'd barely turned sixteen
  She was hailed as England's Queen,
Reigned for nine days — full of dread —
  Then lost both her crown *and* head.

1649:
Charles the First, of royal blood,
  One day found his name was mud;
Parliament had got quite tough
  When he tried to treat 'em rough.
When on Church Reform he frowned
  Cromwell sent his Roundheads round;
So poor Charles made his adieu —
  Felt a proper Charlie, too!

Come into the Garden more
By Greatrex Newman (1981)

A garden is a joy indeed
  Where grubs and slugs and earth-worms breed
And teach their progeny to feed
  On root and shoot and sprouting seed
With shameless gluttony and greed
  While I — with back a broken reed —
Must bend and endlessly proceed
  To weed — and weed — and weed — and weed.

'A garden is a lovesome thing, God wot' . . .
  God, what a lot of loathsome things *mine's* got!

Motor-mower! Motor-mower!
  How I hate that chap next-dower
Who gets up each Sunday morning
  Early dawning starts his lawning
With his noisy self-propelling
  Evil sounding — evil smelling
Motorised decapitator
  Guided by it's navigator
Up and downing — down and upping
  With it's motor's loud hiccoughing
Round and round the same location
  Ceaseless peaceless irritation
Calling forth my foulest curses
  As the fellow re-transverses.

If he were *your* neighbour, Percy,
  Wouldn't *you* feel cursey-cursey?
Wouldn't angry Mr. Thrower
  Damn and blast his blasted mower?

Attempting to grow a new dahlia
  With seed upside-down, seemed a failia;
But to my surprise
  For GIGANTIC SIZE
I won a First Prize in Australia.

The cabbage, curly kale and sprout
  Have lots of vitamins no doubt
But something's lacking in their *looks*
  Which makes discerning chefs and cooks
Prefer the *cauliflower's* appeal
  And groom it for some *special* meal
Embellishing it's floral crown
  With cheesy fragrance — tinted brown
To titillate the appetite
  And gourmet's palate to delight
When served as solo dish complete
  (Not just auxiliary to meat)
But with a culinary pride
  That other 'greens' are all denied.

For though in shops they've fraternised
  There's only one *au gratinized* . . .
While products of the self-same soil
  Are bunged in some old pan — to *boil!*

Cucumbers never can disguise
  Their wrinkles — long and narrow;
No matter how a young one tries
  To put on weight and boost its size
It never wins a Flower Show prize
  As vegetable marrow.

Wakey! Wakey!
By Greatrex Newman (1981)

Each morning there's a hubbub
  That awakes the sleeping subbub
As the sons of toil their labours all begin;
  They open wide the peepers
Of the slumberers and sleepers
  With a daily doze of devastating din.
Announcing their arrival
  At an early hour a.m.
The noise annoys the neighbours —
  But the noise *delighteth* them.

They're boys wot enjoys a noise,
  All slumber they quickly destroys;
The quietude urban

They're happy disturban,
  They're boys wot *enjoys* a noise.

In meadows the cows
  Contentedly browse
While cheerfully chewing and mooing;
  Cows haven't a clue
How noisy a brew
  Their chewing is silently brewing.
But milkmen delivering bottles
  Outside some secluded abode —
All gleefully clang 'em
  And bash 'em and bang 'em —
No rest for the rest of the road.

They're boys wot enjoys a noise,
  They're early to bed and to roise;
They rouses the houses
  With juice from the cowses —
They're boys wot *enjoys* a noise.

When daylight begins
  They empty dust-bins
With grins while the family drowses;
  Their method contrives
To wake up the wives —
  Whose grouses arouses their spouses.
By banging the bins on the pavement,
  And dropping the lids with a thud —
All slumberers thinkin'
  Of just forty-winkin'
Are blinkin' well nipped in the bud.

They're boys wot enjoys a noise,
  Their pleasure they do not disgoise;
The bins get a bashin' —
  It really sounds smashin' —
They're boys wot *enjoys* a noise.

Whenever a train
  Decides to remain
At Crewe or the Junction of Clapham,
  A wheel-tapper kneels
To bang on the wheels,
  And grimly continues to slap 'em.
Though nobody knows why they bang 'em —
  I'll tell you in confidence now —
It's 'cause the poor puff-puff
  Can't make noise enough-nuff,
So squeals from the wheels join the row.

They're boys wot enjoys a noise,
  In noises they all specialoise;
With wheel-tapper's hammer
  A deafinite clamour —
They're boys wot *enjoys* a noise.

When blokes see a street
  All natty and neat
They're willin' to start with their drillin';
  They rip it in ruts
And tear out it's guts,
  The skill in their drillin' is thrillin'.
They take a real pride in their prowess,
  No wonder they swagger and swank —
They drill with 'pneumatic'
  The din is ecstatic —
They quivers like Chivers blank-mank.

They're boys wot enjoys a noise,
  They're proud of their loud little toys;
They love to embellish
  The symphony hellish —
They're boys wot *enjoys* a noise.

They're boys wot enjoys — a n'ell of a noise —
  A n'ell of a noise them boys enjoys —
They're boys wot enjoys — enjoys — enjoys —
  They're boys wot *enjoys* a noise.

Hat Trick

By Greatrex Newman (1981)

When I was just a little chap
  I always wore a small school cap,
But graduated to straw-boater
  As early school-days got remoter.

As I advanced to Man's Estate
  Hats more sedate appeared on pate;
As junior clerk I wore the stock
  Black bowler — alias 'billy-cock'.

But when towards the girls I gazed
  A 'trilby' was the hat I raised;
Till up the aisle — with borrowed plume —
  In Moss Bros. 'topper' went the groom.

To me, a hat is still a 'must'
  No parting until death us doest;
Despite perpetual cloak-room fee
  For re-uniting hat and me
At club, hotel or luncheon dive,
  Where serfs or vassals all contrive
To seize my hat with eager zeal
  (As I approach to order meal),
Thus leaving head uncovered, bare,
  With 'titfer' in the bandit's care
Until I finish meal or snack
  Then have to buy the damn thing back!

Animal, Vegetable or Mineral?
By Greatrex Newman (1981)

Here's a General Knowledge Quiz:
　CROC-RIG-AR? — What are or is?
Have you read — or have you heard
　Of this unique animird?

A famous Professor, renowned at all colleges,
　Made a life study of two of the ologies;
Ologies prefixed by 'Ornith' and 'Zoo' —
　He knew all the birds and the animals too.

He'd studied cross-breeding, since learning at school
　That donkey and horse have an off-spring called
　　mule;
And for his degree he had written a thesis
　On specialised spouses of specified species.

Suggesting a crocodile 'cross' as a test,
　His choice of a mate brought derision and jest;
Zoologists felt he had gone far too far —
　A crocodile 'crossed' with a *budgerigar!*

They said his ambition was frankly absurd
　To try to produce a quite new animird —
But when the Professor succeeded — 'Hurrah!'
　They cheeringly greeted the first Crocrigar!

Of course, the Professor was thrilled and delighted,
　For breeding a Crocrigar — instantly knighted;
And when — at each lecture — he placed it on view —
　The Crocrigar spoke the one sentence it knew.

But at the Professor's first lecture abroad,
　The Crocrigar listened — although looking bored,
And as the Professor got more and more wordy —
　It bit off his leg and said *'Who's-a-pretty-birdie?'*

No News is Good News
By Greatrex Newman (1981)

Look through the day's papers and read all the news —
　If your name's *not* mentioned — contentedly snooze;
You've not been accused of some meddlesome prank
　Like coshing old ladies or robbing a bank.

You've not pinched a loaf from some big Supermarket,
　Or left your jaloppy where you shouldn't park it —
No H.P. instalment-arrears still unpaid —
　No Maintenance Order that's not been obeyed.

No cause for your feeling depressed or despondent —
　You haven't been cited divorce Co-respondent;
You haven't been pictured protesting with banner
　Demanding more 'perks' — or in works goes a
　　spanner!

You're not in the news, so be thankful old son,
　And grin that old grin while you're still having fun;
There's only one item should make you feel solemn —
　It's finding *your name* in to-day's 'Obit.' column.

Sour Grapes
By Greatrex Newman (1981)

It's strange that people seldom buy a bunch of grapes
　　until
　Somebody's ill;
They buy all kinds of other fruit — assorted sorts and
　　shapes —
　But don't buy grapes —

Until their rich Aunt Agatha's relieved of her
　appendix,

Then off they rush to buy a bunch, and in one-fifth
　of ten-ticks
They're at dear Auntie's Nursing Home, with hushed
　bed-side decorum,
　(Annoyed if other relatives have left *their* grapes
　before 'em.)

For old Aunt Agatha has got most numerous relations,
    Each one of whom is cherishing most hopeful
    'expectations';
And all of whom send 'Get Well' cards, with verses
    sweet and moving,
    And even sweeter hot-house grapes, with hopes that
    she's improving.

Then early on the 'phone each day they're anxiously
    enquiring
    As to the likelihood — or not — of their dear Aunt
    expiring?
And when informed dear Auntie still is very much
    alive —
    More produce of the vineyard then continues to
    arrive.

But Auntie is a tough old bird, and as they bring each
    bunch in
    Her molars grimly tread the grapes, with
    masticating munchin;
And daily — while dear Auntie rests from surgical
    incision —
    The grapes arrive at bed-side with conveyor-belt
    precision.

But one day — after tributes from her faithful kith and
    kin —
    Fate struck a blow below the belt — although above
    the chin —
And Auntie's pulverizing jaw came suddenly to rest
    As by ten thousand demons her poor mouth became
    possessed.

Her screams of pain rushed nurses in — who found
    that misadventure
    Had forced some most abrasive pips beneath poor
    Auntie's denture;
And lacerated tender flesh beneath that cruel plate
    Had turned each loving bunch of love to hateful
    bunch of hate.

Poor Auntie's language would have shocked all
    Members of the Cloth,
    As she vituperated on those blasted Grapes of
    Wrath;
She summoned her solicitor — and made a codicil —
    And all who'd bought those ruddy grapes were
    wiped out of her Will.

That's That!
By Greatrex Newman (1981)

All girls should take care — of a stranger beware —
    Especially when at the sea-side;
But round by the Band — well, you know how you
    do —
    I noticed a fellow — I fancied I knew:

And I looked — and he looked — we both looked;
    I thought that he looked — rather nice;
Then he smiled — and I smiled, — and I smiled —
    and he smiled —
    We both — sort of smiled — once or twice.
Then he turned — and I turned — we both turned;
    Then he — sort of — half — raised his hat;
As he — hesitated — well — I — hesitated, —
    Then we both said 'Hallo' — and that's that!

We went out to lunch, — and he took me to tea, —
    And then we had dinner together;
And then he suggested a run in his car, —
    I said 'Well — I might — if we don't go too far.'

Then he sat — and I sat — we both sat;
    The car started off, with a bang;
Then he joked — and I joked — and he smoked — and
    I smoked —

And 'Love's Old Sweet Song' we both sang.
Then he stopped — and I stopped — and the car
    stopped!
    He thought p'raps a tyre had gone flat;
We just talked — together, — we talked of — the
    weather, —
    Then the tyre seemed okay — and that's that!

We got home at twelve — or it may have been one, —
    I know it was late, — perhaps later;
He drove me right home — to the door of my flat —
    And lingered — to wish me 'Good-night' — and all
    that; —

Then he looked — and I looked — we both looked:
    The moon was brand new, in the sky;
So he wished — and I wished, — and I wished — and
    he wished —
    The magical moments flew by.
Then he sighed — and I sighed — we both sighed, —
    I paused — with the key of my flat —
I knew *he* was thinking — the same as *you're*
    thinking —
    So I just slammed the door — and *that's that!*

Prehistoric Prattle
By Greatrex Newman (1981)

The Dodo now is quite extinct,
    For years its numbers shrinked and shrinked;
They shrinked and shrinked and shrunked and
        shrunked
    Till every Dodo was defunct.
And recent census figures show no
    Descendants of departed Dodo.

A Lion met a Dinosaur . . .
    The Lion gave a frightened roar;
The Dinosaur his dinner saw . . .
    For Dinosaurs like Lions raw.

Pterodactyls were remarkable,
    (Wing-span over twenty feet!)

Now-a-days they'd be unparkable
    Anywhere near Oxford Street.

In the jungle, when out hunting,
    We heard strange primaeval grunting;
And were scared, as there before us
    Stood a herd of Brontosaurus.

When the Brontosaurus saw us
    Some pretended to ignore us;
Others — who were less suspicious —
    Ate us, and remarked, 'Delicious!'

The Big Tale of Hoo Flung Mud
By Greatrex Newman (1981)

'Tis a Tale they tell in Shanghai,
    At the Sign of the Scented Skunk;
'Tis a Tale they tell
    Of a deed of hell,
In the wilds of Clapham Junc.

At the House of a Hundred Hiccoughs,
    By the Gate of the Gilded Ghouls;
In robe of blue
    Sat Wun Lung Too,
At work on his Football Pools.

He'd a daughter named Chili Bom Bom,
    Of pedigree Chinese blood;
And Wun Lung said
    The girl must wed
The Mandarin Hoo Flung Mud.

But the laughing Chili Bom Bom
    Had a secret boy-friend, Ben;
An affair discreet
    (Told round the Fleet)
With Midshipman Brown, R.N.

They'd planned to elope together,
    For they made an ideal match;
They'd hoped to bunk
    On a Chinese junk,
Or hijack a yachtman's yatch.

'Tis a Tale they tell in Hong Kong,
    At the Sign of the Unwashed Neck;
'Tis a yarn they spin
    With a fiendish grin
In the Tea-House of Tooting Bec.

This night was the Feast of the Fowl-Pest,
    At the Banquet of Bluest Blood;
And Wun Lung brought
    His Bom Bom daught.,
And with her came Hoo Flung Mud.

They sat at the Tip-Top table,
    According to pride of place;
And chopstick Chinks
    Stood Wun Lung drinks,
And Hoo Flung Mud said grace.

Then crash went a window behind them,
    And showing remarkable nerve —
Young sailor Brown
    From the roof jumped down,
Right into a dish of hors d'oeuvre.

His strong arms seized his Bom Bom,
    And carried her out, alone;
He was, by gad,
    Some hefty lad,
For she weighed nearly sixteen stone.

'Tis a Tale they tell in Foochow,
    At the Sign of the Whispered Hush;
While Shepherds bright
    Watch flocks by night
In the silence of Shepherds Bush.

With Bom Bom in his arms, he ran
    Down the Street of the Swiping Sword;
But in pursuit
    Ben heard the 'toot'
Of a second-hand Chinese Ford.

They knew 'twas the car of Hoo Flung Mud,
    And he drove like a fiend of hell;
'Twas a race for life
    For he'd brought his knife —
And his fork and spoon as well.

The car was nearly upon them now,
    But Ben had a sailor's wits —
With one mad whirl
    He flung the girl —
And her weight crushed the car to bits.

Then he picked his Bom Bom from the wreck,
    (She seemed just a shade concussed),
With a dark red mark
    From the plugs that spark,
And a number-plate on her bust.

'Tis a Tale they tell in Peckham,
    At the Sign of the Pye Hi-Fi;
With whispered word
    Of what occurred
When Comin' thro' the Rye.

Then Chinese Wedding Bells ting-ling,
    For Bom Bom — Queen of Vamps;
Her Dad gave Ben
    Ten thousand yen,
And twenty-five Green Stamps.

For dangerous driving — Hoo Flung Mud
    Got fifteen years in clink;
And Ben — outside
    With fist — black-eyed
The Green Eye of the Little Yellow Chink.

Piscatorial Pastime
By Greatrex Newman (1981)

Around the shores of England
    With hook and line and bait,
Beside canals and rivers
    And on sea-side piers they wait.
In ev'ry kind of weather
    They just sit and freeze, outside —
The Fishermen of England
    Should all be certified.

To save their plight
    When fish don't bite,
A simple plot they hatch:
    They call at some fish-monger's shop
And then take home their 'catch.'
    Then in their beds, with sleepy heads,
As blissful hours go by —
    The Fishermen of England
All lie! And *lie!* And LIE!

With patience monumental
    Quite half their lives they spend
In silent solemn solitude,
    Completely 'round the bend.'
Unlucky, but undaunted,
    Undismayed and undeterred —
The Fishermen of England
    The Band of Hope deferred!

Mr. and Mrs. Whistler

By Greatrex Newman (1981)

*(In an Art Gallery, a shabbily dressed little man is gazing at
a famous painting of an elderly lady. He turns from the
picture, and explains to other onlookers:*

She's not Mona Lisa — she's not Cleopatra;
   She's not Ena Sharples — (*she's* bigger an' fatterer);
That picture's *related* to someone or other —
   She's not Charley's *Aunt* — no, she's *Whistler's Mother.*

Yes, she's Whistler's Mother — she's quite a big pot,
   But I'm Whistler's *Father* — the man they've forgot;
I don't want no fame, but I'd like to make clear
   That paintin' that picture was all *my* idea.

Our son was a nice little lad; no complaints;
   An' so, for 'is birthday, I'd got 'im some paints;
'E'd never 'ad lessons in wot they call 'Art' —
   So I said "Paint yer Mother — she'll do for a start".

The Missus agreed, an' sat still all the day,
   While I washed the dishes — 'e painted away;
An' when it were finished — I said to the lad:
   'I think you're improvin' — so now paint yer Dad'.

'E wasn't too keen — but said 'e'd 'ave a bash —
   Providin' I'd let 'im leave out me moustache;
Me shirt — nor me trousers 'e didn't admire —
   An' said as 'e'd paint more attractive attire.

I felt quite relieved, for although I'm no prude,
   I didn't much fancy be'n' done in the nood;
I posed as 'e'd chosed — an' 'e soon got absorbed —
   In glorious technical-colour 'e daubed.

'E soon dashed it off — an' I'm bound to admit
   I felt that 'e'd flattered 'is ole man a bit —
When — in the Academy — lookin' all coy —
   I saw meself labelled as — *'Gainsborough's Blue Boy'.*

Cursory Nursery Versery

By Greatrex Newman (1981)

Little Bo Peep
   Fell fast asleep
While counting the sheep she tended;
   Georgie Porgy — passing by —
Kissed the girl and made her cry —
   And got six months suspended.

Humpty Dumpty wrote on a wall
   A very rude word in a juvenile scrawl;
His Head Master said it was quite indefensible —
   From School (Comprehensive) quite
      incomprehensible.

Hush-a-bye Baby, poor little mite,
   Mummy is out playing Bingo to-night;
Miss Baby-sitter is drinking her tea
   So please don't disturb her, she's watching T.V.

Twinkle twinkle little star,
   I don't wonder what you are;
Satellites around you whizz —
   Don't *you* wonder what *they* is?

Little Boy Blue come blow your cash,
   Carnaby Street has some fabulous fash. —
Rings on your fingers — long hair without bows —
   Transistor music wherever you goes.

Mary Mary quite contrary
   How does your garden grow?
'In window-box of Council blocks
   With dust-bins all in a row'.

There was a little man
   And he had a little gun
And he shot a little copper in Belgravia;
   The Magistrate — in Court —
Said he really didn't ought
   And cautioned him regarding his behaviour.

There was an old woman who lived in a shoe
   And so many Children's Allowances drew —
That when overcrowding became too acute
   She purchased a very nice Council-house boot.

Rub-a-dub-dub
   Three men in a tub;
The fat one protested
   'This bath's too congested —
But if we'd one more
   We could have a Bridge four.'

Hi-diddle-diddle
   An Income Tax 'fiddle'

Is wangled by tax-payer gaily;
   The Revenue laugh to see such fun
When he's in the dock at Old Bailey.

Hickory Dickory Dock!
   The workmen watched the clock;
The clock struck one . . . so they struck too.

Turn Again Whittington
By Greatrex Newman (1981)

As Principal Boy in the Panto,
   Dick Whittington's always a hit;
I face the footlights
   In my second-hand tights
But dare not sit down or they'd split.
   I have to say 'Good-bye' to Alice
To seek fortune over the sea —
   A tear she will wipe
As I sail on the shipe
   And promise to come barck some dee.

Oh Turn again Whittington
   Turn again do —
The pantomime public
   Are faithful and true —
I'll hear the Bow Bells
   And I'm bow-leggèd too
So Turn again Whittington
   Turn again do.

The boat is afloat for Morocco,
   The anchor is weighed and we start —
I'm leaving my gal
   And I haven't a pal
Excepting my dear pussy cart.
   But when we are nearing Morocco
We're shipwrecked upon the Mor-rocks —
   The Captain and Mate
Have lost count of the date —
   They consult: Is it ult. inst. or prox.?

Oh Turn again Whittington
   Turn again do —
Kiss Alice 'Good-bye'
   And then kiss all the crew —
Just murmur 'Tat-tah'
   To each sailor's tattoo —
And turn again Whittington
   Turn again do.

Come pussy dear — up Highgate Hill — and then
   'We'll gather lilacs in the Spring agen' —
I'm hungry Puss — no food has passed my lips —
   Oh for the joy of heavenly chish-an-fips —
I'll be Lord Mayor — of London town — as planned
   (When Fairy Queen has waved her magic wand) —
Hark! Hear Bow Bells — we're nearing Shepherds
      Bush —
   I'm tired — we've *walked* from Ashby-de-la-Zouch.
Come Pussy dear, let's sleep on yon green hillock —
   And you shall dream of saucers full of mil-luck.
Home from the sea! — all doubts and dangers
      scorning —
   I'm 'Off to Philadelphia in the morning'.

With my bundle on my shoulder
   As each Christmas I get older —
To quit as Richard Whit. I know there's been talk —
   With my surplus human paddin'
I'm too fat to play Aladdin —
   So now — I'll be the *cow* in Jack-and-the-Beanstalk.

INDEX OF TITLES

INDEX OF FIRST LINES